BLOOD OF THE DRAGON

FRANCESCA QUARTO

Blood of the Dragon
By Francesca Quarto
© 2017 Blood of the Dragon
Swartz Creek, MI 48473

Cover design by Clarissa Yeo

Thanks to my ever patient and encouraging husband whose love is steadfast in all uncharted waters.

Thanks also to my editor for her contributions and going the extra mile in helping me grow as an author. There is always better to be found within.

Chapter 1

I moved into the ice-blue light reflecting off the walls of the cave. I never expected to find the missing women alive, but there they stood. They looked petrified, eyes wide and mouths stretched away from their teeth as if groaning in agony. Their skin had taken on the blueish tint of exposure to extreme cold. As I came within reach of the first girl, a green, reptilian-like creature, with a flat-shaped head and scaly body slithered across her shoulders. It slowly wrapped its spiked tail tightly around her exposed neck, then casually dropped its hideous head onto her breast. I felt it challenging me to come to her aid, watching me with eyes the color of clotted blood.

I was screaming out a ward to protect her when Jason shook me awake, saying over and over, "It's OK, honey. It's OK."

I laid in his arms for more than an hour before I fell into another restless sleep.

I'd been back four days. My investigation involving the kidnapped women was still playing havoc with my sleep cycle.

It's time to get a grip I scolded myself, feeling embarrassed at what I saw as unseemly behavior in a witch.

I made a concerted effort to start readjusting to life in my cozy home, deep in the forests of Appalachia.

I decided I'd begin by opening the mail that had accumulated on my kitchen table like the dust bunnies under my bed.

My boyfriend, Jason, was watching me as I stood frowning down on the pile, distractedly twisting a long strand of my dark auburn hair around my finger.

Shaking myself out of my disturbing mind drift, I gave Jason a forced smile.

This earned me a chuckle, as he moved closer and loomed over me from his lofty six feet four. Of course, at only five foot four, mostly everyone looms over me.

"Welcome back to the real world, Magic Girl," he said, touching my cheek with his warm fingers.

He wrapped his arms around me as I leaned back to look into his lone green eye. A black eye patch snugged up against an empty eye socket. He'd lost his left eye in a freakish accident. The patch actually gave him an air of mystery that complimented our unorthodox life together.

I leaned into him, wrapping my arms around his well-toned frame.

"You feel wonderful, Jason." I almost purred as he held me tighter.

"There were so many times I wished you'd been with me on this last case. But most of all, I missed your arms around me, just like this."

Jason let his hands drift down to the curve of my butt. He gave it a gentle squeeze as he brought me even closer. I closed my eyes as he pressed his mouth down on mine.

He broke away long enough to mumble something about a more comfortable place to continue. As I turned to head toward our favorite place in front of the fireplace, I nearly tripped over my long-time companion, Ollie.

He sat looking up at me, whining softly to make his own needs clear.

I frowned down on my dog, mumbling something about bad timing, while Jason continued to kiss the back of my neck. All I could do was sigh in frustration.

Ollie cocked his head, his black face and thick ginger-colored fur reinforcing the impression of a fluffy stuffed toy. I gave Jason a quick peck on the cheek as I passed him to open the back door.   Our romantic mood had to be put on hold because my dog couldn't hold it any longer.

I readjusted my clothes and my thoughts and looked back at the waiting mail.   Jason refilled our mugs and squeezing my shoulder as he passed, whispered in my ear, "Later, love."

When I moved to Iron Mountain, the deep snows and bitter cold winters weren't the only challenges to survive.   I was unwittingly drawn into a case of paranormal activity in this turn-of-the–century town that clearly called for a protector's intervention. After that, my *shadow career* was born and a pack of werewolves was destroyed.

Jason sees this covert life I lead as both exciting and important and nicknamed me the *"Witch Sleuth of Appalachia."*

I belong to a very specialized group of magic users that honor the Green Mother as source of life in the natural realms. We are actually called the Guild of the Green Wizards.

Though dating back to before the Dark Times, we are known to relatively few outsiders in this realm.   We practice our skills secretly, shunning any public notice, acknowledging our sworn duty as protectors, guarding the non-magic users from the dark forces.

These evil beings constantly make forays into the vulnerable, first plane of mortals. Here, they move like shadows across the moon, darkening the world as they pervert the innocent and destroy the natural world.

Happily, I work better in the shadows.

I was trained from a very early age by my father, Liam O'Brien, a Celtic Mage, whose powers were recognized beyond his own Irish homeland. He passed his secrets on to me, even though they would normally have been instilled in a male offspring from his clan.

My parents moved to the foothills of the Alleghany Mountains in Pennsylvania, leaving the verdant hills of Ireland just months before I was born.

Though not a native of that wind-swept isle, I have wandered its curving landscape over many years of long visits to my father's family, joining the ubiquitous sheep herds in my unfettered roaming.

My Celtic roots were richly fed on the endless Clan stories told by my paternal grandfather, Connor O'Brien. I heard stories of magical battles between the Demons called the Fallen and my grandfather, a Master Wizard. He was still here; they weren't.

My mother, Brighid, is also a trained Celtic Wizard, practicing her unique brand of what she calls *"This and That"* Magic. Many Sorcerers have tried their skills against mom's quaint-sounding Magic and were destroyed in a blink of her beautiful, sea-green eyes.

I'd been in Iron Mountain just over a year when the first letters seeking my help began to show up. By a twist of fate, I'm already quite wealthy, so money is not a factor when accepting these assignments as a detective of the paranormal.

I realized my thoughts were drifting around like the snow outside, making me restless. I broke discipline, leaving the table to look out the window over the sink. A letter from San Francisco sat on top of the dwindling pile and I was definitely putting off opening it.

Jason brought me back to the present, wrapping his arms around me. I leaned back, enjoying the warmth from his body as he pressed closer to me.

He asked "Hey, where'd you go, Cathleen? I was asking if you were going to take the job in California."

"I'm sorry, honey. Guess I was thinking about life and us."

He looked pleased and turning me back to face him said, "I've been thinking about *us* for quite some time lady, but it's not easy to talk to you when you're chasing down bad guys with long fangs."

I laughed, adding, "And dogs with bad timing? Give me time to get settled in and I'll give you one-hundred percent of my attention, promise."

"Will that be before, or after, you go to California on your next sleuthing job?"

I looked up at him and gave a weak smile. He knew me so well.

"Let me brew us up a fresh pot, Magic Girl. It might make that letter you've been avoiding like a Timber Rattler, a bit easier to handle."

In fact, my hand was still prickling like I'd just picked up a thistle bush, confirming that another Magic User had handled the envelope with the San Francisco post mark.

I walked back to the table and looked at the letter.

Well, this could be interesting, I thought, as I reached for the butter knife.

Chapter 2

I slipped my make-shift letter opener into the flap of the sealed envelope and took out the folded letter.

My Dear Cathleen O'Brien,

My name is Dr. Chung Wu. I am Host Curator of the "Chinese Royal Arts and Artifacts" Exhibit, currently on display at the San Francisco Gallery of Ancient Cultures in California.

A piece from this collection, of incalculable value and age has been stolen from the exhibit. I return to China soon and cannot take part in a search.

You are known in certain circles, where I hold a place of some prominence and long standing. Your reputation as an effective detective, as well as your repute as a Celtic Mage and sworn Protector, have led me to ask you to undertake the recovery of this art work.

The stolen piece is known as "Blood of the Red Dragon"; a porcelain statuette, measuring two feet and weighing 25 pounds. Dating back to the Dynasty of Emperor Qin Shi Huang, it was created by Court Artist, Feng Xi, a formidable and evil Wizard. This statue contains the considerable Magical power of Feng Xi, being produced as it was in the year of his reported death. Feng's body was never seen to confirm the report, however. My fears are well grounded, young Wizard, that if this statue falls into the wrong hands, it will be used in diabolical ways and have disastrous consequences.

There are important maps and information on the back of this missive. The "Blood of the Red Dragon" must be found, before it can wreak havoc on the mortal and unsuspecting world.

Most Respectfully Yours,
Chung Wu, PhD.

Chapter 3

I had taken a seat at the table across from Jason as I read and then re-read Dr. Chung's letter. I looked up at Jason.

"Well?" he asked, studying me intently.

"You were right to think it was about a potential case," I said, as I passed the letter in question over to him.

"Wow! This sounds pretty exotic even for you, Cathleen. How good is your Mandarin?" he asked, with a tight smile.

I could tell he was intrigued, but his comment was laced with concern.

As something of a twenty-four-year-old homebody, I don't just take to the highways and byways on a whim. I wasn't concerned about my language skills and San Francisco would offer a great relief from winter in Iron Mountain, but I needed more than good weather to act on.

I gave Jason a challenging look saying, "So, Sheriff. Give me your insights on this case from what you've read."

"It seems that Dr. Chung Wu is himself a Magic User. I'd guess his assignment to act as Curator in San Francisco was purposely made because of his abilities as a trained Wizard."

I sat quietly, letting him gather his thoughts. He continued.

"If Dr. Chung is to be believed, the piece called "Blood of the Red Dragon" has been zapped with some heavy duty Dark Magic by its creator, the Wizard, Feng Xi."

While Jason saw the statue as being "zapped" like some bug flying too close to an insect light, his meaning was clear.

He concluded, "The statue likely had a spell on it that has already lasted untold centuries, so it had to be really powerful.

Whatever that spell protects inside the statue must be very evil and lethal to our world if released."

"Whoever has the Red Dragon knows of the spell and the potential powers it holds. They have powers of their own and will be trying to unleash Feng's sorcery for their own Magical enrichment."

Jason's face reflected the possible effect of the theft. We both knew it was even more sinister in its potential impact.

We sat silently sipping from our mugs, listening to our own internal dialogues.

A strong wind rattled the window panes and shook the trees outside the kitchen window, freeing them of their white burden as it howled like a tribe of Banshees.

I was considering what wickedness could be inflicted by someone wielding Feng Xi's stored powers, when an explosion of sound brought us to our feet.

The storm door was banging against the side of the house and the heavy front door was blown open with the force of Thor's Hammer.

We ran into the living room and a wall of frigid air and blinding snow was turning the room into a winter landscape.

Jason already had his gun out of its holster.

He pulled the storm door shut, struggling against the force of the wind.

I quickly went to the picture window, peering out onto the desolate scene. I was just in time to see a figure wearing a hooded cloak slip through a curtain of snow that clung to the pine branches, swaying with the strong gusts.

"Jason, someone is out there. He disappeared into the woods. Let's get Oliver back inside!"

We rushed back to the kitchen where I called to Ollie to end his adventuring. He came readily, encased in a layer of snow. He looked like an ice carving until he shook himself and dislodged the load onto my floor.

"That wind wasn't normal, Jason," I was saying as I wiped first the dog and then the floor.

"I want to know who our mystery visitor was, too."

"Well, I can't answer that question, but he seems to have left you an early Christmas present."

He nodded down at the table.

"He must have put it in here while we were closing the front doors," Jason said as he studied the bundle.

My doors are usually unlocked so that explanation worked.

I jumped to my feet and took a strange, round package from Jason's hands.

I placed the package on the kitchen table, shoving mugs and left-over muffins aside.

It might have been glass, as light as it was. It had no sender's name; only an address in San Francisco which I noted was written in the same careful script of Dr. Chung Wu's letter.

"Hey!" I said, turning to Jason who was watching me carefully for information on this mysterious delivery.

"This has to be from Chung Wu."

He looked on patiently, while I cut through the wrappings with my Dad's old Swiss pocket knife. "Never start yer day without this in yer pocket and a strong cup of coffee in yer hand!" dad always told me.

The heavy paper wrapping fell away as I slipped my knife through the shipping tape. In a few seconds, I had a blue, spherically shaped projector, in my hands; that is what I instinctively understood it to be.

"What the heck is *that,* Cathleen?" Jason said as he came closer to examine the ball-like object.

"Well, I'm pretty sure it's a projector and I think I know why Dr. Chung sent it." I replied as I slowly rotated the ice-blue object carefully in my hands.

"What are you looking for?"

By now Jason was leaning very close to me and I could feel his warm breath on my cheek as he lightly brushed against it.

I wished we could make a different kind of magic just then.

Reluctantly turning my attention back to the object, I used my fingers to locate a mechanism to trigger what I knew had to be a hologram. I was rewarded with a soft humming, followed by a sharp flash of light shooting from between my fingers.

We both looked up. There was a shimmering projection of an Asian man, wearing what appeared to be a richly made, authentic Chinese robe.

He sported a mustache that hung down past his chin like strands of grey spaghetti, blending into an equally stringy goatee. I put his age at seventy-five to a thousand. My senses locked onto an ancient gray aura surrounding his lean body.

"He's pretty old," Jason was saying close to my ear.

"He can't hear us sweetie, but we'll be able to hear him. If this had been a *live hologram,* we could have spoken with him, but he already wrote he's on his way back to China.

"I need to signal him to begin his message" I said.

Jason had stepped back to give me room to operate. He's very careful around me when Magic's in play.

Chapter 4

I studied the figure being projected onto my kitchen ceiling and slowly revolved the sphere until I had the image planted on a sunny yellow wall.

"There, that's better," I said.

Jason moved his chair to face the new angle, looking like he only needed a box of popcorn for the movie to begin.

Moving my hand in a slow exploration of the blue projector, I felt the slightest depression and pressed. Bingo! The image was animated and we both became fixated on someone who looked like he'd just stepped off a Ming Vase.

Chung Wu wore semi-formal court robes, in a soft apricot-yellow. The rich garment was decorated with a Dragon motif and an impressive depiction of the cosmos. This garb signified his high station at Court, as only the nobles were permitted the privilege of such robes. The Dragon symbolized the Emperor himself, the Son of Heaven. Only he could have granted this honor to Chung Wu, but that would have been hundreds of centuries ago!

How old is *this guy?* I wondered in amazement.

After a slow, dignified bow from the waist, the shimmering image stood erect and spoke in perfect English, with only the slightest hint of accent. His cultured, deep voice filled my kitchen.

"Cathleen O'Brien, daughter of Liam and Brighid, Celtic Wizards of the ancient clan of Brian Boru, High King of One Ireland, I humbly greet you."

I glanced over at Jason to see his reaction to the flowery, "Hi there!"

Jason wasn't a history buff, so I quickly excused any indifference to my Royal blood.

The phantom-like visitor continued in a precise, unhurried manner.

"I am Dr. Chung Wu. You are now in receipt of my written introduction.

The letter described for you the unique circumstances of my request for your services as a Protector. However, I believe you need a fuller picture of what and who you are being asked to face in this quest.

I must first enhance your knowledge of Feng Xi's masterpiece, "Blood of the Red Dragon".

Throughout the centuries, scholars of the Mystical and the Magical have tried to unlock the secret behind the name of the statue.

Many learned men of the period believed the Emperor killed a second wife and had her blood mixed with Feng's pigments to complete the work. I know beyond a doubt that Qin's second wife did disappear from the Court just before Feng presented the Red Dragon to the Emperor. Coincidence?"

Chung paused, to let it sink in I supposed. Jason shot me a quick look.

"As owner of the Ancient Books Conservatory located in Xian, China, I have access to manuscripts, scrolls and books of every century in China's history. Many Courtiers of Feng's day are recorded in one text or another.

These testimonials all reflect the conclusion that the Wizard-Artist, Feng Xi, imbued his work "Blood of the Red Dragon," with his Dark Magic and the evil cunning of conspiracy, treachery and murder.

Among the more disturbing reports are allegations by Court members of Feng's demonic practice of ritualistic cannibalism. I know this is shocking, but it must be considered when dealing with this creature.

Some of Feng's contemporaries in the Emperor's School of Arts and Sciences, hint at the disappearance of less notable students. Likewise, some of the models he used also had a similar way of vanishing.

You can interpret these Court murmurings with the eyes of a 21st century woman, or use your skills of wizardry and clearly understand these as echoed warnings from the Emperor's Court and Feng Xi's peers.

Something else you need in your understanding of Feng Xi relates to his ability to *race through time.*

Feng Xi is a *Voyager*!

Voyagers move at will from place to place, from time to time. Only a rare Wizard can perform this travel with spells alone; most can only obtain this skill by employing the Black Arts.

Feng Xi is a Master of Dark Magic.

Feng is still at work in this realm, His access to the powers held within the Red Dragon   would insure his continued Immortal status and allow him to turn his enhanced Dark power upon all realms of life and spirit.

You must view the Blood of the Red Dragon not an artifact of a Dynasty, but rather, a Magical key that will unlock Feng's immortal power. If he holds this key, he will cross into the world of light forever and will leave a trail of Darkness behind his every foot step.

With this foreshadowing, I must leave you, Cathleen O'Brien, but not without direction for the journey that lies ahead. Use the map on the back of my letter and it will point you in the way you must go.

Upon your success, the statue can be given to my agent for transport back to me. You will know this agent when the time is right; it is they who have delivered this device.

When I have presented the Blood of the Red Dragon to its owner, it shall be destroyed and your task as the Witch of Appalachia will be completed.

Chapter 5

The hologram seemed to give itself a shake and then abruptly vanished.

We sat staring intently at the wall for a few seconds.

I felt Jason looking over at me and turned my head to him.

"Cannibalism?" he said, in a subdued voice tinged with the horror of the thought. "Cathleen, I'm not sure this is a case you'll want to take on, is it?"

I can't think sitting down. I didn't answer, but stood up and walked into the living room. I stared out the large picture window at the snow piling up and obliterating my world.

The woods had gone very still. The wind seemed to be finished with lashing the trees, at least for the time being. It was as if nature was holding *Her* breath.

I began to go over what Dr. Chung's hologram message had divulged and more importantly, what it didn't!

There was no mention of the owner of the collection that exhibited the Red Dragon among the other artifacts. Who was Chung really working for? Was he an Immortal, or just a long-lived Master Wizard?

Jason had followed me into the front room; standing next to me, looking out. He didn't speak or ask any questions.

I could use Jason's uncanny power of recall if I had my own questions. Along with his extraordinary physical attributes of speed and strength, he always brought to mind a kind of "Super Man" character; masquerading behind his Sheriff uniform as a mere human.

I sometimes wondered if the love of my life had deeper secrets for me to uncover. I looked quickly in his direction.

Jason smiled at me asking, "Are we ready to talk, Magic Girl?"

I put my arms around him and gave him a hug, breathing in his tantalizing scent.

Lifting my chin and looking into my eyes he said, "You're going to take this, aren't you."

It was more of a statement than a question. He knew me so well.

"I have to, Jason," I said softly. I knew this was not the answer he wanted to hear. I quickly went on to defend my position.

"Jason, the evil that would be unleashed by Feng Xi if he has the Red Dragon in his possession would be like . . . like a Magical Armageddon to life in this realm and all other realms!"

I knew he was convinced by the dire situation, but still had some doubts and lots of questions.

"Let's go back to the kitchen," I said. "I think we need to make our plans."

He smiled broadly at the reference to the "we" in that planning process. He wrapped his arm around my waist, drawing me closer.

The blue sphere sat mutely on the table. It had a lovely silvery glow under the glimmer of the ceiling light, but the message it held was a vision of unleashed horrors if I failed.

Dr. Chung had referred to me as the "Witch of Appalachia" which almost made me wince. It made me imagine an old crone squatting in front of a black cauldron full of snake eyes and bat guano. I did notice as he said it that he had given a slow bow to me. *Hmm, that part I liked,* I thought with a small grin.

When Jason caught me smiling slightly he raised a quizzical eyebrow. "Just happy you're my back-up Jason." And I was.

I started a fresh pot of our favorite Sumatra bold, as I didn't want to arm wrestle Jason for the half cup left from the four o'clock brewing.

The blue orb sat between us on the table.

We tried to act like we weren't about to discuss a powerful and evil Sorcerer, or the mystery of a statue that likely held the key to releasing death and perversion upon all living worlds.

I thought I should begin. Jason rarely put his two cents in until I opened the bank for business.

"Here's how I see this case, Jason." I sounded like my best friend, Joanie, launching into one of her folksy lectures.

"Feng Xi sent an accomplice or accomplices, to steal the Blood of the Red Dragon from the art gallery in San Francisco. The statue is fairly substantial in height and weight, but somehow, it managed to evaporate into the hazy California air without a trace."

"At least not a trace that's been uncovered by others," Jason said with confidence.

"Right!" I agreed.

I continued. "Dr. Chung has made it clear; this statue is vital to Feng Xi. Though reported dead centuries ago, Chung thinks Feng has somehow achieved some kind of Immortal status. More importantly, Feng will use all the enormous powers stored in the Red Dragon, so he can remain in this realm, or any other plane he chooses.

I suspect he has been crossing between the Dark and Light Realms, aided by this henchman of his, but he still needs the statue to complete his transformation to a Wizard with a beating heart."

Jason looked unsure. "Cathleen, are you saying you suspect Feng Xi is some kind of Zombie?"

"Not a Zombie, but something even stronger. He's his own master, Jason, unlike Zombies that are manipulated like puppets by their makers. I suspect Feng Xi may be a *Chi Vampire*. He's only able to survive on life force energies; the souls he consumes from other living creatures. That's not like Vampires that drink the blood of their victims for sustenance. And he won't have to feed often like the other kind of Vampires. He can capture and drain his victims over long periods of time, leaching their life force as slowly as he wants to keep their hearts beating longer."

Putting his mug back carefully in the center of the daisy yellow place mat, Jason looked at me and barely breathed the word, "Wow." He sat still for a moment and after processing my comments, went on.

"OK, I agree with that assessment as far as you went, but have one question. Have you got any idea who, what and where the Wizard's helper might be?"

"We're looking at another Magic user; perhaps not as powerful as his or her master, Feng Xi, but someone to contend with. So that answers part of your question.

I believe we'll find this Magic User in the San Francisco area where the statue was located before it was stolen. I also think we'll be looking for a person from Chinatown; because I'm certain they'll be of Chinese heritage."

"My thoughts exactly," Jason interjected, "but I think they may have moved out of that area after they took the Red Dragon from the Gallery. We'll need a good map of the area near and around the Art Gallery too. I don't think this is a woman as that statue would be difficult to lug around, even for a man."

I went to retrieve my lap top from the Deacon's Bench by the kitchen door. That was my catch-all for everything I was too lazy to walk through to the living room and my desk.

I booted up and went to Google for a complete map of San Francisco's China Town.

"Better get another view further out from that point, Cathleen. If this guy is known to that community, especially if he was hauling even a well-wrapped two foot statue around that could spark some unwanted interest."

I looked over at Jason who had moved his chair beside mine so we could look at the search results together.

"Hey, how about searching out the various coastal towns large enough for a sea faring boat to come into port and yet small enough to offer some degree of anonymity," I said.

That's when I noticed he'd taken out his ever-present notepad and seemed ready to interrogate me. "I'll make a list for later research and I'll get maps of all the areas we think pertinent to our investigation."

Every time we worked a case together, I had to grab control back from my bossy boyfriend. Without sticking pins in his macho armor, I'd always been able to rein in his natural enthusiasm for detecting and reassert my position as the witch in charge.

"Jason, how about you getting some sleep and we'll get back together before you go on duty later? I need time to look over the map and instructions, Dr. Chung sketched on the back of his letter."

He gave me a lopsided grin as he closed his notepad.

"Sorry, love. Didn't mean to muscle in and take charge of your investigation."

"Jason, I trust in your insights and never want you to hold back on your observations, or suggestions."

He brushed a long strand of hair off my forehead and gave me a kiss which said all I needed to hear. As his hands began drift down my back, I had to use all my discipline to throw on the breaks.

"Sorry, to turn off that particular switch, sweetie, but it's time to send you home so I can get my head wrapped around this job."

Jason gave me his best movie lover leer. Stepping over to the sink he looked out to where his SUV sat, transformed into a small mountain.

"It will take a good twenty minutes to get my car defrosted and drivable." He reported back to me after pressing the automatic start to begin the process.

He looked down at me and without a word passing between us, we headed back to the warmth of the fireplace and the inviting comforter spread out in front of it.

The work of finding a Dark Wizard's power trove would have to wait for another twenty minutes!

Chapter 6

After Jason left for home, I decided that my internet search should include some history of San Francisco's Chinatown, along with pertinent maps that might prove helpful when we were wandering its historic streets.

Dad always preached, you could never have too much information when preparing to meet a demon, or preparing to meet life. Both can get pretty terrifying.

I was printing several pages of information and maps at my desk, when headlights cut through the lingering gray morning, creeping slowly up my wall. I went to the window, moving the curtain slightly, to look down my driveway.

There were deep trenches marking the snow packed drive where a long, sleek car had plowed through. It seemed to magically appear from behind a white curtain of dense snowflakes.

Its dark shape squatted in the frosty, pale light as it came to a stop, nearly level with my front window. The engine made that deep purring sound of all expensive automobiles.

I kept to the shadows of my living room, studying the scene through the prism of frost covering the glass.

There is no way this can be good, I thought, reaching for my cell phone inside my pocket. I had Jason on speed dial.

Between the haze created by the blowing snow and the patch of fog I was making on the window with my breath, I could only see dark shapes inside the vehicle. There were two people silhouetted against the watery light filtering through the car.

I noticed the wind picking up again, after Jason left. Now, it seemed to have reached a manic pitch of wailing. I hesitated to press Jason's number as I hated waking him when he probably just got to bed.

The driver's-side door suddenly opened and was nearly ripped out of the gloved hand of a short, darkly-dressed figure. He had taken the time to bundle himself to the eyeballs. A scarf that must have been a yard long was wrapped several times around his neck and struggling to stay draped around his shoulders like a bad imitation of *Dr. Who*.

The wide-collared coat he wore resembled a woolen Navy Pea coat in style. Even with the dark knit hat he'd pulled over his ears, this ensemble was barely enough gear for our mountain weather.

The driver shut his door, a gust of wind immediately tearing at the long scarf as if it wanted to drag him away into the bleak woods. Clutching the quickly unraveling muffler in one hand, he crossed in front of the idling car, to the left rear passenger door and closer to my line of vision. His face was still obscured even though I had kept a tiny peep hole open, but I saw him struggling with the buttons on his coat as he passed.

When he reached the passenger side, he bent down to lay his jacket on the snowy ground like an offering to a god, and opened the rear door.

Unbelievably, he bowed even further down as the passenger stepped out.

The woman emerging from the car was wrapped up like a mummy in a long fur coat that actually swept the snow as she moved. Even with my bad optics, it appeared to be made of the whitest ermine, and was complemented with a large matching hat with feathering white fur concealing all but the lower half of her face and a hint of red lips.

Blending with the snowy world as she did, it was as if she had risen out of a drift; a fully formed "Snow Queen"; and she had a groveling minion to prove it!

She stood for a moment, turning her head in a slow scan of the area, while a small snow mound was forming on the back of her kowtowing driver.

Guess he can't move till she does I thought.

My curiosity satisfied, I began a ward of protection.

Just as I finished, the driver stood and closed the door. He immediately went around to the back of the car. Opening the trunk, he retrieved a snow shovel which he began using to clear a path for his waiting mistress to my front door.

Wow! That's what I call service, I was thinking as the minion-driver worked like a man possessed, to clear a suitable path before his mistress could be chilled, though I doubted even the original owners of her furs would have been warmer.

As he got closer to the front porch, I was able to make out his features more clearly.

He appeared to be a fairly young Chinese man, perhaps in his mid-twenties. Though not very tall, he had a body builder's physic. I saw his impressive muscles flexing under a tight black turtle neck sweater as he plowed through the heavy snow. I noticed his tight black jeans, tucked into high, black leather boots were very fashionable, but definitely not Appalachian winter appropriate. He must have been freezing assorted parts off!

He finished his marathon shoveling sprint, re-wrapping his scarf. His waiting mistress swept past him as he again assumed the kowtow position. I noticed she was wearing white leather boots to match her remarkable outfit. *She's quite the fashionista* I thought a tad impressed.

She stopped just short of the step and her minion, as I'd come to think of him, carefully moved around her onto my porch and pressed my door bell.

Comfy in my favorite sweats and battered fleece-lined slippers, my long, unruly hair was in a ponytail so that it wasn't covering half my face in curly auburn mayhem.

I pulled out the scrunchie, deciding that without the benefit of makeup at this early hour it might be wiser to use my hair as camouflage. Raking my fingers through it, I went to greet my mysterious visitors.

Chapter 7

I answered the door with some foreboding as I finished my last ward. Without opening the storm door, I gave the driver a good once over so he'd know his muscles didn't impress me.

He announced in a loud, heavily accented voice, "Lady Bao Gu, "The Immortal Lady!"

Now *that* piqued my curiosity!

Forgetting my father's constant nagging that my curiosity was "…like a shovel; always digging holes for ya to fall into!" I opened the storm door.

The driver quickly stepped aside and held it for his mistress to enter.

The moment she placed her tiny booted foot down in my entryway, I think I broke out in a sweat.

My senses surged into high gear and I had to struggle not to show my alarm. I moved back a few feet to better appraise my visitor and my gut reaction to her.

She glided into the room. Her head was slightly bowed so I couldn't get a look at her face. I was staring intently at the top of her fur hat when I heard the storm door, then the front door, firmly shut behind the lady's driver.

As if on cue, my Immortal Lady visitor raised her head and looked at me from under slightly lidded eyes, giving her the appearance of being somewhat shy or humble. This was definitely not the vibe I was picking up from her Ladyship.

She was an ethereal beauty, with the delicate features of a porcelain doll; in fact, her pale coloring seemed even whiter than her furs. She wore deep red lipstick on a sweet, bow-shaped mouth and had a small, but perfect straight nose.

Her eyes stopped me from doing a fuller inventory of her looks. They had been made-up expertly, with a fine line emphasizing their almond shape and just a hint of a natural eye shadow. As I looked into them, I saw the fringe of thick dark lashes, outlined eyes so black, it was like staring into bottomless pools of water at midnight--the only difference being the lack of reflected stars, or any light for that matter. In fact, her eyes appeared devoid of life as she returned my appraising stare.

I wanted to squirm under that dead gaze, but she broke the silence between us.

"Forgive my intrusion at such an early hour, but my business with you is of an urgent nature, Wushen, Cathleen O'Brien."

I had studied the history of witchcraft and wizardry extensively during the long days of my apprenticeship in Magic. I recalled that "Wu" was the Chinese word for Shaman, or wizard, with its roots in the ancient folklore of China; "Wu-shen" translated as "wizard or sorcerer".

Obviously, this mysterious lady knew more about me than I knew about her at this point in our acquaintance; which was exactly nothing except that she was some kind of nobility in the ancient Chinese tradition. No one in modern China would be referred to as "Immortal Lady" that was for sure!

I didn't acknowledge her calling me Wizard. I wanted to hear about her urgent business before I committed to being a Magic User.

She seemed to have read my mind and immediately continued in a flat voice. "Your reputation as "The Witch of Appalachia" has passed over many mountains and waters to reach my ear, honorable Wushen, as well as your discreet investigative talents. I am in dire need of both your Magic and your discretion."

I had noticed the driver had taken a position in front of the door, standing like a soldier on guard duty.

I tried to phrase my next comment to reflect a certain respect that I knew was expected by this visitor. I needed time to study her more closely. My senses had already alerted me, this was a woman of exceptional powers.

I said, "Lady Bao, I am unsure how my name came to your attention, but I welcome your visit and invite you to refresh yourself with a cup of tea."

She seemed pleased with my invitation as a smile played briefly on her perfectly shaped mouth. I noticed it never brought a flicker of life to her dead gaze and filed that away for further observation. I was already formulating some not-so-nice opinions about the Lady Bao, as I carefully slipped my cell phone into the pocket of my sweatshirt with Jason's number still only a finger touch away.

While I led the way into my softly lit kitchen, I saw Lady Bao flick her finger at the driver who stayed rooted in place at my front door. *Guess he doesn't get any tea,* I thought, kind of feeling sorry for him. After all his shoveling, he probably needed it more than his fur-clad mistress. That got me to thinking about something else that was nettling me.

I began filling my tea pot. Looking back over my shoulder to ask her my question I saw that she stood near the table, but didn't sit. *Must need a special invitation,* I decided, but I wanted some information and let her stand.

"Lady Bao, I've enjoyed a limited study of the unique customs of your country. I discovered the role that colors play in acknowledging occasions of import and signs of station and, of course, the more spiritual aspects of your ancient culture.

I would like to ask, if I may, how you come to wear white fur, considering it's the color of mourning and death."

This question was met with stony silence and lifting of one perfect eyebrow. She seemed reluctant at first to give me an explanation, but finally answered.

"You are quite correct, honored Wushen; the color I wear is for showing reverence for the dead during funerals, or periods of mourning their passing. I consider myself a modern women, however, and have no fear of insulting those whose spirits have joined their ancestors."

"Ah!" I said like she had just pronounced some deep truth and I was showing solidarity with her twenty-first century attitude. Modernity always sounded too much like "maternity" to me and her comment was definitely "pregnant" with some untold truths.

I tried not to look too deeply into her eyes, so I looked away and fussed over our tea cups and searched for some chamomile as the water came to a slow boil.

I turned to her saying, "Lady Bao, please, be seated, this will be just a minute."

In the next instant, the driver was pulling out a chair and bowing so low his forehead barely cleared the floor.

Geeze, can he move fast, I thought, as I watched the Lady primly place her royal bottom on one of my well-used wooden chairs. Lady Bao flicked another manicured finger and the driver was back in the front room standing with his feet apart and his arms crossed in front of him; awaiting her next finger flick I assumed.

Every time I got close to the Lady, or her man, I felt some kind of strange surge radiating from them like a cold draft whooshing by me.

"Your driver has remarkable abilities of movement," I said, looking back at his expressionless face.

When she didn't respond, I turned my attention back to her. She had the collar of her heavy fur clutched tightly around her throat; almost as if she couldn't get warm after her brief exposure to the snowy morning.

"I hope you aren't too cold, Lady Bao. I notice you still have your coat on and wondered if you'd be more comfortable in front of my fireplace."

She smiled back at my concern. "I thank you for your attention to my comfort, honored Wushen, but I am sure my chill will pass with the tea you are preparing for us."

With the whistle of the kettle, I turned off the gas and put the pot on the trivet in the center of the table and placing the tea bags into it, to let it sit and steep.

"I apologize for my use of tea bags, but I don't have any lose tea on hand," I said as I took my place across from her.

"Please, don't distress yourself. I welcome the hospitality you offer."

With the graceful movement of a dancer, she reached up to remove the fur hat, releasing her hair to cascade in a torrent of black rain, covering her back and draping over her arms and shoulders.

Now, only an arm's length from her while I fiddled with the tea pot, I became aware of frigid air emanating like a blast of ice rays from her body. I tried to suppress a shudder and thought I saw a glimmer of a smile cross her red mouth as I shifted uneasily in my chair.

I picked the tea pot up and began to pour slowly into the two cups, feeling my uneasiness increasing with each passing moment.

When I finished pouring, I looked up and said, "Lady Bao, I wish to discuss your visit to my home. I am naturally curious that you have come here to seek me out, but I need to know your exact needs to determine if I can, or would, choose to lend my particular services."

A flash of emotion turned her eyes into shards of polished obsidian.

"Most honored Wushen, know this, your Celtic ancestors have *already* committed their Magic to my needs, before the light of civilization was put out," she said sweetly.

Did I hear her correctly? My ancestors?

The gleam died in her dead eyes almost before I had time to form my thoughts. I sat there immobilized by this assertion. It seemed both preposterous and unsettling in its possibility.

She went on, "I have no time to waste on explaining in depth, the history that has passed between your ancients and me. Let it suffice to say, there was a pledge, made by your clan founder, Brian Boru. In compensation for my aid to him and his own warrior Wizard, he would commit his clan's Magic to me, once only, at the time of my choosing. This is that time!"

"Brian Boru! You're talking about *centuries* ago! How could there be a connection to your country, or to *you* for that matter? It's not possible!"

I was so undone by her comments that I found myself almost stammering.

Lady Bao hadn't moved a muscle during this mini-tirade. She merely scrutinized me, a detached look on her beautiful face.

I needed to put a lid on my emotional response to her outrageous claim.

I also needed to view the situation at hand with my more discerning eyes. Just who and more importantly, what, was Lady Bao?

I slipped into my Inner Eye with a slow blink. Looking away from her for a second, I saw that her minion had moved into the kitchen as quickly and silently as a whiff of bad odor. He stood ramrod straight, like a blunt object waiting to be hurled in my direction.

I refocused on my royal visitor.

"Honored Wushen," she said softly. "I have not come to you out of malice, but of need. I have nothing but respect for your revered ancestors and indeed, for your esteemed self."

While she was speaking these platitudes, I was scanning her, still aware of the unmistakable vibration of magical power I'd felt radiating from her from the first.

And now, finally, I saw the "what" part of my question. Lady Bao was indeed the *Immortal Lady*.

She was a Vampire.

Chapter 8

My visitor watched my face closely as I tried to conceal my discovery from her. I needed a minute to organize my thoughts and, more importantly, to dredge up any information dad might have shared with his inattentive daughter.

I stood up, abruptly grabbing the kettle off the table. Walking over to the sink I slowly began rinsing and refilling it.

Shooting a brief look over my shoulder, I casually said, "I'll need time to shed some light on your claims and also to get answers to some pertinent questions, Lady Bao."

I noticed the driver had moved himself, with the same slithery grace of a hunting shark. He now stood behind his mistress. I went on filling the pot and placing it on the stove.

A low droning sound was coming from my guest, but she didn't speak. I felt her watching me with those bottomless eyes.

I turned my back to the odd couple and began to rummage through my pantry for some tea cookies. By the time I had carefully arranged them on a plate, I had resurrected my father's words on Vampires and their unique magical strengths and weaknesses.

Right now I was interested in their vulnerabilities, because I was pretty sure I had two of them scrutinizing my every move.

I came back to the table with my plate of tea biscuits and putting them down, resumed my seat across from my guest.

I decided to be direct in the hopes of disarming her little surprise secret.

"Lady Bao, you have told me who you are and now I understand "what" you are."

The beautiful Lady merely nodded slightly as if she approved of my information gathering technique. The slight curve of her perfect mouth hinted at a smile. I went on.

"I am aware that vampires have been a part of the magical fabric of this realm since the dawn of mankind, but your own country of China, is not known to harbor many Jiangshi as they are named in your land. Frankly, you hardly look the part."

She inclined her head and I continued, snatching quick looks at the minion who had subtly moved closer to his mistress.

My kitchen clock seemed to be ticking off the points as I made them.

"It is reported that Chinese vampires or Jiangshi, are stiff, unable to move arms or legs and are hideous in appearance with greenish-white skin believed to be the result of a fungus that grows on dead bodies.

The Jiangshi were not known to be blood suckers of the living, but were raised from the dead by the use of supernatural arts. It is also said that it takes decades for the deceased to become a Jiangshi and it is thought that their appearances began with the Qing Dynasty."

When I finished, I felt like a grade school teacher, telling the kids about the history of Abe Lincoln.

"You are well informed, Wushen, but I expected no less. You are aware of my history and have your answers to some of your questions. But now, please allow me to instruct your inquiries to both our satisfaction.

Though it is true that I am not entirely of this realm any longer, understand that my antiquity precedes even your most ancient Celtic Mage. I was known as a Lady Doctor in ancient China, famous throughout the empire for my skills with potions and skilled in herbs and plants.

My turning from Lady Bao, Doctor, to Lady Bao, Jiangshi, occurred after I succumbed to a plague that blistered my skin like a million suns had touched it.

My servants refused to come near my fallen body and left me exposed where I lay in my secluded gardens. I had taken refuge there when all ran from my presence in fear for their lives. My body lay upon the soft earth and after a time the sky blackened like a pustule and a storm broke open above me, battering my still form.

A powerful Wizard, named Feng Xi, a great artist and doctor to the Emperor Qin Shi Huang, had heard of my work in the mysteries of medicine and also of my great beauty, which I mention humbly here, to help you to understand his interest in me.

Word had reached his ears from his many spies at Court, that I had fallen gravely ill. He decided to offer me his own medical expertise and healing powers.

And so, the Wizard Feng Xi came to my house and finding my servants emptying it of any valuables and carting off my furnishings and wardrobe, flew into a rage at their disloyalty. He had his own servants subdue them and bind them and under painful questioning, they told him of how my body still lay unburied in my Secluded Gardens.

His guards were ordered to destroy all of my servants for dishonoring me, while Feng came into the Secluded Gardens alone, to find my exposed body."

She paused here in this dreary narrative and hung her head so that her hair covered her face in a midnight veil.

I took the opportunity to ask, "Did he come to bury you, Lady Bao? I know your folklore speaks of the transformation into a Jiangshi occurring if the soul of the deceased fails to leave the body due to improper death and burial."

Looking sharply at me for a moment, as if my very alive human body was an affront to her, she said "This information is correct, yet it was the raging storm which stroked at my fallen body with long tentacles of lightning, that brought about my transformation.

By the time Wizard Feng Xi found me in the Secluded Gardens, I was already sitting up and wearing the pale skin and beauty of my former life; only now, I wore it as a *Jiangshi Immortal.*

The Wizard took me into his own household and I became his servant in all things and protected his life from threats of other Magic Users. I tell you now, Feng Xi was a prideful man.

Though I was bonded to him as mistress-servant to master, he was jealous of my own skills in the mystic arts. As he aged and I did not, his envy began to grow in proportion to his already great age; for only his Dark Magic was keeping his delicate heart beating.

He was desperate to preserve himself from the long reach of mortality, and so, plotted an evil and obscene way to reach his goal of immortality.

He would take the powers from every other Wizard, draining the energies from any Magic user within his Emperor's kingdom and beyond.

To complete this audacious plan he schemed to trick all Wizards, Witches, and Mystics, inviting them to come to the Court of Qin Shi Huang to be rewarded for their service in the *Order of Magical Defenders of the Empire.*

They would each receive a drop of blood from the last Dragon; a Dragon, Feng claimed to hold in his sway. He swore them to secrecy as the Emperor had forbidden any, other than himself, to benefit from the powers granted by the Dragon's life blood.

This was naturally a trap.

He knew that the other Wizards could not ignore such a tempting bounty of Magical power as Feng Xi proposed to bestow upon them. The Wizard Feng understood that the greed for more power would overcome any fear of entrapment and the others would step into his carefully laid snare, blinded by their unbridled gluttony for magical prowess."

The vampire became silent and seemed to be fascinated by a scene playing out before her that only her lifeless eyes could see.

I shot a quick glance at her driver. He stood rooted to my kitchen floor, looking oddly like a muscular undertaker. His eyes seemed fixed on the back of his mistress, waiting for the next finger twitch to signal a new task.

She sat as still as a marble statue. This reminded me that I needed to inquire about Feng's missing statue, "Blood of the Red Dragon". I knew that line of questioning would have to wait until Lady Bao reached the end of her saga.

I filled in the silence with a quick sip of tea, trying to keep things as normal as possible for myself.

As if she sensed my wish that she'd complete her story, Lady Bao broke her silence.

"The Wizard Feng Xi was renowned and feared throughout the Empire for his ability to subdue any person or animal to his will with his enchantments. And so, the other Magic Users believed the story he spread to their ears, that he held a young Red Dragon under his command.

This feat was last accomplished when dragons flew free over vast wild lands; before the Zhou Dynasty began at the beginning of antiquity in China.

He hinted that this dragon was the offspring of the mythical *Hong Wang* known throughout the centuries as the *Red Dragon King*. This creature was possessed of fantastic mythical powers. He ruled over all other flying dragons, as well as lesser magical creatures of light, water, air and fire, such as Hu Far, Tiger Flower, the beast of the hundred deaths.

The wizards secretly came from every corner of the empire to claim their drop of blood of the Red Dragon. They were all given a poison by Feng Xi, disguised as the potent blood they eagerly sought.

When they left the secret chambers of the wizard, Feng, they held death by the hand and walked among the mortals, until their last breath. No longer capable of calling up their charms or spells, wards or protections, they were quickly vanquished by the small army of Immortals such as me, sent out by Feng to destroy all who had been drained of their Magic.

This was done to prevent them from warning others that would follow; blind beggars, each holding the shoulder of the one preceding. All doomed to eternal darkness."

She seemed lost in the memories she had dredged up from a past so distant, I couldn't begin to fathom its relevance to my modern world.

I noticed that as still as she sat, her hands seemed to tremble slightly like delicate river reeds in a breeze. I almost felt the chill of that wind as I looked at her dead-white face and began to experience a pang of sympathy for this young immortal woman.

"I was a tool for Feng Xi to wield," she continued. "My life as a mortal had ceased. Now I was truly the Immortal Lady.

The great wizard, Feng XI, desired me for my beauty and skills and bonded me to himself, as I emerged from my human mortality, into everlasting life as a *Jiangshi, a* vampire. "

I'd never met a living vampire. My experience was limited to folklore and a smattering of instruction by my father, on best ways to destroy them. None of those included a cup of tea and tea biscuits.

"Have you come here on your Master's business?"

"I have." she answered.

"My existence is intertwined with the Wizard's wish to preserve me in this endless cycle of time. However, know this: While I am his agent still, I too have my own purpose for being here. I would call upon the sacred vow made by your ancestors, deep in time; a promise to aid me in a single request."

I tried to shake some information lose from memories I had stored away of my clan's own folk lore.

Our tradition as *Protectors* and members of the *Guild of the Green Wizards* had led many an O'Brien kin into dangerous and often murky waters. Defending the *Green Mother's* natural world was our pledged commitment.

Now, I was sitting across from a vampire claiming rights to my magical intervention based on a promise made in a long ago world.

"What exactly are you asking from me, Lady Bao?"

I decided a direct approach was the only way I could understand what my involvement might be and if, in fact, I was bound to honor a family pledge.

She turned her head slightly and her silent companion knelt at her side, head bowed. Without looking at him, Lady Bao spoke a few words and in a blur he was back to guarding the front door, looking ready to intercept a missile if one was lobbed in this direction.

Wow…two vampires in one day! I was thinking, as I used my Inner Eye to scan the driver and verified my suspicions.

I had remembered something else my dad had said about vampires.

"These creatures are probably the least happy of any denizens from the Dark Pit of the Sleepless Dead."

At the time, I thought this an odd comment since I saw little cheer in any demon. But upon reflecting on the kind of existence a vampire led, I began to understand how life itself could become an endless burden of loneliness and pain. They were doomed to eternally recall a humanity that held laughter and happiness and appetites normal to all humans. None of these could be felt or experienced as a vampire, but all would be remembered.

The lady was rising to her beautifully booted feet. I was a bit alarmed at this shift in position until she said, "Wushen, I wish to present you with this scroll to authenticate my claim to your service."

Here we go, I thought with rising apprehension.

Chapter 9

She deftly produced a rolled parchment from the sleeve of her white silk gown and held it out to me.

What once was probably cream colored paper was yellowed, with spots of encroaching brown on the most exposed areas. It felt brittle and I held it as gently as possible so that I didn't crush it, destroying any possible evidence of her "claim" as she put it. I was sure she would see that as an act of aggression and I couldn't imagine a good outcome in that scenario.

As I began the slow process of unrolling the scroll, Lady Bao moved back to her seat, standing there like a patient, waiting for her doctor's diagnosis. I managed to open the document without tearing any of its corners and began reading the old language of my Celtic-Druid heritage. Translating slowly, I studied every sentence carefully to get the true meaning of the ancient words.

"*We*, the Clan of O'Brien, known in this land as "Exalted Ones" descendants of *Brian Boru*, of the fabled Harp Totem, firstly King of United Ireland in the time marked as the tenth one hundredth year, hereby pledge to repay a debt of honor to the Immortal Lady Bao in answer to a singular request by *The Lady* to render her aid and comfort. This obligation will carry through the ages, until a time The Lady Bao acknowledges the need for fulfillment by a Mage of the O'Brien line. Be it known the origin of this indebtedness lies with the dust and bones of Brian Boru, High King of all Ireland; he who sought out the Magical powers of *The Immortal Lady* to subdue and vanquish

Cu Roi of the fabled Salmon Totem, Druid King of Munster who opposed Brian Boru in His just Royal Quest.

Any of the O'Brien Clan is sworn through the ages to answer the summons of The Immortal Lady Bao in one stroke and one stroke only that will render this debt fulfilled.

Brian Boru, Ainmire Clan O'Brien~
Liam O'Brien, Master Wizard and Witness

I walked over to the kitchen window where a thin winter light was beginning to stream into the room. Studying the parchment closely, I was sure of its authenticity. The archaic language hadn't been in use in Ireland for hundreds of years except by the *Guild of the Green Wizards* as part of our training in the Celtic Mystic Arts. While the text was beautifully executed in a deep black ink, the signatures were written in a rusty shade of red with a Celtic symbol of the Harp of Brian, drawn in the same flaking ochre. He had signed himself "Ainmire" which meant "Great Lord".

Was it done in blood, I wondered? Knowing full well the answer. And there was dad's familiar handwriting, bold and sure.

Oh, Boy, I thought with some real trepidation seeping into my bones.

I was concentrating on the signatures, when I felt a stirring of the air around me and looked up to see Lady Bao standing beside me.

Her eyes shad taken on a resemblance to glass beads, the black showing flecks of red. Her lips were pressed into a hard red slash. She must have anticipated some argument from me about my duty to her.

"Lady Bao," I spoke into the stillness she seemed to create in the room around us.

"I accept this document as a legitimate heirloom of the Clan O'Brien, but I require a fuller explanation of how it came to be. How did my ancient ancestor, Brian Boru, even know of you or the circumstances of your powers? And even more importantly, how did my father come to be a signatory to this instrument?"

The Lady's mouth relaxed from the hard line of determination and a small smile brought back the lovely curve of her lips.

"Your esteemed noble ancestor and father were both powerful Mages in their own right. The High King was able to bring peace where only chaos prevailed by the use of his magical skill.

At a turning point in his efforts to gather the warring clans of his country together under the banner of the Harp, Brian Boru was struck down by a mysterious ailment that brought him to the precipice of death.

He would linger in this state between the light of the living world and the shadows of the dead throughout a long winter.

I had become aware of Brian Boru and his powerful Sorcerer's skills. I crossed often between the realms of the sentient beings and the dark void that holds the cries of the lost souls.

When I felt his life force begin to flicker like a flame in an odious wind, I traveled to his side to offer my aid.

There I found your own father trying to keep him from crossing over into the dark realm before his task of union was met. He was working with a green liquid fire which he poured into the dying king's panting mouth; his spells were powerful, but nearly useless against the long reach of the *Bleak Gardener*."

She paused, giving me a sharp look before saying, "Of course, your father knew better than the sick king that there was a cost tied to my proposed intervention. You now hold that price in your hands."

"What did you do for the High King?" I asked.

"I stayed the hand of the *Gardener* as he came to collect his bounty. I snatched your revered ancestor from his fingers by giving him the life force of my body guard. You see him here today, serving as my immortal protector and companion."

That seemed rather brutal on her part; as if the man held little value in her eyes. But then, she was a vampire, and human life had little meaning and less worth than the shadow she used to cast in the living world.

My suspicions of Feng Xi as the maker of the vampire driver were as ill-founded as my first impulse to pity Lady Bao.

"And my father, what was his part?" I asked, afraid at what I might hear.

"The High King asked your father in his failing breath to help him sign the pledge and to sign his own name as witness and participant. Your father was like an angry bull, stubborn and fearless, demanding more time to vanquish the enemy. In the end, he capitulated to his liege and placed his name beside the king's, insuring the victory I could help achieve.

Her face took on a dreamy look.

"I was then free at last to continue my own quest between the worlds."

"And what exactly do you search for, Lady Bao?" I asked, while carefully rolling the scroll back into its cylindrical shape.

I could hear the kitchen clock as it ticked away seconds that could never be retrieved no matter how strong the Magic. It occurred to me that Lady Bao, this vampire from an ancient civilization, existed in a world without the structure of time. She could never know the boundaries of life as it passed into the next realm of existence. She was a beautiful artifact from the past, present and future.

I looked up from the rolled parchment as she answered in one word.

"Death," she quickly added, "But if not my own mortality, where I can find a longed for peace among the shades of my ancestors, at least the death of my wretched master, the wizard, Feng Xi.

He hangs onto this realm of life like a barnacle to a great leviathan, feeding from its strength. He has been the ruination of many men whose greed for power and wealth made them vulnerable to his manipulations over many hundreds of years. His words, dripping into their ears like poisonous dew hidden in the glow of a soft dawn, led them to their own dark corner of the Pit. He gathers their strengths unto himself, until he can tap into the ultimate powers stored within the last of his great works, the Red Dragon."

She reached over toward me and I placed the ancient paper into her small, pale hand where it disappeared in the hidden pocket of her gown.

"Now that you understand the claim I make upon your powers, Wushen, I believe you have already guessed at my purpose, at least in part."

"I presume you want me to destroy the wizard, Feng, and find the Red Dragon before he does," I said.

"In this you are correct," she said with a slight bow of her head.

"There is, however, one element that I need to share with you now, as it will prove significant to your undertaking.

Feng was not being totally deceptive about the blood of the Red Dragon. He in fact had the last drops from that noble beast frozen inside the sculpture he created, sealing it cunningly into the statue with his strongest spells and wards.

He always planned to keep the power of the Dragon's blood for himself. But first he needed to destroy the other sorcerers and absorb their life forces and magical powers to enhance the blood's magical potency."

I knew there was more to this story, but a question kept nagging at me that needed answered.

"I know dragons were symbols of power and wisdom in Chinese folklore," I said, "and their own magical powers were legendary. How did Feng manage to destroy such a strong being?"

A fleeting look of anguish passed over her lovely face.

"He lured the Dragon King, *Hong Wang* to a cave where he had scattered the bodies of many of the local peasants. These unfortunates had succumbed to a red death that scoured the land like a wire brush.

The dragon had not eaten the flesh of man in many centuries, since his kind were pledged to protect the frailer humans.

The last dragon was very old and weakened by infirmities. It had been many months since he had eaten. The wizard, Feng, spelled the bodies of the dead with the richest scents of roasted meats and succulent fowl.

The Dragon King was driven mad by an all-consuming hunger and fed ravenously upon this tainted feast."

I imagined a macabre scene of rotting death and feverish crunching of disease-covered bone and flesh.

"After many days of consuming these human remains, the Dragon King became aware of himself. He knew he had broken the sacred pledge and he fell into a torpid state of grief.

There was a deep pool of water in this great cavern, filled from a sweet underground spring. The once mighty Dragon King spied his reflection in this mirror of water where he had sought to quench the fire of his thirst. His heart broke with the image of the gore covered creature peering back at him.

Hong Wang died in that cave of desolation, as his life force drained away with the tears he shed from his golden eyes. These things I witnessed myself.

Feng knew the dragon would disappear into the ether as he succumbed to mortality. I was hidden there to gather some of his power-rich blood before it turned to dust."

Lady Bao seemed unaware that she was gripping the back of the chair and had closed her eyes. When she spoke, it was as if she was watching a horror movie, her face strained and frightened.

"I approached the fallen King while he lay quivering in his death throes. Piercing the great tale, I took a vial of blood and brought it to my master."

I waited for more to be said, but Lady Bao had turned away from me and sweeping her fur hat off the table had begun to leave the kitchen, like an actor exiting the stage after a dramatic performance.

I put my cold tea back on the table and followed.

"But how did Feng lose possession of the statue containing the Dragon blood?" I asked her retreating back.

"It was stolen by a fellow courtier of the Emperor's inner circle.

His name was Chung Wu; a scholar and sorcerer of ancient years even then. I knew him as a deadly enemy of Feng Xi, who hated him with a blindness that darkened his vision to Chung's plots and schemes, until it was too late."

"This Chung Wu stole the statue?" I hoped my voice didn't betray my alarm.

"Chung Wu overpowered the men set by Feng Xi to guard the Red Dragon statue as it stood drying on its pedestal. It was rumored he ripped the eyes from their heads and opened their throats as if by a lion's claw, before they could make a sound.

Feng Xi burned the bodies so this could not be verified.

The statue and Chung Wu vanished from the court and the city and eventually, the land. He didn't leave as much as a grey hair behind. Feng Xi was maddened with hatred of the old wizard who had beaten him at his own game of magic. He took revenge on any he suspected of aiding the old sorcerer."

We both stood motionless. Shadows changed places as the low morning light crept into the room. All seemed to be waiting breathlessly for the next word. I had to ask more questions if I was to understand just what lay ahead for me and this latest discovery really set my skin to tingling with anticipation.

"Lady Bao," I said, as she began to turn toward the door once more. "I want to know what you intend to do with the Blood of the Dragon if I am successful in finding and retrieving the statue; and what will I encounter during this mission by way of other Magic Users?"

The beautiful vampire turned slowly back to me and I saw a spark of anger ignite those inky eyes for a brief second. The lady didn't like being quizzed.

"You will most *certainly* succeed, Wushen, and as to Magic Users, they will be less of a challenge to your own powers than a breeze is to a stone tower. When I am in possession of the Red Dragon, I will destroy it, of course. That will mean Feng's end and my freedom from his control.

"But what about the spell and wards placed on the statue by the wizard? How can they be breeched?"

"Why, *you* will break through his wards and undo his spell."

Just what I didn't want to hear, I thought bleakly.

"We shall speak again Honorable Wushen," she said somewhat dismissively.

I said hurriedly, "I'll need more information if I am to undertake such an assignment, Lady Bao. And there are questions I have regarding a message I just received from *another* who searches for the Red Dragon. Perhaps you know of him?"

She was floating toward my front door, like a skater without the ice, followed by her silent driver. She stopped and turned slightly toward me. Her eyes focused like lasers on me.

"Who is this person you speak of, Wushen?" She spoke with the harsh edge of implied threat.

"He owns a book store specializing in ancient volumes of Chinese literature. He has asked for the same help you seek from me. He is no friend of the wizard, Feng, as far as I know, but like you he wants to destroy the statue of the Red Dragon."

"What is this person's name and where does he reside?" she asked firmly, demanding my response.

I didn't want to divulge too much information and thought it best to protect Dr. Chung's identity for the time being. I'd give her a few tidbits of the information Dr. Chung shared in his message.

"I was told by this person that Feng created the statue in the year of his *death*, yet you've told me he still lives. Is he also a vampire?"

Again, I felt the knife-like stare.

"Feng uses a small army from among The Fallen. They search out and capture beings from the realms of the living, especially *Wizards* like you."

I felt a shudder at the thought of this fate. The Fallen were demons who carried the seeds of hate and greed like a terminal disease; to release the "dogs of war" upon any vulnerable society so they can reap the harvest of death.

"Feng consumes the energies that animate each victim. The blood I took from the dying, Hong Wang, will make this unnecessary. He will emerge from his shadowy world like a viper from its shell, to walk in the Living Realms once more. His chosen will be restored to serve him in an army of vampires. They will devour all, as a tsunami devours all that stands before its might."

She seemed to be gazing through a crystal ball, foretelling a horrific future. I could almost smell its corruption and death.

I thought she was finished when Lady Bao added, "Now, for him, there is only a life hiding in shadows, or everlasting life in a body quickened by the blood of the dragon, where all other beings will become his slaves in an eternity of his making."

The blood locked inside the statue held an immense evil. The statue of the Red Dragon had to be utterly destroyed and Feng along with it.

My visitor I included among those that had to be sent to the Dark Realm. She couldn't be allowed to walk in this plane forever.

I hoped fervently that she couldn't read minds as I stood under the glare of her ebony eyes.

Chapter 10

I broke off eye contact with the Lady and asked her if she would be providing me with more information.

She turned to her driver and said something in Chinese. He bowed low and went back into the frigid air where he immediately started the engine. I could hear its smooth hum through the storm door and watched the wipers laboring to clear snow from the front and back windows.

The driver sat behind the wheel with a blank expression on his pale face, just as he had stood throughout the discussion between his Mistress and me. The condensation forming on the storm door glass quickly obscured his expressionless face.

Lady Bao closed the door with a flick of her hand. I felt immediately on guard at her casual use of Magic in my house.

"I do not wish to chill your home, Honorable One, and so have taken the liberty of shutting out the cold." I wondered again if she had read my mind.

She smiled at me after offering her explanation. Seeing her small, perfect teeth as they peeked from behind her perfect mouth, brought to mind the mouth of the King Cobra as it prepared to strike an intended victim.

"Lady Bao," I said, allowing some irritation to seep through in my tone, "All I need from you, is the name of the last place the statue was seen. I believe it was in San Francisco, but…"

"In China Town, more precisely, in the *Historic* China Town, found *under* the existing city," she said, interrupting me.

"My agents have reported that it has made a meandering journey, below the modern tourist center and was last seen in the possession of an elderly Chinese scholar. Perhaps this might be the gentleman to whom you have alluded, Wushen?"

"I can't be sure, Lady, but it is a possibility I will have to explore."

I now had a mystery within a conundrum to investigate.

My dad always warned, "Never jump into an inviting pile of fall leaves unless you're sure that nothing nasty lay under the lovely colors."

Was Dr. Chung what he purported to be, or was I being hauled in like a bass on a good fly reel. I wondered if he had other motives for finding and possessing the Red Dragon.

The sound of the vampire's long fur coat sweeping my carpet brought me back to my current mystery, Lady Bao.

"I will leave you now, Honorable Wushen, to give you an opportunity to consider your plans. You will find my driver has left a copy of the pledge of Brian Boru on your table by the lovely tea set. Your mother's, perhaps?" Her smile seemed genuine, though fleeting; almost like it had pained her to acknowledge a sweet feeling.

Without waiting for my answer she opened both doors with that annoying flick of her hand. I noticed the driver must have used his trusty shovel to remove even more snow and now Lady Bao was gliding over a pristine path of driveway. The rear door was open and she flowed into the back seat like a white cloud across the face of a pond. I noticed the driver had laid his jacket back on the ground and retrieved it quickly when shutting her door. Not a flake to mar her lovely boots.

Before I could blink, the driver had accomplished a difficult U-turn and was heading out of my drive toward the empty road leading out of town.

Pushing the heavy curtains aside, I watched the heavy snow as it slowly reclaimed my driveway.

I had just entertained a vampire in my home, actually two vampires.

When I turned back, my kitchen was still a sunny yellow, and mom's tea set sat on the well-used oak table.

The promised copy of the parchment was lying beside the tea biscuits. I gave it a cursory glance and then proceeded to more enjoyable tasks.

Rinsing my cups after emptying Lady Bao's untouched tea down the drain helped to steady my jangled nerves. Her touch had left an echo of energy on the delicate porcelain, reminding me this would not be our last encounter.

I understood that I needed to begin a journey of honor; a journey fraught with danger and the magical challenges of vampires and dark wizards wielding vast powers.

And then there was the mystery of the man who brought the Blood of the Red Dragon and its sordid history to my door, Dr. Chung Wu. What did I actually know about him except what he chose to share in his letter and hologram?

Holding my mom's tea pot in my hands I ran my finger around the smooth, clean circle of the spout, it dawned on me that I did have some allies in this investigation. One was a very good looking Sheriff and the other was a Master Wizard of the *Guild of the Green Wizards*.

I grabbed my cell phone out of my pocket and dialed the second person on my short list. After two rings it was picked up.

"Hello, Mom?"

Chapter 11

My mother's homeland is the Emerald Isle. She practices a high voltage magic that she named "This and That". It's a mishmash of magical idioms culled from centuries of sorcery and witchcraft, with a heavy emphasis on the Druid tradition.

To mom, magic is indeed a craft; one that she's perfected with the help of my father. They both "fiddled just a wee bit," as mom so coyly phrased their battles against some of the most terrifying demons to ever cross over from the Dark Realm.

Although dad has passed onto the next level of being, mom remains deeply committed to the *Guild of Green Wizards* in service to the *Green Mother*. This seemed a good time to ask her to reach into her recipe box and draw out some powerful Magic for me.

"Ah, Cathleen, love. Is that truly you, girl?"

I loved to hear her sweet Irish brogue. It seemed to have been fully restored to her after her long absence in the USA. In fact, it sounded even broader to my ears since her return to Ireland nearly four years ago.

"Hi, mom! Glad you can still recognize my voice since we haven't talked in a few weeks."

"And so, whose fault might that be, dear girl? I was certain you would have need for me sooner or later, when the little folk told me you've been doing magic in the strangest of places."

The "little folk" she referred to were the Faeries from the surrounding clans, who often visited "Brighid the Beauty" as they adoringly call her.

They were horrible gossips and carried tales of other Magic Users back to her eager ears, where she rewarded their information with sweet treats like honey pies and sassafras tea.

"I'm glad you're keeping tabs on my work mom, because I have a rather unique investigative assignment that will be of interest to you."

"Oh, that does sound intriguing, Cathleen. Let me get myself a "cuppa" and then we'll proceed."

As she put her tea kettle on to boil and gathered up the makings of her wonderful green tea, I answered a few questions about Jason.

"Are you still mad about the dear boy? Should I be looking about for a proper Mother of the Bride dress?"

I was able to answer a succinct "yes" to the first question and "no" to the last.

"Mom, Jason is the one for me, no doubt about that. But we're not ready to get married yet. He's not going anywhere, believe me! We've talked about our future together and for now, that's enough."

I heard the clinking of her spoon on the side of her cup as she sighed deeply and said, "Of course, dear. Just don't wait too long, as the tree doesn't look as grand with too much moss climbing up its backside!"

I said a quiet "Huh?" and said aloud, "Are you comfy, mom?"

"I am indeed, my girl. You can continue."

I had already plopped down on the couch in the living room.

I tucked the old quilt around myself after I made sure the fireplace was well fed for the long conversation ahead.

"I've been asked to locate a statue taken from an art gallery in San Francisco."

"Well, that doesn't sound too challenging, lass," she broke in.

"Except, this particular statue carries spells and wards, placed there by the artist, a dark wizard named Feng Xi. He did this to protect the last drops of dragon blood; drops he infused with his own powerful magic, perverting the dragon's noble magic."

There was a moment of silence before my mother said rather haltingly, "Cathleen, did you say, "Feng Xi" was the name of this sorcerer?"

"Yeah. He's an ancient Chinese Wizard, with a really nasty reputation. Among his more notable acts of Magic is turning unwilling humans into Vampires, enslaved to his will."

Again, there was a deep silence from my otherwise talkative mother.

I said, "Mom? You still there?"

"Of course, dear, but I must confirm something before we go any further.

This wizard, Feng Xi, sounds quite ancient, but the only wizard of that name that I have come across was once a part of the Court of the Qin Dynasty. That would make him a powerful Immortal indeed!"

"He's not an Immortal quite yet, mom! He's kept himself alive using his powers to drain the life force of others, including any Magic Users he can get his hands on. How is it you know of this guy?"

I heard her put her cup down on the saucer with a tiny clink, before she answered.

"Well dear, I'm glad I fixed my tea before this conversation started. I hope you are situated for the next few minutes."

With that she launched into a history of the wizard that more or less coincided with what I'd already heard from Lady Bao.

Mom told me Feng came to the attention of the *Guild* just at the dawning of its own coalition; at the time that the clans of Ireland stopped slaughtering one another and joined under the banner of the Harp.

"You see, dear," mom was saying in her best story-telling mode, "Brian Boru was not only very charismatic, but a Wizard warrior King, who saw Ireland as weakened by the incessant fighting between the clans. He had a clear vision of uniting all the clans under his own leadership and used an iron cudgel to do just that."

There was real admiration in her voice when she related the narrative of the High King, Brian Boru.

"Not only was he the founding rock of the country of Ireland today, but he established the O'Brien clan, of which you are a member through your dear da, rest his spirit in the Realm of Reason and Light."

"Mom," I asked, "how did the Guild know about Feng? He was so far away in China and I can't draw a line to his involvement with our own Magic Users."

"Well, dear, the *Guild* has always had its spies even in its infancy. On the whole, these were sorcerers who were proficient in the art of the devious. They were sent out by the *Guild* to infiltrate the Courts of various countries and times, where the use of magic had been detected or, in the case of Feng Xi, where evil from the Dark Pit had clearly been released upon this realm.

It wasn't difficult for these Spy Masters to locate the Wizard Feng Xi; he operated openly in his country. He had won great favor from his Emperor, Qin Shi Huang and was seemingly untouchable.

As the first Emperor in China, you might recall he had over 7,000 warriors, soldiers, horses with chariots and many kinds of weaponry, created by the artists of his Court.

The Wizard Feng Xi was among this elite group. Through his manipulations and skullduggery, he was able to eliminate all other artists with any power at Court; setting himself up as the Emperor's favorite."

She was quiet again and I visualized her sipping her cooling tea.

"Mom, I've had a visit from another Magic User known to the Court of Emperor Qin, but more importantly, to Feng Xi."

"Cathleen, if this is true dear, you have met with a true Immortal."

"Guess that's another word for her. Her name is Lady Bao, known at that period in time as "The Immortal Lady." She's extremely beautiful and very elegant. Not qualities I expected to find in one of her kind."

I left that hanging out there and mom asked, "What kind might that be,Cathleen?"

"The vampire kind, mom."

Chapter 12

"A vampire you say! By the *Green Cloak of the Mother*, I hope you are mistaken daughter! This is a nasty pot you'll be stirring otherwise, dear girl!"

"Don't worry, mom. I am fully aware of the dangers of dealing with a vampire, but I was hoping to get some background information on Lady Bao and her Master, the wizard, Feng Xi, before I left for San Francisco."

Mom was undoubtedly trying to sort through this new information. I could almost visualize her jumping to her five foot nothing feet in her excitement.

She declared, "Cathleen, you must listen to me closely in this matter. While you are certainly an accomplished Master Wizard, you have never dealt with the likes of a vampire, and especially an *ancient,* therefore, more powerful one."

"I know that, but I don't really have a choice. It's a matter of a solemn pledge given and signed by Brian Boru, to the Immortal Lady on the eve of his last battle at Clontarf. He likely knew he'd be dead soon thereafter, but this ensured his army won the day against the Vikings.

"Have you actually seen this document, Cathleen?" she asked.

"I have a copy of the original, which I held in my hands, when it was presented by The Immortal Lady. It's authentic. It commits the O'Brien Clan to a one-time obligation to Lady Bao, for a service of her choosing. She just made that choice and I don't see any way out of the sworn pledge."

I wandered back into my kitchen, sitting down in front at the cloned document left there by the driver

"Mom, there is something else," I said, trying to keep the alarm out of my voice.

"What is it, daughter?"

"The document has two signatures on it, Brian Boru's and dad's!"

"Ah!" I heard her exhale with a tinge of resignation in the sound.

"Cathleen, it seems the time has come to share a bit of a family secret with you, dear. This will take some explaining, I think."

I was on my feet the minute she said, "family secret," but told her I was fine to listen to her tale, however long.

"Your father, bless his bones, was a most cunning chap when need arose and was considered a Supreme Master in the *Guild.*"

"Mom, just tell me what the secret is," I said. I was getting edgy with anticipation.

"Of course, dear," she said quickly.

"Your father had discovered that it wasn't necessary to be an Immortal to have your way with time. With specialized charms and spells he devised a way to command and *bend* time and space, to his needs. In short, he was a *Voyager.*"

I had been leaning against the sink while mom was talking and my unfocused eyes nearly missed a quick shadow pass over my dormant garden and disappear into the thick trees.

I gave myself a mental shake and asked mom to stop for a minute so I could check something out.

There was no evidence of foot prints in the deep snow and my garage door was snuggly in place, but I felt there was someone watching my house. The tire tracks left by Lady Bao's car had long filled in and were barely visible. I moved to the front window to check things out from that vantage.

"What's going on, Cathleen? Is everything alright, dear?"

Mom sounded very worried, so I was quick to put her at ease.

"It's nothing mom; probably just a raccoon trying to get in my garbage cans."

She wasn't buying that explanation.

"Cathleen, I want you to put your phone down and perform a protection ward right this minute. It can't hurt to be extra careful considering your recent visitors."

"OK," I said, as I placed my cell phone on the window ledge. I raised my hands to the four directions and breathed out the Druid words, *"faaal faaarc,"* building an invisible barrier around myself. I felt it close around me and reached for the phone.

"Mom, did you hear?"

"Yes, dear and that ward should do nicely if anything is amiss there. I have contacted the Little People to see if they have any knowledge of this Lady Bao that they can share with us. I will call you as soon as I have information, dear, but until then do be careful and keep your wards in place."

With that quick directive, mom disconnected from the call and I was left holding my cell phone, listening to dead air. I was also left hanging without an explanation of dad's ability to travel like a silk worm down the threads of time.

Pick that up later, I thought grimly.

I was just turning to go back to the kitchen, when my front window exploded into the living room, scattering shards of glass in every direction.

My invisible barrier stopped any of the pieces from penetrating my flesh; instead they fell around my feet when they broke to dust upon my ward.

The wind that swept through the room stirred the flames in the fireplace to burn more intensely. The curtains that hung on either side of the shattered window twisted and flapped in the frigid gusts.

Thank you mom, I was thinking as I surveyed the room, searching out the intruder I sensed was now with me.

I caught a slight movement from the corner of my eye and slowly turned my head toward the stairway leading to my second floor.

That's when I saw two cat-like golden eyes staring back at me from within a swirl of green mist.

"You could have just knocked, Feng," I said softly to the dragon taking shape a few feet away.

Chapter 13

The golden eyes were suddenly peering over a long green snout. The greenish body emerging from the mist was long and thick, pooling, serpent-like around the floor.

Its legs were stubby, but muscular, ending in large splayed feet with six curved talons on each foot. The massive jaws were filled with several rows of bone-white serrated teeth.

It was perfectly still except for a forked tongue the color of mashed plums darting in and out of that awesome maw.

Studying it closely, I realized it looked like the Imperial Dragons I'd seen depicted in ancient texts.

I stood my ground, protected by my ward and called out, "You've made an impressive entrance, Feng Xi."

As if in response to my remark, the creature let out a stream of gray smoke between the rows of teeth. I wondered if it was smiling, or just heating up its fires to roast me.

I waited for something to happen.

The dragon surprised me when a reedy, heavily accented voice said, "There is no need for your shield, Honorable Wushen. The wizard, Feng, wishes no harm to befall your person."

"Well, I'll just keep it in place if you don't mind," I said, and immediately chanted a second ward to send the *Mother's* energy through my spell. Anything touching it would turn into an ash heap.

"As you wish. The Great Wizard has sent me to bring the Immortal Lady back to him as he now has need of her services. It is known that Lady Bao has been searching for you. I feel the echo of her presence still clinging to this place and have come to take her to the Great Feng."

I thought better than to deny this observation; mostly because Feng's buddy already knew the truth and would catch me in the lie.

Instead, affecting a calmness I wasn't particularly feeling at the moment, I said "The Lady Bao was here, but that is of no concern to the Dark Wizard. I want you gone from my house. Now!

The dragon began to uncoil itself and slowly rose to the height of my twelve foot ceiling, where it had to hunch its scaly back to accommodate at least another foot.

It blew another charcoal cloud of smoke in my direction. I knew it was testing my defenses. My Irish temper began to rise like the smoke drifting through the dragon's jagged teeth.

I said firmly, "I don't appreciate your master trying to intimidate me by sending a messenger with such bad manners to speak with me."

I suddenly dropped my ward and raising my hands threw a nasty bolt of energy directly into the dragon.

The creature tried to lurch back from the full kick that the bolt carried. I increased the voltage and in less time than it takes to spit, the dragon winked out leaving me alone with the acrid smell of sulfur clinging to the cold air.

I knew this was probably only the first of what might prove to be many such visits by Feng Xi's avatars.

I called up a repair charm, bringing the shards and dust of scattered glass together and re-hung the window snugly into the frame. The wind had deposited a light covering of snow in my living room. I held a radiating hand over the indoor winter scene and it all evaporated.

I went back into the kitchen and after flopping back into my chair, fished my phone out of my sweatshirt to call Jason.

"Hey, you." he said, his voice thick with sleep.

"Jason, I'm so sorry to wake you, sweetie."

"No problem, love. Is everything alright over there?"

"Only if getting a visit from an evil wizard's pet dragon is alright!"

Before he began to jump into his clothes, I hurriedly went on.

"It's OK, really, Jason. I dispatched the scaly bugger and sent a message to his handler."

"I'm coming over, Cathleen! You'll need to explain all this in person, so no arguments."

I heard lots of scurrying about as he was probably gathering up some clothes and getting dressed. He'd have one more shift before he could take off for a few days, but he still needed to sleep.

"Jason, please don't come over yet. You won't be any help to me if you're falling over on your face from sleep deprivation! And besides, I've already got this under control. I just wanted to ask you to come earlier than we planned, so I can bring you up to date."

"Cathleen, I will be there in less than 15 minutes and you'll have that coffee pot brewing your strongest for me; then, we talk. I want to be with you so I can judge for myself the threat level of this Feng guy. Anyone that uses a Dragon has got to be pretty powerful I'd guess. Do *you* have dragons doing your bidding?"

With that last comment, I picked up his ritual gun check, before he put it in the holster that always hung on his bed post.

"No, but I know where I can get one if I need to," I answered belatedly.

"I bet you do, Cathleen. I'll be there soon and keep yourself in a bubble or something until you see my headlights!"

I smiled to myself at that suggestion. Jason had been with me inside of a Dome of Safety a few times, but always referred to them as "bubbles".

I assured him I'd be safe and the coffee was on. With that I heard him mumble a quick "See you soon, love."

What was I getting my wonderful man involved in?

Maybe love really is *blind, but it shouldn't be dangerous, for Mother's sake!*

Chapter 14

I went back upstairs to do the minimal amount of fussing over my hair and face. It was a good thing Jason loved the natural look.

The coffee pot was sending fragrant messages throughout the house, reminding me that Jason would be here in ten minutes. I ran into the bathroom to take one last swipe at my unruly curls when my reflection began to shimmer. I could barely make out the expression of surprise on my face when there was a sudden rippling of the glass.

A second later the face in the mirror wasn't mine!

I was staring into the yellowed, rheumy eyes of an incalculably old Chinese man.

His face was crisscrossed by wrinkles, sagging in an ashy yellow from his cheeks and neck. There were a few watery-white wisps of hair, clinging to the shriveled dome of his head. They closely resembled strands of bleached moss, frozen in death on their climb over a knobby rock.

I got over my shock long enough to gasp out a quick ward.

"You are an unwelcome presence!" I said as harshly as I could, considering my shaken state.

The hideous face staring back at me had the same reedy voice I'd heard earlier from my scaly visitor,

"My apologies, Honored Wushen. I regret that my first communication with you . . . ended in such . . . discord." He spoke haltingly as if he'd just run a marathon, but I realized it must have been his great age.

He blinked slowly as if it was a terrific effort.

"You have . . . obviously identified me . . . as Feng Xi, Physician and Royal Artist . . . to the Court of Emperor Qin Shi Huang."

He sounded like someone had his hands wrapped around his throat in a strangle hold.

He continued in that irritatingly broken and scratchy tone.

"Having established my identity, you know I am, like you, familiar with the Mystical Arts."

"Perhaps you suffer from a touch of false humility, Feng Xi. Your reputation as a Dark Wizard has been widely reported. Just state your purpose in appearing to me in this manner."

I was purposely goading him, hoping he'd blurt out something about himself I could use later.

"You speak with much disrespect, Wushen O'Brien, but I will attribute that to your tender years. I am aware that my protégé, the Lady Bao, has been to see you and suspect that she wishes to employ your services to locate a certain item of value to me. You have already guessed at some of my powers, but I assure you, I will move the heavens and the earth, to bring it back into my possession. I reach out to you in this passive manner since my Avatar seemed, shall we say, a bit disconcerting to you, Wushen O'Brien, but now--"

I interrupted him, saying, "I wasn't the one who got a trifle rattled in that meeting. Your dragon was well done I'll grant you, but send other nasty messengers and expect more than lightning bolts coming your way."

He was silent for a minute, but I thought I heard the grinding of his teeth before he spoke.

"Forgive me for underestimating you, but please, do not fall prey to the same mistake regarding me. I am determined to reclaim what is mine and there is nothing in this realm that can prevent that. I am extending to you this courtesy of warning you off any arrangement you may have foolishly reached with Lady Bao. She is *my* servant and cannot act on her own accord, or for her own benefit."

"Funny," I said with a sneer I hoped the old windbag could read in my voice "she didn't seem to profess any particular allegiance to you. In fact, I got the impression she had escaped her bondage to you and had no intention of remaining your "servant", as you call her. She is an Immortal in her own right, so why would she need you?"

"Because, Wushen, I have the power to bring her immortality to an end. I am certain she is enjoying her life as a woman of means in this existence; a woman of greater wealth than any queen. Her life on this plane is of my making and can be undone at a word."

Two points now formed in my mind after hearing Feng rant.

First, Lady Bao was very wealthy, but I suspected she lived like a recluse to hide her secrets. She likely sent her driver out to *shop* when she needed to feed.

Also, Feng revealed he could take away Lady Bao's status as an Immortal, bringing her existence to an end on this plane. *Could he really get the better of an ancient vampire?*

Yet, the Immortal Lady was willing to give up all she was and had, to be free of Feng's authority over her. He claimed the beautiful vampire as his creation, no less than the Red Dragon was of his making.

"Feng, I have no interest in continuing this conversation. You are wasting my time and whatever you have left of yours."

With that I drew back my right arm and slammed the mirror with a flash of green lightning, melting the glass into a puddle that ran down the wall into the sink. I called on a mending spell, cleaned up the mess and used the congealed silvery puddle to re-make my mirror.

Taking a deep breath, I went back downstairs to the kitchen where I stood, moodily watching out the window, thinking and watching the woods.

The spruce trees swayed like huge ships, heavy with their cargo of snow, buffeted by strong winds as they endured a churning sea of white foam.

Watching triggered mom's revelation earlier about my dad's secret ability.

He could move like the wind, through time and space.

I still needed to process the fact that he was a *voyager*; a time traveler. Why the heck I never knew of this talent before was a mystery, but my parents did love their mysteries.

I took a quick look at my clock, expecting Jason to come rolling into my driveway any minute. As if on cue, I heard the sound of heavy tires plowing the roadway.

Looking out my window, it was like some crazed sculptor had been throwing heaps of white clay into lumpy shaped beings.

While I felt badly that he had to deal with the white-out conditions, I was happy Jason was going to be with me.

The tea set had dried in the dish drainer, reminding me of my beautiful, but very dead visitor. It struck me that from here on out, I could expect big trouble to come calling until this investigation was concluded, one way or another.

As a precaution, I slipped into my Inner Eye to scan the room for any unwelcomed visitors. I came up empty, but did pick up the faint glow of energy residue from where the Immortal Lady had sat at the table. This is something like a jet trail left by high flying planes; reminders of a powerful object's recent presence in space and time.

As I leaned over the sink, I saw Jason's SUV pull onto my long drive and pull into his spot.

I opened the back door and unlatched the storm door, watching him park the big vehicle and trudge his way through boot-high drifts.

Jason came into the kitchen wrapped in a flurry of white flakes. He quickly slammed the storm door, latching it automatically.

He was securing the heavy kitchen door, when I stood on tip-toe to give him a welcoming kiss on the cheek.

He turned and smiling down at me, grabbed me into his strong arms and kissed me hard and long on the mouth. I ignored the cold clinging to his coat and hugged him tighter.

"Hi again," I said softly.

He had a dreamy look in his eye. I was hoping it was from seeing me and not from being roused out of his bed.

"Hey, Magic Girl. I'm really glad you called. I want you to know about something I haven't shared with you yet."

While he was talking he slipped out of his coat and boots.

He had piqued my curiosity when he said he had something to tell me, but I knew better than to try to drag it out of him before he was ready to share.

Jason was a rare man, who took his time to judge the moment.

He pulled out my chair, waiting for me to get the cream and put the coffee pot on the table between us. I took my place, but now, instead of sitting across from a vampire, I could enjoy the company of my very alive boyfriend.

Jason had taken the seat occupied by the Lady Bao, but he shot back to his feet almost instantly.

"Wow! I felt like I was just given a jolt from a Taser!" he said as he stood frowning down on the offending chair.

"Jason, I don't know how you felt that!" I said wondering yet again, at his sensitivity to Magic.

I explained "There's always a residual energy signature from Magic Users. What you just felt was left by my recent visitor, Lady Bao."

Since I hadn't shared that particular story with him, Jason had a question planted squarely on his handsome face.

"Lady Bao?" he asked. "Is that a Chinese name and when was she here? Is she connected to the Dragon thing or--"

"Slow down, sweetie. I need to start at the beginning so you can put new eyes on what's looking like a double-edge sword hanging over my head."

Jason grabbed for my hand across the table after taking the chair next to me. He was looking deeply into my eyes and I could almost feel the churning emotions he was experiencing, just under the rough surface of his palms.

"Cathleen, I think I should start first. I need to tell you about one of my visions. I had it just before you got back home from your last investigation. I didn't put much store in it as premonitions go, because it seemed just crazy to me."

As I stirred cream into my mug, Jason sat quietly, waiting for me to speak.

"OK, Jason. I'm ready to listen to your premonition. Don't leave anything out, or try to protect me from any of the ugly stuff."

Chapter 15

He took a deep breath and a sip of coffee, peering at me through the cloud of steam.

"While you were away on your last case, I was investigating my own mystery. We'd had a series of break-ins at remote farms around the outskirts of town. I spent a lot of my night shifts driving around the back roads, looking for any suspicious activity.

During one of these night rides, as I backed my SUV up against the tree line I saw what I thought was a fire in the woods behind me.

Jason's solitary green eye took on a faraway gaze, as if watching an internal video.

"I got out of my car and ran as fast as I could, but could barely lift my legs out of the high drifts. I checked to see if the fire had spread and was relieved when the glow seemed to be fading.

I got to an opening in the woods and saw a cabin, so decrepit it could have been there since the last century. I realized the glow I'd seen earlier was actually a reddish mist, covering the shack. Somehow, I knew the mist was keeping someone inside from getting out.

I stood there, staring and wondering what the heck I was seeing. That's when I saw you step out of the front door."

I sat straighter in my chair when he said that. I was sure this wasn't going anywhere good, but I kept quiet so he could finish.

"You looked like you were running from something, Cathleen; something pretty scary from the look on your face.

That's when I saw a creature come out from behind the house and head straight toward you."

"Jason, can you describe the creature?" I asked anxiously.

"Yeah. It was dark red. It had a thick body; reminded me of a huge moray eel, with a mouth full of teeth. I was surprised how short its legs were, but they were powerful looking. The entire body was covered in scales that looked more like armor. I yelled out to you, but you didn't seem to hear me and looked unafraid.

As soon as I yelled your name, the mist started to dissolve and so did the rest of what I was seeing."

"Did you see if the creature was attacking before it all faded?"

Jason was looking down at his coffee, searching for the memory on the black surface.

He shrugged as he answered, "No.

I reached out for his arm and laid my hand on it to try to reassure him.   Unfortunately, I wasn't feeling particularly reassured myself. I hate trying to figure out visions, especially when they concern me and creatures with lots of sharp teeth.

"Jason, we'll think about your vision, but I need to tell you everything that's happened since I opened that hologram with you. I'd better get you caught up with my early morning visitor and the mirror trick Feng Xi played on me after."

Jason looked worried as he said, "Let's take our mugs into the living room so we can sit in front of the fire. You know that's our best "war room."

"Jason," I said, after we settled in, "your vision, as worrying as it seems, can help me in what I have to face eventually. I think you under-estimate that the more I know, the more focused my magic can be when it actually happens."

Jason leaned down and kissed me gently. Looking intently at my upturned face he said, "I hate seeing things like that, Cathleen; things that might hurt you, but I'm certain this vision has something to do with the new investigation."

"I clearly felt danger, Cathleen," he continued, "but strangely, it didn't feel like that creature was the source."

I began to wonder what I'd found inside the cottage and whether the red creature was really dangerous to me.

Another mystery within a mystery.

"Now, tell me what's been going on here since I left you earlier," he said.

I related everything about the visit by the mysterious Lady Vampire and her eerie driver, to the annoying use of my bathroom mirror by Feng Xi.

He listened attentively, without any visible reaction to what I was saying; even when I mentioned that the Lady was very ancient and therefore, extremely powerful.

"Cathleen, I think we need to bring some heavy guns into this case. How about we contact your mom as back-up?"

"I've already spoken to her, so she knows some of the particulars. I called her right after my visit from the Lady Vampire and her weird driver. She told me some interesting stuff about dad."

"I've had a few thoughts of my own regarding your dad. I think your dad travelled back somehow, to the time of Feng Xi and the Lady Bao. That would explain how his signature was on that pledge."

"Wow! You're spot on, sweetie! Mom told me my father was a *Voyager,* but not in the sense of the vampire, or Feng Xi.

He was able to manipulate the time continuum with secret spells. He used his magic to "bend time".

According to mom, dad was with the High King, at his last battle. He and the King both signed the pledge to insure Lady Bao's aid in securing their victory against the Norsemen and to insure the foundation of the O'Brien Clan. There might be other reasons we can only guess at."

I was certain my mother knew the whole story. She and dad had no secrets from one another. He believed, "If you need to hide something from yer mate, yer in the wrong bed!"

Jason had stretched his long legs toward the fire, leaning back on an elbow as he listened. I was having troubling doubts about involving my love in what could be my most dangerous investigation to date.

It was going to be a lethal game, with all the players looking for the weaknesses in the others to give themselves an edge. Was Jason going to be *my* weakness?

"What are you thinking about, love?" he asked.

"I was just going over some of the characters in this weird drama and how they all seem to know a lot about me. That means they also know about the man I'm crazy in love with."

Jason sat up and wrapped his arm around my shoulders. We sat quietly for a moment, watching the fire consume the last of the logs.

"Listen, Magic Girl, I know you're worried about my involvement in this case, but I have my visions and that might give us an edge, like you said."

I couldn't argue with that. It's good to know when there's a cliff ahead before you take the next step!

Besides his visions, I'd begun to notice that Jason seemed to be evolving in his abilities to sense the presence of magic; he was becoming more tuned into my world. In fact, sometimes I wondered if he was sharing everything about those abilities with me.

Usually, when I mention his new-found talents, he shuts down the conversation with some joke about being a direct descendent of some long-dead Gypsy King.

Makes me laugh, but with his dark looks and penchant for seeing into the future...stranger things are believable to a Wizard.

I was thinking how little I knew about his parents, or family history, when Jason started to stand up.

Ruffling the top of my head, I knew he was going home. No questions would be asked or answered. Whatever his story, Jason was definitely part of the magic in my life.

Chapter 16

Just before he left, Jason added new logs to my fireplace. With the comfort of the roaring fire, I curled up with the blanket in my overstuffed chair, letting my mind wander to the mysterious Chung Wu.

He was more of an enigma than the vampire, or Feng Xi.

Was he also an Immortal? If he was, did that mean he was also a vampire?

I speculated about underlying motives Chung might have in locating the Red Dragon. By his own admission, he was a sorcerer. The fact that he called upon my help made me wonder about his powers. Perhaps he was limited in them by some sort of spell. There was a chance that the *Guild* might have interacted with Chung Wu somewhere during his long life and he was paying the price for bad behavior. The *Guild* had its tentacles everywhere and wasn't restricted in their reach to this realm alone.

I wondered if Dr. Chung and the Immortal Lady sought me out because I looked like an immature mage to them, posing no real threat if I decided to keep the statue for myself.

Another question just dangling out there, I thought glumly. I hated dealing with so many unknowns, but then, I didn't write the script.

I had already done preliminary research into the area in and around San Francisco's China Town. After refilling my mug and grabbing my laptop and the new information, I returned to my little nest in front of the fireplace.

I was about to type Chung Wu's name into Google when I had a memory blip; Dr. Chung had called Feng a *Voyager* in his hologram, saying Feng Xi used the Black Arts to achieve that feat.

I now knew my dad was able to travel in time, using spells. I speculated that dad's path might have crossed with the infamous Feng, making the Lady Bao the common denominator in that equation.

Dad didn't have to travel to China; only back in time to the decisive battle that led to the unification of Ireland.

Not for the first time, I wondered what part dad had taken in that final battle. Maybe he worked his magic alongside of the Immortal Lady to win the day for the king's men.

I typed in the words "Qin Dynasty Court Artist, Feng Xi," and began taking notes. I found nothing significant except that he had a fearsome reputation for being ruthless in gaining favor with the Emperor.

After nearly two hours of trying to refine my search, I gave up on trying to get more solid information on the Wizard. He must have been a mystery even to his contemporaries. There was little written of him and most of that was speculation on his origins and death, especially the disappearance of his body after this was reported.

I worried that I'd have to look to Dr. Chung to help supply the particulars.

Unfortunately, I had my doubts about him as a source of information. He was definitely more than just the loyal art agent working on behalf of his employer.

For all I knew, Dr. Chung and the owner were one and the same person. It seemed feasible that Chung Wu had stolen the statue from the gallery himself and was hiring me simply as a smoke screen, to appear above suspicion.

Leaving off my search on Feng, I went on to the Immortal Lady where I easily confirmed her historic role in ancient China.

She held an honored place as a healer and medical pioneer, and was highly regarded by both the peasants and nobility. Folklore rose around her even in death, when it was reported she succumbed to a devastating plague. It was noted her body, like Feng's, had mysteriously disappeared.

Sightings of Lady Bao were reported by local peasants and recorded by palace Scribes. Her beauty it was reported was undiminished even after death had claimed her body.

As with all people from our earthly past, Lady Bao slipped into history, as a ghost slips through a locked key hole.

The peasants were right about the noble Lady. Now that she had made herself known to me, I had a new respect for the truth behind many folk tales.

I wondered how much the *Council of Green Wizards* knew about the quest for the Red Dragon by the three Magic Users.

It was time to get my mother fully involved. She could tell me everything she knew about the players in this unfolding drama. Oddly, I couldn't shake the feeling that she had secrets she hadn't shared. This was going to be like panning for gold and that doesn't always end well.

Chapter 17

Dark forces gathered in preparation for the approaching storm of evil.

Feng Xi, or for that matter, any being that had twisted the natural cycle of life such as a vampire, held an unnatural place in a realm in which there was a natural order and a natural life span for all life forms.

I called mom's cell phone, though it had been "tinkered with a trifle". She placed a charm on it so it couldn't be triangulated for positioning.

"Why would I want anyone to know where I was at any given moment?" she'd asked indignantly, when I questioned her *improvements.*

She must have been holding her phone in her hand. She answered almost before it rang.

"Hello, Cathleen dear. I expected you'd call back after you had a wee bit of time to consider your position."

"Yeah, mom. I've been talking things over with Jason too, trying to get his perspective. And there's been another development that I need to share with you."

"Ah, I expect that this has something to do with the Wizard Feng Xi, dear."

"Yes, but how did you guess that?"

"The Little People from the County Clare clan wasn't it. They were fizzy with excitement yesterday when they flew over for a bit of biscuit and honey.

They spoke of a sorcerer with ancient powers using his Dark Magic to travel like a bleak wind. He has reportedly established a kind of Royal Court and stronghold. I'm certain it's that rascal, Feng."

"Did the Faeries of Clare happen to tell you *where* Feng was locating his power base, mom?"

"Indeed. They say his stronghold is hidden from all eyes, it being the case that the modern China Town in San Francesca is directly *above*!

What was once a sprawling neighborhood of early Chinese immigrants is now buried beneath today's China Town tourists attractions. The Faeries report that it is not unlike the catacombs of ancient Rome, and you know how they *hate* those!"

I interjected, "Mom, rumors about a secret underground China Town have been floating around since before the establishment of the current community. Supposedly it existed all along, from the eighteen hundreds, until the great earthquake in 1906. I've read the original catacombs hid gaming houses, opium dens and just about any other kind of criminal entertainments.

But between the destruction of the earthquake and the general erosion of time, I can't imagine anything exists but rubble and ruin down there."

"I'm happy you've been studying up on this dear, but the Little People have been informed by the highest source among the Fey, the *Teacher*."

I took a breath and held it a second. The shiver running down my spine had nothing to do with the winter chill.

I asked in a wavering voice "Did you just say the *Teacher* is involved?"

The *Teacher* isn't a caring kid, fresh out of college, trying to hammer some rules of English Grammar into a room full of squirming third graders.

The *Teacher* was anything but caring, or patient. In fact this post was held only by the scariest from the Faerie Clans, usually a sorcerer with probable sociopathic undertones to his personality.

He only held that position after passing through a hierarchy of leadership levels, plus life and death challenges to his magical abilities.

There was no gender or origin bias in the position of *Teacher* so any from among the Faerie Clans could apply to the deadly selection process. The sitting *Council of Green Wizards,* with all their Magical cunning, would act as opposition to all candidates, hurling incredibly complex spells at them, each becoming more lethal as they progressed onto the last stages of selection.

This would eventually leave two candidate combatants. They would battle under diabolical conditions, where both would be given several handicaps, such as blindness, or paralysis. Finally, after relying on their individual prowess, the process of elimination was complete.

The one left standing, if he could, was granted the status of "Fey Gladiator," kind of an Oscar at the Academy of Awards," except with ultimate magical powers.

The *Teacher*, having achieved such a pinnacle in the world of Magic took up permanent residence among the clans of the Faeries. There, he or she (there has only been one female in this ancient ritual) begins their role of *Teacher* to the Fey; guiding and protecting them with godlike knowledge of the four planes of life and unparalleled use of magic.

The Faeries keep the location of the *Teacher's* forest home a secret under penalty of death. In return, they are privy to everything happening in the world of Magic from the crossing over of a Demon from the Dark Pit of the Sleepless Dead, to the presence of Immortals in this realm.

Mom was saying, "There is something very pertinent, Cathleen, to your search for the Red Dragon and its connection to the *Teacher*."

That got my attention.

"When your father voyaged back to the time of Brian Boru, he didn't travel alone. He took two of the strongest from the clan of County Clare Faeries. They had proven excellent warriors and as brothers, they fought like one being.

When they arrived with your father at the Battle of Clontarf and sought out Brian Boru, they placed themselves at his service. The High King asked that your father send the two warriors to reconnoiter the Norsemen's battle positions.

Unfortunately, the Wizard Feng detected the presence of powerful Magic Users entering this plane.

He sent a small contingent of Immortals led by the Lady Bao to capture and bring the interlopers to his secret dungeons beneath the Imperial Court. They traveled in the same way your father did; back and forth in time as needed to achieve their ends.

Your dear da' never forgave himself for what befell the two brothers while he stayed behind to act as Warrior Wizard to the High King.

The brothers were lured into a trap by Lady Bao, posing herself as an injured runaway slave belonging to a lord from the invading army. She captured them both at one stroke, using eye glamour to disarm their natural wariness until she could overpower them.

They were taken back to her Master, Feng Xi, frozen by the glamour charm and utterly defenseless."

"Mom, that sounds terrible, but what does that have to do with the *Teacher*?" I asked trying to contain my impatience at the long story.

"Cathleen, Feng tortured one of the brothers terribly; ripping off his arms and pouring acid into the stumps and sealing them to keep him alive to endure more agony.

Feng used many spells to hurt and maim the one brother, forcing the other to watch in horror; only able to make futile threats of revenge. Just as the tortured brother expired, Feng was able to cast a spell and capture his spirit, placing it into a dark lifeless state; depriving it of re-birth into the next plane of being.

This was the ultimate torture. The lone brother swore eternal vengeance on Feng Xi and his followers, until all were destroyed."

"Did the last brother escape, mom?"

"Oh, indeed he did, Cathleen. Your father was made aware of the capture of his friends by the Lady Bao herself, when she secretly traveled to join him and the High King to move her scheme along.

She wanted to assure your father's help in securing the pledge binding the O'Brien clan to her service. She is a most patient and devious woman, the Lady Bao."

"So," I said thinking out loud "she engineered the capture of the two warrior Faeries, to get dad on board with signing the pledge. She created her own blackmail using the brothers as both bait and pawns."

Mom said softly, "Your father tried to save the tortured brother, but was unable to. On one of his first trips back, he was able to overcome Feng's guards and destroy the part of the dungeons holding the surviving brother, rescuing him and sending him back to his Clan.

He continued to voyage back to Feng's time over and over, until he was able to destroy the whole network of cells, but was never able to locate Feng Xi."

That explained many of my dad's "business trips" while I was growing up. I never could figure out just what that business was; now I knew he'd been on a search and destroy mission.

"And what about the brother whose spirit was held by Feng?" I asked, hoping for a better outcome.

"His spirit still languishes in darkness, awaiting release, Cathleen. His brother has said he intends to join your assault on Feng's hideaway and free his brother's spirit into the next realm of life and peace. This will be accomplished with Feng Xi's destruction."

As I was processing mom's story, it dawned on me who the second brother was.

"Mom, the brother that escaped is the *Teacher*!"

After she confirmed my guess, she told me he was determined to complete his revenge on the Wizard at any cost.

"You know lass, if the Faeries heard this information from the *Teacher*, you can certainly rely on its validity. The Dark Wizard is burrowed deep beneath the modern streets of China Town and I fear he has several minions to do his bidding."

I moved out of the living room where the fire had burned itself down to red embers, climbing the stairs to my bedroom. I wanted to change out of my sweats and put some heavy clothes for a trip I needed to take into town.

"Mom, I'm going to put you on speaker so I can change."

"That's fine, pet. I'll try to repeat everything the Little Folk shared with me regarding the Dark Wizard."

That said, she described how Feng Xi had established hive-like quarters, clearing some of the old tunnels and opening primitive passageways deep beneath San Francisco's modern China Town.

"It looks alarmingly like he is making this a permanent residence, dear."

To create his worker-army, Feng captured the life force of any living creature that fell into his hands; even the rats that scurried throughout his maze of tunnels.

He instilled that energy into mindless creatures to carry out his will. They had supernatural strength, working like tireless moles, beneath the earth. From the description that mom repeated to me, Feng designed these beings from the sludge found at the bottom of the Dark Pit of the Sleepless Dead; a place he traveled to with ease of practice.

They were living-dead; their grey, hairless bodies covered in seeping pustules that carried the odor of rotting corpses. Feng had created them all alike; flat, featureless faces, limbs knotted with ropy muscles and walking in a shuffling gait like zombies. He obviously liked the mold they were cast in, because he'd made several dozen; a small army of demons right beneath the streets of a major American city.

Feng was close to sending his dark creations up to the light of our realm, to hunt down the statue of the Red Dragon.

"Mom, did the *Teacher* say how much time we had before Feng releases his demons?"

"They don't know, but it sounds like they are moving swiftly toward finishing the crude network of passageways down there. And one other thing dear, Feng is on his own quest; he'll be hunting down his old nemesis Dr. Chung Wu."

There's my mystery man again.

"Mom, how's your calendar looking right now?"

"I've already booked my ticket to San Francisco, dear. I just love to travel you know." she said with a smile in her voice.

She finished telling me how the Grant Hotel was strategically located when I interjected.

"What do you think I should do about Lady Bao? I'm pretty sure she'll be back in touch, or maybe even come visiting again."

"Unhappily for us, the Lady is correct in her claim to our help, Cathleen, and there's naught to be done for it I fear.

When your dear da' took his first of many historic "voyages" he returned with quite a tale to share with me. You were a wee lass at the time and won't recall the stir he created in our house." I heard her softly chuckle at the memory.

"I won't go into it until we are together dear, but suffice it to say, it is a true document she gave you and the O'Brien Clan is committed in blood to fulfill that pledge."

I didn't like hearing that, especially the "committed in blood" part.

"When she gets in touch with me for her answer, I guess I'll have to say yes," I said without much enthusiasm in my voice.

"Cathleen, you are clearly a fine Wizard and come from a long line of Wizards serving the Green Mother with distinction. Do not think for a moment that you will be outwitted, or outdone, by these other Magic Users. They have only the Dark Arts; you, my darling girl, have ME!"

After mom's many warnings to stay safe, I went to check out the itinerary she had emailed to me, just before I called.

She knew me like the clapper knows its bell.

Chapter 18

Jason called a few minutes after I hung up with mom. I laid out our travel schedule and he said he'd take care of getting our tickets.

My next call was to Joanie. I gave a quick synopsis of our plans and the investigation. She nearly broke my eardrum with her answer when I asked if she was interested.

She wasn't the least bit put off when I mentioned vampires and immortals and I wondered if her heavy diet of zombie movies made her blasé about creepy creatures.

Joanie was going on about the thrill of the mission, while I was thinking about how to keep a low profile. Her job as an ER nurse must give her nerves of steel; a thought I've had on many occasions over the years.

After what felt like hours on the phone arranging for mail and Ollie's stay with the Vet, I was ready for nasty weather, hoping that was the only nasty thing I'd be running into.

I knew I'd find Jason at the Iron Mountain Fidelity Bank.

The Bank had a small Travel Agency located just off the lobby. This innovation coincided with the return of the Bank President's daughter to town with her newly minted certificate as a Travel Agent.

I hoped Jason had handled any nosey questions about our trip, when I spotted him sitting in the small "Excursions Unlimited" agency office.

He had one leg crooked across the other, supporting his heavy jacket and knit cap. The two young women working there were standing side by side, dimpling like two fourteen-year-olds.

I stood just outside the open door until Jason turned his head, following the direction of their distracted looks.

"Hi, love," he said, standing, throwing his coat and hat onto the chair as he leaned in to kiss my cheek.

I smiled up at him. "Thought you'd be done here. You finish up and I'll see you back at the house later."

Both girls were trying to look like they weren't eavesdropping, but failing miserably. Jason reached into his shirt pocket, pulling out a folded paper.

"You'll want this, Cathleen."

I slipped it into my coat after scanning the schedule for my flight out of the tiny Iron Mountain Airport, to a private airport near Pittsburgh International. I'd planned to meet up with Joanie at PIA.

"Thanks, sweetie," I said, as he bent down to receive my goodbye kiss.

The weather had continued to get meaner as the morning wore on, with the prediction of another two inches of snow reported by my radio-heads back at WHIP.

It was fun to tune into a radio station that I owned, though I rarely visited the office these days. Fortunately, I have a top notch staff looking after the day to day business of running the place, but I decided I better put in an appearance, to let the Station Manager know I'd be out of reach for at least a week.

I had hired Virginia Connell away from a mid-size station in Massachusetts for two reasons: she knew how to run a successful radio station and she loved the snow.

I got to the station and was pleased to see that the parking lot was recently plowed, though the snow was relentlessly covering it over as I pulled into my parking spot.

I still laughed with Jason about my being a "media mogul" now, but we both knew this was only a good cover for me and my real work, magic.

Our receptionist, Martha, a delightful older woman in her mid-sixties has the dignity of a Dowager Queen. She maintains a serene, unruffled manner, no matter what challenges come across her desk.

After a quick gossip with her, I gathered up the pile of mail she handed off to me and proceeded up the worn marble staircase to the second floor and my office.

"Oh! Ms. O'Brien!" Martha called out as I made the first landing. "You had a visitor yesterday evening, just as we were closing the office. Guess they didn't mind the storm. Anyway, since you weren't here, I had him leave the package with me so I could get it to you today if you stopped by, or deliver it later at your place."

With that, Martha poked her head under her desk for a minute and pulled out a small box wrapped in brown shipping paper and bearing some odd looking stamps.

"It appears to be from China!" Martha said with a tinge of awe in her voice.

I always wondered why people were so impressed by the arrival of things from distant countries; especially when almost everything seemed to be from somewhere else.

I returned to Martha's desk and took the package along with the rest of the mail to my office. I didn't get there for another five minutes as I had to pop into various offices and studios to check in on staff. They were gratefully low maintenance as far as personal attention from me.

On entering my office, I threw my coat and scarf on the guest chair, dumping the mail on the desk. There was a pile of pink phone messages, but rather than plow through them, I buzzed my Administrative Assistant, Darla Stinson.

As she came into my office I looked up and, as usual, was greeted with a cheery smile.

"Welcome back, boss!" she said.

She took my coat and scarf and automatically hung them up for me. I thanked her, rather embarrassed at my own laziness.

I noticed that her hair was now a distinctive shade of red and cut into a kind of spiky, punk style. Pretty radical for Iron Mountain's one and only salon.

Darla was a size zero and looked like a stiff mountain breeze would whisk her into the next state. But looks are deceiving. She has a black belt in Tai Kwon Do and runs five miles every day, using the indoor track at the high school in winter. I got winded just thinking about her daily routine.

"Darla," I said smiling back at her "it's good to be back but it'll only be for a few days."

I went on to explain a quick business trip I'd be taking to the west coast. Darla took the pink message slips back to her office to cull out the ones needing immediate answers.

When she left I turned my attention to the small package postmarked China and grabbing my pocket knife, began to attack its multi-layered security tape. When the heavy brown wrap fell open, a plain wooden box was revealed, reminding me of the rough crates used to ship fruits.

If this is any kind of fruit, it has to be midget melons I thought as I rummaged in my desk drawers for a tool to open the mystery box.

I settled on my letter opener, already a bit mangled from other incidents of ill use. Expecting an ornate Chinese fan, or a replica of the Great Wall with a panda sitting atop, I was stunned when the lid joined the rest of the packing mess scattered on my desk.

I lifted out a highly varnished cherry wood box. It was inlaid completely with a lustrous Mother of Pearl and what appeared to be, semi-precious stones embossing its lid. These were artfully placed to create a strikingly beautiful mosaic of a fire-breathing red dragon. The deep colors of the stones against the creamy pearl tone, set off the intensity of the fire and I imagined I could almost feel the heat.

"Wow!" It was Darla returning to my office and looking with wide eyes at the fantastic artifact on my desk. I was certain it was no replica, but an original and could only guess at its age.

"Yeah, it's really something isn't it?" I said trying to cover my true emotion of alarm at what I feared was a Trojan horse.

"You must have done something really nice for someone, Cathleen. Were you ever in China? I noticed the postmark."

"I've never travelled there, but hope to one day. I haven't found any card with this yet," I said, as I shuffled through the wrapping paper and tape.

"Why don't you open the box, Cathleen? I'll bet they put a card inside." She closed my door and watched while I shoved the mess to one side.

I had wanted to do this in private in case my suspicions proved correct and this was no gift, but a warning.

Unfortunately, Darla was firmly planted in front of my desk and obviously was not going anywhere until I unmasked the sender.

I lifted the ornate lid expecting some kind of nasty surprise, but I wasn't prepared for the hideous phantom face of Feng Xi staring up at me.

It opened its shriveled mouth, shooting out a yellowish stream of gas.

Immediately, an overpowering odor of rotting corpses escaped into the room. We both began to experience uncontrollable gaging and coughing. My lungs were being squeezed and I knew my airways were closing off. My throat was on fire as the cloyingly sweet scent was all I breathed in.

I looked up at Darla and saw that her face was turning a deep shade of red. Her eyes bulged as she doubled over, clutching at her throat, trying to pry ghostly steel hands as they strangled the life out of her.

I slammed the lid down, but not before I spotted a piece of tightly rolled parchment paper through the blur of tears streaming from my eyes.

"Darla, you'd better leave the office so I can open my window and air it out. I'll be out in a minute."

I was wiping away the tears from my face trying to look only mildly concerned; she wasn't buying it.

"I'll get the window," she said as she sprinted over to the window behind my desk. Before I could object, there was a cold breeze stirring the back of my hair.

"Thanks. Something very potent must have been released when I opened this darn thing up." That sounded pretty lame, but I was trying to keep any panic from building up.

I came around to the front of my desk and grabbed my coat off the hook by the door.

I slipped into it again saying, "I may have Jason look at it, in case there's of some kind of terrorist activity involved."

As goofy as that idea sounded to me, Darla seemed to think it was plausible since we were "part of the media" as she was quick to remind me. Sometimes, the more farfetched you make something sound, the more believable it seems to become.

My throat still felt like I'd swallowed sandpaper with an acid chase.

Darla's voice was scratchy sounding as she wiped delicately at her eyes.

I asked her to take the unopened mail back to her office and deal with it. She cleared her throat and made a face.

"I can *taste* that smell, if that makes any sense." She scooped up the pile of envelopes and left for her own office, but not before giving the offending cherry wood box a look of deep mistrust.

"Well, that was fun," I mumbled to myself. I usually loved surprises, but this one pretty much stunk.

I needed to retrieve that parchment to find out who sent me a beautiful trap. Whoever it was, didn't intend it to be lethal, only damaging.

I used a ward to prevent any other release of noxious vapors from the box.

I breathed out the words in a long exhale, *"Breaaac traath."*

This enchantment would cause the pungent particles to coalesce, colliding together into a tight, nearly invisible ball.

I slipped into my Inner Eye to verify success and gingerly lifted the ornate lid.

A ball of inert elements had rolled into the corner next to the parchment. I reached in and carefully removed the scroll.

Using both hands, I laid it on the desk and slowly uncurled it until I could hold it flat at the edges.

The vapor's scent clung to the paper, though thankfully only as a vague odor. The hand writing was almost classically beautiful on the parchment, written with soft swirls and sweeping curves.

Geez, looks like a Monk transcribed this from some medieval text, I thought, as I let my eyes take in the script.

That's when I saw the signature at the bottom, written in a sure flourish... *Feng Xi.*

Chapter 19

No matter how I looked at it, Feng had reached out his withered, evil hand to me and I took it in mine.

I felt embarrassed at how easily he had captured my curiosity by placing the Red Dragon on top of the exquisite wooden box. I was too entranced by the richness and artistry of the gift, to slow myself down long enough to ward it properly. What a truly bone-headed move my dad would be saying to my red face about then,

How can I hope to find the statue and defeat a legion of bad guys, when I can't even control my impulse to see pretty, shiny things!

I sighed then refocused on the text of the parchment.

Wushen O'Brien,

I trust your breathing has returned to normal. Understand, I predicted your rash action and knew you would open the beautiful box I prepared for you. Consider this a warning of how easily I can reach out to you, and to those you cherish. You have little chance of finding the Red Dragon, but if by some fluke you do, I will quickly reclaim it and I assure you, you will be lying at my feet when I do.

Feng Xi

I reread it. I'd have to share it with Jason and let mom know the Dark Wizard had made a fool of me and that I'd exposed my Assistant, Darla to the same danger.

I was trying to mentally prepare myself for an ego-deflating lectures when my cell phone rang. I saw who it was and after taking a cleansing breath of the frigid air answered.

"Hi, honey. Did I ruin Gracie's day too badly?"

"I think she'll survive, although I think she might have found a better deal on our tickets if I had been more receptive to her sashaying about the office."

We both laughed though I wondered how long he watched her swinging her hips. I hate that little twinge of jealousy when it pops up like an annoying zit.

"Jason, something has come up that directly impacts our investigation."

I heard what sounded like a car door slam shut and asked, "Are you in your squad car now?"

"I'm just turning onto Main and will be at your place in twenty minutes, love. Don't let anyone in, but me!"

With that he hung up. I buttoned my coat and grabbed the booby-trapped box off the desk.

Poking my head into Darla's office, I gave her some specifics on my upcoming trip and said I'd be gone the rest of the day. I was relieved to see she'd fully recovered and quickly made my exit.

I had neglected to tell Jason I was coming from the station and he'd probably assume I was home. I drove a bit faster anxious to get there before him.

The wind was picking up the fluffy tops off the snow mounds and causing dangerous white-out conditions. I was barely able to see ten feet ahead of my Jeep's headlights.

I was pumping my brakes as I neared a sharp curve, when something came out of the swirling veil of snow directly ahead. Whatever it was, was heading straight at my car.

Swerving wasn't a good option, so I kept pumping the brakes, hoping to pull over toward the trees. I knew the road's shoulder was a safer alternative than hitting an unidentified object.

The Jeep jerked when I pressed the brakes a bit too hard, slid and bumped to a stop.

Taking a second to collect myself, I looked in the rear view mirror to see what I had avoided hitting.

I blinked my eyes. The lumbering shape of a battle-dressed Chinese warrior stepped out of the blurring white screen like a phantom onto a stage.

He looked uncannily like one of the Painted Terra Cotta Army created by the first Emperor, my old friend, Qin Shi Huang. He had an army of thousands like this guy, created as guardians of his elaborate underground burial site, more than 2,000 years ago. I quickly recalled mom's comments on Feng Xi being one of the artists on that project.

If this guy was one of that bunch, I could be in for some trouble. That would mean Feng had access to a whole army and had found a way to bring them to life.

From what I knew of this fabulous archaeological find, there were likely 8,000 warriors guarding the tomb complex along with chariots and horses. Each soldier was as individual as a snow flake and was fully armed with swords, spears, axes, and whatever else they used to slice and dice enemies back then.

I noticed the soldier was approaching me very slowly. The sword held at his side was cutting a deep gouge in the snow piles he stomped through. His other hand held some kind of battle ax. Maybe he thought I wouldn't go down easily.

Right he was!

I jumped out of my car, nearly falling face first into a snow-covered depression.

Righting myself, I raised both hands and shouted "Claiomh Solais," calling down the Druid *Sword of Light,* to stop the unwavering clay killer before he got any closer.

A searing flash of light forced me to slip into my Inner Eye so I wasn't blinded. The long sword hung directly in the path of the advancing warrior. It was at least four feet from bejeweled golden hilt, to the tip of its deadly four feet of curved blade. Dad told me this weapon would open a stout tree to its very heart as if it was a stick of butter.

It hung suspended in the blinding white-out. The wind whipped around my head, snapping my long hair into my face like a cold slap.

The soldier seemed unperturbed by the dangling threat and came steadily toward me. I figured he hadn't heard about this famous magical device since he approached so calmly into its range.

We were close enough now that I could make out his features. His eyes were a dull black, like thin drops of dried tar splashed on the ochre colored skin of his face. His nose was broad and flat. A well-sculpted mustache drew my eyes toward the cruel sneer twisting his mouth; the only emotion he displayed.

He was dressed in quilted armor, his hair pulled up into a tight, bun-like style that could easily have been some sort of skull cap.

Just when I thought he would advance on me, ignoring the *Sword of Light,* he came to an abrupt stop and drove his own sword deeply into the snow in front of him.

He was waiting for someone, or something. I did a quick scan around the area with my Inner Eye to search for a possible attack from the sides, or my unprotected rear. There were no other threats that I could see through the heavy, whirling flakes, but I still didn't like being so exposed.

I called *Green Fire* to my hands knowing I could defend myself quickly. If I had to throw it at the thick looking body of the soldier, it would dissolve him, armor and all.

The silent warrior seemed to be weighing his options for the expected conflict. He brought his battle ax up along his side and raising his arm, began to twirl it around his head turning it into a blur as it spun faster and faster.

Those flat, pitch-black eyes never left my face. I held my hands up waist high, with only a small flame licking at the frigid air.

I might have blinked, but I totally missed the *Sword of Light* when it swung around once, as if by the mighty arm of Brian Boru himself. Its sharp blade now pointed at the heart of the soldier. The whirling battle ax was released and seemed to fly over the sword like a metal snowball. It hurtled toward my face and I barely had time to bring my hands up to meet its smashing force.

The *Green Fire* flattened out into a wall of flame as I kicked it up a few notches to meet the incoming missile. They connected in a burst of vivid green, fragments of dark metal collapsing into a pile of dull ash at my feet, covering the tops of my boots.

While I was protecting my head from being transformed into a smashed kumquat, the warrior saw his opportunity to make an all-out assault. His scream of blood lust tripled in volume as it bounced off the walls of snow-heavy spruce trees surrounding our battle ground. He charged with his sword held high, his intent clearly not to take prisoners.

I took an unconscious step back as he covered the space between us.

I turned up the intensity of my flames. I'd have to spread fire over him quickly, to stop the sword from connecting with some part of my body. My head for instance.

Because my focus was on killing, or being killed, I had ignored the *Sword of Light* that still remained motionless. I mumbled something out loud about its being pretty much useless, when it dawned on me, it needed a command to strike!

I frantically tried to recall the proper words needed to release the spell suspending the Magical Sword. Until then it looked as threatening as a crescent moon over the scene.

Thinking of the various old-language trigger words I watched with half an eye as the soldier began a head-long charge. He too, had lost sight of the sword hanging above him. He ran forward, completely absorbed in his intent on slaughter.

I quickly screamed out the words in the old tongue as they finally became unscrambled in my head.

"Claiomh Folamort!"

*T*he sword swung in a perfect killing arc, slicing the warrior's head from his padded shoulders. It rolled to a stop at the foot of a large Spruce several feet away. The body fell beneath the blade which hung again in some kind of lethal repose.

The soldier's arms were outstretched, but his hand still gripped his now useless sword. There was no blood spilt on the frozen ground, in fact, after a blink, there was nothing. The would-be assassin, vanished as I watched, not leaving so much as an impression of his heavy body where he fell.

The *Sword of Light* disappeared as soon as I stepped forward to inspect the ground for any trace of the Terra Cotta soldier.

I understood that Feng was already sending his minions into this realm to hunt for the Red Dragon and me it seemed.

That made a sure targets of Jason. When mom and Joanie joined our little task force, they'd also be in Feng's cross hairs.

I extinguished the green flames still dancing around my fingers. I knew it was time to get serious about finding the cursed statue.

I jumped back into my idling Jeep and using my tire tracks to guide me, backed onto the road.

While I was duty bound to fulfill the blood pledge to Lady Bao, I believed she was as dangerous in this venture as Feng and possibly, Dr. Chung Wu as well. They both stood like shadowy presences in this unfolding drama.

But now I knew two things for certain; I had assassins on my trail, who threatened me and those close to me and, I needed destroy the Red Dragon before it became the ultimate power source for one of the unholy trio.

Chapter 20

Jason was peering out of the living room window, the heavy curtain held back in his hand. A look of relief was apparent on his face as I slowly came up the drive toward the garage.

He was standing at the open door by the time I rounded the slight curve to the back of my house, a weak smile on his tightly set mouth.

I parked next to his Police SUV and practically sprinted to the welcoming glow of my kitchen and his waiting arms.

He grabbed me up into a tight bear hug, deliciously taking my breath away as he always did. In his anxious state, he kicked the door shut and held me closer.

"Where the heck have you been, Cathleen? I was about ready to call in an all-points bulletin on you!"

I had to laugh. Jason only had one Deputy and Max was probably sitting somewhere on a country road working his much loved crossword puzzles.

"I'm so sorry, sweetie. I didn't have a way to call you when something big came up."

He gave me a quizzical look and asked "What was that something *big,* or should I ask, *who?*"

"Jason, I ran off the road on the way home. I was trying to avoid someone coming straight at my car." I paused, but Jason knew better than to interrupt my stories so I went on.

"I know this will sound weird, but it turned out to be a soldier… from the Qin Dynasty…a Terra Cotta Warrior to be exact."

Jason looked down at me intently as if trying to make sense of a lunatic's ranting. He took a deep breath, preparing himself for what was coming.

"OK, love. You have my attention, but I'm having trouble trying to visualize this character who stepped onto the roadway. How did you come to recognize him as one of those warriors?"

I was relieved Jason didn't question my eyesight, or sanity, or both.

Jason always left the window of credibility open a crack. He understood my version of reality was not going to be considered a normal interpretation. I saw things other humans couldn't. Lucky them!

"I've been researching the first dynasty in China because that's where the wizard, Feng Xi, belonged in history."

I was talking while Jason helped me out of my heavy coat, hanging it and my hat and gloves over a kitchen chair.

"Feng was Court Artist to Emperor Qin; he likely had an active part in making the Terra Cotta Army. That may be how he was able to animate the one that was sent to do me in. He's probably used an animation charm on other soldiers, so he could call on them when needed."

Jason said, "Makes sense to me, but I want to know about this attack on you. You've got me itching to grab my gun and go hunting."

He stopped and looked at me closely. Guess my touch of make-up didn't hide the apprehension the attack caused in me.

"You look pretty wound up, honey."

Jason took my hand and led me into the front room. The fire was crackling and snapping, giving the air a cozy, languid feel. We took our usual places on our comforter and that's when it hit me.

The adrenaline rush, combined with my magic, had given me a kind of gladiatorial strength. Now I was totally drained and felt exhausted. I related the entire story told without any embellishment, quickly moving on to its head-rolling conclusion.

Jason had been watching me closely; suspicious I might leave out some imagined injury. He's a natural worry wart, but when I accused him of that once he was quick to put me straight.

"Gotta watch out for the cracks in the ice."

Which was as mysterious as this guy gets for me.

"Cathleen, it seems this creep, Feng, isn't waiting on you to arrive on his home turf in San Francisco. He's proving he can reach you wherever you are and deal you a death blow. Boy, did he underestimate my girl!" He said this last with a sharp laugh and then got serious again. "What's our plan, love? Leave earlier for California?"

I sat for a moment considering my options. Did I really want to speed up my preparations to go rushing headlong into territory I didn't know?

"Jason, I don't much like other people setting, or rearranging, my agenda; so no.

We'll stick to our travel plans and leave on Friday. Besides, our tickets are purchased and so are mom and Joanie's. Let's just stay focused and stay put until then."

"Good," he said firmly "And both your mom and Joanie will need to be brought up to date on what we'll be facing."

"I've already got mom pretty much in the loop and Joanie and I will have a long trip from Pittsburgh and I can fill her in," I said.

But he had a good point. I still needed to sort through the bag full of mysteries that I'd be lugging around China Town in the next few days.

I hadn't heard from Chung or Lady Bao since their first contacts with me. Only Feng seemed interested in staying in touch and that's because he wanted to scare me off, or kill me; whichever came first. Though with the reputation he brought with him over the centuries, Feng's favorite form of persuasion was deadly.

With all the excitement of the past few hours, I had totally forgotten about the reason I had called Jason to begin with; the cherry wood box sitting on the floor of my Jeep.

Jason had to leave to get some sleep before he took over from Max to work the night shift. I asked him to stay for a minute so I could show him my "gift" from the Dark Wizard and threw my coat and boots back on to retrieve it.

I grabbed the box and just to be sure opening it wouldn't release other unpleasant surprises, I covered it with my trusty spell, suspending anything trying to drift out. I shook it gently to assure myself the parchment was still inside.

Jason had slipped back into his outdoor gear and stood by the stove.

I placed the lovely box on the counter and carefully opened the lid, but not before Jason had admired the beautiful inlaid work on the dragon.

"Do you think those are real gems, Cathleen?" he asked, a bit of amazement in his voice.

"Oh yeah, they're real; probably a part of Emperor Qin's treasures. I'm sure Feng knows where all the wealth is hidden."

I'd already told him about the noxious gas that had Darla and me choking for air.

I reached out my hand, feeling the force field I created with my spell. I immediately relaxed as I lifted the lid.

When I started to lift the scroll out, it crumbled like an over baked taco shell and fell into a grayish heap on the red velvet lining.

"Geez, guess Feng doesn't want me to share his warnings," I said, looking down at the disintegrated scroll.

I looked up in time to see Jason smile.

"I think Feng is feeling kind of insecure about now, Cathleen. He knows you dodged a bullet and he doesn't want to chance you sharing anything about him with others; just in case you have allies of your own."

"Hmm, that sounds about right. He knows I've already been contacted by Lady Bao and he knows he can no longer trust or control her. He also suspects there are others hunting his precious statue, but like the Lady, he's not sure of their identity, or how helpful they'll be to me."

I closed the lid with a quick snap, staring for a second at the dragon and wishing I had a better plan of where to start my hunt.

"Jason, when you come over in the morning," I said, slipping my arms around him, "I think we need to talk more about another weapon that Feng and the others don't know I have on my side; your visions."

I saw his deep green eye flash a subtle light that I'd never noticed before. I suspected it had something to do with seeing into a murky future.

Jason was my first experience working with a clairvoyant and I needed to keep him under wraps.

"Listen, love," he said looking concerned "I don't think I can turn on my visions like a faucet. They just come over me like vivid daydreams."

"Can you think of anything that might trigger them though?" I asked hopefully.

He looked thoughtful as he covered his thick black hair with his knit cap and put his gloves on.

"I know I am always thinking of someone close to me and picturing them in my mind. When I was little, the visions were always about some family member, even if I hadn't seen them in a while. The last one was about you, but then, I always have you on my mind."

With that he leaned down and kissed me deeply until I stopped thinking, or breathing.

"You sure make it hard on a girl to say goodnight, Jason," I said, in a breathless rush.

We both chuckled at that obvious fact. I knew he could feel my body mold into his arms like silly putty.

Knowing how much I hated our goodbyes, Jason smiled down at me as he gently brushed a long strand of hair from my forehead.

Without needing to say more, he opened the kitchen door and stepped into the endless white of Iron Mountain.

Chapter 21

Now that I was alone, I went back upstairs to throw a few things into the washer for the upcoming trip. Ollie was disturbed from his dreaming by my commotion and his head resurfaced from under the bed skirt. This reminded me that I needed to pack up his food, biscuits and favorite bed for his own trip to the Vet's.

Since Ollie was one of the staff's favorites, a long stay for him was not a real hardship; they treated him like a furry potentate and lavished him with affection and treats.

I pulled my battered suitcase out of the closet and set about my usual over-packing process. This consisted of making piles of clothes on my bed.

I had just put some newly washed items into the dryer and was back to sorting through my clothes piles when I heard my front door bell chime.

Ollie did his usual retired guard dog trick and scooted more of his body under the bed skirt.

I looked at my watch and saw it was getting close to three. With the days so darkened by the endless winter storms in the mountains, it was hard to judge just when we slipped into evening from late afternoon.

I threw a pair of jeans onto the bed next to the suitcase and went to the bedroom window to check out my visitor.

I wasn't really surprised to see the long, sleek limo sitting in my driveway. I couldn't be seen by whoever was ringing my doorbell because of the porch roof. If Lady Boa sat in the back seat as she surely did, she wouldn't be able to see up to my second floor.

I was shifting from one foot to the other, wondering whether I wanted to answer the door, when I heard a noise downstairs. I immediately placed a strong ward to guard my room so Ollie wouldn't be involved in any mischief making. He was totally fearless because he loved everyone which made him an easy target.

After placing the ward, I tiptoed toward the hallway and heard a second sound coming from the living room this time. A minute later I smelled the scent of pine and heard the crackling of a large fire, I hoped in my fireplace.

What the ...I started for the stairs when I heard my name called out.

"Wushen O'Brien. You must join me as my time with you is limited. I know you are hesitating, deciding on your next action. Please, come and sit before the fire I had my driver prepare for us. The pine cones are delightful to smell. I have much to share with you regarding our current situation."

The Immortal Lady didn't leave me much choice. I had to find out what she knew. It really got my Irish up that she thought she could just glide into my home like we were old buddies.

I was trying to think of a good way to tell her she'd better confine her visits to invitation only, when suddenly, the lady in question was standing inches away from my nose.

"Apologies, Honored Wushen," she breathed the words softly into my startled face, "but as I have said, my time is inadequate with you, so you must permit my assistance."

Without another word, I felt myself being lifted by some invisible force and carried like dandelion fuzz on a strong wind, downstairs and into my living room.

Before I could strenuously object to my newly found locomotion, I was gently deposited into the armchair in front of the fireplace and its unnaturally intense orange and yellow flames.

The muscle-bound driver was standing stoically beside it, blackened poker in hand as if he guarded the holy fire of Ra.

He still wore the all black outfit of earlier, only now I noticed something different in his sphinx like face. His eyes were a bright red. I knew this indicated that he had recently fed and I prayed it wasn't on a neighbor!

Lady Bao must have noted my look of apprehension, probably a look she was very familiar with.

She said, "Do not be alarmed, Honored Wushen, my driver has only tasted the blood of a four legged being; not one of your kind."

"Did you forget, Lady Bao, *you* were one of my *kind*, once?"

She turned away from me and said something in Chinese to the driver. Without a sound he returned the poker to its stand. It didn't look quite as deadly then.

Before I took my next two breaths, he was outside in the cold. I had barely registered the door opening.

Lady Bao seemed pleased with herself when she turned her attention back to me.

With a small smile she said, "I believe privacy is important to our discussion. My driver has been serving me for centuries, yet sadly, I am not totally convinced of his loyalty. While I brought him to his Immortal state, Feng Xi had a hand in, shall we say, *instructing* him, in the finer points of surviving as a Jiangshi, or *vampire* as you know us.

She certainly is chatty today I thought, shifting in my chair to avoid staring into her eyes. I had already noted their appearance; a blackish-red like clotted blood. She must have feed before her driver. He got her left-overs no doubt. A class thing even among Vamps!

I watched her carefully posing herself like she'd just entered stage right to deliver her lines. I was picking up some unsettling vibes from her, immediately regretting not putting a ward around myself when I did my bedroom. There was my *Green Fire*, but that does take a few seconds to conjure and she had incredible strength and speed.

Maybe I can finagle a way to get back up there, I was thinking frantically, as the sense of danger increased with each tick of the old Grandfather Clock.

I said stiffly, "Lady Bao, I want to know why you felt it necessary to return here. I fully understand your demands regarding the O'Brien pledge."

She seemed almost offended by my comment. *Maybe she thinks we bonded over tea this morning,* I thought, as she continued to study my face.

"You are quite young, Wushen, but I believe you have the capacity to understand many things beyond the restrictions of age. I shall not to take your comment as being dismissive of my own powers, but rather, attribute them to a lack of experience in matters of honor."

Now, I was the one who felt insulted! But, hey, she was the ancient power and I was just a very well-trained Celtic Mage a bunch of centuries younger.

She had no idea how her condescending comment had irritated me. I wasn't about to let on that it had. *Let her think I was humbled by her "forgiveness" of my youthful ignorance.*

I took a calming breath and said, "Perhaps it would be helpful if you explained this second visit, Lady Bao."

I had decided not to aggravate this mercurial being since I wasn't prepared to deal with the result of her anger just yet.

She seemed placated enough by my milder tone, to take the seat opposite of me. I was rather annoyed that she had her driver move my furnisher into this current configuration, but I did sort of like the look.

My fluffy blanket was folded neatly on the couch so she probably thought I was a bad housekeeper along with being immature.

"I have returned with news that will aid your search for the Red Dragon, Wushen."

I was immediately all ears and looked at her attentively for any sign of devious story-telling. I knew she wasn't concerned with my well-being, but she'd be sure I knew enough to protect her real interests.

She looked away from me long enough to smooth the silky material of her ankle length skirt. She still wore the beautiful fur, but had left off the matching hat. Her midnight black hair shone as glossy as the creamy skirt that seemed to caress her thighs with a subtle whisper when she moved. She was truly one of the most sensual women alive, but then I remembered, she wasn't…alive that is!

"You will be pleased to know, Wushen O'Brien, that the statue we seek has been located within the labyrinth below the modern city of China Town. I know you have made plans to travel to this American city two days hence, therefore, I wanted to extend the offer of my private jet to you and your party for that purpose."

Holy crapski! I thought frantically. She knew I wasn't working this gig alone.

I was biting down on my lower lip when she added, "Your mother is not unknown to me, or to those like me, Wushen; in fact, her reputation is one which encourages, shall we say, certain precautions in dealings with her. She is as formidable in her Magic as was Liam O'Brien, your honored father."

"My mother is not a part of this, or future conversations, Lady Bao. I have no intention of involving her in any capacity in fulfillment of this pledge."

She cocked her sleek black head to the side with an almost amused expression on her face.

"Don't take me for a fool, young Wizard." Her words sounding like sharp needles going through my ears.

"I knew you would reach out to the Lady Brighid, for she has a role to play not only as your mother, but as a *Protector of the Guild of the Green Wizards*."

I could only sit dumbly looking at her and wondering how she had come by this intimate information. She continued, but now her face wore the serious expression of finality.

"Wushen, you will use your mother as a tool; just as I use you. She is already a passenger on a flight from her Celtic homeland, to San Francisco, this Saturday, and has reserved two rooms at the Grant Hotel."

I gave an inward sigh of relief. The Lady had only counted mom and possibly Joanie, without realizing Jason would be flying out after us. Sharing a room with my old friend was proving a good move after a long argument with my boyfriend.

This was the only bright spot in the information dump. It was infuriating that she knew so many details and really irritating that she was so arrogant about showing me her long reach.

"I don't use my mother as a *tool*, I said, looking at her steadily.

"If she cares to lend her insights to our search, so be it. But I think you are assuming too much. No one ever tells Brighid what she must do! Her only concern is that the pledge tying my family's honor to your service, be met and done with. I can't and won't commit her to anything she won't give freely."

"Spoken like a truly respectful daughter, young Wizard. I too had a mother in the natural realm. I no longer carry any feelings toward such tenuous relationships, but then, you are only mortal. Something I advise you to keep in mind."

She made this last comment while staring like a crow considering a rabbit carcass at the side of the road. I had to fight the urge to squirm under that hungry gaze.

"Perhaps, if you are finished here, Lady Boa, you'll excuse me while I prepare for my coming trip."

With a slight flick of her wrist the fire in the grate was turned to smoky ash and she was standing at the front door within my next blink.

Dang! I hate the way she can move like that! I was thinking, when the door opened and the driver was in his usual groveling bow.

She turned slightly, looking back in my direction.

"We shall meet soon in the Chinese city beneath the earth of China Town. I regret you will not accept my offer to fly you there, but then I didn't expect that you would. So like your mother I suppose. You will be contacted after your arrival, Wizard; enjoy your journey."

With that little speech the doors closed behind her and a few minutes later the luxury car make another careful U turn out of my driveway, heading toward the highway out of town.

I decided it was important to find out as much as possible about dealing with her kind.

It was time to dig out my dad's *Shadow Box Library of Celtic Magic and Folk Lore.*

Chapter 22

The Protectors have always kept interventions in this realm out of public view.

Things like the disappearance of a popular D.J. personality on a Radio station in Pittsburgh. He was also a notorious *Athelmort,* an Irish *Shape Shifter,* who spun severed heads like records. He would lure unsuspecting fans to his studio after his late-night show "Music of the Spheres," then change into the lowest kind of demon a *Rathripper.*

Guess he worked up a big appetite because eight people vanished before dad could stop him. Mom said dad never trusted that "New Age" music.

Now, I needed to bring some of those secrets out of the dark, so I could learn a new trick or two.

I began rummaging through my memory, trying to remember where I'd stashed my dad's things after I moved to Iron Mountain.

Mom went back to Ireland and O'Brinnion Keep. She was quick to unload lots of family treasures onto me saying my new home *was sufficient to the task.* This from the lady with a small castle!

My wizard father couldn't swim a lick, yet worked as a part-time flunky on board various shipping boats and fishing vessels because he loved to be on the water.

Dad always warned me against using magic to help prolong our time in this realm, reminding me that we lived an allotted time and no more. I wished his time would have been longer, but he always said, "Pack your suitcases well in advance of any journey lass and you can spend more time looking forward to the trip." I hoped he was enjoying the journey.

I put my suitcase on the floor near my bed trying to judge its weight while moving it, wondering if the airlines had pictures of people like me they depended on to pay fees for over-weight bags.

I stayed down on the floor and peered into the murky land of dust angels where I found a few errant socks and a box of family photos.

Sadly, whenever a wizard passes onto the next realm, any pictures of them begin to fade over time, until there is no physical record of them occupying a place in the natural world.

I took out several pictures of dad and could still make out his features, but they were already washed-out around the edges. Soon, I'd have only my imprecise memory of his handsome face and open smile. I sat for a moment and wiped the tear that had crept down toward my chin.

"Get yourself together, Wizard! "

I jerked so abruptly that some of the photos scattered around the floor.

"OK, I know I didn't imagine hearing you! Identify yourself now, or when I find you, pay the consequences."

"Tisk, tisk! You surely have your mum's temper, lass. But to satisfy your request, I shall do even better than naming myself."

With that, the late afternoon gloom that had settled around me was transformed into day-glow colors that splashed over the entire room. Sitting cross-legged in the middle of my bed was *Crom Croich,* earliest god of religious cults before the appearance of the Druids in ancient Ireland.

I knew him instantly from the huge oil painting of him that once hung in our secret kitchen library. Mom had camouflaged this room to look like a pantry. It protected all of their books on Celtic Magic and Myths, along with her favorite "This and That" recipes that she didn't want known to the *Council of Green Wizards.*

I leapt to my feet and was unconsciously backing toward the doorway when my visitor spoke again.

"There's no need to flee lass, I surely have not come to do harm. Nay, I am here at the request of one you shall meet upon your journey."

His face turned a rosy pink along with the deep fur that covered his bear-like round body.

*Does **everyone** know I'm going on this trip!*

I'd only been contacted by other Magic Users so far. This would be my first god from the pantheon of Ireland's ancient history. Kind of thrilling, really.

I meekly returned to the center of the room and tried to sound completely at ease when I said "I welcome you, Crom Croich, god to the ancients. I am honored that you should enter this realm un…"

"Uninvited? I do believe that was the word you seek, Protector, but that is far from the truth. You see Cathleen O'Brien, daughter of Liam and Brighid, I became aware of your unique challenge when you called upon the *Sword of Light.*

You touched off a series of alarms throughout the echelon of gods and demi gods. I was one who heard.

You used an old, and rather outdated spell I might add, but then your sire was known for his love of history."

"But how did you hear about my trip, if I may ask?" I tried to sound humble before this mighty god of Irish lore.

The unpredictable God of Storms, Crom had a reputation for demanding admiration and good etiquette. He was proud of his fearsome status for bringing the Bleak Gardener along on his wild rages, both in this realm and the third, where he normally dwelled.

He grabbed my pillows and pushing them into place behind his back, leaned against the head board and sighed.

"Ah, rather cozy little cottage my young friend, and the weather here is fine enough to make me a tad envious."

When he said this, his face and fur turned a deep shade of green.

He gave a snort of laughter and suddenly I could see my breath steaming out of my mouth and nose, as if I was on a mountain top instead of a temperature-controlled house.

I remembered how dad joked about this mischievous god; saying he had the humor of Loki and the hammer of Thor!

"Well, young Wizard, as a *Protector of the Green Mother* I assume you are well versed in the High Magic of the *Green Council.*"

"I was apprenticed to my father, Liam, and also trained by my mother, Brighid. But then, you know this. "

"Indeed, young Wizard. Your family history is recorded and known within the Second, Third and even into the Fourth realms. Because of this, I have come to offer my aid in your quest to find the dreadful Red Dragon."

I stood as rigid as the statue he'd named; wondering who else knew of my family's pledged involvement in this search.

I had unconsciously moved closer to the storm god when he raised a glowing yellow hand to warn me to step back.

"Close enough mortal!" he said, the cold air shifting with his words. "I will tell all and then I must leave you to your own devices until I am needed. At that time you may call upon me once and only once, as I promised the *Teacher*. I am curious about his interest, but then I have never understood the Fey."

Now I knew for certain the *Teacher* was an undeclared ally.

He must have taken a breath. Suddenly the air felt like it was stirring and small items on my dresser shifted and spun for a second. He continued.

"Your father imprudently signed a pledge with a vampire well known to the pantheon. Doing so, he embroiled your family down through the ages, ensnaring them in a web of increasing evil, corruption and death to many, both mortal and otherwise.

This pledge was made because of one mortal king's vanity and your own sire's need to aid him in founding your family's line.

The *Teacher* would have his revenge on the brigands that assaulted and slew his brother. The very same beings you are now committed to serve in this quest."

I stiffened up at that comment.

"Just so you understand, Lord of the Storm, I have no intention of handing over the Red Dragon to any of those seeking it for their own. I understand how dangerous it would be if it fell into the hands of Lady Boa, or the wizard, Feng Xi."

"Ah," he said, with a hint of a smile on his purple lips. "And what about the third party to this triangle of seekers? What of Dr. Chung Wu? Have you placed him on that list as well?"

"I must admit," I said, "I don't know much about Chung. If you care to enlighten me about his part in all of this, I could determine how to deal with him."

"Oh, I'd better warn you, young wizard, if you ask this of me now; I will not be available to aid you in some future crisis. Remember what I said, I have promised one, only one, intervention in these affairs of you mortals."

I didn't want to play that Ace before I needed and said, "Thanks for reminding me. Will I see the *Teacher* any time soon?"

"That information is still locked in the *Teacher's* little Fey head and he chose to keep me in the dark."

Suddenly, my room turned pitch black as if he was illustrating his annoyance at not being enlightened.

I stood still until his attitude brightened, along with my bedroom.

"And now, I must depart this too-cheery abode. There are storms to brew and winds to churn the very clay of this realm. The *Green Mother* allows this as these are natural occurrences on this plane."

The furry god was now a scintillating shade of gray; his body shifting like quicksilver as he moved his immense bulk off my bed and toward the window. As I began to ask one last question of him, the window flew upward and he spun out into the darkening sky.

How do I let him know if things turn to scary crap for me? Yell at the nearest dark cloud? I wondered, as I watched a dark swirl of sooty looking snow rush into a foreboding sky.

Chapter 23

I slammed the bedroom window shut against the swirl of snow flakes and tried to refocus on packing, not easy to do after meeting a god.

I let my mind drift through the mental storage rooms of my brain and into the murky places that occupied my thoughts.

I now had one more character to acknowledge in this strange investigation turned saga.

On the positive side, Crom could be trusted to blow in, to help me out if things got really dicey.

The *Teacher* had not made his appearance yet, but I guessed he would remain out of the picture until I was in China Town and on Feng Xi's trail. His thirst for revenge on the Wizard and Lady Bao would be a powerful influence on his actions. I just hoped he wouldn't be blinded by that dangerous emotion and bring more trouble down on my head than I was prepared to meet.

By the time I finished my packing and had done nominal chores around the house, a deeper darkness was beginning to gather in the corners of the rooms.

I didn't expect Jason for several more hours so I decided I had better take advantage of some down time to locate dad's Shadow Box Library.

An hour later, I reemerged from my basement with nothing but cobwebs clinging to my clothes and a bad case of the "creepy crawlies" in my scalp.

I flopped down on the chair near the fireplace, dangling my legs over the cushy arm. I felt chilled after that time spent below ground, so decided to start a fire to warm myself.

Shivering on the back porch while retrieving an armload of logs, it occurred to me that I had put some of dad's belongings in a small storage cubicle behind the bed in the guest bedroom. At the time, I figured I wouldn't need anything in the boxes, but couldn't bear to part with any of his things.

After dumping my wood onto the cold grate, I used a quick spell to light the logs.

I didn't have any trouble moving the bed from in front of the hidden alcove and was inside on my knees in a matter of minutes. There was a pull chain on the low ceiling connected to a bare light bulb. The tiny space was quickly illuminated so I could see into the crowded interior.

I was just starting to go through the five or six boxes jammed in there when my skin began to tingle like I'd taken a shock from a bad switch. The hair on my neck began to stir and I knew I wasn't alone in my house any longer.

I decided it wouldn't be a great idea stay in the tiny space since it could become a trap. I crept backward on my knees and closed the small door behind me. I wanted to push the bed back to conceal the cubby, but that would have given my location away. Instead, I got to my feet and made my way to the hallway and peered over the banister into the front entryway below.

My dad had trained me to feel changes in the movement of the air, using the skin's surface as my barometer for shifting air currents.

I called up a quick ward of protection and was instantly enclosed by a golden dome of light.

Descending the stairs slowly, I distinctly heard a sharp clattering sound coming from the front room. The wall between the stairway and the sitting area in front of the fireplace prevented me from seeing my visitor, but my nose was on fire with a noxious odor of dead fish. *Crabslayer!*

I stepped around the corner and was staring at a single red eye of one ugly demon!

The *Crabslayer* brings a whole new dimension to the species of crustaceans.

It scuttles along the ground like any crab, giving the impression you might out-run it. It's another story when it rears up on scaly hind legs. It has six of these and stands seven feet or more.

It was impossible to look into the creature's bulbous eyes, because they dangled from long stems protruding from a flat saucer shaped head.

While I couldn't read its next move, I knew it was frustrated; waiving its claws wildly around.

I stood perfectly still inside my golden dome, watching as it went into the equivalent of an arthropod frenzy, knocking over everything including my desk, turning its wood to splinters.

I had enough of quiet observation at that point. I moved back a few feet so I could call up Green Fire to fry his hard-shelled butt!

Unfortunately, that's when the mailman showed up and began pounding on my storm door.

Because I didn't move to answer his repeated banging (something I really hated about this guy), he leaned to the side to peer into my front window.

My demon visitor took an immediate interest in the postal intruder. It spun on its bristling appendages to investigate the interruption of its attack.

I took advantage of his shift in attention and dropping the dome, turned up the fire, spreading it so it could consume his vast mass and eat through his heavy red shell.

That accomplished I now had a large pile of smelly residue in my front room and a paralyzed mailmen to deal with and quickly!

I decided on a favorite spell of mom's when she was inconveniently disturbed while using magic. It causes the sensation in a person that things are "not quite right," but not being able to understand the source of the disquiet.

I opened the front door and as I did, whispered, "Ai teacht neach."

The postman had turned his terror-frozen face to me when he heard the door open, but immediately his expression turned to confusion.

"I...I...think I saw…something…" he stammered and then shook his head making the ear flaps on his hat look like they belonged on a beagle.

"Hi Fred, sorry you have to be out in this storm. How's everything down at the Post Office? Marla doing well?"

Using the name of his girlfriend, who worked as a clerk at the Iron Mountain Post Office, seemed to put him in a better frame of mind. He smiled ruefully and grinned from ear to ear.

"She's terrific!" he answered, as he shuffled his feet like a young boy. They were now happily the talk of the small town gossips.

The fear had drained out of his eyes and wishing him a great day I grabbed the mail and shut the door behind his waving hand.

The ash pile was quickly disposed of, vanishing down a temporary hole in my floor.

I began to wonder who had sent this last messenger. Seemed like Feng Xi had already tried to make his threats and Lady Bao was here a short time ago. If she'd wanted to do me harm, she certainly could have had a good run at me! Was there another mystery player in this drama?

Had to be Chung…but why? He'd hired me for *Mother's Sake!*

Who wanted me turned into chunks of Wizard didn't really matter. I couldn't trust any of them.

Chapter 24

I hunched over and re-entered the low-ceilinged cubicle, grabbing an old blanket from the top of the heap to keep off the cold wood floor.

I had just opened my third box when I felt something like a mild tingle in my hands. *This is it,* I thought with a broad smile. I carefully got into a crouch and carried the box out and into the room, where I placed it on the bed.

This wasn't like opening a present on your birthday. This was going to take some finesse and speed. Finesse, because it had to be done with the right combination of magical skills, and speed because I had to move like a flame on a match stick, or get caught when all that magic collided.

I didn't really want to turn this bedroom into a repository of ancient books, so I decided the only real choice I had was the basement.

Not wanting to lug the unwieldy box down two flights of stairs, I conjured one of mom's favorite *House Buddies* to do the grunt work. What's the use of being a Witch if you can't enjoy a few fringe benefits?

Normally, a *House Buddy* is around for more than the five minutes it took to get the box downstairs and into my rather creepy basement. I didn't want any distractions when I began the incantations and those guys love to talk and visit. They are very charming, in a green, gnomish sort of way. I especially like the tufts of dark green hair that looks like grass sprouting on their soccer-ball-sized heads.

I gave this guy two extra arms so he didn't have to struggle as he carried his burden. His flat feet were broad enough to make a flapping sound on the stairs and I heard him faintly humming to himself. These guys are just nice to be around.

As soon as we reached the bottom step, I directed my helper to carry the box to the middle of the floor. My basement was not a place I often frequented. Frankly, I have an aversion to dark, damp and moldy-smelling places.

My hundred-and-fifty-year-old house came with an old fashioned "cellar" that the realtor blithely named a "basement," for my sake. It had walls constructed of heavy, misshapen stones that looked as if they had been quarried in Roman times.

After my *Buddy* deposited his burden, I thanked him and he winked out, leaving me to unpack what would become my dad's prized possession.

Tossing some old rags and other packing material aside, I removed a rectangular container made of a rich, black walnut, carved with hundreds of intricate Celtic symbols and runes.

The legend of Celtic hieroglyphs found on the lid read:

"*Ye seekers of Knowledge and Secrets behold the words of the ages and be fearless to speak them in the name of the Goddess Mother.*"

I traced the deeply carved symbols with my finger and read them again, this time in the Old Druid Tongue. The awkward words seemed to slip off my tongue as I went into a trance-like state, under their influence.

My eyes became unfocused and heavy. After a third recitation of the words, I became aware of a movement under my fingers as the lid began to slide open. I brought myself back to the moment and took three steps away from the box.

The basement, with all of its cobwebs, musty smells and stained cement floor, disappeared in a flash of white light. I stood transfixed for a moment; as blind as a mole and feelings as defenseless.

It took me a minute to process that I was now surrounded by books, scrolls, open parchment papers lying helter-skelter on several heavy wooden tables. This would have been how dad left them on his last visit here.

I stood transfixed by the novelty of being absorbed into this new environment. No longer in the mortal realm, I was clearly occupying space inside the Shadow Box Library!

There was an air of antiquity about everything, including the lighting provided by oil lamps hanging from cross beams of roughhewed timbers. They lent a smoky essence to the stale air. There was also the sweet scent of tea steeping in a pot that sat on a grate in a large corner fireplace.

My head nearly spun around on my neck as I tried to take in the room that had replaced my dingy cellar.

I'd never stepped foot in my dad's Shadow Box Library, just read some of the treasured books he'd bring out from time to time to advance my training.

Dad told stories of the treasures it held among its many papers and leather bound volumes. Works by some of the Masters of the art of Magic and Sorcery: Merlin, the Greek Alchemist, Phariditus, even Galileo, who had to carefully hide his magic under the guise of math.

I turned in a slow circle trying to take in all the works of the ages that were written about one thing: Magic.

My father's Shadow Box Library was one of only five known to the magic community. He was bequeathed his, just as his father was, down through the centuries of clan O'Brien.

And now, it was mine.

I took a deep breath, feeling the dust motes tease my nose as they swam lazily through ancient air. The books were calling out to me and my curiosity was stirred like a blue propane flame in a winter gale.

Glancing over at the stone hearth, I could smell the effects of the fire as the tea began to bubble with robust flavor.

I now had only one thing to do.

I sat down on a three-legged stool among countless treasures and waited for the Custodian of this Magical domain, the *Librarian*.

Chapter 25

There are no accounts of personal meetings with the *Librarian* by any Wizards, including my dad.

No description of the *Librarian's* appearance has ever been recorded. The fact that there has always *been* a Librarian over more than a thousand years indicates a being of incalculable age.

He is allegedly of the Fey and lives in close proximity to the *Teacher,* though this was likely pure conjecture and a bit of romanticism. Some in the community of Magic Users believed these two entities were lovers, who not only shared trade secrets, but lived an idyllic life of passion and adventure.

I had quizzed my dad about those theories because they appealed to my dreamy teenage imagination at the time.

When he stopped laughing, he said "Cathleen, lass. All who have met with the *Librarian,* including yer old da', are forbidden to speak, or record anything of their encounter. This honor comes with the threat of expulsion from the *Guild of Green Wizards* if the secret encounters are documented."

I had no idea what I was going to see when the Librarian finally showed himself. It was disconcerting as I sat on my perch with visions of the hideous creature that might appear at any moment to start lectures on Wizardry, while gnawing on a bat wing.

I was leaning my elbows on the rough surface of a table covered with books and scrolls with strange symbols. As I was trying to decipher what some of the arcane symbols meant, my skin began to tingle, alerting me to the introduction of a new presence.

Turning slowly on the stool, I was face to face with a creature so handsome, he was almost beautiful.

His golden hair came down to his shoulders. Its thick yellow strands seem to float around his shapely head like gilded rings around Saturn. He was not very tall, as I found out when I jumped to my feet upon seeing him.

A forest green cape was draped over a set of pleasingly broad shoulders and broad chest. It reached to his ankles, revealing matching boots of lustrous leather, with braided gold buckles shaped like vines across the tops.

When he reached out a hand to me, I saw he wore a simple white tunic, cinched with a braided gold belt fashioned in the same vine motif.

I instinctively gave him my hand in what I thought would be a milk-toast handshake. Instead, he turned it, placing a firm, moist kiss on my palm. I was too shocked to pull away and we stood for several moments with him gently holding my slightly grungy paw.

I gave myself a mental shake and slowly withdrew my fingers.

As I looked into his eyes, they changed from blue, to green, and then back to blue.

"I hope I haven't alarmed you. The last time the Library was opened was when your father, Liam, was researching how Pledges cast their long shadows over off-spring. In this case, that would be you."

"Please believe me, Librarian, I'm not alarmed by your presence. Do I call you "Librarian," or should I use another name?"

His voice was like a silken scarf wrapping itself around my head. It was deep and sensual and seemed to reflect the power radiating from his body.

He smiled and, naturally, his teeth were perfect in size and a dazzling white. He answered me with just a bit of a twinkle flaring, as his eyes turned green again.

"You are most welcome to call me by the name I am known among my clan; "Ban Briathar"."

I translated his name in my head from the old Druid tongue and said aloud, "White Word."

"Yes, indeed it means thusly, but you may address me simply as "Bandi," if you are so inclined."

He had a smile on his face that told me he preferred this shortened version, but it seemed weird to be calling such a powerful being "Whitey"

"I am honored to meet you, Bandi. I am Cath…"

"Cathleen O'Brien, daughter of Liam and the lovely, Brighid. Yes, I am aware of this. I also know that you are a *Protector of the Guild* and on a quest; a quest that requires arming yourself with something stronger than metal armor and wiser than mortal cunning. In short, knowledge of your enemies. And so, you have opened the Library to seek my assistance. Am I correct in this conjecture? "

He said all of this with a rather smug look of self-satisfaction on his very handsome face.

"While you're correct about my quest, perhaps you are unaware that I am dealing with an ancient wizard named Feng…"

"Yes" he said interrupting me again. "Feng Xi and the vampire, Lady Bao. But there is another, another you have to include in this reckoning, the elusive Dr. Chung Wu. Have I missed anyone, Wizard?"

I felt a prickling of annoyance run through my head.

"Actually, you forgot the Lady Bao's driver," I said a bit too proudly of my insider's knowledge.

`His mouth gave the tinniest quirk of a smile as if he was trying hard not to laugh at my show-off comment.

"Ah, I see you have been made aware of the mysterious, Chung. But then, he would have contacted you regarding the missing statue, the Red Dragon. Good, that shall make my instructions easier as you are already conversant with the players in this sad drama."

"Sad? Why do you call it that? And how do you know about Chung soliciting my help in securing the Red Dragon for its owner?"

The Librarian had wandered over to one of the other desks in the furthest part of the large room.

I had been asking questions while following behind him like a bleating sheep.

As he approached one of the large desks, he lifted his right hand and moved two stools over from the nearest corner and motioned me to take a seat opposite him.

I watched as he nonchalantly arranged his long cape so that it fell just right, looking like he was readying himself to do a photo shoot.

"Um, Bandi, if you wouldn't mind answering my questions. I have to finish getting ready for my trip. I'm sure you already know about *that* too."

He ignored the touch of sarcasm I couldn't keep out of my voice and gave me the benefit of a patient smile and a nod.

"You are indeed a unique person, Cathleen O'Brien. I believe living in these remote climes has made you into a most daring Witch. Not many would try to dictate my actions. But then, Liam, your honorable sire, often "pushed my brooches" as the saying goes."

His mouth twitched but wasn't quite smiling. I didn't dare correct his fractured idiom.

"Let us begin with the wizard, Feng Xi, who came to my attention while a novice serving the last Librarian, over a thousand of your mortal years. This was during a time of great strife in the first realm.

Feng Xi is a diabolical being who created the statue of the Red Dragon to conceal and hold his many powers, along with the drop of blood from the last Dragon King.

But from the way you are squirming on your seat, I gather this is known to you."

I merely nodded my head and he continued in his deep, rich voice.

"My Master, the first Librarian, tasked me with closely monitoring the Dark Wizard and to record his habits, plots, desires and especially, his weaknesses, as I discovered them.

Lady Bao is, or shall I correct myself and say, *was*, the protégé of Feng Xi. He was there when she was transformed from mortal, into the vampire she is today. Her life depends upon the procurement of unfortunate beings, mostly acquired by her driver, himself a vampire.

Her goal is to take possession of the statue and the power it holds. She would use this to become untouchable and would be a pestilence, moving relentlessly through the realms unless she is eradicated

Lastly, the shadowy Dr. Chung Wu. He too has come to my attention, but more recently than the rest. He is what you might term a modern Sorcerer.

He only came to notice when he stopped Feng Xi's efforts to animate an army of terra cotta soldiers buried with the first Emperor of China, Qin Shi Huang. Feng was only able to enliven some few dozen."

"But what is Chung's part in my quest?" I asked when he finally took a breath.

"I still haven't discovered that secret, but fear not, I am not leaving off from this realm while you are in need of answers and aid."

"Bandi, would it be possible for me to look at the material you already have here so I can get a better handle on how to proceed?"

He got up from his stool and walked over to the tall bookcases. He pulled out two books and a scroll. I followed behind and he put the three items in my hands.

The scroll looked as if it was just placed there and the books, bound in fine dark leather with raised embossed lettering, smelled and looked newly printed.

He must have seen my surprise at the fresh look of the items as he said, "This is a timeless environment, Cathleen O'Brien. The Library never reflects the passage of the ages."

I looked up at him from my study of the items and said, "I was under the impression that you were the first and only Librarian, but you mentioned another. May I ask what became of him?"

"Part of my interest in this investigative effort of yours, Cathleen O'Brien, hinges on the death of Fionn, the first Librarian and my mentor.

You see, while this is a lifetime appointment, the Librarian may choose to take an occasional sabbatical to visit other planes and gather more information about the worlds we visit. That is why the Librarian usually trains an apprentice; to step into the Library during his absences. I have not found the right assistant yet, but my search continues.

In any case, Fionn was absent from the Library and as arranged he was in contact with me over a great span of time, as you understand it. Then, our mental connection was suddenly broken. It felt like a sword had severed us and I was as alone as the last star in your galaxy!

I used every spell and charm to reach out to him, but Fionn had vanished into a Blackness I could not penetrate.

Since I was now the Librarian by default, and without an assistant, I could not leave my post to make an extensive search of the homelands of life where I thought he might have traveled. His silence was unprecedented and my fears grew with every passing eon."

"How is Fionn's disappearance connected to the Red Dragon?" I asked.

"I uncovered a tenuous connection between Fionn and the Lady Bao."

He saw my surprise, but hurried on.

"The Librarian keeps a close scrutiny of all Magic Users and records their incursions into realms where they don't belong. In return for the protection of the *Council of Green Wizards,* the Librarian informs them of Demon infiltrations and use of the Dark Arts on this or other planes.

I made a thorough study of the relevant happenings during the period Fionn went missing. I discovered that he had encountered the Lady Bao during his information gathering of the war to unify Ireland.

According to his sparse writings, she came to his knowledge as he recorded data on the battle in progress. The Lady Bao must have discovered his presence, though he would have been concealed from mortal eyes. She surely spied Fionn as he wandered the battle field.

I would guess he let his guard down in her presence, and though I don't know what she has done with him, I fear she may hold him captive in some manner."

When Bandi finished we sat together at the desk I related all the paranormal activities I'd encountered to date since starting my investigation.

"All the creatures you have described were conjured by Feng Xi, Cathleen O'Brien, for the sole purpose of doing you great harm, but also to test your defenses against his future attacks. It is obvious that the Wizard Feng has underestimated your abilities. He won't make such a mistake in future. For now, he is only testing a foe."

"And what about the Lady Bao?

"Lady Bao needs you alive. She'll try to use your skills as well as your magic to achieve her own ends. Her greed for power matches Feng Xi's, evil for evil. You cannot trust her, but she will do you no harm so long as you are searching for the statue."

"Well, that hardly makes her my champion, but it beats a poke in the eye with a sharp stick!"

The Librarian looked at me like I'd just said something deep and wise. Guess he wasn't up on human sarcasm.

Chapter 26

We studied the scrolls written by Fionn, and others, by nameless historians over eons of mortal time.

As I translated the arcane language used to describe Feng Xi, I began to come across references to a powerful vampire, suspected of serving his will.

I can almost smell her Jasmine perfume, I thought, furrowing my brow.

We skipped over the Court gossip and searched other historic chapters, until we came across the battle to unit Ireland, the Battle of Clontarf in 1014.

And there she was again, the "Beautiful and Deadly Jiangshi."

She was described as being as savage as she was exquisite.

"This exotic creature, with astonishing physical speed and strength, fought in the battle of King Brian Boru against his enemies, the Norsemen."

This could only have been Lady Bao.

It was clear from what we hungrily translated, that she was always accompanied by a tall, powerful wizard, throughout that long battle that won the High King his empire.

The pair of them were reported as seen in close contact, flying into the heat of battle and hurling fire balls at the enemy's army, triggering a breakdown in formation and order and raining down a fiery death.

In one account, Bandi read aloud scribbled notes written by the old Librarian, describing how my father had caused great storms of lightning to break over the heads of the Norsemen, generating enormous fear and panic among the fighters.

Lady Bao was reportedly "…holding fast the hand of the tall wizard to fill him with hellish fires."

I couldn't discount this testimony as being relevant to Lady Bao's connection to my dad, and ultimately, to me.

Bandi broke into my mental ramblings.

"You understand, Cathleen O'Brien, this was *faisneis*, an eye-witness account by Fionn, and puts him squarely in the vampire's sphere at the time of his own disappearance. "

I had been staring down at the clutter on the desk, letting my mind wander around a battle field, imagining my father and his vampire guide standing side-by-side overlooking their handiwork.

"Bandi, do you suspect Fionn was discovered by Lady Bao while he was making this account of the battle and the use of Magic by the Vampire and my father?"

"There can be no other logical alternative to that scenario, I fear. In fact, I have wondered over many of these past eons, as I fulfill Fionn's obligation as Librarian, if he may actually be hidden away with the Teacher's brother."

He stopped speaking for a moment and added, "You know of his capture and death I presume?"

"I know of the betrayal of Lady Bao of the two brothers to Feng Xi and the ultimate capture and torture of the Teacher's brother, while he escaped. I'd like to know why my father allowed them to fall into Feng's hands."

Bandi sighed deeply.

"Your father lived in a state of constant shame after that incident, Cathleen O'Brien.   Do not fault him for wanting to serve his liege Lord, the High King, Brian Boru."

I must have looked less-than-satisfied with that reasoning as he continued.

"Lady Bao has the sweet words of the caring physician she was in mortal life, but the tongue of a slithering viper, poisoning her prey even as they stand by, believing in her good intent.

I would council, do not judge him harshly. Liam, though a Master Wizard, was still a mortal. As such, he was susceptible to the Vampire's machinations and likely saw her as an invaluable ally against the hordes of Norsemen doing battle with his King."

Saving Ireland and the O'Brien clan from being wiped out of history had to be his primary goal.

"Thanks, Bandi. I appreciate your wisdom and insights into my father's actions. I know he was a faithful *Protector* and he would never put any member of the Faerie clans in jeopardy, if it was unavoidable."

I was quiet for a moment before I asked something that was deeply troubling to me.

"Did the *Teacher* hold my dad responsible for what happened to his brother?"

"The *Teacher* has always held him, and now his blessed memory, in the highest regard, Cathleen O'Brien. And you, of all Wizards, should know the close relationship your family shares with the Faerie Clans."

I was becoming antsy and needed time to plot my next moves.

I made some not-so subtle comments about doing serious research on my own, and the Librarian said he'd be leaving me for a bit.

He gave me a short lecture on handling the ancient texts and made his way toward a chair tucked into the shadowed corner of the large room. I noticed it earlier because it was the only real chair, while there were only stools scattered around the room.

As he approached this solitary piece of comfortable furniture, he raised both his hands and it became luminous, lighting the gloomy corner.

The Librarian took the edges of his long cape and pulled it closely around himself, as he lowered his body into the now dazzling chair.

Tucking his arms carefully at his sides, I saw his mouth moving and heard bits of a Druid chant. Within a blink of a lizard's eye, he and the chair had vanished.

I stood transfixed for a minute, then started browsing through the shelves.

I was running my finger over titles when I came across two books of interest, "Vampires, Wizards and Dragons of the Jiang Dynasty." These were books I and 2 of that study.

I made an opened hand gesture, sweeping them both onto the closest desk. Sitting gingerly on a wobbly looking stool, I turned to the front of each volume, carefully using my index finger like a wand over each delicate page; turning them without touching their pristine surface.

It seemed like the pages were made up of notes and quick jottings that at first I thought of as unimportant until I began to read a short passage by *ACF, Librarian*; it could only be *Althar Cron Fionn*, the missing Librarian.

I was eager to read anything he had written, especially if it touched in some way on my father and Lady Bao.

Having trouble reading the narrow, slanted writing in the dim light of the hanging lamps, I had almost pressed my nose to the page. Something made me jump back, nearly falling off my stool. It was as if I'd hit a glass wall as I leaned in to better see the script.

I slipped into my Inner Eye and saw an unfamiliar aura around both volumes. I tested the mystical shading by tracing it with my finger and it shivered like the face of a still pond as a wind passes overhead. Then I knew.

There had to be a hologram inside the books waiting to be activated.

I wondered briefly why Bandi hadn't discovered this before, but likely, he'd never had an occasion to open these obscure writings.

I waived my hand over the open pages to try to locate the strongest point of power. I scanned the Index and the name Brian Boru popped out at me. This seemed a likely place to look and I moved my hand over the slightly rustling pages.

I was rewarded with a glimmer and then a bolt of light shot out of the pages projecting the words *"The birth of Ireland and death of Brian Boru."*

I needed to find its activation mechanism. I began by reading the title and then the text out loud in the language of the ancients.

This was no mere cataloguing of facts, but a vivid description by Fionn, the author, of all the horror and misery of war.

I could almost smell the dead, with their entrails spooling around their feet like slimy snakes devouring their legs and feet. I heard the battle cries and blood lust ringing in the ears of the Norsemen, as they surrounded two of the High King's butchering their fallen bodies.

Fionn went on to describe how *"These dead were being gathered up like logs and limbs of felled trees. The being responsible for retrieving the fallen, the Wizard Protector, Liam O'Brien."*

156

Chapter 27

I blinked. The words must have blurred; they seemed to float off the page.

When my vision cleared, I re-read my father's name. Fighting back my initial reaction that this was completely wrong reporting.

I calmed myself and tried to understand why he would do such a gruesome thing.

Then it came to me. He was traveling with a known vampire of extreme power.

I thought *If these dead were left, she might have gathered them herself, to bring to her Master Feng for re-animation.*

This would allay Feng's doubts about her loyalty to him. She was cunning and my dad would know her intentions would all be self-serving.

Writing, Fionn went on to describe how dad used a far reaching spell that opened the earth under each body and body part and all the dead were absorbed into the earth where they lay scattered.

Lady Bao would have no power to stop this cleansing spell because the *Mother* would totally sanction dad's Magic.

I hadn't found a way to start the hidden hologram yet and figured that only the old language that Fionn used to seal it, would open its message.

To find those words, I needed Bandi.

"Ban Briathar, I call upon you to return to the Library to aid me."

"Well, I surely expected to be called sooner, Cathleen O'Brien." Bandi said sounding a bit peeved by my neglect.

He stood behind me and I nearly jumped out of my skin when he spoke.

"Bandi, you must have been close to get here so quickly."

"Actually, I have never been gone. The light coming from the book you have been perusing is me."

"Ha?"

"I have devised a way to live inside these many tomes so that I never have to leave the Library, unless called to duty elsewhere."

I told him I thought a hologram had been attached to the books. He explained it was merely his life force I picked up. Then he congratulated me on my keen perception, even if it was ill informed.

He seemed fascinated by what I learned from Fionn's notes, especially dad's part in securing the dead before the vampire could harvest them for Feng Xi's army.

I asked if he had any information about the Lady Bao that would relate in any way to my investigation.

Bandi gave me a dark look, like I'd just suggested he smelled as musty as the books he said he lived in.

"You ask the right question, Wizard!"

With that, he stalked over to the dark wooden bookcases at the back of the room. There was only one oil lamp suspended from a cross- beam, dangling several feet away. This afforded only a moderate ambient light, but Bandi went without hesitation to a volume stuffed into a bottom shelf.

After he pulled it free from the tight grip of its neighbors, he marched over to the nearest table, his long green cape sweeping the floor.

He began turning pages, using his index finger in a sweeping motion

"There she is!"

I assumed it was the information I'd requested on Lady Bao, but couldn't be certain since he had signaled me to stay put and not to follow him.

He mumbled something about "protocol" and then began an ancient Druid spell for casting images.

The beautiful vampire, seemed to take shape from of the shadows gathered like spider webs around the chanting Librarian.

Just as I was about to leave my assigned perch and take a closer look, Bandi held up his hand.

"You shall not come closer, Cathleen O'Brien! This is delicate work I undertake."

With that the Librarian entered into the vaguely shimmering form of the Lady, forcing it to expand to accommodate his presence. Just as he entered what appeared like a projection upon a wall, I saw another figure materialize close to the Lady.

I gulped air and gasped back out, "Dad!"

My father and the vampire were in what appeared to be, a heated conversation. I couldn't hear words exchanged, but they moved around each other like boxers, making angry gestures; their faces distorted in unmasked hatred.

Their constant shifting of places allowed me some ghastly glimpses of the aftermath of human warfare.

I was enthralled watching this young version of my dad. He was in command and unafraid.

Even as the vampire leaned into him in a threatening manner, her beautiful face spattered in blood and her eyes wild with a dark lust for more death.

Suddenly, off in the background, I noted movement among the corpses. It wasn't Bandi. I'd nearly forgotten about him, watching the scene between my father and the angry Lady Bao.

This had to be *the first Librarian, Fionn.*

He appeared to be skulking about, trying to remain undetected during the argument between my father and Lady Bao. This proved he was present during the battle; an historic event he would *never* have missed.

My attention left him for a minute. I resumed watching my dad's interaction with the vampire.

She had gone stone-still. I sensed she would make a strike like the viper she was.

Dad's arms flew up at the last instant. A barrier of Green Fire separated them as she lunged for him. She seemed to bounce back like a rubber ball off a wall, landing on her back. She looked more surprised than hurt and launched herself onto her feet in a blur of speed.

Dad was gone by the time she righted herself.

Lady Bao stood alone among the slaughtered of the battle. Those few bodies dad wasn't able to bury in the *Green Mother's* earth were now vulnerable to a different kind of *Bleak Gardener.*

The vampire would now harvest these souls to bring back to Feng Xi, her Master and most hated nemesis.

I sat without moving a muscle throughout this drama until I noticed a slight shift in the perspective of this remarkable hologram.

It was Bandi, crossing back into my field of vision as he once more stepped into the Library and out of the history books.

Chapter 28

"So, my fine young Wizard, you now have an accurate accounting of some of your father's history with the Lady Bao. As you have likely guessed, the hologram was the work of Fionn, though I fear, his next movements took him out of this realm."

"But how can you be so sure he's no longer on this plane? Perhaps he's hiding from the vampire and her master."

"Trust me, my dear. He has left no trace of his life force where I could have detected it. He may still be gathering history and facts that will one day become a part of this Library, but that will be long after the *Green Mother* has cleansed this plane of all diseased souls."

"Do you mean to take the Library with you when you leave here?"

I'd been worried that I'd lose this resource before I had a real chance to delve into its hidden secrets.

"You shall have use of this Library as long as your own life cycle, Cathleen O'Brien. It was bequeathed to you by your father. I shall make it quite portable for your trip so that you can access its many resources."

I had gradually shifted over to the back of the long room to be closer to Bandi as he spoke. He gave me a wide smile and gestured to a stool which I promptly sat on. I knew he had important things to tell me and I wanted to make myself as unobtrusive as possible as he began to pace back and forth in front of me.

"There may come a time, young Wizard, when you'll return here to this place of knowledge; most especially when in need of *sanctuary*!

You see, only the Librarian or a *Sworn Protector* of the *Guild of the Green Wizards* can ever enter this place; it is sealed by many wards and spells to any others.

When you are on your quest, this can become a personal refuge, if needed."

"I don't have the time to sift through these thousands of books, Bandi. I need to leave here in less than two days."

He gave me a curious look and then chuckled. It sounded like a bird warbling to my sensitive ears

"You do like to worry, Cathleen O'Brien. Very endearing trait, that" he said still smiling like an indulgent parent.

"Of course, I shall take the books you need for research and separate them out from these thousands."

Saying that, he went down the aisles like he was on roller skates and with an outstretched hand, four books flew off the shelves and onto the table in front of me.

"That should do it!" he said cheerily.

"You have these slim volumes to peruse at your leisure, and the Library with you as your stronghold in time of need. And, naturally, I will be here whenever you might find a reason to call upon me. Look for the book that's glowing, just as you found me before.

Until that time, Cathleen O'Brien, may the *Green Mother* hold you in her safe and loving embrace and strengthen your magic. Happy hunting, young wizard!"

He blinked out of sight like a lightening bug and I immediately saw a yellow glow in a book lying on the table beside me; ***Life and Death of the High King, Brian Boru"***

While I stood there staring at what was the Librarian's life-force radiating from the volume, I felt the Library begin to vibrate. It was as if a strong wind was battering at the structure.

Suddenly, the walls began to vibrate, spinning faster and faster around me. I grabbed for the books.

The whirlwind sounded like a jet engine roaring through a tunnel. It acted like a black hole as it scoured the complete contents of the Library; books, tables, chairs, even the lovely fire and tea.

As it spun around me, it was shrinking in size until it became a pinprick of violet-blue light.

I jumped as the vivid light stopped circling my head and slammed into the top book, instantly disappearing inside.

Now that the noise had stopped I could hear my own sharp intake of breath with the relief that surged through me.

"Now, that's what I call cleaning house!" I said into the emptiness of my shadowy basement.

I had to get my own show on the road and make final plans to hop a plane in less than thirty-six hours.

I was ready to get myself back upstairs when I heard a popping noise.

I didn't have time to consider the source of the new sound, because the pale light in the basement went out completely.

I switched to my Inner Eye to catch anything that might be creeping up on me in the inky swell of musty air.

Nothing stirred except for the increasing beat of my heart rate in my eardrums.

As I was about to place a protective ward around myself, I finally picked up a small life force moving in a straight line and coming at me.

"You!" I cried out sharply and felt the vibration of my words humming in my ears.

"Althar Cron Fionn!   The First Librarian at your service, *Protector* Cathleen O'Brien."

Chapter 29

I was staring open-mouthed at the pleasantly round face of the long-missing Librarian.

"It is delightful to meet the daughter of Liam O'Brien, Celtic Mage and Protector for the Guild of Green Wizards" he said, sweeping back a long black cloak in a quick bow.

He was probably as tall as Bandi, but a stooped back made him look almost dwarfish. His long hair was a rich chestnut color, falling in soft waves around his shoulders and framing the unlined face of a young man. But time meant nothing to a Librarian.

His eyes did that same color change I'd seen in Bandi, but they had a mischievous twinkle in them no matter the color. I liked him immediately.

"I am only with you a few short moments, young Wizard. I have been forced to use much of the power I had stored in my First Librarian medallion, to make this effort. But, here we are at last!"

He seemed so pleased to meet me that I was embarrassed at my own silence.

I managed to finally stammer, "You do me a great honor, Fionn! Your protégé, Ban Briathar was with me a few moments ago."

"I did not come to see him, wizard's daughter, but you alone. Bandi needs no interference from these old bones. He is now, in truth, *the* Librarian.

You have been called to a dangerous mission, Cathleen O'Brien and I knew I must shed some light on the darkness surrounding your search."

"But, how did you learn about my investigation, Fionn?"

"Whenever the Library is opened for any reason, I am made immediately aware. I retain the abilities needed to extend my life force into any realm of my choosing and thus am here with you in this form.

I have come with information and warnings. I have been waiting eons for this hour, Wizard O'Brien!"

While I liked the part about information sharing, I definitely didn't like hearing that there would be warnings attached. Then it dawned on me, he said he'd "been waiting eons for this hour." Now, *that* really grabbed my attention.

"Did you know about the Red Dragon while you still lived in this realm?"

"I not only knew of it, but I knew of its creator, the Dark Sorcerer, Feng Xi. And by association, naturally I knew of the once mortal woman he enslaved to his will; the Vampire, Lady Bao.

Your dear father manipulated and used the Lady, but I hasten to say, to the most honorable ends. I'm certain Bandi has given those details to you, however."

"He has told me my father saved many of the fallen from being harvested by Lady Bao and how he worked beside her to win the Battle against the Norsemen."

Fionn was nodding his head in the affirmative, acknowledging this part of history as correct. That's when I noticed the small hour glass hanging from a heavy gold chain around his neck.

As I watched the grains of sand, they were rushing toward the bottom. When they were gone, my visitor would be also.

"I have brought to you some instructions on how to destroy Feng's Red Dragon along with the twisted power locked within."

With that, he fished around inside a voluminous sleeve of the long brown tunic he was wearing. He pulled out a tightly rolled scroll secured with a dark green wax seal.

I immediately recognized the imprint of my father's Celtic Name in old rune calligraphy. This would have only been used in his role as a *Principal Protector to the Council of Green Wizards*.

The physical seal vanished upon his death, as all such seals do. These personal silver discs held the name and rank of the holder. There were never any duplicates.

I took the document from his hands and held it with a deep reverence along with a deeper pang of sadness.

"Your father prepared this for you, young Wizard. He knew, by my own instruction, that you would be called to this journey of discovery and destruction. I made him aware of Feng's plans and how he was draining more and more power from other Magic Users for his own malevolent ends.

You should find everything you need within this document to destroy the Red Dragon upon taking it into your possession."

I was just about to ask if he could help me locate the statue when Fionn turned to the hour glass and blurted out "Ah! My time is done here *Protector*. May the *Green Mother* guide your steps upon this quest and shelter you always against your enemies."

He disappeared so quickly that I almost thought I'd only imagined the whole encounter.

Holding what was likely my dad's final message to me while he was in this realm, brought me back to a hard reality. I stood in among the shadows of the cellar and made a silent pledge.

There is no way in the four realms, dad, that I'll fail you in this mission.

My resolve cemented well in place, clutching the scroll and four books, I headed back upstairs.

My head was now stuffed with more questions that I hoped I could answer before I had to leave for San Francisco. This trip was beginning to feel like a life's work and I felt like Alice in Wonderland. *Nothing is as it seems,* I thought as I patted the top book to assure myself by the faint glow that the Shadow Box Library was still there and with it, my access to Bandi's help.

Carrying the books and the scroll from my dad, I made my way back to the kitchen.

Ollie was waiting patiently by the back door and gave me a look that seemed to accuse me of doggie-neglect.

I ruffled his furry head and sent him out into my snow obliterated back yard.

Now that I had the resources, I needed to make some plans. With dad's unopened message and the four books selected by Bandi, I had some serious homework to do!

This called for some serious help from a very helpful Sheriff. I took out my cell phone and hit speed dial.

Chapter 30

"Hey, Magic Girl! I was just picking up the phone to check in on you. I was thinking of coming over, but didn't want to interrupt any research you were doing."

"Actually, honey, I'm calling to ask if you'd give me a hand in that particular undertaking. And, of course, I want to see you."

"I'm slipping into my coat as we speak and my car is already warmed up. See you in fifteen minutes."

It seemed like Jason was here more than his own place. I wondered when we'd get around to finishing the conversation about making this arrangement legal, as well as permanent. Shades of mom! I hoped she had nothing to do with this new domestic feeling that seemed to have taken hold of me. I got out my vacuum before that domesticity could fade.

I heard the crunching of snow as Jason's heavy SUV labored up my drive.

When he came bursting in, Ollie was right behind him, excited to be with his two favorite humans.

Jason reached for my arm and pulled me close. We kissed until we both needed to come up for air. Jason held me at arm's length for a minute and said, "You are a real Irish beauty, Cathleen O'Brien! If I wasn't already in love with you, I'd be falling right this minute."

"Jason, you could be Irish yourself, with all that "blarney!"

I was feeling the warmth he always stirred in me, pulsing through my body like liquid fire.

He drew me closer again, putting his mouth close to my ear, whispering, "I meant every word."

It wasn't easy to turn my attention back to the reason I needed to see him. I definitely didn't want to throw cold water on our intimate moment. It just felt too good!

Reality set in when Jason followed my look over to the table. He saw my newest acquisitions of the books and scroll. Then his eye registered the very faint glow in the top book and I saw his eyebrows raise slightly with unasked questions.

We settled down in front of the fire place. It was comforting to have the cozy warmth radiating back at us, while we composed ourselves for a much needed strategy session.

Jason listened attentively as I told him about the Shadow Box Library and my encounters with the two Librarians. I handed him the book where the Library was now only a vague glow.

"It's really amazing, Cathleen, that the Library as you described it, could be contained in such a small object. Magic is really handy!"

I smiled at that observation and then went on to open dad's scroll for the first time.

I used four stone coasters to hold the parchment flat. We both were leaning in to read the message. My dad's very distinctive hand writing jumped off the paper. I read out loud.

"To my darling lass, Cathleen O'Brien,

I pen these few words to aid in the quest you are about to undertake. For I know without a doubt, that it has fallen upon you to see an end to Feng Xi and his monstrous statue, Blood of the Red Dragon. I also am preparing you for your encounter with the Lady Bao, an extraordinary vampire, who has sought revenge upon Feng for enslaving her for untold centuries, to his will. While she has come to me, to lend aid to the High King during his battles, she has shown her duplicity and is, sadly, untrustworthy. Beware of her machinations daughter and remember my teaching on the undead, "Life has no meaning to them." Guard against her as you will against Feng Xi and his Dark killers. You will enter an area unknown to me, but which I have seen from another plane. Do not enter caves or dungeons unless armed with Green Fire and the placid spirit of your champion; whomever they might be. Destroy every particle of the statue, for it is an abomination in nature and not of the first realm. Guard against the glamour of the Vampire; she is both beautiful and deadly. Lastly, if Brighid, your dear mother and my dearest wife, is to accompany this quest, heed her words on patience. You were ever the impatient student my darling lass and that could be your undoing. Go with the Green Mother lighting your steps in the darkness to come. I have always believed in you, Cathleen. Be strong and you shall prevail."

~Liam O'Brien, your Da' now and always

I filed away dad's warnings and directives. I now had no doubts about the challenges ahead of me. I had already made a judgment on Feng Xi and Lady Bao and they lined up with my dad's.

Since he never referred to Dr. Chung Wu, I had to infer from his silence, that he wasn't aware of the man who had sought me out to find the statue. I was disappointed and curious.

I knew that Chung was a contemporary of Feng XI. I wondered for a moment just what Dr. Chung did for his Emperor, but didn't want to be distracted by yet another trail to follow.

It was obvious that I needed to hit the books and learn everything I could before I left for San Francisco; and the clock was ticking.

Jason moved the coasters off the scroll and picked it up to read again; nodding his head occasionally as if in agreement with dad's warnings and assessments.

He turned a serious gaze on me. Even with one eye, Jason had a way of locking a penetrating look on anyone and right then, it was on me.

He said quietly, as if he didn't want the dancing flames inside the fireplace to overhear.

"I can see your dad was a very smart guy, Cathleen. I think he had a feeling I'd be the "placid spirit" that would be with you during your search. What do you think?"

"Yes. He was very smart and yes…you are definitely my peaceful companion."

He leaned in and gave me a soft kiss.

"Thank you for knowing how much you mean to me, Cathleen. You may be the finest wizard this side of Pluto, but sometimes you don't understand how important you are to me and how much I need to keep you safe."

He had reached out to hold my face in his hands. Searching his solitary eye, I saw more of his placid spirit than ever before and felt a deep calm come over me.

I've got this now, I thought, smiling back at my remarkable man.

After we compared notes on the scroll, we began opening the books provided to me by Bandi. We were able to finish perusing them in an hour, taking notes on the legal tablet I'd snatched off my desk on the way back from refilling our cups.

We covered several pages with information about Feng Xi and Lady Bao, but found only a passing reference to Chung Wu. He seemed the biggest enigma and I didn't like those kinds of mysteries.

I felt more settled inside about our travel plans. I knew mom had booked an earlier flight so she'd be at the hotel. Joanie would be flying out of Pittsburgh. We planned to meet at the gate and board together. I was flying out of Iron Mountain Airport to a small private airfield and would drive the forty minutes to Pittsburgh International to meet her. I was trying to keep her under the radar if possible. I had insisted on buying her ticket as an early birthday present. We were going first class so I could have the space to spread out my research. Jason refused to allow me to treat him and he'd fly Coach. He said he was "tough enough" to withstand the rigors of "steerage".

Because we'd been at it for several hours, we decided to take a break and stretch our legs.

"How about taking Ollie out walking in the woods behind the house before it gets too dark?" Jason asked.

I never pass up an opportunity to be in the thickly wooded area around my house and readily accepted the invitation.

Bundled up, we left only the tips of our noses exposed to the single digit temperatures. Before we left, Jason stoked the fire and added a few logs, hoping to keep the downstairs warm for our return.

We were a few feet away from the shelter of the house and were disappointed at how the wind had picked up. Trudging toward the tree line, we had our heads bent against the strong gusts. I was struggling to tuck my thick knit hat over my ears and piles of resistant hair.

Ollie galloped in a circle around me through the heavy drifts, delighted with the adventures found in the ever-changing winter scene.

We headed toward the path Jason and I had carved out of the woods last summer. With three feet of snow, we relied on the canvas flags we had hung on several branches, marking the outline of the trail.

In the natural twilight of the deep woods, we found something else besides. Something that nearly stopped my heart as effectively as coming into contact with a two-twenty electrical line.

The body of Dr. Chung Wu.

Chapter 31

It was easy to identify Chung. We breathed out his name like a chorus of morbid singers, the words freezing into crystals of vapor above his head.

We had spotted our canvas flag hanging from a broad blue spruce and saw his head poking out from the snow mound below it.

Using our gloved hands, careful not to move him, we dug Dr. Chung out of snow that had drifted in a soft curve up to his chin. I was reminded of a white shroud.

There was a stark contrast between his milky-blue skin and blue-black of his mouth. The snow around his face and stringy white beard and mustache was tinted watery pink. The bruised looking lips were drawn back in a snarl of rigor mortis, showing teeth, stained brown from long use.

Silently, we stood shoulder to shoulder and studied the scene of his death.

He'd been propped against the tree's stocky trunk. Almost like he'd been on a picnic under its wide umbrella of branches.

We stared down at his corpse. I thought distractedly, about how his mysterious letter and hologram had started the investigation. Now, it was rolling like a fat snow ball downhill, gathering the dark debris of evil along the way.

Jason's voice cut through my thoughts.

"OK, Cathleen. We need to look at this like a murder investigation now."

He had a grip on my arm trying to focus me. Ollie had come to stand by my side, curious about the discovery.

Jason was basically talking to himself as he ticked off the process, since I wasn't listening.

I was in shock at finding Chung's body on my property, especially when he was supposedly back in China. I wondered what other lies he'd told me.

I was considering the possibility I'd been duped by Dr. Chung and my eyes wandered back to the victim.

He wasn't there.

I yelled out, "Jason!"

We had turned away from the scene for only a few seconds.

"Not to state the all too obvious, Cathleen, but he's gone. Did we imagine finding him?"

He asked this while slowly scanning the area in a slow circuit.

I noticed the snow that had been turned a pale pinkish color presumably from Chung's blood, was also gone. New snow was already beginning to cover the supposed murder scene.

"Jason, I know what's happened!" I said hurriedly.

"Dr. Chung has been removed from this plane since his mortal being is no longer a viable vessel for his spirit."

"Uh, care to explain?" Jason said looking even more confused.

"I suspected that he was an Immortal, Jason and like other immortal beings, Dr. Chung Wu had achieved a measure of power that only his ilk can enjoy. He was able to maintain a presence in this realm of life, because of his original physical make-up. Once that was destroyed, he'd be relegated to the second plane, or maybe even the third. That means he will no longer be accessible to mortals in this life. Unfortunately, that also means I can't find out what he knew about this investigation unless…"

"Unless what?"

"Unless I find a way to communicate with him wherever his life force has journeyed."

I took in a deep breath of the frigid air, trying to stay clear-headed.

"Whoever did this to him obviously didn't want him to contact me again. The fact that he made the trip in his mortal form, knowing he was vulnerable to dark forces like the Vampire, indicates he thought it worth the risk."

"It also means he lied to you about going back to China." Jason added decisively.

I could see the doubt on his face, but Jason and I were always a bit leery of Chung.

"Jason, Chung, like Lady Bao, would have the ability to travel using *time-bending* achieved through powerful spells. He would have no problem leaving China for a few minutes and traveling here.

I have to admit, I wasn't sure if Dr. Chung had those kinds of magical abilities," I concluded.

We were looking at the impression in the snow left by the newly dead Dr. Chung Wu. It seemed as though he had been laid out for our discovery. I was certain I knew who killed him and I knew she did it to cut off my access to other powerful resources.

Lady Bao wanted me to have to rely on her for any information pertaining to the Red Dragon.

We started to search the area around the tree, finding nothing secreted away by Chung that might have indicated his mission. Jason suggested we widen our search to include more of the woods and then circle back to the tree where we found Chung's body.

"By the way, Cathleen, if Chung's remains could no longer be maintained in this realm, why didn't they just disappear after he was killed? I mean, he'd been there under the tree long enough to stain the snow with his blood and be buried up to his chin."

"He was laid out for us to discover him, Jason, and held in place until that was accomplished. Lady Bao must have placed a binding spell on his body which would have included his vanishing act as soon as she was satisfied that we found him."

"The more I hear about this lady, the more concerned I am about you crossing swords with her."

"Leave worrying about Lady Bao to me, sweetie. She's going to be astonished at how much power will be hurled at her when we've joined forces with my mom."

Lady Bao had bested another powerful Magic User and another ancient one at that. My young years would not be very intimidating to her that was for sure!

If this murder was the vampire's doing, she had sent me a clear message; "Don't mess with me, Wizard. I can kill and control the dead."

My fears were shifting like sand under my feet, giving me a feeling of uncertainty I hadn't experienced since ending my apprenticeship.

I gave Jason a quick peck on the cheek and told him to go to the left of the tree and we'd meet back here in twenty minutes.

When I called out to Ollie he appeared like an apparition out of the shifting shadows, his thick fur holding the snow and freezing around his warm mouth.

He was giving me his happy smile and I envied his innocent life.

Chapter 32

I quickly lost sight of Jason's receding back as he moved off into the dark green shadowing of the trees. Ollie stalked silently beside me as we began our own reconnaissance of the area. Even he seemed more alert to our surroundings.

After five minutes of slogging through heavy drifts and around fallen forest debris, both Ollie and I stopped as I sniffed the air. There was a spicy odor riding the frigid air currents.

It became stronger as we mushed through the deeper drifts. At one point, I could almost taste it; jasmine.

I was immediately on my Magical toes. I recalled where I had smelled that particular fragrance before. My house. Lady Bao.

Stopping again, I made a slow scan of the trees, watching as they swayed, shifting their snowy burdens like tired workers under an unseen lash.

I switched to my Inner Eye to detect any presence that might be lurking.

An immediate chill ran up and down my spine as I spotted a set of flaming red eyes glaring back at me a few feet away.

The driver!

The thought shot through me like an arrow as I began to back away to put more distance between us. The minute I began to move, he understood he'd been spotted and came out from behind the masking of tree branches.

"The Lady has sent you a message, Wushen O'Brien."

He looked into a distant spot above my head and began in a monotone voice, sounding devoid of any life, which of course he was.

"The death of Dr. Chung Wu is a sampling, of what to expect if you fail to secure the Red Dragon for me. I will not permit any other Magic User to have access to the statue under penalty of death, as I have demonstrated with Dr. Chung Wu."

As I listened, my mouth slightly gapping at the oddity of hearing the driver speak, I understood that Lady Bao was more than a Vampire. She was a master puppeteer not unlike Feng Xi.

The driver continued in his lifeless voice.

"Chung Wu has departed this realm forever and your connection to him is henceforth severed."

With that, the Driver, still dressed in his black Goth uniform, blurred out of sight, practically leaving skid marks on my Inner Eye.

"Wow!" I said more to myself, though Ollie responded by wagging his bushy tail enthusiastically.

"Well Oliver, guess I've been warned."

Taking one last look around, I approached the trees where I'd first spotted the driver, hoping to find some clues to where his mistress was hiding. I could smell her jasmine scent strongest where two sets of prints marked the snow, big ones and very petite ones. *Huh,* I thought, nodding my head, agreeing with my conclusion.

The vampire had been there all along, likely under some kind of invisibility spell.

She was definitely trying to intimidate me.

Guess she's not as smart as she believes she is I thought as I resumed my search.

Ollie had walked off on a private adventure leaving me to continue alone. He probably felt like I had everything under control and he wasn't needed as a witness, if I didn't.

I was getting closer to the large spruce tree where Chung met his earthly demise. There was the sound of crunching snow under a heavy boot and I knew Jason must be close by.

Just as I opened my mouth to call out to him a bolt of lightning seared the trees to my left, missing my arm by a good frog's leap.

I threw up my arms and shouted, "Scail sciath," covering myself in shadows and darkness.

Hunched over and carefully probing the woods with my Inner Eye, I found the driver once more, but this time the vampire stood beside him.

She seemed perplexed at my disappearance as her eyes narrowed and darted around the space she last saw me occupy.

I decided I didn't have time to dawdle here as Jason was bound to be close by and I didn't want him to stumble into this standoff.

I threw my voice so it would come from behind the two un-dead.

"I thought you wanted me to help you, Lady Bao."

She spun around toward the sound of my voice only to find herself looking at a dense wall of fir trees. The snow had helped me to pitch my voice as it deflected off the thick surface on the branches.

"How can I ever trust you, now that you've both threatened and tried to kill me?"

"Honorable Wushen, you were not the target of my bolt. Look at the place where it touched the trees."

While I suspected her of some chicanery, I didn't want to appear afraid and dropped my spell.

Lying across a burnt tree limb, smoke rising from its thick, worm-like body was the scorched remains of a *Blood Wart.*

These evil creatures wrap themselves around their intended victims, causing hideous blood-filled boils to erupt on any exposed skin surface. It was an excruciating death because the hundreds of sharp hooks on the underbelly of this beast, could tear away any protection provided by clothing, even armor. The Blood Wart was a favorite minion of the Dark Sorcerers that harassed Merlin and other Green Wizards.

She noted my reaction to the charred remains and likely saw my nose twitch at the wretched smell rising off it.

She called over to me, "A messenger from Feng Xi no doubt. He has sent others?"

I didn't bother to answer, but said "Lady Bao, I appreciate not having to deal with the Blood Wart, but I most certainly could have. While you are here, perhaps you could tell me why you removed Dr. Chung Wu from this realm."

A slight breeze stirred among the trees and suddenly the vampire was standing a few feet in front of me.

Geesh, I hate that! I thought, annoyed at her show of skill.

I noticed she wasn't exactly standing in front of me, but rather floating on a current of air, her white leather boots unsoiled by dirt, snow…or blood. Her driver stayed put a short distance away.

"You have only to look at the slight Dr. Chung Wu to think him kindly, yes? But I tell you now, Wushen, Chung Wu was as unpredictable as the cobra and as lethal as a cup laced with hemlock."

I took a small step away from her while she went on in a heated tone.

"I encountered Chung Wu when Feng brought me to the Emperor's Court. I was another of his many glorious prizes, to flaunt before the peacocks among the nobles. Naturally, my altered state was kept secret.

Chung Wu held great influence over the Emperor Qin, though Feng worked to undo that at every turn. I was supposed to dispatch Chung Wu at a crowded banquet honoring the Emperor's youngest son. My attempt, however, came to naught when he discovered me feeding on one of his servants after I had *questioned* him at length."

She must have seen my face reflect disgust at her reference to bleeding a mortal dry, and smiled coyly at me saying, "Even I become hungry, Wushen, and must eat to sustain my life flame."

Guess she thought that explained her vampire ways sufficiently as she continued in her melodic voice.

"I was forced to leave the Court after Chung Wu made it known to the Emperor and the Imperial Guard Captain that I was a Jiangshi, a Vampire.

Feng Xi saved himself, claiming I must have cast a spell to conceal my true dark nature from him and others.

I was made to flee Court like a common cur. I traveled ahead in time to our present day and with my wealth, I lived independently for hundreds of years, until Feng Xi reached out to me through our link and brought me back to his side. I was hidden away in his darkest sanctuary. And today…today I have collected the debt Chung Wu owed me by revealing my secret, his mortal life."

I said, "Lady Bao, I will be leaving here in less than 24 hours and I don't want to see, or hear from you until my investigation is completed. That means no more surprise visits to my home to protect me and no more killing of your competitors. I really don't care if you foul creatures decide to send each other to the fourth realm of the Dark. I just won't allow your intrigues to hurt me or those I care about."

When I finished talking, the vampire stared daggers at me. When her lips pulled back over her teeth, she revealed the long incisors her kind enjoyed using as they nibbled upon and drained their victims.

I subtly moved my left hand and before she could react threw a fist-full of Green Fire bolts at her. She reacted just as I knew she would, vanishing like a vegetarian at a hog roast.

I got back to the designated spruce tree and found Jason crouched down, searching the spot recently occupied by the dead sorcerer, Chung Wu. He sprang to his feet, obviously worried at my coming late to the rendezvous.

"Cathleen! I was beginning to worry, love. Everything alright?"

He took hold of my arms, studying my face closely. I could never hide anything from his keen scrutiny.

"Tell me what happened."

I gave him the abbreviated version of my encounter. He thought that I might have been too hard on Lady Bao, saying she did save me from the *Blood Wart*.

I explained that she was probably the one who conjured it so she could "rescue" me!

I reminded him that she had lots of ulterior motives in her line of work and she *was* a *vampire* let's not forget!

After he agreed you couldn't be too hard on a Vampire he said "Found something, you'll want to see, love."

A piece of cream colored silk, no bigger than a thumb nail had been found stuck to the bark of Chung's last resting place. I took it from Jason's gloved fingers, amazed that he saw such a small object with only one eye. But then, he was a methodical man and would have gone over that tree with the scrutiny of a hound dog searching out scent.

Within a few minutes of joining Jason, Ollie came hurtling through the snow.

"Guess that's our cue to get back home," Jason said, taking my gloved hand in his.

I was ready for a cozy fire and a cup of green tea. Which reminded me, I had to call mom and bring her up to date, especially about the demise of Dr. Chung Wu.

As one of my favorite literary sleuths, Sherlock Holmes would often say, "The game was afoot!"

Chapter 33

After recharging the fire with some stout logs, Jason left for home. He wanted to finish packing. Like any soldier going into the field, he'd only take bare essentials in his old army duffle. There was no way he'd approve of what I considered necessities, but he was wise enough not to mention it.

I returned to my bedroom after confirming Ollie's drop-off time at the Vet's.

I finally shut my suitcase and called that job finished.

Grabbing my lap top and some research papers I'd downloaded for the investigation, I shoved the lot into leather tote big enough to carry a "Smart Car."

The Shadow Box Library was tucked in among the papers, looking like any other book. I smiled to myself at that practical touch of magic.

Finally, I felt like I was really taking this trip and not just talking about it. Snatching my tickets off the dresser, I zipped them into an inside pocket of the tote.

I had decided earlier, against opening the Library for Jason because it stirred up the Librarians.

Jason had been slipping into a mood the last few hours I was with him. I'd seen that out-of-focus look come over his face before. It meant he was working something out in his head. Something he hadn't shared with me yet.

While I ruminated over the subtle change in my boyfriend's behavior, I went back downstairs to the kitchen.

It was getting close to seven-thirty and pitch black outside. The only things visible from my kitchen window were millions of snowflakes that whirled like tiny dancers under the glow of the porch light.

A thin scrap of moon hung like an afterthought among the scudding clouds. I noticed the trees behind the house were so heavy with snow their branches swept the ground. Eerily, they resembled a row of zombies on the move. That thought brought on a mental shiver. I wrapped my arms around myself, wishing it was time for Jason's predawn visit. But that was many hours off.

Jason always made me light up inside. With his wavy black hair and his strong chiseled features, he was easily called a "hunk" by any standards. He confided in me once that he thought the loss of his left eye was disfiguring. In reality, he was so handsome I felt downright frumpy around him. Luckily for me, my Adonis saw me as sexy, smart and totally his.

Dad instructed me about love's mystical charms when I was still young enough to hate most boys, and one in particular. Looking at me with his most serious gaze, dad said he understood my heartbreak.

"You need to understand lass, love can be a fearful master. To know it truly, you need to be brave enough to embrace it without reservation, in total commitment of the mortal and Magical."

I turned away from the chill of the frosted window, grabbing the tea kettle I'd put on to boil when I got downstairs. I pulled one of mom's good china tea cups out from among the bland, white ceramic ones and poured in a fragrant chamomile tea.

I was ready to curl up for a bit and think about the coming trip and looming investigation.

I still had the three books chosen by Bandi that I would go through once more, hoping I missed something in the first reading.

I plopped down in front of the fireplace with the small stack of ancient volumes and the notes we'd taken earlier.

The first small volume, titled "The Dire Cost of Founding a Kingdom: Brian Boru, High King of Ireland.'

Wow! What a mouthful! I thought with a sigh.

Twenty minutes after starting, I was pleasantly surprised with something new.

Fionn, ever the observant historian, had described in detail Lady Bao's role as an ally to the High King. He recounted the vampire's methods of infiltrating the enemy with her own chosen henchmen, vampires under her control. They brought death by the hundreds in their feeding frenzy, causing panic and mayhem among the warriors who fled from the blood orgy they witnessed.

She had undoubtedly broken the opposing army of Norsemen and Boru would have given her anything.

Luckily, my father wasn't charmed by her, though she used a form of *Infatuation Spell* to overcome resistance in others.

By returning several thousand fallen warriors to the Green Mother, dad prevented a legion of walking dead being sent to Feng Xi. What I suspected at the conclusion of the book was that Lady Bao would have retained full control of that army and turned them on Feng when he least expected it.

Over the next two hours, I'd re-read all books, did more copious note taking, and was going back upstairs to stuff them into my carry-on bag. I stopped mid-way when I felt a familiar and unwelcome chill.

There was someone up there, or perhaps more alarmingly, *something* up there. It was waiting very quietly for me right now.

Standing on the staircase, holding my notes and the three ancient texts close to my chest, I tested the air with my deepest senses. Nothing screamed out monster!

OK, this is weird, I thought, creeping up two more steps. Why wasn't I picking up a threat?

Then I got a whiff of something I hadn't smelled since my last investigation among the wild beauty of Utah.

My mom's distinctive perfume, wafting on the chilly air coming from my room.

Could it be?

Chapter 34

When I finished my creaky ascent, I heard the sweet melody of an old Irish lullaby being hummed from various parts of my bedroom. Just as I was about to step in, one hand clutching the books and papers the other holding Green Fire in a defensive position, I heard, "Come in darlin' girl. We don't have much time!"

I poked my head around the corner, looking into my room.

Perched on her old rocking chair was Brighid O'Brien.

"Mom!" I yelled as I ran toward her dumping papers and books into a messy pile on the bed. Throwing my arms around her as she stood up to her five foot nothing, we hugged and pulling away and mirrored broad smiles.

"Well, pet, before you ask, I know you wonder why I'm here rather than on my way to San Francisco."

"Yes, I am wondering, but it's wonderful to see you."

"And I'm very happy indeed to be with you, Cathleen, but I won't be here long as I've only bent time for a wee bit and…"

"Whoa. You know how to bend time like dad?"

"So, who do you think taught your da' how to perform the spell needed for that particular bit of magic? Just one of my better recipes, love."

She said this with just enough humility to make me smile.

"Mom," I began, as I finally let go of her hands. I sat next to her on the bed when she motioned for me to join her. "There have been some happenings around here that I'm sure you'd be interested in hearing about."

"I assume these "happenings" have something to do with the demise in this realm of Dr. Chung Wu, dear."

Once again, mom had learned about my significant news before I could blurt it out. Quite annoying actually!

"Oh, don't look peaked, my darlin' lass, you know I have the ears and eyes of the little people to gather intelligence."

By "little people" mom was referring to her numerous friends among the Faerie clans. She had achieved an almost rock star status among them.

"But I think we would both feel better if I heard all of the details from you, pet."

I knew she was trying to assuage my feelings. I hated to have details of my life and work floating around like tufts of milk weed fuzz.

After recounting Lady Bao's latest visit and the removal of Dr. Chung from this realm, mom held up her hand.

"I think it's time for a cuppa, Cathleen. Lead the way to your kitchen dear and let's brew some of that fine green tea you always have at hand."

Mom sat looking rather pleased with my bustling about. She was dressed in a winter-white sweater in a complex cable knit pattern. A well-fitting pair of black jeans and knee high boots finished her perfect ensemble. I was sorry I didn't inherit at her fashion sense!

As I was putting the tea set on the table, mom gave me an approving smile. I was using this treasured gift from her as she wanted. She was probably afraid I'd store it away because I'm not one for too much fussing.

I noticed her long dark auburn hair had sprouted a few silver strands since I'd seen her last. As much as she hated aging, I hated witnessing it.

We sat facing each other over the pot and a small dish of scones. From the look of concern that drew her eyebrows toward the small line between her eyes, I knew mom had something important to say.

"Cathleen, dear, there is something I should have shared with you sooner, but it needs to be told now." She took a deep breath then looking at me intently, went on.

"Dr. Chung Wu was an agent of the *Shadow Walkers*, an elite group of Wizards from among the *Grand Masters.*

As you know, the *Grand Masters* were the founders of the *Guild of Green Wizards,* Cathleen. They formed this as an exclusive group, during the Dark Times in this realm. Chung was also one of the *Guild's* first *Voyager's.*"

She hesitated as if expecting me to shout out some expletive. I couldn't have interrupted her if I wanted to. I was stunned into silence.

"The *Shadow Walkers,* as part of the *Guild*, operate from the third plane and never venture into this realm unless they detect forces of corruption at work. They cannot meddle into the affairs of men, except upon discovery of demons, or evil powers being used to thwart the natural course of mortal life.

Chung was acting on behalf of the *Grand Masters* when your da, bless his bones, met him during the battle that won Brian Boru his kingdom.

Prior to that voyage, Chung had gone back to the dynasty of the Emperor Qin of the famous Terra Cotta Warriors."

"Yeah, they're really famous now, mom. In fact, I met one here who tried to slice and dice me, but I'll tell you all about that later."

"Oh, dear, you have been busy, lass. I any case, the *Grand Masters* became aware of the Wizard Feng Xi because of the brutal tyranny he practiced with his Magic. They sent the *Shadow Walker*, Chung Wu, to put an end to Feng's evil scheme of achieving Immortality and subjecting mortals to his will.

Chung Wu voyaged back to ancient China, where he used his own powers to become a close and trusted advisor to the Emperor.

While at the Royal Court, he unearthed the plot between Feng Xi and his vampire mistress, Lady Bao, to secure all the dead from a battle that had not yet occurred. This scheme would have been perfect as there would be no way to predict events in yet another country far into the future.

Because Feng Xi traveled in time's currents by using spells, he knew exactly when armies would clash. Going forward in time, Feng's plans could not be thwarted or interfered with by his enemies.

The battle the Dark Wizard chose was between Brian Boru and the Norsemen. The dead from this ferocious encounter between the warriors, were to be reanimated to serve Feng Xi as his own army of unstoppable undead.

Chung Wu voyaged forward and took this information to your father on the battle field. Together they returned the fallen by the thousands to the *Green Mother*."

I finally interrupted, "So, Chung Wu was trying to stop Feng Xi *before* he became an Immortal?"

"After Chung Wu successfully denied Feng his army of the dead, he knew the wizard had not been stopped in his ultimate quest of Immortality. He watched and listened, using his own spies at the Emperor's Court, alert to any new attempts by Feng Xi to move ahead with his evil purposes.

"And *that's* how he must have learned of the Red Dragon!" I blurted out; excited that some of the pieces in this puzzle were falling into place.

"That's right, dear. The *Grand Masters* had the *Shadow Walker*, Chung Wu, advance to the present day, where he had traced the statue, called "Blood of the Red Dragon", to a small gallery in San Francisco's China Town. It was on display with over one hundred artifacts from the Qin Dynasty. Of course, this was a clever way of hiding it in clear view."

I knew our tea had gone cold, but we both picked up the delicate porcelain cups and sipped while we reflected on the unfolding story.

"Mom, who put the statue in that gallery and for that matter, who do you think stole it?"

She carefully placed the cup back into its saucer and seemed to be studying the lovely floral pattern.

"Cathleen," she replied in a soft voice "I don't know who the thief is, but I can tell you who placed the Red Dragon among the artifacts and art works. I did."

Chapter 35

I blinked.

"You did *what?*" I finally asked, a squeak entering my voice like I was choking on the question.

"You see lass, your father, bless his spirit, was most grateful to Chung Wu for his intervention during the battle and for protecting him from Lady Bao's schemes. Although, he had already signed the cursed *Pledge of Service* to her and there was no way out of it.

When Chung voyaged back to this realm, not long before your father left it, your da' felt obliged to accept a new commission brought by him, from the *Grand Masters*, a commission not unlike your own.

The *Shadow Walker* told him about the Red Dragon. He explained how it held one drop of blood from the last Dragon to fly free. He explained to your da' how Feng Xi had imbued the blood and statue, with the darkest magic he could conjure, corrupting its purity and its immense powers.

Though it was his creation, Feng Xi could not access the powerful Magic in the statue until he bound it to himself in this time and on this mortal plane. This was to be his eternal Empire.

Feng Xi's plan was to lead an army of Vampires and undead after he absorbed the evil powers he placed into the statue. With all the wars that had ensued in this realm since Clontarf, Feng could muster unimaginable numbers with his new powers."

"Did Chung Wu steal the statue in the first place, mom?"

"He was instructed to destroy it by the Grand Masters, Cathleen, but on his return to the Court of Emperor Qin, he found it on open display; a beautiful gift to the Emperor from his Court Artist, Feng Xi.

A most cleaver ploy to keep it safe among the Emperor's other guarded treasures."

I considered Chung's dilemma for a moment. He now had to steal the statue from under the very noses of the Emperor and his whole Court. Placing it into the Emperor's hands, had relieved Feng of the burden of guarding it. Pretty smart move I thought, begrudgingly.

Mom continued, "But, Feng was outsmarted by the Shadow Walker once again!" she said with an admiring tone.

"Chung merely produced a second statue by using *image manifestation* spell, placing a charm over it making it radiate a false presence of power whenever Feng was nearby.

He later cast a sleeping spell over the Emperor's elite guards and made the switch. With that done, he transported the original to a chamber deep within the castle so that he could destroy it.

Unfortunately for Chung, Lady Bao was not as easily duped as her Master.

She had been watching his every move. Naturally, as a vampire she never slept and kept Chung under constant scrutiny.

She already deeply mistrusted him after the battle of Clontarf, where she learned of his interference. The slaves she had placed around the court and palace followed the *Shadow Walker's* every move, while she was hidden away by Feng in his secret rooms.

Chung Wu understood the deadly capabilities of the vampire. He thought her loyalty to Feng Xi was unshakeable, only to discover her ultimate goal was to own the Red Dragon and possess its powers for herself."

Mom took a sip at her cup, giving me a minute to process all this information.

"Lady Bao set a clever trap for Chung Wu. Coming out of hiding long enough to use her powers of allure, she subdued one of his most trusted personal guards. She turned his allegiance from the *Shadow Walker* to herself, alone.

When Chung Wu entered the secret lower chamber carrying the real Red Dragon, he found his guard waiting for him as planned. Telling the guard to lock the heavy door behind them, he walked into the small room where Lady Bao waited to spring her trap."

I was mesmerized by mom's recounting of the story. So much so, that I almost missed hearing the faint crunch of snow under a heavy weight. It came from the woods closest to my back door. Whoever it was, they were careful to stay out of the pale yellow pool of the porch light.

Mom had already registered the sound and was on her feet peering through the heavily frosted window over the sink.

"Why, Cathleen. I do believe you have a shy visitor crouching behind that lovely row of spruce."

I looked over her shoulder and spotted a darker patch between the branches as they moved sluggishly in the wind.

This can't be good, I thought, as I sensed a sinister force peering out from the shadows.

I had no doubt this was another of Feng's emissaries. The fact that it didn't register on my *living things* scale, could only mean it was one of the soulless servants he'd been using as his enforcers.

"Mom, how do you want to handle this; bring it down for good, or bring it in for interrogation?"

"Naturally, dear, I would prefer to gather more intelligence for the investigation ahead, so perhaps we might stun it and bind it with your da's delightful, "Iron Bands" spell."

She sounded downright chipper about the prospect of facing a bad guy. I felt more apprehension than elation, but was ready to ask some pointed questions. The opportunity had presented itself nicely and it didn't hurt matters that mom had my back.

Mom stepped away from the window saying "Let's finish this lovely tea dear, before it gets too chilled. I'm certain our visitor will make its appearance shortly. After all, it's on some sort of mission and won't want to dilly dally."

Pouring some hot tea into our now tepid cups, I took the seat across from her.

I had a clear view of the kitchen window, the frost sparkling in the shallow light of the porch. It was high enough up from the ground that all I could easily see was mid-way up the line of pine trees and the snowflakes, as they whirled past.

Fortunately, the light reflected off the blowing snow seemed to dispel some of the darkness of the back yard. If our visitor approached the window for a better look, I'd spot it.

We sipped our tea, smiling at one another as if something amusing had passed between us. Mom had actually been telling me what defensive spell she'd be using and found my own "Quite acceptable, dear."

We had already slipped into the Inner Eye, when a rounded snout popped up over the window ledge, followed by a huge wedge shaped head.

I watched without seeming to and still smiling inanely said, "Our visitor is reptilian, mom, and it's slithering up the side of my house. I don't think we'll be asking this creature any questions though."

"Oh well, but we can finally get off our posteriors and go into demon destruction mode, Cathleen!"

With that, she jumped to her feet and with me on her heels, she threw open the kitchen door.

We were both casting our chosen spells and from the size of the Komodo-Dragon like creature climbing up to my second floor bedroom, we had picked our poison correctly. The beast was immobilized by mom's freezing spell and we were able to look it over before bringing it back down.

It had dug sharp claws, deep into my wood siding.

Mom turned to me and I carefully began to remove the creature, not wanting to damage my siding any more than it already had.

I used my wind spell, wrapping the frigid air around the thick torso to lift it away from the house.

It floated like a really creepy Macy's Thanksgiving Day Parade balloon, toward my garage. Mom flipped her hand to open the garage door and it sailed through.

Luckily, my garage had served the previous owner as part workshop, so it was oversized and could accommodate what turned out to be a fairly large beastie.

As it lay upon the oil-stained cement floor, mom closed the garage door with another flick of her hand and we began to study our stupefied captive.

I had mistaken its dark body as black in color, but saw upon closer inspection it was a deep, midnight blue. The mouth was wide open, exposing more teeth than a couple of chain saws. Its four muscular legs and splayed feet were bristling with bone-like spurs, these also protruded from a humped and scaly back.

Cold, reptilian eyes followed us as we moved around its immobilized body. It was sizing us up like entrées on a buffet line.

Mom stopped circling. Using a special voice technique that prohibited eavesdropping, asked "Did you notice how intently it is observing us, pet?"

When I told her I had, she said "I do believe this particular being was sent by Feng Xi as his personal observer. In fact, I'd wager the Wizard is watching us this very moment.

Let's finish up with this bad boy, shall we? I will need to return to my correct time stream soon."

In the language of our Celtic ancestors, we shouted in unison, *"briocht bruane,"* causing the inert demon to burst into flame and then, to a black sludge resembling a gooey oil slick on the garage floor.

Mom reopened the door with another flick. Using a sweeping motion, she sent the remnants of Feng's spy outside into the murky night it came from.

I began to feel a deep chill seeping into my body, becoming aware of my lack of a coat. I looked over at mom who was scanning the shadows that swayed and bent and rose again like courtiers of a Dark Lord.

Chapter 36

Returning to my cozy kitchen, I looked at the clock on the stove and saw it was nearing time for Jason to show up. I got the coffee pot ready to switch on.

Sitting back down across from mom I said, "Mom, finish your story about Chung Wu and then we can discuss our visitor."

"Of course, dear."

Mom loved storytelling and picked up the thread of the story.

"As I said, the vampire, had set a trap for Chung Wu, however, as clever as she was, she didn't understand the powers of a *Shadow Walker* such as Chung Wu.

After the turned guard had bolted the door, the *Shadow Walker* used the Inner Eye and spied the vampire in the shadows of the deep chamber. He heard the slithering sound of a sword being drawn from its scabbard and immediately threw an invisibility spell over his body. Not wanting to kill his guard outright, he took him to the ground with a binding spell.

Lady Bao didn't have the Inner Eye of course, so she flailed around trying to catch hold of Chung Wu to plunge her own dagger into his heart. Chung still had hold of the statue having veiled it under his spell and put a wall of Green Fire between himself and the enraged vampire. That done he carried himself and the statue through the quickly unbolted door and made good his escape."

"But how did you come by the statue?" I asked trying to keep hold of the various threads of this tale.

"Oh, my. I don't have time to relate the entire story, pet, but suffice it to say, the *Shadow Walker* came to this time stream, sought out your father, and asked him to take the statue and destroy it as directed by the Grand Masters.

Before your da could carry out the task, the cruel waters of the Alleghany claimed him and the task fell to me.

I carefully hid the statue, thinking to bring it to the masters as soon as I received word from them to do so. Several years flew past, I was already in Ireland and you had moved to Iron Mountain, when I finally heard.

I was told to bring it to the Art Gallery in San Francisco as the perfect lure to capture and destroy its creator, Wizard Feng Xi."

Now I understood why this evil artifact was openly displayed among the other art works from the Qin Dynasty before it was taken yet again.

The *Shadow Walker* must have known the Grand Masters sought Feng's destruction and permanent removal from this realm. That explained why he didn't just do away with the statue when he first possessed it. Dr. Chung Wu had taken on a whole new role in this dark drama.

A plot, within a plot, within a scheme. I was thinking about Chung Wu in more complimentary ways.

Mom drew me back from my speculations and asked if I enjoyed my perusal of the Shadow Box Library. I had begun earlier, to relate my exciting experiences there with both the first and present Librarian and she smiled throughout my recap.

It turned out mom was well acquainted with dad's magical book conservatory and had a long term friendship with both Fionn and Bandi.

"I'm sure you found both Librarians quite cordial, Cathleen; though that Bandi is something of a flirt."

She blushed ever so slightly and I reflected on the fact that I too had found him very handsome, as centuries old Librarians go.

"I've packed the Shadow Box up in my carry-on and will have it with me at all times," I said.

This reminded me that time was shrinking and mom had a time thread to catch! She'd promised to teach me all her time-bending recipes.

"Thanks for coming, mom," I said, feeling suddenly a little anxious of what lie ahead for me, for us.

She took my face into her hands and said, "Don't fret, Cathleen. I think Feng Xi will have decided to wait until you are on his turf before sending out any more of his unpleasant creatures to harass you. And by then, daughter, I'll be on hand to get in a few good whacks!"

We both smiled at that comment, knowing her role would be far more significant than a little Magical muscle.

"I must leave you now, my darling girl, but I'll be waiting for you to arrive at the Grand in less-than a day. May the *Green Mother* watch over you, daughter."

With that said, I felt her hands slipping from my own and she was suddenly spinning in a blur of colors and motion. I heard a sudden *pop* and she was gone.

Chapter 37

I stood at the kitchen sink washing our cups when I picked up the sound of a heavy vehicle crunching up the road. A few minutes later, Jason's large SUV pulled into sight.

I felt a familiar warmth surge through my body as I watched his tall, lean form get out of the car. I smiled when he stooped down by the wood box, to grab an arm load of logs before coming into the house. Watching him move toward the door made my heart beat just a little faster. Anticipating his arms wrapped round me and his mouth on mine, I already knew this was a magic that could never be undone.

I opened the back door and even with half a dozen logs wedged between us, Jason managed to give me a long, satisfying kiss.

"Good morning, love. I've missed you. Let me dump these and show you how much."

He was giving me his mischievous grin as he walked toward the fireplace in the front room.

He had kicked his boots off before he came through the back door. I scooped them up from the small porch, standing them by the heat vent where they puddle-up immediately on the boot tray.

I filled our mugs and joining him, settled back against the over-stuffed chair, sipping quietly and holding hands.

I gave him a concise version of mom's recent visit, relating the important information on the newly departed, Dr. Chung.

After I told him of mom's role in all of this, I realized he hadn't commented on what was some pretty exciting stuff.

I looked intently at him and said, "You're awfully quiet, Sheriff. Did you hear what I've been telling you?" I gave his hand a squeeze and he looked over at me.

"Cathleen, while I was at the office, just before I came over here, I had another vision."

Before I could say anything, he placed his finger gently on my lips and said, "I'll tell you, but don't interrupt, or I might leave something important out."

"OK."

He took a breath and focused on the flames waving like sea weed, ebbing and flowing within the fireplace.

"I was sitting at my desk back at the station when I began to feel kind of light headed. I put my head back against the chair and closed my eye until it passed; except it didn't. It got worse.

I felt like I was in the spin cycle of the washing machine. When I finally opened my eye, a chill had settled over me, warning me I was about to have a vision.

I saw you and me, in an old fishing boat. There were nets and baskets hanging over the sides, and a small outboard motor. It seemed only big enough for a two or three man crew. I noticed how warped the boards were on the floor boards and how it looked as if it hadn't been painted in decades.

We were bobbing in the waters off a small island, with only a smear of a shoreline.

I remember thinking it looked tropical, with dense vegetation, a thick, sultry air hanging over it. Nothing moved or swayed. I felt it was *waiting* for us."

I had been watching Jason closely while he relived his vision. He was clearly recaptured by the intensity of the experience. I barely breathed as I was transported to that silently rocking boat. I smelled the sea water splashing up against the sides and the fishy odor of the nets. There was an utter stillness in the air around us.

Jason must have given himself a mental nudge and resumed his description.

"While we sat in the boat without speaking, the boat began to drift toward the island as if pulled by some unseen force. When we first came into view of it, the island was several yards away, but now, the boat's bottom scraped on the coarse sand of the shoreline. I jumped out into the water and pulled the boat further onto the shore and you got out. There was a scream."

Jason seemed to be hearing the phantom echo of a shrill cry. I thought he would stop speaking. His hands clenched around his mug tighter.

"Suddenly, I was alone, crashing through dense trees, toward the sound of several more screams of pain, or fear. I felt like I'd been swallowed up by the island's foliage; the smell was overpowering in there, like rotting fruits, or the sickening sweet smell of decaying bodies."

Now, I did begin to squirm! I didn't want to break his concentration, but I was feeling pretty uncomfortable with the direction his vision was going.

"Just as I thought I was lost, I stumbled out of the gloom of the woods and into a clearing where I saw a cave in the side of a low hill."

I felt it was safe to speak at this point as Jason seemed finished. He turned to me, his face relaxing as he visibly shook off the remnants of the all-too-real vision. He glanced over at my rapt face.

"Go ahead, Cathleen. Ask away."

He had a tired look in his beautiful green eye. The reflection of the fire on his eye patch, made him appear vulnerable and I quickly leaned in and kissed him. My hand on his cheek, I hoped I was reassuring him.

If the screams he heard in this vision were someone we cared about, I was glad I had added one more thing to my magic arsenal, the Shadow Box Library.

Then I thought, *some of those screams might be mine.*

Chapter 38

"No matter what you saw, or heard, Jason, we'll be ready."

When he gave a mirthless chuckle, looking into his mug, I understood that he felt out of his depth in this mission.

"Cathleen," he said turning to me. "My biggest concern is that you will practically be facing this Feng character and the Vampires on your own. Joanie is no Wizard and could become a liability to you. Only your mom will be able to fight beside you."

"Jason, every time you can share your visions, I am more prepared to face those odds. Your gift is a kind of magic. Even my dad didn't see coming events like you do."

Jason reached for my hand and gently squeezed it to let me know he accepted my judgment of his value, saying, "OK, Magic Girl, you've convinced me."

Unfolding his long legs, he stood and gave me a hand up.

We wandered back into the kitchen after Jason put more logs on the fire. I noticed he'd saved the biggest ones for when he planned to leave, making sure I'd have a good fire going to keep the rooms warm.

I could hear the wind swooshing around my backyard, rattling the storm door like a mischievous kid.

Jason and I sat quietly sipping our re-heated coffee, while he picked at a scone. We were deep into our own thoughts.

I was trying to outline a plan of action when the time came to face the real thing. I had already made my mind up that whatever I would be facing in that cabin of his first dream, I wouldn't do it without some heavy-duty magic on hand.

The idea that there was a dragon involved wasn't as alarming as what was happening inside the rooms of the cottage.

The second vision needed more translating. Jason had heard screams coming from the cave on the island. Joanie's face had flashed through my mind when I first heard this, but then I realized it could be anyone caught up in this drama, human and non-human alike. The vampire had already suffered at Feng Xi's hands over her centuries as his mistress. Though it was hard to see her as defenseless, the Wizard had controlled her before. He would know of any flaws in her powers and use them against her.

I knew that I could never trust her, but Lady Bao was a victim herself, caught in an everlasting existence. Never dying, always dead.

Jason's chair scraped on the floor as he stood to take his mug and dish over to the sink. I guess I looked startled.

"You seemed deep in thought, love. Sorry if I gave you a jolt."

"You're fine, sweetie. Guess I was out there, somewhere..."

"Somewhere near that cabin or the cave," he added.

"Cathleen, we both know there are going to be unknown dangers waiting in San Francisco for you. But I'm beginning to understand that my visions could shed a light on some of the unknowns."

I had collected my own mug and stood at his side by the sink.

Looking up at him I said, "I have the Shadow Box Library. I also have allies with powers committed to helping me succeed, plus your clairvoyant abilities. I have a real edge."

Jason pulled me into a comforting hug and without speaking we returned to our cozy nest in front of the fire. His need for some rejuvenating R & R was contagious, and I turned toward him eagerly. We could make our own magic, and no force on earth, dead or alive, was stronger than our love.

Chapter 39

I had decided it was time to provide Joanie with a ward to keep her safe when I couldn't protect her outright. I grabbed a pendant from my jewelry box that she had admired over the years, a gift from my dad. He always said Joanie was their second daughter. The fact that she looked like a walking add for a, "Come Visit Ireland" brochure didn't hurt either.

I held the selected piece up to the light. At the end of its long gold chain dangled a two inch raven, carved from the black thigh bone of a *Branan*.

The *Branan* is an elusive bird living in the lush forests of the third realm. Its long, missile-shaped body is covered in flaming red and yellow feathers, making it look like a fire arrow as it streaks across the topaz skies of its home world.

Though the size of a park bench, the *Branan* is as timid as the rabbit-like creatures it hunts, in the blue twilight hours of those woodlands.

I conjured my favorite *Body Blessing* to infuse the pendant with a protective shield. This would activate whenever Joanie faced any danger of the magical kind.

My packing was done except for what I'd throw in the leather bag I was using as my carry-on. It was one of the first extravagant gifts I gave myself when I came into my inheritance. The fact that the name of the famous designer was plastered all over it was rather annoying, but it clears an aisle quicker than a defensive tackle.

Our flight into San Francisco would take over four hours. I wanted to use that time to get Joanie updated on what had transpired thus far in my investigation.

My dad always said, "Too much knowledge is as bad sometimes, as too little." So, I'd omit the part about dead warriors and giant lizard creatures visiting me. No need to scare her half to death while flying at thirty-five-thousand feet.

While she wasn't blessed by the *Mother* with magical gifts, Joanie was smart and had an uncanny intuition about people. I felt secure about involving her in my current investigation because I knew she wouldn't step into any demon dodo when I wasn't looking. Joanie had common sense enough for both of us.

Our phone call lasted long enough to figure out where and when we'd meet. I planned to get to the airport by 8:00 that evening, factoring in the winter conditions.

I wasn't looking forward to the flight from the mountain-top airport in Iron Mountain. I kept remembering the wind socks and thinking they looked like some of Jason's old pairs. The puddle jumper planes were six seaters, and the two pilots that ran the shuttle from Iron Mountain to Pittsburgh, could have flown with the Wright brothers!

I was tired and ready to turn in for my usual few hours of sleep. That was one of the best things about being a wizard. I needed little sleep to feel rested because my energies were so closely attached to the rhythms of the *Mother*.

I went back downstairs, turning off lights as I walked through the rooms and making sure the fire was down to embers and headed on to bed.

I stopped halfway up my creaky wooden staircase and decided to place a ward at the kitchen and front doors. I also placed a ward at the windows as well. Content with my security measures, I retraced my steps back up the stairs to my bedroom.

Thirty minutes later, I drowsily looked over at my bedside alarm and saw it was nearing midnight. I yawned contentedly, snuggling deeper under my down comforter.

As I began to doze off, I picked up what sounded like a scratching noise coming from below.

My eyes flew open and I lay still, listening to the dark. *There! I heard it clearly this time*, scratching like a large cat clawing at the front door.

It can't get in, whatever it is, I thought, trying to keep calm while getting out of bed and slipping into my robe.

I felt secure that whatever wanted in would find their way barred with magic.

I reached the bottom step and was about to step onto the foyer floor when the scratching sound abruptly stopped.

Maybe it was only a raccoon.

That random thought stirred a feeling of relief, just before I heard a distant thump. It was coming from above me, something on the roof.

"Well, unless this is a *troop* of raccoons, I've got a persistent visitor," I whispered to myself as I looked up toward my ceiling.

I still felt safe behind the magic I'd placed earlier.

Padding softly into the shadows of my front room I noticed how chilly it was without my logs heating it up. I looked over at the fireplace just in time to hear something clawing at the cooled bricks on its way down.

"Oh crapski!" I half shouted, then groaned.

Dad always told me not to overlook the chimney as a port of entry in a storm.

I figured this wasn't Santa dropping by, so I did what any self-preserving wizard would do; I started a big fire to warm up my visitor.

Chapter 40

The green flames were licking at the uppermost part of the fireplace and heating the brick until they glowed red, then white. Because I had used the *Mother's* own fire, there was no possibility of destroying the stone work unless that was my choice.

The flames were dense and constant; not dancing with every shifting of the air.

I was pleased with the demon retardant and began to approach the fireplace to get a look at what was caught up in the blaze. I didn't want to turn it into a briquette until I had a chance to look it over.

Just as I stooped over to peer up the chimney, something dropped to the log grate.

It was as black as a lump of coal (maybe it was Santa) and only slightly larger.

It layed inert for a few breaths, then slowly began to uncurl itself, stretching like silly putty until it took a form resembling a small hunched-backed man, wearing monk type robes with a cowl covering his head. Whatever, or whoever, it was, it had the curve of its back to me.

The flames were still intense, but the thing obviously wasn't afraid of them. That's when I understood. *This isn't real. This is a hologram!*

The three-dimensional image slowly rotated until it faced me.

I automatically jumped back from the gruesome face that peered out at me from behind the wall of Green Fire.

I could see the back of my fireplace through the shimmering image and understood this wasn't the perfected work of a hologram user like my mom. This doppelganger was not perfect, but I got the point.

Staring back at me was the deeply creased face of an ancient Chinese man. A long, wispy mustache drooped down mixing into a sparse beard, the color of wet cement.

The eyes of my conjured visitor glared at me through the flames. They were a deep red with an odd black marbling. I found them almost mesmerizing in their intensity.

Watching the projection I saw the black streaks were moving in and out of each eye ball. This hologram was not a perfect twin of the Wizard, Feng Xi, but it definitely exuded his evil nature.

"Greetings, young Wushen."

My hyper-sensitive ears felt like shards of ice had been jabbed deep inside, them like frozen Q Tips. His comments were choppy as if he wheezed through a tube in his throat to breath.

"I regret disturbing…your slumber, but… the need to speak with you, far outweighs… your *mortal* needs."

Feng's hologram had succinctly told me he was calling the shots and that I was a mere mortal. Nice.

"I have nothing to say to you, Feng Xi. I don't appreciate your intrusions, whether made by your unimpressive hologram form, or by one of your demon flunkies."

I was letting just enough of my annoyance show through to let him know I wasn't going to be easily intimidated by his magic.

"I have perfected this communication, so that I may give you an opportunity to save yourself and those you care for, from the deadly consequences of your actions.   It would be *wise* of you to hear my words."

I stood firmly on my now chilled feet and decided to show the stuff I was made of.

Raising my hands, I removed the Green Fire from the grate.

This wasn't as brave as it looked, since I was in no jeopardy from his image. It made me feel more in control though.

"My presence here should demonstrate my reach, Wushen. I have sent others to keep me informed of your activities, including your visitors over the past days."

I didn't want him to think he'd gotten to me, or that I might be frightened by the ease at which he spied on my life. I decided to turn the tables.

"I'm certain you believe you know about me Feng, but you seem to have overlooked one thing. Your once loyal servant, Lady Bao, has informed me of your past, present and future plans. All most helpful to my own strategies I might add. I also have a great deal of information on you as well."

I acted as nonchalantly as possible, letting the bite of arrogance, creep into my voice. I think that did the trick, along with mentioning his once loyal Mistress.

Feng's projection started shimmering, as if blown by the force of my boast. Then, it began to lose its human shape and form; becoming as squat as a toad. A rather fitting end to this nocturnal conversation I was thinking.

I turned my back on what was left of Feng's quivering image and started for the stairs. As I placed a foot on the first step the hair on the back of my neck bristled like a dog's will when detecting a threat.

I spun on my heels, calling down the first ward I could think of to cover myself.

"Closfiurt!" I shouted out in the old tongue.

A prickly arm was trying to grab my throat through my hastily conjured shield of barbed silver mesh. As I instinctively leaned away from it I realized I was barely shielded from another attempt at me.

I had to act fast, forming a gossamer-like webbing, inside the silver mesh to strengthen it. I was a second too slow as the creature was pushing it inward and I felt a long nail scratch my face.

I'd have to deal with that later. Right now, I had to defend against a new threat.

At first, I thought, Feng was some kind of shape shifter. He'd already demonstrated he could summon and command some fairly nasty creatures, so I wouldn't be surprised if he'd gained this particular magical ability. Shifters are found in most magical cultures, so it wasn't that improbable.

Glaring back at me now through my stronger barbed coral was something else entirely. *This,* I thought, *is a Grotesque Hag!*

I hadn't seen its kind since I was knee high to one, actually knee high.

I was about 6 years old when dad and I went foraging for mom's favorite hooded mushrooms in the wooded area behind our farm.

"As rare as Irish hooligans," dad always told me before these hunts.

Dad had warned me not to wander too far ahead of him, or get out of sight, so naturally, I did both. I heard him calling my name and decided it was a good time to play "hide 'n seek". I crouched down behind the first mossy green boulder that caught my eye as I went deeper into the woods. It was very large and I was easily concealed.

As I held my breath trying to stifle giggles, the large rock began to vibrate under my hands. I jerked back and looked closely at it. Using one pudgy finger to move the lank green moss aside, I was sure I'd find a chipmunk hiding from me, the way I hid from dad.

That's when the boulder slowly rose up on two gnarly green feet.

Suddenly, it sprouted two stubby arms covered in prickly bumps as it continued to rise off the ground. The green moss fell away from a green, leathery face, covered in oozing pustules the size of robin's eggs.

I sat back on my heels, mesmerized by the slow moving creature until it opened its eyes.

The pupils were shaped like a cat's. They shifted in color between blood red and deep amber. That fascinated me until a fat worm came slithering out of one of them. This immediately prompted me to scoot back, screeching like a banshee for my dad!

I stared into those captivating eyes and continued to shuffle backward on my knees and feet, only to get tangled in the exposed, twisted roots of the large surrounding trees. I ended on my back looking up at a Witch known in the world of Magic as a *Grotesque Hag*.

The *Hag* wore a rough-looking garment in a sickly shade of green that I mistook for moss. She rose to her full height, glaring down at me with a twisted smile exposing a mouthful of sharp black teeth.

I lay there frozen with fear, but still shrieking like a fire alarm.

One pimply arm shot out toward my legs. Before I could gather my wits to move, seven thick fingers wrapped themselves around my exposed ankle. I was lifted upside down and moving inch, by agonizing inch, toward the *Hag's* face,

Her skin was the color of pond scum and a foul odor of rot was coming from her gaping mouth. Combined with the stench from the yellow ooze dripping from her open sores, I began to feel nauseous.

I heard soft plops of secretion as the thick drops fell among the pine needles on the ground. There was a sharp reek of putrefaction left behind, when that puss burned deep holes in the *Mother's* sweet earth.

The *Hag* still moved sluggishly, like she was treading her way through a thick swamp. She seemed ready to take off with me and rotated unhurriedly toward the dense woods behind us.

I was shrieking over and over' "Dad, Dad…she has me!"

Looking at the topsy-turvy world was beginning to make me dizzy and my screams began to get softer until I was just whimpering.

The creature was slow moving on those stumpy feet, but we drew ever closer to the dark patch of woods.

I knew I would die if dad didn't find me in the next few minutes.

The *Hag* began to mumble a verse through thick purple-black lips. I knew just enough of the old languages to identify this as *Coilia;* the language of the ancient Witches of the Woodlands.

It held the power of the Dark Times, when these Witches roamed throughout the primordial forests found in the third realm, protected from death by the *Guild of the Green Wizards.*

Only in the last 1200 hundred years, according to my dad, had the *Grotesque Hags* begun to shamble into the first realm of man. They found the rugged mountain forests perfect habitats since few humans ventured deeply into them.

They had begun to raid small hamlets and remote towns around the earth scouring them for food. Now, I was about to be eaten by one like a picnic lunch.

I had given up seeing mom and dad ever again when a fire ball came crashing into the *Hags* back.

Because she was dragging me like a rag doll by this time, I was not touched by the flames and scooted away when it howled and let go of my numb ankle.

Crawling away as fast as I could, I heard dad's voice as he hurled another fire ball at the Witch, this time catching her brittle green hair on fire. She immediately began to turn in circles trying to flail at the fire.

The sound of her screeching became hundreds of finger nails across a chalk board. I felt all the hairs on my arms rise up in abject fear.   The Hag stopped whirling and was quickly consumed, becoming a pillar of flame and acrid smoke.

Now, all these years later, I stood looking at my second *Grotesque Hag.* I recalled how dad had dispatched the first, using fire.

Though I was secure enough behind the sharp points of the barbed silver mesh, I couldn't stay there for long.

The *Hag* had begun to mumble some kind of chant in the same Coilia of the Witches of the Woodlands. My safety ward began to tremble. Her words took on a persistent, jagged pitch until I was ready to box my own ears to silence the sound.

I began my own chant. I knew for my fire to be effective, I'd have to drop my protective enclosure. That meant the *Hag,* standing only a foot from my face would have an opening to open me!

To avoid that particular unpleasantness, I put up a quick screen to cover my actions.

I shouted my command and a thick wall of inky black smoke obscured me from being observed. And where there's smoke, the fire is sure to follow.

Suddenly, the *Hag* lit up like a Teakwood Torch!

She reached through the green flames, making a grab for any part of me, only inches away from fourteen razor-sharp nails, I leaned back as far as I could while the Hag began to screech another spell to counter my fire.

Suddenly, the floor beneath my feet began to melt like hot wax and I felt myself losing my footing.

The *Hag* was able to take advantage of my momentary loss of concentration. My fire wavered and flattened out and turned downward. I was now sinking into the melted flooring, and totally vulnerable.

The Witch's screeching changed to what definitely sounded like a gurgling laugh coming from her blackened mouth.

This can't be good I thought looking down at the goop that was once my floor and was now consuming me inch by inch.

The *Hag* still burned like a cheap candle; lots of greasy smoke and sputtering flame. She was using some kind of ward to keep the green flames from consuming her body, letting the mossy green rags burn around her misshapen form.

Through the smoke and flame, I saw that the Hag was covered in pustules from head to gnarly toe like I remembered. As they heated up from my fire, they began to bubble and erupt like mini volcanoes, each shooting its yellow load and stinking like a sulfuric bath.

I had sunk up to my shins into the melted floor. The *Hag* seemed quite pleased with herself. I had a bad feeling that Witch knew something I didn't.

I knew I couldn't let the soupy mess make its way up to my chest. That would pose a whole new threat to my life in this realm!

I had decided on using the one option open to me under the circumstances; I called out to *Crom Croich*.

He had promised me one intervention to save my butt. I hated to use that aid even before I left for San Francisco, but I was sinking fast. Placing a dome over myself wouldn't keep me from being absorbed into the waxy goop as it climbed steadily up my thighs.

I shouted at the top of my lungs for the god to show himself.

All I got for my efforts was more screeching from the *Hag*, I took a deep breath, gagging on the tainted air.

I screamed louder than the Witch.

"Come to my aid as promised *Crom*, as you pledged to *The Teacher*!

By now I was struggling to breathe, the yellow muck spraying around me gave off noxious fumes. I had to clear my mind so I could think of another spell to save myself.

The thick sludge was now chest level. My lungs began to burn and felt like they were being crushed in a vise. Things were going dark and my vision blurred.

Just as things began to wink out, a huge crack of thunder and a cyclone force wind sprang up around the Hag and me. The wind was so strong that we both began to spin in a blurring rotation. I felt like a spoon in a thick milkshake!

A deep, rumbling voice called out in the tongue of the ancient clans of Ireland. With the last word, the floor was restored to its natural wood, with me standing firmly on its dark surface.

My fire still burned as brightly, but now it had rooted itself inside the *Hag*. Flames poured from the stretched mouth as the *Hag* howled in anger and pain.

When I was certain the pile of black soot accounted for the entire Witch, I opened the nearest window and flicking my wrist, sent the remains into the snowy night.

Crom was hovering over me as I checked my appendages and found all accounted for.

His voice was still too loud, but I couldn't exactly tell him to pipe down after what he just did for me.

Instead, I bowed low to him and said "Your pledge is now fulfilled Crom. The *Teacher* will be satisfied."

Rather than telling me I was on my own from here on out, the god smiled indulgently.

"You are mistaken young mortal. My promise to the *Teacher* was to come to your aid while you searched for the Red Dragon in another part of this realm.

I answered you this time because I hate *Grotesque Hags* so much. They held my people in terror for centuries until they fled back to the third realm. And now, I find one returned!"

He sounded furious and the house vibrated with another clap of thunder.

When he calmed he said, "I will be at your service once more Wizard, as you pursue the Dragon. The *Teacher* is pleased."

With that promise, the ancient god vanished.

I looked around me and sighed as I saw the upturned furniture and scattered objects around the room. After ten minutes of magical intervention, all was placed in order and I was barely keeping my eyes open.

Geez, I want to get a decent night's sleep, I was thinking as I returned to my bed. I tossed around for a few minutes as thoughts of Feng Xi tumbled around in my head.

At first, he only wanted to dissuade me from attempting to find the Red Dragon; now, he wanted me dead. Guess my persistence was ticking him off. Go figure...

Chapter 41

My interrupted sleep of the night before slowed me down some the next morning. I couldn't push myself out from under my pile of blankets until after 4:00. Luckily, part of my DNA was just fine with a few hours of shut-eye; the other part was on autopilot.

I wrapped myself up in my bulky bathrobe, shoving my quickly chilling feet into my slippers as I did so. Ready to face a busy morning, the wafting aroma of fresh coffee floated me downstairs to the kitchen.

Leaning on the counter, sipping from my steaming cup. I was trying to pierce the heavy curtain of shadows among the pines. After my recent encounters, I was on high alert for anything of a paranormal variety.

I was packed and ready to go.

Ollie had been dropped at the Vet's the afternoon before, so I wouldn't have to rush my goodbyes to my "furry son". Though he was in relatively good health, my canine companion of many years was very old now, and every trip away from him, brought a sense of impending loss.

Joanie would meet up with me at around 6:30 that evening, for a light dinner, and I'd start filling her in on the investigation.

As my closest friend, Joanie had seen her share of Magic performed around my house when we were growing up. Her friendship never wavered over the years; even when faced with the unexplainable or terrifying.

I always believed her profession as an Emergency Room nurse prepared her for the unexpected and constantly changing scenarios.

My mind wandered back to Fionn and Bandi. I had been tempted to open dad's *Shadow Box Library* after Crom dispatched the *Grotesque Hag* last night. I wanted to contact one of the Librarians to ask about old charms and spells that I might find helpful against my adversaries.

I suspected that Feng Xi had been preparing himself for my eventual appearance.

Now that Dr. Chung Wu was taken out of the equation, I felt I had lost at least one ally that I didn't even realize I had!

Having learned from mom that Chung was a secret agent, a *Shadow Walker,* working for the *Grand Masters* of the *Guild,* I understood how important this quest was to the entire *Guild of Green Wizards*. That realization only made me more determined that I had to succeed.

Jason had not stopped over after his last shift. I needed to do some more research on China Town's historic underground site and get a handle on the geography of the area.

I couldn't start my day without first hearing his voice though and he would be in bed in a few hours.

Since Jason wasn't flying out until later, we were hoping to keep his participation in the investigation under the radar. I wasn't sure how that was working out for us. Feng Xi seemed to already know a good bit about my plans.

I had gotten a little complacent living here, in the vast wilderness of the Appalachian Mountains. It seemed like my existence went pretty much undetected by other Magic Users who might be trying to scope out power sources.

Dad always warned me about complacency.

"If you sit around feeling secure and happy lass, you've already opened the door to the Dark ones."

My troubles with Feng and Lady Boa proved his adage correct as my feelings of vulnerability seemed to be growing with each encounter.

Jason picked up on the second ring.

"Cathleen, is everything OK, love?"

I always appreciated his concern for me, but I think sometimes he forgets I'm more than just the owner of a radio station.

"Everything is fine, or will be fine when I get to see you." I answered.

"Miss our morning coffee break and visit did you?" I could hear his smile in his voice and was starting to feel better already.

"Our morning is my favorite part of the day, Jason. But as to "visits", I wasn't lonely for company."

I gave him an abbreviated version of my night caller ending with a lame "It's all good now though."

There was a pause before he said "Better let me finish some paperwork for the office, Cathleen, but I'll be over in an hour. Are you OK until then?"

I felt guilty. I was listening to the voice of my *needs*, rather than to my practical voice; something dad often called my "confessional" expressions.

"You don't need to be telling all, Cathleen. The bits and pieces will do for most folk."

Ignoring my momentary pangs of conscience, I quickly agreed that he should come over. Even the best of intentions fall prey to human frailty.

Good to his word, an hour later I was enjoying my hiatus from worry and fear, while Jason listened to a fuller version of my latest encounter.

I had Jason put my suitcase into my Jeep, keeping my leather carry-on with me since the *Shadow Box Library* was inside.

He kept checking around the property and then did a complete search of my house. After a particularly long time spent in the basement, I got worried that he might have actually found something.

I called from the top step, scanning the visible area in the murky light.

When he didn't answer, I immediately called up my Inner Eye to see anything other worldly, hiding in the far shadows of the large musty rooms.

I took two more steps down and waited for anything to show itself.

There was a dark shape standing in front of some old moving boxes. I scrutinized the figure and realized I was looking at a very still Jason.

I became alarmed when he didn't answer or move as I came down the stairs. He stood rigidly. His eye was wide open, though unfocused, his eye patch reflected the glow of the single light bulb on its black surface. It almost made it appear like there was a light radiating out of the empty socket.

I still searched with my Inner Eye, probing the area around Jason and the darker recesses of the basement for any surprise visitors. We were alone.

I looked closely at him and saw that he was breathing normally, but was unable to speak because he was in some kind of trance.

That's when I understood; *he's having a vision.*

235

Chapter 42

I came close to his face, but was afraid to startle him in any way, so I didn't touch him, or speak. From his descriptions of his visions, I knew he was in the midst of one.

It seemed like an hour of silent standing and waiting for him to return from wherever his dream trip had taken him.

Just as I was beginning to get anxious that Jason was too deep into this subconscious -state, he blinked his eye. He shook his head slightly, before he actually saw me standing there a few feet away.

"Cathleen, are you real?"

He reached for me and we held each other tightly.

"Jason, you were having a vision."

"I was looking around, when I began to feel drowsy. I knew I'd be going into my walking-dream state, but couldn't stop it from happening and had no time to warn you. Sorry if I scared you, love." He held me tighter and I felt him begin to relax.

"Let's go back up, sweetie. I need to hear about this last vision and you need some of mom's calming tea."

We went back up to the kitchen where I put the tea kettle on. I had several hours before I had to drive to our local airport and could let Jason take his time in retelling his vision.

Jason took a few thoughtful sips of tea and with a far off look of a man under a hypnotic spell, began.

"I was standing in front of a cave. I could hear the ocean at my back. The air was very still, and felt heavy with salty moisture. I could taste it on my lips. It was completely silent.

No wildlife rustled around in the trees, or along the sandy ground, no seagulls swooped, or called from the shore.

And then I heard your voice, or *thought* I heard your voice. I wasn't sure, because it came from deep within the cave and seemed to be bouncing off the walls till I swore there was more than one of you! I couldn't make out the words, but I knew it was you."

He paused for a second to take another sip.

He resumed, his hands wrapped around the mug as if he needed an anchor.

"I entered the cave and within a few feet, stood in almost total darkness. There was a smell. I remembered the stench from every road kill I'd encountered over my lifetime. It was rotting death."

I couldn't suppress the shiver that ran down my spine like cold water on a hot day. I was completely absorbed in Jason's vision. Fear crept into my mind and like a phantom limb it throbbed with a life of its own.

Jason seemed oblivious to the effect his vision had on me.

"I reached out my hand to connect with the side of the cave; using my sense of touch to guide me further into the darkness. I heard you call out, only this time I was able to understand. You were speaking in another language. I was sure it was the ancient words you use when casting spells.

Walking in complete darkness, feeling my way, I came to what seemed to be a split in the passageway. I listened for your voice again and followed it down what felt like a narrow passageway. When I reached the bottom of a steep incline, there you were!"

Jason stopped talking which immediately brought me back to reality.

I watched his face for any sign that he was going to continue, but he was looking down into his cup and seemed finished.

"Ah…Jason? Is that all there is to your vision, honey?"

I was hoping he'd say no. I wanted to know who, or what, I was throwing my magic at in that cave.

He raised his eye to my face.

"That's all I saw. You, standing there with your arms raised and shouting in your old language. I never got to see what you were facing down there. Not much to go on is it?" he said despondently.

"Actually it is. Now I know where Feng and probably the vampire will be waiting to trap me. I'll be ready for them. Besides, you'll be coming to my aid, right partner?"

He leaned in to kiss me. I could taste the sweet scone on his lips and put my hand on his neck to bring him in closer for a deeper kiss. Jason smiled back at me when we drew apart.

"I needed that," he said dreamily, taking my hand and leading me into the living room and the cozy comforter, warmed by our fire. We hardly needed the heat.

Chapter 43

It was getting closer to my drive time. We tried a lighter banter to ease our minds before we had to say goodbye. He'd be with me in San Francisco in less than 24 hours, but I'd be missing him every minute.

I locked up the house, leaving timers on several lights throughout the rooms, just as Jason reminded me to do before he drove off. My garage was unlocked now, but there were only some gardening tools in there and if anyone wanted them, they were welcome to take them. The closest I ever get to gardening is collecting my vegetables off a salad bar.

My Jeep had been tuned up and gassed up and was ready to go. It sat warming in the driveway as I made a last minute sweep, unplugging things as I went.

"Wow! This traveling thing is exhausting!" I said out loud as I climbed into my warm car. The defrosters had been blasting and any ice that started to form was sliding down the windshield. It was time to drive to the Iron Mountain Airport

I switched the Blue Tooth on and carefully pulled away from my house and onto the road.

I had touched base with Joanie already, but I thought I'd give mom a quick buzz to assure myself of her arrival. I didn't think that the Wizard, Feng Xi, was aware of her intent to travel to San Francisco. He might suspect as much, but mom was a slippery Wizard. She would have covered her true destination on the off chance that she was being watched.

As *Protectors* working for the *Council of Green Wizards*, both mom and dad had access to arcane and potent spells and enchantments. I was counted among the *Protectors*, but hadn't yet achieved either of my parent's higher rank. I'd be depending on mom for some of the heavy lifting, magically speaking.

She picked up on the first ring of her cell phone.

"You always seem to know when I'll be calling, mom" I laughed.

"That's what mothers do, pet. It's good to hear your voice, Cathleen. Are you on your way to your little airport?

"I am, mom, so I should be arriving around 5:00pm Pittsburgh time. I'll be meeting Joanie around 6:30 before we board our flight. How are things with you?"

I asked this with some trepidation, afraid she'd say she was still in Ireland. Mom's very reliable, but have a rather capricious nature and has been known to change plans on a whim.

"I checked into the Grant yesterday and did some early reconnaissance today. I think I can say, my time has been well spent. China Town has been most forthcoming in giving up some of its secrets."

"Sounds like you've been busy. What's your room number, by the way, so we can call you when we get in this evening?"

The sky was gloomy, full of heavy, low hanging clouds, pushing each other around like school yard bullies. I hoped our flight wouldn't be cancelled due to bad icing on the runways, or plane wings.

Our plans as we went on to discuss them were pretty straightforward. The statue of the Red Dragon had to be found and secured by us. Once we had safeguarded this potential threat, mom would transport it to the *Grand Masters*. As the elite of the *Council of Green Wizards*, it would fall to them to destroy the statue for all time.

The statue would pose a tremendous temptation to anyone who had it within their control. They had to be of unshakable character to withstand the pull of Immortal life and awesome power.   Mom was the one for the job.

"Before I go, have you had any luck gathering leads for us, mom? I'd like to hit the ground running so we can wrap this up quickly."

There was silence from the other end. I suspected she could no longer talk openly about the particulars of the investigation. Instead she began speaking in her best Irish brogue.

"'Tis a fine and glorious city, luv…so much ta sees and the street cars are surely a delight."

She went on like that, with me trying to ask pointed questions that she could answer with a yes or no. Her deep Irish accent was quite charming, considering her normal brogue was mitigated long ago after twenty years of living in the U.S.

This charade only lasted long enough for her to actually hop onto one of the "delightful" streetcars. A minute later, she was telling me about being followed on her walk by a Chinese man wearing all black, with the look of a body guard about him.

"The driver!" I shouted into the phone.

"And whom might that be dear?" mom asked.

"He's Lady Bao's driver. I'm certain he was turned by her."

"Oh, so he's also a vampire. He and his mistress certainly don't live up to the old wives tales about not being able to walk in daylight. He's been following me at a respectful distance from when I landed at the airport, dear. He was definitely waiting for my arrival."

"I guess we can't keep you a secret from Feng, either." I said despondently.

"I don't believe the Lady will share her information with her old master, pet. I suspect she'll use any information to her own ends. Well, well…"

"What's up, mom?" I asked sensing she was distracted by something and feeling a bit distracted myself as I waited for her response. It was turning out talking hands-free didn't help me over rough ice patches as I narrowly missed hitting a snow bank in a slide.

"It appears the *driver* has managed to board this transport vehicle, dear. His speed is quite impressive."

"Get off as soon as you can, mom" I was saying as I approached my turnoff to the airport.

"I don't want him to know that I am aware of his shadowing me, dear. I will take this trolley down as close to the Bay as possible and then disembark. Not to worry. Well, ta darling. See you soon."

I must have been gripping the steering wheel like I was clinging to the side of a cliff! My fingers felt stiff as I made the sharp turn into the parking lot.

I knew mom was more than capable of handling the driver, or just about *anything,* for that matter. I was afraid, however, that she'd find herself outnumbered. Lady Bao was an ancient power and not to be taken lightly in the threat she posed to this mission.

An hour of fairly easy flying, despite some unsettling strong wind gusts at the lower altitudes and we landed at a small private airfield near Pittsburgh.

I quickly lugged my bags over to what passed as a car rental counter and rented a non-descript vehicle from their fleet of fifteen, for my drive into Pittsburgh International Airport.

Joanie would be meeting me in front of the elevators near long-term parking.

As I was pulling into a spot, my cell phone rang through the Bluetooth.

"Hi, love! Are you there yet?"

"Hi, honey. Just parked in long-term. It's so good to hear your voice, Jason!"

"I've just received a packet of information, Cathleen, from my good friend Perry at the University of Southern Cal.

I asked him to do some research on the history of the original China Town… before the big earthquake."

"That's great, honey. Bring it along and we'll review it when we're settled in."

I had to make it a short conversation because I didn't want Joanie to get antsy if I wasn't exactly on time.

We said our goodbyes and decided he would get to the Grant via rental car from the airport.

I still wasn't sure how much Feng or Lady Bao actually knew about my plans. It couldn't hurt to keep Jason undercover while we could. If I was a gambler, he'd be one ace to hold back.

The life of a Wizard-Sleuth could definitely get dangerous for people who were too close. I needed to keep Jason and Joanie out of the line of fire. Mom and I are both expert at returning that fire, and it was as green as the *Green Mother* Herself!

Chapter 44

My best friend is always prompt, or very early, depending on how anxious she is prior to an appointed time. Not surprisingly, she stood several feet from the elevator door as it opened.

Her carrot-red hair was cut in a short bob, framing her freckled cheeks and emphasizing her amazingly blue eyes. Though not more than five foot seven, Joanie was so slim that she looked taller. I always felt like a dwarfling when we were walking together.

I got out of the elevator, propelled forward by the crowd of people jammed in with me. I was wrestling with my carry-on and over-stuffed suitcase when she yelled my name.

"Cathleen!"

I waved back to her as we scooted around milling people and finally connected in a long hug. We were absorbed in our happy reunion, while people streamed around the small island of laughter we had created.

Still chattering like magpies, I felt a sudden chill raise the hairs at my neck.

"Joanie," I said through my smiles, "just keep laughing and don't look around for a minute, Ok, sweetie?"

I kept my arms around her shoulders in another hug, my smile firmly in place. She nodded back at me, only now her grin looked as wooden as a ventriloquist's dummy. For a natural kind of girl, Joanie is awful at *acting* natural.

With a quick scan, I saw a dark, Asian man approaching our friendly cluster. I looked down at the floor noticing short, dark boots with full-legged trousers tucked into them.

I casually stood back from Joanie and got a better view of him when I stooped to pick up my bags.

Joanie continued to smile broadly and to chatter on about the delay she'd experienced trying to drive through heavy traffic coming into the airport.

"I wasn't too worried though, since our plane doesn't leave for another two hours," she said, almost breathless in her effort to appear relaxed.

She knew me well enough to understand when I needed her to act casually for the sake of misleading a potential threat. It sure put a strain on her though!

By the time our little performance had become difficult to maintain, the stranger had moved to stand in front of the elevator. He looked up casually, as if watching for its arrival.

I grabbed Joanie's elbow, steering her toward the nearest flight monitor. So far, our flight was still on schedule. We had enough time for a bite after we went through security.

Joanie had stored her suitcase in a locker. We'd planned to retrieve it as soon as I got in.

I dropped my leather bag on the floor, pretending to rummage around in it for something. This gave me a chance to take a closer look at the suspected agent of Wizard Feng Xi.

He had turned fully around to observe us.

A light bulb of recognition flashed in my mind.

His strange clothes, minus the sword and assorted knives, looked like those I'd seen on the Terra Cotta Warrior the night I was attacked by that ancient killing machine.

While no one in this large International airport paid much attention to his odd attire, I knew I was looking at another animated slave of Feng Xi.

Now I was certain the Dark Wizard was aware of Joanie's involvement. I got back up and as I did so grabbed for my carry-on from Joanie.

Still smiling like the cat that ate the canary I said, "Joanie, I'm so glad you're going with me! But I have to tell you, they now know that you are part of my team on this investigation."

"You'll take care of any bad stuff coming my way, Cathleen. I'm not worried."

I nodded my head and we headed for the nearby lockers.

After retrieving Joanie's bag, we walked toward the first restaurant in view. I took a last glance in the direction of our shadow. He never made eye contact, but I understood we were under surveillance.

Bringing him to life and binding the warrior to his will, Feng Xi had displayed great skill and power. I was trying to recall the best wards to protect my friend and me while we headed for the typical airport dining experience. Maybe we'd lose our buddy after we went through Security. I wasn't counting on it.

As we waited to be seated by a hostess, I looked over at Joanie and saw the tell-tale flush of excitement on her pale, freckled cheeks.

"How are you doing, Joanie?" I asked, with a tinge of concern in my voice.

"I'm fine. Just want to eat our dinner and catch up before we have to board. By the way, that funny looking Chinese gentleman is following us, isn't he?"

"Wow! I'm impressed, Joanie! I didn't think you'd noticed him."

"It was fairly obvious, Cathleen. You wanted me to act naturally, but I already spotted him watching me before you got here. So I figured when he seemed to be attached to our movements, he might be the bad guy."

"I think I've underestimated your sleuthing abilities. I'm happy for the extra pair of eyes," I said seriously. "I only wish he hadn't already seen that we were together."

"Oh, he's been hanging around by the entrance from long term parking since I got here. At first, I just assumed he was meeting someone too," she said, in her usual calm manner.

I knew then that Feng had dispatched his ancient thug to spy on my friend. So much for keeping her out of his line of vision and safe.

We were seated by a very thin hostess. I noticed a tattoo of a raven on her left inner wrist when she handed us our menus. I commented on her unusual choice of body art; remarking that it was quite well done.

She immediately lost the fake hostess smile like I had just insulted her mom's parenting skills.

Then she looked intently at me and everything around us disappeared and my focus was concentrated on her piercing gaze.

"Cathleen O'Brien, the *Teacher* has sent me to gather information on the evil one, Wizard Feng Xi. My directive from the noble *Teacher* is to aid you in the Dark Lord's destruction. I shall be in contact with you soon."

I realized that she hadn't spoken to me verbally, but connected directly to my mind to deliver her message.

I blinked and looked around me for any sign of others overhearing. Joanie was still looking down at her menu as if time had skipped two ticks backward. I cleared my throat.

My comment about the tattoo was completely erased in that hiccup in time.

When our waitress came over, we both ordered a chef salad and Joanie seemed in the dark about what had happened.

The hostess passed our table once and looking over at us with a broad smile said, "Enjoy your meals ladies!'

"She seems pretty chirpy," Joanie commented watching the girl return to the front desk.

"Yeah, must be having a good day," I replied.

Chapter 45

The *Teacher* had a red-hot vendetta against Feng Xi for the torture and murder of his brother. Now, this girl with the raven tattoo had revealed herself as my new ally, sent by the *Teacher* himself.

I was wondering how the hostess really looked, so I slipped into my Inner Eye to scope her out as Joanie looked around the large dining area.

"Wow!" I didn't realize I'd said that out loud until I saw Joanie's expression.

"Is the weird Chinese guy here, Cathleen?" she asked with a worried look, her eyes darting around the restaurant.

I shook my head in answer as I was trying to recover from the shock of seeing my first *Colossus Faerie*.

I had only seen them sketched in my book "Arcane Magic and Magic Users," and now, I had just had a conversation with one!

The Colossus is human-sized and able to take the form of any human within its immediate sphere for purposes of disguise.

This Colossus would have stashed some unsuspecting young woman somewhere, placing a deep sleep charm on her, so she couldn't revive and blow the "hostess" cover.

Because the *Teacher* had sent her as back-up support, I knew she would follow any orders I gave her without hesitation. Doing battle with a Colossus was pretty scary stuff as they had uncanny speed and agility. I'd heard stories from dad about seeing a young Colossus run up and down walls like he was skipping up a street. They were known as fierce fighters who never gave quarter to an enemy unless directly ordered to do so by their Master, the *Teacher*.

I sincerely hoped he gave no such order to her. I needed all the nasty advantages on my side when I had my inevitable face-off with Feng-Xi and the Vampire.

We finished dinner and paid our waitress. We were leaving the restaurant when I stopped by the hostess station on the pretext of asking the location of the nearest coffee shop on the concourse.

While Joanie moved ahead of me into the traffic flow, I quickly spoke to the hostess in the old tongue.

"Please, tell your master that I appreciate his sending you, a fine *Colossus* warrior, to assist me in my work."

She turned pale grey eyes to me and gave me a curt nod of understanding as I went to join my friend.

Nice to know I have some heavy-hitters on my side, I thought, as we made our way through Security and to our gate.

Joanie smiled over at me.

"The weird Chinese guy is behind us, Cathleen," she said with her grin fixed in place.

"I noticed him when I left the restaurant. Wonder how he got through the Security checks?"

He's a magical creature, Joanie."

She bobbed her head saying, "Oh, yeah. By the way, what's with the hostess back there?"

"Geeze, I thought I was being pretty sneaky."

"I know you well enough after all our years to intuit when there's something up with you, Cathleen. And besides, I saw you watching her after we sat down. Is she another one of the bad guys?"

I told her no, but I'd explain after we were seated on the plane. I didn't want to take the chance of being overheard by our persistent shadow.

We claimed seats over-looking the tarmac; my carry-on securely tucked between us. The baggage trailer was being unloaded onto our plane. I checked the over-head wall clock-- twenty minutes until boarding.

I took advantage of the crowding of the other passengers as they began to assemble in the waiting area, searching faces for Feng's spy. He stood beside a post and was looking down at something in his hand.

I figured it wasn't going to be a cell phone, but whatever it was he was absorbed in what he was viewing.

The other passengers seemed to unconsciously move away from him as he stood like a rock amid a sea of multi-colored faces.

While I tried to make out what he was holding, the soldier blinked out of existence.

I had forgotten I'd been watching him through my Inner Eye. When he disappeared, I knew no one else had seen him vanish. He would have made no more than a ripple in the air around the spot he had vacated.

Now I knew what he had been so engrossed with; some kind of Voyager mechanism provided to him by Feng Xi. Moving him from San Francisco to this airport to do surveillance on Joanie and me, would have been a simple trick of time wrapping for a Wizard of Feng's skills.

I was wondering where else that Dark Lord had sent his warrior minion. Had he already been to Iron Mountain, spying on Jason?

With the sudden disappearance of our Chinese warrior pal, Joanie visibly relaxed.

"Hey, Cathleen" she said craning her head around to locate his whereabouts. "I think we've shaken our tail."

"Actually, he was taken out of action by Feng Xi, Joanie."

She looked confused, but knew whatever happened, we were safe for now.

I heard them announce our plane was ready for boarding. We were sipping a glass of Chablis before we were airborne.

Joanie leaned over to me and thanked me for the novelty of flying with all the leg room she needed for her long limbs.

"Sure beats hanging with the common folk, Cathleen!" she said, grinning broadly and taking tiny sips at her wine glass like a freckled humming bird.

While I was very happy that this part of our experience was fun for her, I didn't lose sight of the real danger I was allowing my friend to walk into.

With that gloomy thought, I told the passing cabin steward that my friend and I would like another glass of wine. Joanie raised her red eyebrows at the request.

"Don't worry, Joanie" I said in answer to her questioning look. "We have a long flight and I think we both deserve to relax a bit before we land."

Looking back at me she said very primly, "Cathleen, relaxed is one thing; unconscious is entirely something else!"

Two minutes later she was sipping her second glass of the crisp wine and sinking with a sigh, deeper into her leather seat. Life as a rich girl does have its advantages.

Chapter 46

During the long flight into San Francisco International, I was able to get Joanie filled in on all the events leading up to our trip. I tried not to minimize the risks involved for all of us, but if I worried about her reactions; I needn't have.

Our bags made it off the plane quickly and after a short shuttle bus trip to Sand Dollar Car Rentals, we picked up our rental.

The time difference made it three hours earlier, but there was a heavy look to the sky, like a storm was going to blow in, making it fairly dark.

Our arrival seemed to be uneventful and unnoticed. Such thinking only gets wizards into trouble according to my dad. Once again, he was proven correct.

As I turned out of the car lot onto the exit ramp heading for San Francisco, I noticed a car pull out directly behind of us. It was still following several minutes later. Not too unusual given we were on a major freeway into the city, but this car had a very familiar look; long, black, sleek.

When I had a chance to look back again, I saw that they had dropped back and there were now several cars between us.

There have to be thousands of luxury cars around these parts, I was thinking. *Yeah, but why do I get a vibe off that one?*

I hadn't said a word to Joanie, but when I glanced over, she seemed to be watching her side view mirror.

"So, Cathleen, that black limo that followed us out of the rental car lot… I noticed it's still behind us. Do you think it's another tail?"

I saw the black car slide into the right lane as we took a curve. It was too dark to see a driver unless they pulled up next to us.

The limo stayed in the outside lane, keeping pace as we ate up the miles.

We began seeing highway signs for various downtown streets. Famous names like Embarcadero, Fisherman's Wharf, Ghirardelli Square, began to pop out along the roadway, indicating upcoming exists.

Joanie was very quiet as I began to make the turns and jogs necessary to follow signs leading to our final destination, the Grant Hotel.

I glanced over at her to find her eyes were still fixed on the side view mirror and I supposed the black limo.

It was much lighter as we entered into in the city proper, with street lights and several store fronts still lit up.

"Joanie, is that limo still tailing us?"

"Yup! But I finally got a look at the driver. He looks Chinese. So maybe he's just going home to China Town. You think?"

"Let's just play it safe, Joanie, and stay on the lookout for suspicious activity; especially when we get to the Grant."

I had no sooner spoken, when I spotted the sign for that venerable, timeworn hotel.

The Grant sat like a once sophisticated old lady, rocking in her wicker porch chair, remembering a posh and elegant past.

I told mom and Joanie that the Grant was something of a landmark in the city. Its location was perfect. It was only a two minute walk to China Town and one block from the Cable Cars. Many a tourists has praised this Victorian structure as a terrific home-base for touring San Francisco's many downtown attractions.

I pulled into the parking garage across the street. Grabbing our bags out of the trunk, Joanie and I crossed over to the hotel, pushing open the glass front doors, stepping into a softly lit lobby and back into time.

Overlooking the somewhat *restrained* exuberance of its mostly Chinese staff, a rickety elevator and paltry continental breakfast, the Grant was reportedly the best buy in town.

I saw Joanie unconsciously wrinkle her nose at the musty odor of aging furnishings and carpeting that had seen thousands of visitors trailing in history on their shoes.

When we entered our room, I was pleased to see her expression of apprehension change as she looked around the spacious, immaculate setting and began to smile.

"Wow! This is much bigger than I thought it would be."

She headed toward the bathroom to check out that important facility.

"It's really clean, too!"

I knew that would appeal to her fastidious nature. We were pretty much polar opposites in the tidiness department, but she appreciated when I cheated, using a *house buddy* to clean up after some messy sleep-overs as kids.

Joanie flung her suitcase on the bed nearest the bathroom and began unpacking.

I took advantage of her distraction and began laying a ward. I was whispering the chant, though I was sure Joanie knew I was using Magic. I saw her head jerk up and then, as quickly, she looked away. She knew better than to distract me when I was in witch-mode.

After laying my ward around the rooms and our door, I placed my bags on what would be my bed over the next few days and began unpacking myself.

When we registered, I made a point of asking if we could extend our check-out date if we wanted to do so.

The matriarchal-looking Chinese woman at the front desk gave me a curt nod after the young man checking us in asked her about my request.

When our eyes connected, I felt a slight jolt on my Magic-User detector. Slipping into my Inner Eye with a blink, I checked out the venerable lady and saw the *Colossus Faerie* staring back.

Ah ha! I gave her a small smile and nod of my own.

As I thought about the *Teacher's* involvement in this mission, I began wondering if he would make an appearance. His vendetta against the Wizard Feng was a part of his very existence.

Dad warned me there were two things in life and magic that should never provoke a wizard into blind action, fear and hate. I wondered how the *Teacher* would handle his powerful hate for Feng Xi.

As I shuffled through my suitcase and began putting things in my allotted drawers, I thought back to my own lesson in the fear response. It came very early in my training as an apprentice wizard.

Dad and I were sitting by our fire in the cave we always used for my instruction into the secrets of Celtic Magic. I was about the turn ten and dad believed it was time to introduce me to a *Forest Shade;* a kind of half ghost, half whatever else it was in life. This one was half coyote.

Dad used a yellowed whistle, carved from the finger of a powerful Witch he had defeated in his early days as a *Protector*. He blew on it, making a drawn-out shrieking sound.

The fire jumped within its rock enclosure. Flames shot up red and orange, staining the cave walls and ceiling with dancing shadows reminding me of grasping claws.

The *Forest Shade* slunk close to the ground as it approached our campfire. It stopped just short of dad's reach.

Where its eyes should have been, thousands of small fireflies occupied the empty sockets. The fur was matted around the skull, with clotted blood from a gaping wound in front of the left ear. It looked thick and black as tar in the light from the fire. Its long snout looked torn and ragged from bite marks.

The lower body of the *Shade* was as transparent as a sheet of wax paper, floating behind him, a thin and insubstantial cloud.

The long dead beast hung there, in front of the fire. Slowly, its mouth curled back, revealing rows of stained or broken teeth. I knew this was the grimace of death.

"This is how he would have appeared shortly after being killed," my father told me softly.

From the look of his ragged wound, he'd likely been in a fight with a bear that nearly scalped him with his claws. I felt compassion stirring for the *Shade,* rather than feeling frightened by him.

Dad seemed pleased with me for not trying to bolt as the *Shade* moved closer, but when he saw my expression was one of pity, he understood that his lesson wasn't having the impact he'd hoped for.

He reached down and drew a long thick branch from the flames; its tip was red-hot.

Casually he handed it over to me and said "Cathleen, please take this and shoo the wee beastie away. There's a good lass."

I was still thinking compassionate thoughts toward the *Forest Shade*, but took up the hot brand.

As I stood and began to approach what seemed a cowering coyote, it let out a bellowing roar that nearly straightened my curls! I jumped back expecting my father to put himself between me and the roaring beast. Instead, as I searched for his calming face, I found empty space where he'd been sitting.

The *Forest Shade* began to move on invisible feet toward my retreating figure. I still held the brand in front of me like a smoking sword, waving it wildly in its leering face.

I thought about running for the mouth of the cave, but knew the *Shade* would have me before I could cover the distance. I wasn't sure what those phantom teeth were capable of, or even if I would feel them if they tore into me.

I was so intent on watching in front of me, I didn't notice the small pile of rocks we stored in the cave for our fires. Suddenly I was on my backside and the smoking branch was somewhere behind me.

Some kind of instinct took hold of my senses and I knew I could use the rocks to defend myself against the jaws that now snapped inches from my face.

I rolled away from the slavering mouth and teeth and grabbing a handful of rocks began throwing with all my ten-year old strength. The stones might as well have been made of water as they flew right through the ghost-beast, without altering its direction toward me.

That's when I remembered that I had some Magic I could call upon to defend against this enemy.

Dad had taught me how to call the *Green Mother's* fire to my hands in desperate moments. This was definitely one.

I raised my small hands and repeated the ancient Druid chant and watched in awe as green flames leapt from my fingers. They shot across the small space between me and the *Forest Shade* just as I willed them and it immediately burst into a thousand glowing green shards, decorating the cave floor feet from me.

I had called on the Green Fire before, but only as an exercise in my training. Now, I jumped up, breathless and began shaking from the aftereffects of my adrenalin rush.

My dad was suddenly holding me in a tight embrace.

"You did well, lass. You didn't run out of fear, but used your knowledge to defeat the threat."

He was beaming down at me, then becoming very serious said, "Let's just keep this little test between ourselves, Cathleen darlin'. No sense getting your ma all riled up after the fact."

With that comment I knew my mother would not have approved of his training methods in this particular case, but, then, she seldom did.

Now, zipping up my empty suitcase, I wondered if the *Teacher* would succumb to the other powerful emotion, hate.

With these sobering thoughts chasing each other through my tired brain, I watched Joanie collect the shampoo and soap from the bathroom and snug them into a plastic shower cap.

"I know you only use your own stuff, Cathleen and I do too, so I'll just take these back for the Women's Shelter."

I had to smile at her thoughtful gesture and hoped it wouldn't extend to the toilet paper.

Chapter 47

I had to call my mom to let her know we were settled in. We had decided that I wouldn't contact her until we'd had a good night's sleep.

By the time I poked in her room number, it was nearly seven-thirty. There was no chance she'd still be asleep. She never stayed in bed past six in the morning. Even while keeping to her habit of turning in well past midnight most nights, mom never changed her sleep schedule.

She claimed she worked her best "during the hours most predators were active." She casually put herself into that shadow-hugging category.

She answered on the fourth ring.

"Hi mom! We're in. I hope I didn't catch you at a bad time."

"Nonsense, pet! I am delighted to hear your voice. I was just taking a bit of a soak in the tub, to undo the damages of my day in the city."

"I hope that went well for you. I assume you were able to deal with the stalker yesterday."

"Naturally, dear. I enjoyed watching him buzzing about like a drunken bumble bee from person to person, searching me out."

Though Lady Bao's driver had followed her onto the cable car, she had planned to lose him when they reached the end of the line near the famous Piers lining the Bay.

With evening thinning out the crowds, she was able to shake him by hopping right back on the cable car. He then unwittingly began following a random woman she used as a decoy.

My mother loved to use her "bubble wrap" recipe as she called it, but rarely found the right opportunity.

She would wrap her own body double around an unsuspecting woman with a very short-lived spell, using light and air. As soon as she was clear of any imminent danger, she would "pop" the wrap and no one was the wiser.

The decoy never felt changed and the dangerous hunter would be left shaking his head and turning in circles to locate her.

A pretty clever ruse, though dad always objected to using unsuspecting humans like fun-house mirrors. He said mom took too many liberties with Magic, though I always saw the pride in his eyes as she skirted another potential disaster.

Mom put me on speaker while she finished getting dressed.

"Let's have a bit of a snack, Cathleen," she was saying. "You dears must be a wee peckish after your long trip last night."

We settled on the coffee shop around the corner, deciding to meet there rather than the lobby of the hotel. I glanced over at Joanie to check with her.

"Mom, I think Joanie will be out for another hour. How about meeting in two hours?"

After agreeing to a delay, she said she'd be taking care of any would-be stalkers.

"Let's keep the enemy wondering about our comings and goings, pet. I'll just use an old subterfuge recipe that's handy in situations where we might be followed."

I laid on top of the bed covers, happy to catch an hour of sleep. Joanie was snoring softly. I quickly rechecked my wards before closing my eyes and drifting off.

My last thought was of Jason and my pulse quickened just knowing he'd be with me soon.

My group of allies was nearly assembled. The hunt for the statue, Blood of the Red Dragon, was about to begin.

I was mulling over the logistics of fighting on more than one front when dad's cautionary observation on life floated into my mind:

"If you have placed yerself in the role of victim in this world, there are plenty who are happy to oblige you by making it so."

My role was that of *Sworn Protector*.

As I began to drift off, I felt the slightest nudge against the wards I had placed earlier. The air in the room seemed to push in slightly against my spell like a head on a soft pillow. It shifted, but held firm.

I knew we were safe as I let Morpheus close his arms around me and fell into complete darkness.

Chapter 48

I had never visited the "City by the Bay" as San Francisco is romantically called. After living in the rugged mountains of Appalachia for the past four years, the smells and noise of a big city work day was something of a systems over-load to my senses.

Joanie was thrilled with the local sites we passed walking over to the coffee shop where mom would be waiting. She was enchanted by the trolley cars as they trundled by and the architecture of the buildings, with their elegant bay windows, curving around like sultry, half-lidded eyes on softly colored faces.

Our meeting place wasn't hard to identify. Its front doors were wide open to the cool breezes coming off the Bay, sparkling in the distance below us. The tangy smell of the sea, mixed delightfully with the fragrance of freshly brewed coffee, sweet sticky buns and Danish that swirled around us as we entered.

Mom was sitting at a small round table, sipping a cup of my morning elixir. She seemed to be studying the pattern of paper under the decoupage veneer of the table top as we approached her.

"Hi mom" I said as she turned and looked up at us, a smile lighting up her face.

"Cathleen! My dear girl!"

She was on her feet and giving me a tight hug, kissing both cheeks in the process.

Mom was very "mom-like" first thing in the morning, before she had to deal with life's little annoyances like shopping for food.

"It's so wonderful to see you, pet. And Joanie! Still a lovely Irish lass, I see!"

She had grabbed onto my friend, squeezing her and giving her the required two cheek pecks.

Joanie adored my mother and this was reciprocated. When we were very young, running wild through the woods around our farm like two yearlings, mom always placed special wards over us.

I used to think Joanie was unaware of these protective spells, until one day she said she felt a buzzing around us every time we left the house. That's when I knew Joanie had a seventh sense and was able to "feel" the presence of magic, even if she couldn't practice it herself.

I kept that knowledge about my friend to myself. I didn't want to make her too self-aware of it and somehow block her natural gifts.

Unlike Jason, whose gifts as a seer were very dramatic, Joanie's tingles and slight jolts were a built in warning system.

We grabbed a third chair from a nearby table and stuffed ourselves around the undersized table.

Our coffees miraculously appeared in front of us as we sat down.

Mom put her hand over mine and squeezed saying "I knew you'd be prompt, dear, and I wanted to save our precious time together so we could make our plans."

"Mom," I said softly, taking her hand and smiling into her vivid sea-green eyes. "I'm so happy to have you here with us."

"I wouldn't be anywhere else, lass. Now let's get to the business at hand before we draw any unwanted attention."

With the slightest nod of her head and flick of her wrist, I saw her place an invisible dome over the three of us as we huddled closer together.

I had slipped into my Inner Eye as soon as Joanie and I left our room earlier. I needed to be aware of any of Feng Xi's creatures, or Lady Bao's henchman, on our walk over.

Mom looked over at me. "There we are." She winked and I nodded back.

I saw Joanie give a shiver as if a bitter wind had just blown over her.

She spoke up in alarm. "Magic!" she breathed out the word like an incantation.

Mom was aware of this odd talent of Joanie's from the earliest days of our friendship, so wasn't concerned to hear her identify what she'd been up to.

"Joanie, dear, I'm keeping our little group a wee bit safer by shielding us from sharp ears, like the ones that just entered this fine establishment. He's taken a seat near the door, but believe me, his hearing is better than any *living* being."

None of us turned toward the new arrival until Joanie's vivid blue eyes seemed to be pulled by magnetism in that direction.

From her vantage point, she had a clearer view of the new arrival than I did.

I knew it had to be Lady Bao's driver when mom mentioned his uncanny hearing and heavily emphasized the word *living* when making her comment.

Joanie was becoming a pretty competent spy, nonchalantly looking around the place while pretending to sip at her mug.

She smiled broadly at me saying "It's a Chinese guy, except his coloring is kind of *off*. I've only ever seen that look on *cadavers* at the hospital morgue."

She said the last with a small shudder, looking away quickly.

Mom and I smiled and nodded our heads.

I said "Thanks for the information, girlfriend! What do you want to do mom?"

"Well dear, since this is apparently the Lady's driver, he may become confused at the company you're keeping at the moment. He will need to sort us all out before reporting back to her.

He knows *me* of course. He trudged around town following me most of yesterday. It was like having a faithful dog shadowing my every step.

Let's just finish this wonderful coffee shall we? He'll keep for a wee bit while we talk."

With that, she daintily sipped at her cup of frothy cappuccino and smiled the way she always does when she's planning some serious magic.

We decided we'd split up when we left the coffee shop. Joanie and I would make the short walk into China Town, while mom would take the trolley car down to the shops around Ghirardelli Square.

She'd hop another trolley from down there, trying to draw out any suspected shadows trailing her movements.

I looked over at mom and said, "Ready."

We all got up and the dome vanished.

Joanie and I followed her out the door, into the growing crowds on the sidewalks.

I gave mom a hug, whispering close to her ear, "Be safe, mom. Jason will be here early this evening."

Mom kissed us both and walked unhurriedly toward the trolley car stop.

Joanie and I walked in the direction of China Town and all its mysteries.

Chapter 49

At first, neither of us noticed anyone following, but I kept getting that familiar tingling running up and down my spine like a busy spider on a web. There was a Dark One nearby.

I tried to look around me as if I was taking in the sites. The touristy act didn't last long. I spotted the driver reflected in a store window as he lounged by a store front across the street.

He blended into the crowds of Chinese residents and shop owners like a part of a densely forested landscape. I only picked him out of the milieu because I felt the weight of his stare boring into the back of my head.

I started pointing out items in the window display to Joanie, acting excited like I'd just stumbled on a great buy.

My lifelong friend wasn't fooled. She knew I detested shopping and especially the *window shopping* that most women seem to participate in. She went along with me and peered through the fingerprint smeared pane into the shop.

"I think you picked up our shadow, right Cathleen?"

"Right again, old friend!" I answered enthusiastically. If the store keeper was watching he must have been getting his cash register ready for business.

We huddled closer as I pointed randomly to the silk robes hanging like a rainbow across half the window. This pretense put me at a small disadvantage since the driver could move out of range and I might lose him to the crowds.

I leaned closer to Joanie's ear, flashing a toothy grin.

"The driver has found us and we need to lose him. Let's go in the store and while you talk with the sales person, I'll scout for a back door. I'll whistle when I find it and you take a robe like you were going to try it on and meet me in back."

We entered the shop and the shop keeper moved so quickly to greet us that Joanie gave out a startled yelp at his close proximity.

She began to rub her arms as if we'd entered a freezer and it confirmed my own tingling feelings that we were in the presence of another magic user.

I immediately switched back to my Inner Vision and recognized the Colossus Faerie in yet another guise. While I welcomed the extra magic muscle, I hoped there wouldn't be any repercussions from the *Council of Green Wizards*. They frowned upon using humans like spare tires.

This time the Faerie had chosen wisely, however, scrunching her very tall and muscular body into a small, non-threatening frame.

A Colossus doesn't have wings like its delicately built cousins; instead, it moves with fantastic speed. With a reputation for awesome strength and a mean disposition, it was pretty unlikely this Faerie would ever need to run from a fight, but neither would the vampire watching us from across the street.

After my initial shock at finding the *Teacher's* personal henchman in yet another guise, I placed my hand reassuringly on Joanie's arm.

"It's all good Joanie. This is the *Teacher's* special agent. Just keep talking to her…um him."

Turning back to the Faerie I asked in the old tongue "What do your people call you?"

Answering in the same language she said, "I am called "Anfa."

I knew her name meant *storm* in the ancient language. I couldn't help smiling to myself as I thought she looked more the *tempest in the teapot* at the moment.

"Well, Anfa," I said, "you need to point toward the back of the store and keep speaking with my friend. Please hand her a robe to try on in front of the mirror on the back wall. She and I need to slip out the back door."

The tiny man stared back at me and gave a jerky nod to my instructions.

I started to wend my way down aisles stuffed to overflowing with colorful silk purses, fans, small statues of a pandas and the mystical, Chinese dragons.

Seeing the dragons gave me a mental jolt. I looked back over my shoulder for a second, in time to see the driver crossing the street and coming straight for the store.

I located a door and praying to the *Mother* it was the way out, I gave a bird whistle dad had taught us when we were out of sight of one another in the woods. It wasn't so shrill that it would sound like an alarm, but could penetrate a dense woods or over-stuffed store.

The bird call barely sounded when Joanie arrived at my side and we flew out the back door of the shop.

I didn't have time to see if the driver had entered by then, but knew he wouldn't be far behind. The Colossus Faerie, Anfa, would have to step up at this point. If she couldn't stop him, she'd at least slow him down. In her current form of a tiny shopkeeper, Anfa did have an advantage. She looked like a pushover. And I was hoping the driver would try to push!

Weaving our way down the narrow alley behind the stores we were practically swimming through a thick sludge of odors. Scattered about, along with endless crates of molding food and discarded vegetables and fruits, were cages of live chickens and ducks, raising a cacophony of fowls in distress.

Then we heard the unmistakable sound of breaking glass and screams.

The driver has met the Colossus, I thought, with a grim smile.

"Joanie!" I called over to my friend as she ran to my side.

"We'll only have a few minutes before the driver is free to follow. We need wheels under us!"

She followed me through the back door of the nearest store, trying not to be noticed as we scooted down aisles, trying to avoid collisions with shoppers.

We quickly exited onto the street where we joined the throngs of sightseers and locals, shopping for exotic spices and bargains.

I made a quick survey of the cars and trucks passing by and saw what we needed.

"Joanie, that cab over by the corner!"

We were weaving through the crowded sidewalk toward the cab, just as it began to move. Luckily for us it stopped again, waiting for people nonchalantly crossing in front of it.

I grabbed for the door handle, pulled it open and jumped inside with Joanie close on my heels.

The driver was looking back at us and about to say something when I nearly screamed.

"Golden Gate Park and I'll double the fare if you get us out of here in the next two seconds!"

Without a second glance at me, he laid on his horn and rolled forward into the oncoming pedestrian traffic. People shouted angrily and made rude gestures, but he was able to make a path through the multi-colored human herd.

We were suddenly free of any obstructions and he picked up speed as he left China Town in the rear view mirror and headed toward our destination.

Joanie had collided with me in the back seat when we dove into the moving taxi. Now, she sat wide-eyed and pale, gripping the overhead hand-hold as we swayed with the lane changes the driver took with ease.

She stared silently through the cloudy Plexiglas divider while the driver made some wild u turn and barreled along down narrow, twisting side streets.

After a few minutes of a more regular heartbeat, I poked her gently with my elbow to bring her attention back to me.

"Hey, we made a clean getaway" I said quietly so the cabbie didn't think he was hauling two bank robbers in his backseat.

"I think I saw him just as I jumped into the cab, Cathleen. Do you think he'll follow us? And by the way, why'd you pick Golden Gate Park?"

I gave the driver a quick look to be sure he was watching the road. He was happily zipping along one of the crazy five lane freeways this area was known for. I vanely searched for a seat belt.

"I think Lady Bao told him to keep us in sight no matter what!" I muttered back.

I rechecked that the cabbie was still intent on cutting people off and expertly tailgating like it was an art form.

"I think we lost him this time sweetie, but he'll be waiting for us back at the Grant."

"The hotel feels safer to me, though," Joanie commented while still looking out the partition to the road ahead.

"Hey! There's a sign for Golden Gate Park." Why didn't he get off there?" she asked as she turned her head to see us fly past the exit.

I was about to say something to the cab driver when I saw his eyes fixed on my face while he unerringly swerved between the cars.

OK, I was thinking *the only way he could watch me while driving at 70 miles per hour was if...uh oh!*

Chapter 50

Whoever said, "Magic is a fine journey without end," must have enjoyed the scenery.   Oh, yeah.   It was my dad who said that.

As I stared into the cabby's eyes, it felt like I was being mesmerized by some masterful magician.   There was something familiar in them, something not human, something…dead.

I blinked and was now seeing the cabby through my Inner Eye. Lady Bao was staring back at me.

"Greetings, Wushen.   I see you have discerned my identity. I am pleased as this guise is most disquieting to my aesthetic senses."

With that said, Lady Bao let the skin that had covered her drop away and once more was exquisitely beautiful.

I had gone rigid as I watched her slip out of what had once been a living, breathing taxi driver.   Now, his skin was sloughed off like a snake sheds his old skin, exposing the new, sleeker version.

I understood then, my innate ability to detect another Magic User was blunted by the body that Lady Bao had used as her own.

Joanie had gone totally still.   I gave her a quick sideways looks to be sure she hadn't fainted at what we'd just witnessed. She had gone very pale; even her lips had lost their rosy plumpness as they were compressed into the thin line of a stifled cry.

I reached out for her hand and was happy when she returned my tight grip, letting me know she was still with me.

Lady Bao had slowed the taxi and took an exit ramp off the main freeway. I tried to note the signs so I'd have some idea of where the heck we were, but it dawned on me that it might not matter. We were in trouble; that's where we were!

I knew the vampire would not harm me since she needed my help to find the statue. I wasn't sure my immunity extended to Joanie.

The cab was pulling off the ramp and onto a back road leading into hilly country.

The grasses on the sides of the gently rolling terrain were still green. It looked untouched by any human development as I scanned it from hill to gently rolling hill.

I suspected Lady Bao might have some secluded cabin tucked away in a valley, nestled up to one of the larger hills.

Looking at me from the rear view mirror, the vampire smiled.

"We will arrive shortly, young wizard.

"How did you know we'd use a cab, *this* cab?' I asked, not totally able to conceal my admiration of her skills.

"I have been sitting in this dreadful automobile since you left the coffee shop. I wasn't certain you would need to travel, but felt it best to be prepared. I knew you would discover my driver and guessed you would, in vulgar terms, "ditch him" as quickly as possible. I had followed him through our *connection*, naturally."

I knew that connection was between *slave* and *Maker*.

"So, you murdered the real cabbie to take his place in this cab."

My disgust at her actions was clear; she smirked back at me in the mirror in response.

"For one as powerful as you reportedly are, Wizard, you are oddly reluctant to use it when it is convenient to your ends."

Joanie sat quietly throughout this exchange, but when the cab slowed and then stopped, she looked around like she'd been sleeping.

"Cathleen," she said softly, though Lady Bao could hear her heart beating.

"Where is she taking us?"

Although she was barely moving her lips, Lady Bao gave a tiny gurgling laugh and answered for me.

"The Wizard cannot answer you, but we have already arrived at our destination. Please exit the automobile."

She had already opened all the doors with a quick motion of her fingers. I got out, Joanie sliding out behind me.

We were standing on a dirt road on the edge of a densely wooded area. A sagging barbed wire fence ran along the length of the woods in both directions, disappearing beneath a dip in the ground.

I thought we were likely on the crest of a hill. An uneasy feeling made my stomach twist when I looked into the surrounding woodland.

Without saying a word, Lady Bao moved ahead of us, expecting us to follow her. Joanie leaned close to my ear and hissed, "Let's run!"

The vampire stopped several feet ahead and without bothering to face us, spoke like she was talking to the trees.

"It is foolish to speak of fleeing, as we have already been joined by my friends."

She turned and looked past us. Her beautiful, pale face was distorted with a grin exposing long incisors.

Joanie and I both spun around to see what new threat was looming in our path of escape.

Standing like two thick tree trunks with legs were body builders gone crazy on steroids. They moved together toward us. We instinctively shuffled backward toward Lady Bao.

Stopping short of her reach, I grabbed for Joanie's hand.

I said quickly, not trying to whisper, "Don't be afraid, Joanie. I've got this!"

I knew my *Green Fire* would halt the thugs standing behind us, but I was afraid the vampire at my back would attack Joanie. I made a snap decision and instead of burning them to a crisp, I used one of dad's favorite spells.

Before they could take another step toward us, I held up my arms and screamed out the ancient words "Bilebiss!"

Both muscle-bound brutes looked down. Their feet, legs, thighs and torsos were transformed into a dense wood. They made no sounds as the spell consumed them completely, rooting them to the spot like dwarf redwoods.

"Very clever and amusing young Wushen, but now your friend will find my hospitality less accommodating."

I spun around in time to see Joanie being hauled away like a football, tucked under Lady Bao's arm as she flew like a streak of lightning deeper into the woods. The amulet I had given Joanie for protection hung down, flapping uselessly in the wind.

Chapter 51

The image of my best friend being kidnapped while I stood a few feet away, left me paralyzed.

I began conjuring a wind spell to transport me with speed equal to the vampire's, when the thick line of woods she had run into, completely vanished.

My mouth was still forming the old Druid words for my spell casting, when the dark green of the trees was replaced by the soft curve of a green hillock.

Either the woods had been an illusion, or the Lady had somehow camouflaged the entrance.

I knew I couldn't break through the barrier of Magic she had contrived. I went back to the cab to retrieve my cell and punched in mom's number.

She answered immediately. "Cathleen, where are you dear?"

"Mom, something really bad has happened."

I went on to explain how Lady Bao had taken Joanie hostage to insure my cooperation in finding the statute.

"I was getting ready to follow her, but she shielded the entrance into the woods or else, they never existed. Either way, mom, I need your help.

"I've already found you dear and will see you shortly."

A feeling of relief washed over me, but now I was putting my mom in the direct line of fire too.

I was worried sick about Joanie. Thinking back, I realized she had never called out to me for help. It wasn't likely she had been too afraid to scream. Joanie was pretty fearless when her Irish was up.

I decided Lady Bao had used some kind of suspended animation, putting Joanie into a readily compliant state.

I was staring across several yards of grassy knoll, when I heard the now familiar popping sound that signified a *voyager's* entrance or departure.

Mom was standing like an apparition at the crest of the hill, her back to me.

She seemed to be peering into thin air. After a few seconds of this, she turned at the sound of my voice.

"Mom!" I was shouting as I ran up the slight rise to join her.

"Cathleen, I'm so sorry I wasn't here with you, lassie."

She gave me a quick hug, probably to let me know she was really there.

"Tell me everything that happened, pet, so we can lay our plans."

I repeated the story leading up to of Joanie's abduction, starting back at the store where the driver was intercepted by the Colossus Faerie.

As I spoke, we were facing the open space leading down to another green hill where the wood line should have been.

"Alright, dear, I believe the Lady created the image of the hill we are seeing to deceive your sense of place. It was conjured up like a mirage in the desert. If we were closer, we'd no doubt see it shimmer. But, before she could conceal it, we know she took our girl into the wooded area you first observed.

"But why go to the trouble of conjuring that hillock?

"Why, clearly to give herself a clean head-start on any pursuit and to leave you wondering where to begin. But I can still feel the magic she drew upon, can't you?"

She asked this last looking sharply at me, reminding me that I was a wizard myself, with the same abilities. I only had to stop my panic long enough to use them.

I was mentally slapping my own forehead for giving into the fear factor. I opened my senses to all magic stirring in the area.

There it was! It was something like a painter's wash splashed over a canvas, covering a wide swath of grass. It led down the knoll for several yards, ending at a thin shimmer that must have been the entrance to the woods.

Mom had been watching me as I tried to follow the clues left by the use of magic. I looked back at her and smiled.

"OK. I know where they went now." I started to move forward when mom grabbed my arm.

"No, pet. We cannot approach just yet. We must first learn how the land lies. The vampire would have secured a remote place in the thick of the woods. We need to reconnoiter a bit before we go charging in."

"But what about Joanie, mom? She may be in real danger. What if Lady Bao gets...hungry?" I said the word with true dread coursing through my body.

Mom was peering intently ahead and I wondered if she even heard what I said.

Turning back to me she answered.

"She will not attack Joanie, Cathleen. She understands you will never turn the statue over to her if she harms your friend in any way. The Lady is very clever. She won't risk Joanie's life and lose her chance to possess the Red Dragon. Remember dear, she is hungrier for the power it holds, than she is for the life of a mortal."

With that, she started back toward the taxi, parked as if waiting to pick up a fare.

I had begun to follow her down the gentle slope when mom stopped suddenly and I heard her whispering in old Druid, a ward of protection. Or maybe one to conceal us…I wasn't sure because suddenly, I couldn't hear anything but a roaring like a waterfall.

The wind had suddenly picked up in speed and volume. We were fighting to stay upright!

"Let's get inside the cab, Cathleen, before we're blown off this hill!" mom screamed.

We dove inside the yellow car, slamming all the doors before the wind could shear them off. As it was, the taxi was rocking back and forth like a baby's cradle. There was no way we could exit the vehicle now.

It seemed like the swirling gusts were concentrated on the cab and us! Everything beyond was like a still-life painting.

"Don't worry, pet. My ward will keep us safe inside here." Mom must have been watching my concerned face.

Just as I was beginning to unclench my fingers from the door handle, the taxi was picked up. We were shot like a loaded sling, straight for the blank space previously occupied by the woods. A sharp intake of breath was the only sound either of us made.

We found ourselves hurtling through a heavily wooded area. Branches and leaves blurred as they were beaten away from the cab.

Suddenly, there it was.

The cabin in the woods; the cabin of Jason's vision.

Chapter 52

After our blindingly fast trip to a narrow patch of clearing just above the log cabin, the doors to the cab flew open. I hardly took notice. I sat staring at the solitary building.

I was trying to catch my breath after our rocket-ride, when I realized Mom was already outside the cab.

She had her hands outstretched, ready to call Green Fire. A bolt of lightning seared the ground near her feet, announcing the appearance of a rotund figure covered in thick grey fur, looming over her.

I jumped out of the cab and got to mom before she toasted Crom's blue toes.

"Crom, I'm so happy to see you again!" I called out while scooting to mom's side.

Mom was looking from the corpulent god of storms, to me, and back again, when she said, "Again?"

I ignored her for a minute and continued addressing him. I didn't want to tick him off before I asked him for that one favor promised to me.

Thinking of that, I looked up at him and said "While I am honored you have sought me out, Crom Croich, I didn't summon you."

"I am here because you continue to upset the *Teacher's* plans in the matter of the Red Dragon, young Cathleen. He dispatched a team of Faeries to invite my interventions once again." He said all this in something of a huff.

"Does this mean I can't call on you for that one *promised* intervention?" I asked.

Mom had been looking between the god and me, trying no doubt to get the gist of our conversation. It was time to make introductions.

"Mom this is …"

"I am well aware of who this is *now*, Cathleen," she said, interrupting me.

"The *Protectors of the Council of Green Wizards* have often sought your intercessions, Crom Croich, God of Storms. But I have never been honored by your presence."

Crom seemed very pleased with my mother's quick recovery of her manners, with just the right amount of awe.

"Brighid, Master Wizard and wife of a favorite, Liam O'Brien, I greet you now with warmth and delight."

I felt an immediate heating up of the air around us, as Crom turned a hot shade of fuchsia.

"Crom, is this then, your last intervention?" I asked, half afraid of his answer.

"I have been asked by the *Teacher* to help you unravel this bit of treachery by the Lady Bao. I delivered you to this place, so you can choose whether you want me to proceed further. I will do so, if you so desire. Only, be aware, this will be my last intervention as I tire of all these mortal quandaries."

My mom looked up at the fearsome figure of the God of Storms and meekly asked a few moments to consider.

Mom turned toward me.

"Don't use the promised help now, dear. I am positive Joanie will be fine until we secure the Red Dragon. I fear we may need Crom's assistance in that endeavor as we will be treading upon unknown ground."

The thought of being unable to help my friend that second, was nearly unbearable. She trusted I'd take care of her with my magic, but now I was being asked to put off her rescue until we had the statue in hand.

Unfortunately, it made good sense. The Red Dragon was the perfect bargaining chip with the Lady Bao, or the Wizard Feng, for that matter.

"I suppose you already know my decision, Crom."

He'd been watching us intently through a light gauze of fog he'd created, probably out of boredom.

"I will await your call in future, young Cathleen. You may both reenter your transport and I shall return you from hence you came."

We were no sooner seated in the yellow cab then the same whooshing sound surrounded us and we were flying backward out of the woods. I was looking back at the lonely cabin as it blurred and disappeared.

Will Joanie forgive me when she realizes I had to leave her in the vampire's hands?

Mom must have read my mind as she did so often.

She reached out and gave my hand a squeeze saying, "She'll understand darling."

When the cab settled back on the hillside, mom and I decided to mark the spot with a magic symbol.

Choosing our own Celtic Dragon as our signpost, we placed that image on a nearby mound tufted with long, swaying grasses. The Dragon seemed to flex its leg muscles as the wind gently nudged the wheat like stalks.

We were careful to ward our work against any interference and got back into the cab.

By now, it was nearing the time for Jason's flight to arrive and I needed to get back to the Grant to meet him.

With a last, but determined look around, I started the engine to begin our forty minute drive back toward China Town and the coming darkness.

Chapter 53

Leaving Joanie behind was overshadowing my excitement at seeing my boyfriend.

I felt guilty about being happy to have him hold me tightly in his arms, while my friend was being held against her will!

Jason was also very concerned about Joanie's situation. He suggested we use his rental car and make another rescue attempt.

"We can't do that yet, sweetie," I said, resignation in my voice.

"I have to secure the Red Dragon so I'll have something to trade for her release."

"You aren't seriously going to give the statue to that Vampire are you, Cathleen?"

"I can't give that cursed thing to *anyone,* but the *Green Council* and mom will take it to them herself. We need to have it in our possession though, before we can negotiate with Lady Bao for Joanie's release."

I had related the story to Jason about the trip to China Town with Joanie, including everything leading up to her being snatched. He raised his eyebrows when I told him about finding the cabin he saw in his vision.

"So, now that you have marked the place Joanie's being held, what's our next move?"

"I don't trust Lady Bao to do anything, but lie," I answered, "but I still have the upper hand if I have the statue."

Joanie knew there were lots of risks connected with this investigation, risks to all involved. I had to trust that she wouldn't do anything to antagonize the vampires holding her captive.

I called mom's room to make plans to meet. She was anxious for me to introduce her future son-in-law, as she constantly referred to him.

Jason was charming and self-assured, with just the right touch of mystery when they finally met. As for mom, she seemed delighted with my choice of life partner. They got into an animated conversation over a light dinner and I felt like tapping on the water glass a few times to get a word in edgewise.

They'd been discussing fruitful interrogation methods when Mom became very still.

Looking around she asked, "Cathleen, dear. Do you pick up a sense of a Magic User in our midst?"

"It's alright, Mom," I said in a near whisper. "It's just Anfa, the Colossus Faerie sent by the *Teacher.*"

"I see," she said, still looking around the small dining area of the hotel. "Would you point her out, pet? I do hate not knowing all the players in a drama."

I had been using my Inner Eye to scope the room the second I felt the presence of a Magic User enter. I found Anfa in the guise of a small, Chinese busboy. No doubt she stashed the sleeping teen in some broom closet of the hotel kitchens for her new persona.

"She's the busboy over…"

Mom interrupted me saying "Oh! There you are! I just needed to look more closely."

She'd obviously started using her Inner Eye and was now watching the Colossus as she cleared dishes and picked up used flatware from empty tables.

We were the last customers left in the small restaurant. Anfa was carefully avoiding our table until everyone else was gone.

"Good evening, wizards," she said, as she approached our table.

She gave a small bow while picking up the empty bread basket. She then favored Jason with a curt nod.

"A special welcome to the mortal, Sheriff Tate. The *Teacher* has been cognizant of your connection to the wizard, Cathleen O'Brien, for a handful of your mortal years."

Jason looked less than pleased that he was on some Faerie's radar, though he heard it from a Chinese bus boy!

Anfa turned to mom.

"The *Teacher* sends warmest wishes to the *Beautiful Brighid*, wizard and wife of Liam, *Protector of the Green Council*. And an urgent message, that you must gather to meet with him at the appointed hour."

Before I could question her about the "appointed hour" comment, she blinked out of sight.

We sat like three wooden dummies waiting for someone to put words into our slightly open mouths. Mom was the first to recover.

"This is progress my dears! The *Teacher* will be among our small troop at some point. Our mission to liberate the statue and rescue our dear Joanie ought to move along quickly now."

"Mom, since Jason doesn't have Inner Eye, I think we need to fill him in on what we just saw."

It took us another five minutes to explain the presence of the Colossus Faerie, assuring him the busboy was sleeping soundly somewhere safe and would certainly be awakened by Anfa very soon.

Jason looked more perplexed at the end of our lecture, but wisely asked no questions that might delay our leaving.

The *Teacher* obviously had a plan and needed us to set it in motion.

We returned to our rooms, with Jason walking me to mine for a long good-night kiss outside my door.

He said, "Your mom is great, Cathleen. I can see you got her beauty; right down to the beautiful auburn hair."

He was smoothing a long, wavy strand out of my eyes while I stood pressed against him and the door.

"Jason, you are such a charmer!"

I leaned in for another kiss and slipping out of his arms, inserted my key and opened my door.

He sighed a resigned, "Good night, love."

His room was at the end of the hallway. He asked for this arrangement so he'd be close to an exit, he told me.

I thought he just didn't want to be too close to temptation, especially since mom's room was next door to mine. I suspected my mother's presence would dampen any thoughts of romantic nocturnal visits.

After thirty minutes of rolling around in bed, I sat down at the small desk where I had carefully laid out my research papers.

I was struck by the paltry amount I had uncovered about Wizard Feng Xi. It was as difficult to find some decent history on him as it was for his body to be found after his reported death.

He was obviously using his deviant talents to conceal as much about himself as he could without being completely invisible.

"Hey!" I said to the empty room. "He was using an invisibility spell!"

That notion made me jump to my feet and begin a new ward of protection on my room. I had taken a few minutes earlier to ward Jason's room and felt sure he was safe behind it. Mom naturally could take care of herself.

I began mumbling a Druid spell against the monsters or demons that might be searching me out. When I got to the last word I felt a vibration in the air of my shadowy room.

Like the spider that becomes aware of something snagged in the sticky threads of its web, I began to search the small space for my intruder.

Slipping back into my Inner Eye I immediately identified my visitor.

Anfa was standing by the door, holding what appeared to be a willow staff; supple and long, matching her own form.

The full expanse of the staff was expertly carved with a life-like blue snake, its limber body wrapping tightly around the smooth wood, its anvil shaped head decorated with faintly glowing green eyes.

After closer observation, I realized the viper was in fact, slithering along the length of the staff in a continuous blue line. It dropped to the floor with a soft plopping sound and began to make its way toward the desk and me.

I jumped to my feet, instinctively calling Green Fire to my hands.

Anfa stood unmoving near the door holding the now empty staff. The snake left a greenish smudge that glowed as it made a slow, sensuous path across the carpet toward me.

I called out to her.

"Hey! Get your snake under control, Anfa. I don't like slithery things very much."

I turned up the volume of my fire a notch, to underscore my comment.

The blue creature stopped moving and began to curl its long length around itself until it resembled a pile of azure blue yarn waiting to be spun.

I was ready to ask Anfa what she was up to, when the lump of blue lying a few feet away, began to glow in the iridescent shades of the sun on a calm sea.

There was a high pitched hum.

Suddenly, standing before me, where the snake had been coiled, was the *Teacher*.

Chapter 54

He stood well over six feet; considered a giant among the Faeries, but typical for one of his clan. Faeries come in all sizes and shapes. I only had to glance over at the Colossus hovering in the background, to remember that fact.

"Greetings to you, Cathleen O'Brien, daughter and apprentice to Liam O'Brien, *Protector* of the *Green Mother*. I should also recognize your mother, Brighid the Beauty, who is at this moment in the presence of the *Council of Green Wizards* making her report on the progress of your investigation."

I blinked several times trying to take in that last part of his comment.

The *Teacher* was rather a distraction from any rational thought in any case.

His clothes seemed designed to emphasis a muscular build. A dazzling, blue-green mesh armor covered a mid-thigh tunic of teal blue. His legs bulged like a weight lifter and were bare except for the studded greaves strapped to them, matching his body armor.

I was struck by the long, snowy-white hair cascading down his broad back. It contrasted vividly with the youthfulness of his face. His large eyes were green and piercing. I noted his square jaw line which brought to mind a cartoon super hero, drawn to perfection.

He appeared to be barely out of his teens, but then remembered the *Teacher* was hundreds of centuries old. Not a single wrinkle flawed his silvery skin. He shone like a newly minted coin.

I felt the weight of his stare as he coolly appraised me in return with open curiosity. He moved a foot or two closer to where I stood, rooted like a potted plant.

"Wizard O'Brien, you are more youthful and comely than I had been led to believe."

I immediately wondered who was bad mouthing me around the circles of Magic Users.

His smile told me he had a touch of mischief in his nature. Now *that* was something I wouldn't have expected! From all I'd learned about this mythical figure, the *Teacher* was not inclined toward jest.

"My apologies, for this manner of intrusion, Wizard, but…"

"Please," I interrupted, "just call me Cathleen. I would feel more comfortable."

"Certainly, Cathleen. Your name is as lovely as the woman who bears it."

I am pretty sure I fluttered my eyelashes at him, but I'd never admit that to anyone.

My Inner Eye was scouring his body for any imperfections, hoping to find something to distract my growing attraction to him.

Hey, I wonder if he's using a glamor charm on me, I thought with a jerk of my head as my eyes had drifted back down his legs.

"OK!" I said a bit tartly. I was angry with myself for ogling him like some rock star groupie.

"As you surely know, my mission has barely begun and already my friend is held captive by the Lady Bao. I've accomplished nothing, even though my mother is here and now you tell me she's *not* here."

He looked a bit taken aback at my frustration.

He walked over to Joanie's bed. Casually sitting down he leaned back against the headboard. Lifting his long legs, he stretched out full length. The greaves made a soft scraping sound as he scooted around a bit.

"You seem distressed, Cathleen. I understand the weight of the pledge made by your father is a great burden to one so young and untested."

Not only was the *Teacher* turning out to be a hot hunk of Faerie lust, but he was insulting my skills at wizardry.

In my distraction, I nearly forgot to question him about the whereabouts of my mother.

"Did you say my mother was with the *Council of Green Wizards* at this moment?"

"That is correct, Cathleen. Though I suspect since your investigation has not progressed too far along, her return to this realm is imminent."

He became quiet, sitting back up and planting his feet on the floor. I felt his eyes bore into mine.

Gritted out between his perfect teeth, he added, "Until that time, we must begin to lay our plans to secure the statue of the Red Dragon and utterly *destroy* the Wizard Feng Xi and his mistress, the Lady Bao!"

Up until this declaration of war, the *Teacher* had been relaxed with me, almost playful.

The mention of Feng and the vampire had not only altered his expression, but his appearance. His silvery complexion took on a tone of soft crimson and his eyes glowed like hot coals.

I believe I'm meeting the real *Teacher* now, I thought, as I watched the drastic transformation.

We locked eyes for a few heartbeats, our stare broken off by me.

"*Teacher*, I need to understand my mother's role in this mission. Am I correct to believe she's working on behalf of the *Council,* as their agent?"

He seemed to weigh how he'd respond.

"This ever is the truth. When your father, the Wizard *Protector,* Liam O'Brien was taken from this realm, Brighid took his place at the *Council's* invitation. She has acted on their collective behalf since her return to Country Claire, but has kept that position confidential, even from you it appears. But be assured, she would have joined you on this journey anyway, because you are her blood. "

He moved closer to me in one fluid motion. I saw clearly the pain of his own loss reflected in his beautiful green eyes.

This mission was more than revenge for his brother's death. It was to free the *Teacher* from the obligation of that revenge. It had been eons in the planning and now, he could find release from his own pledge of vengeance.

"Will you help me rescue my friend from Lady Bao?" I asked.

"I will leave Anfa for that purpose. Also, Crom Croich has already given his promise to aid you once. Your mother was wise to council against using him just yet. Your need for powerful magic will be great when you face the Dark Wizard. "

"I thought *you* would be with me then, *Teacher*," I said, with a tinge of concern entering my voice.

"Anfa," was all he said in reply.

The Colossus stepped forward, standing slightly to the *Teacher's* left. She was nearly his height, and almost as imposing in the strength she radiated.

"I will most assuredly be there when you confront the monster, Feng Xi, Cathleen. Anfa will take on the persona of your friend until you are able to secure her freedom."

I took a quick glance over at the tall Faerie. Looking back at me when I blinked was my best friend.

I jerked back from the shock of seeing this Joanie clone.

Answering my shocked look, the *Teacher* said, "Anfa will confuse the Lady Bao into believing you have freed your companion. The vampire will surely return to where she is being held to investigate her supposed escape. This will provide an opportunity to fall upon your friend's captors and secure her freedom."

I couldn't deny this was a better plan than I had thought up, which was exactly zip!

It was still weird to think this *Joanie* would be hanging out with me. For a fleeting moment, I wondered if she even sounded like my friend.

As if in response to my curiosity, the new Joanie said, "I know everything will go well, Cathleen. I imprinted many of your friend's mannerisms and speech patterns from the energies and echoes found in this room. I am certain you will find small flaws in my portrayal of Joanie, but no one else would."

My new friend did sooth my fears somewhat and I smiled weakly at her, bobbing my head in agreement.

The *Teacher* had stood silently to allow the new Joanie to answer my unspoken questions. Now, he moved so close, I could feel his breath on my upturned face when he spoke. He took my arms in his silvery hands.

"Cathleen, you are aware of my personal mission here, but fear not. I have no intention of abandoning you, or your friends. No more loved ones will be lost to the Dark Wizard, or the vampire. Your magic is young but powerful, and aligned with Brighid's you will prevail. Of this I am certain."

I sensed he was about to leave me so I hurriedly asked, "Will you be present when we face Feng Xi, *Teacher*?"

He looked back at me and I shivered as a creepy smile twisted his otherwise beautiful, full mouth.

"Naturally, I will mete out just the exact amount of justice Feng Xi is deserving of, Cathleen. When I am certain his suffering is equal to his victims, I will dispatch him to the Dark Pit of the Sleepless Dead. Of this you can be assured."

With that threat ringing in the air, the *Teacher* handed something to the new Joanie and then vanished with the odd humming sound that announced his visit.

Anfa looked down at me and held out her hand.

"For you, Wizard, a talisman of great protection and power."

Chapter 55

I reached for the small object and almost dropped it when she added, "It is from the thigh bone of the great *Wizard Protector,* Liam O'Brien."

Upon touching my hand, my skin tingled with energy. There were small runes carved along its entire surface. I closed my fingers around it and it disappeared into my fist.

"Are you saying this is a bone from my father?"

"When the *Wizard Protector* was on one of many missions attempting to rescue the *Teacher's* brother, he himself was captured and nearly lost to this realm.

Feng Xi was using his Dark Magic to induce the deepest of pain in your father, when the Teacher intervened. He blasted the chains forged by magic that held Liam O'Brien, but in doing so took part of the *Wizard Protector's* upper leg.

He repaired it quickly, but the shard you hold now was discovered amid the filth of the cell and retrieved by your father. If the Dark Wizard had found it, he would have used it to weaken your father's magic.

The *Wizard Protector* gave the bone to his rescuer as a memento of his loyalty."

I could feel the smooth talisman warming. I opened my fingers from their tight grip and brought it closer to my eyes.

The warmth wasn't just from my own body heat. The small shard was beginning to glow like mother of pearl, cleanly washed in the mollusk's shell. It became iridescent under the vague lighting of the desk lamp.

The presence of my father became so strong, I looked up, searching the room for him, but found only shadows cast by the Colossus Faerie, Anfa.

The face of my friend Joanie looked blandly back at me when I mumbled, "Wow." I knew my real friend would have been all over that small bone shard.

Guess Anfa has seen it all before, I thought, as I continued to turn the talisman over in my hand.

After a few minutes of inspection I slipped the magically infused Talisman into the pocket of my sweatshirt.

It had gotten cooler with sunset and I hadn't slept or eaten properly, a bad combination for my body.

"Anfa, do you mind if I just use your own name? I don't really feel comfortable calling you by my friend's."

"As you please, Wizard O'Brien. And now, may I suggest you sleep and renew your strengths. I will have your breakfast waiting upon your awakening."

Before I could respond, Anfa laid down on top of what had been Joanie's bed.

I wonder how she knew that was Joanie's, I thought randomly, as I lay down on my own bed. *Must be the energy markers she picked up. How weird all of this is...*

I woke up to the smell of fresh bacon and eggs and the enticing aroma of coffee.

Rolling over on my side, I saw Joanie puttering around the desk, laying out fork and napkin.

"You are aware once more, Wizard. Your morning meal is prepared."

I processed the unnatural wording and it dawned on me, my best friend was still missing.

"Good morning, Anfa, and thanks for the breakfast."

I got out of bed and sat at the desk to examine a dish spread with steaming scrambled eggs and crisp bacon. I grabbed for the coffee and looked over at the Joanie look-alike. Smiling while I stuffed my face.

Twenty minutes later I jumped into the shower to finish the job of waking up.

Fresh jeans, a new T-shirt with a red Dragon emblazoned across the front and the sweatshirt with dad's talisman snugged into a deep pocket and I was ready.

Anfa and I exited my room and knocked on Jason door at the end of the hallway. There was no need to check in on mom as I knew she would be at the coffee shop by now.

I was anxious to hear about her recent visit and report to *the Council of Green Wizards.* I was also a little unhappy with her for not sharing with me her true role in all of this. But that was mom; she loved to play the undercover operative.

Jason opened the door after my first knock.

I think I stopped breathing for a minute. He looked like an ad for *Gentlemen's Quarterly* magazine, decked out in a dark blue turtleneck, neatly pressed jeans and a tawny leather jacket. Cowboy boots completed the rugged man image. His black eye patch lent him that mysterious, sexy look. I think even Anfa was impressed.

"Joanie?" he blurted out, before I could say anything.

"Sweetie, this is not Joanie."

He gave me a nod and said, "Better come in."

I was happy to be out of earshot of any passerby and we stepped into the small foyer off the bathroom.

"Better give me the short version, love. I know your mom will be waiting for us."

I started with the fact that Anfa was sent by our other ally, the *Teacher*. I filled him in on why Anfa had taken on Joanie's appearance.

"If she does that, we can free Joanie and--"

"Destroy the vampire!" Anfa finished my statement with a deep scowl on my friend's face.

"That too," I added lamely.

"Ok then. I guess you two have figured out the angles. Better get over to the coffee shop. I'd like to speak with Cathleen, so would you mind leaving for there before us? I guess you could use the time to fill in her mom until we get there."

He was a take-charge Sheriff again, and Anfa responded with a quick affirmative shake of her head and a quick exit.

When the door closed Jason grabbed me and gave me a long kiss. I felt my heart beat triple time and my breath became a gasp when I came up for air.

"Wow! How do you do that to me?"

Jason was smiling down on my flushed face and kissed the side of my neck where my pulse was beating like a kettle drum.

"Ok, love. We can leave now," he said with a look of satisfaction. I was far from satisfied, but before I could protest, he was ushering me out the door.

We arrived at the small café where Joanie and I had met mom only the day before.

I thought the *Teacher* was right about smoking the vampire out of wherever she'd gone to ground.

We picked up our shadow almost as soon as we exited the elevator to leave the hotel. When we entered the coffee shop, we spotted mom sitting across from Anfa. They were holding an animated conversation and looked to be greatly enjoying one another's company. I always forget how popular my mom is with the Faerie folk.

Jason and I crossed the room toward their table. When mom saw us she jumped to her feet, giving me her two-cheek pecks. She was dwarfed by Jason's six foot plus height, but somehow managed to look like the regal dame, greeting her knight's return from a joust.

I sat in one of the empty chairs while Jason grabbed another from the nearby table for himself.

Mom quickly installed a *Dome of Silence*. After five minutes of updates, mom reached over and squeezed my hand.

"Well done, dear. The Lady's driver has naturally found our little group and will be reporting back to that our dear friend is somehow free. The Lady will undoubtedly fly back to the cabin, and then we'll have her in our sights!"

Chapter 56

From outside of the invisible barrier, our little group would appear to be enjoying a quiet conversation while sipping our coffees and biting into Danish.

Mom turned to Anfa asking if the *Teacher* had any specific instructions for her.

"The *Teacher* has told me to assist in the freeing of your friend. I am to follow all instructions given by the Wizard, Cathleen O'Brien, and you, as agent of the *Council*."

"Mom, what's your true part is in this investigation? The *Teacher* has already told me that you took dad's place as a *Wizard Protector* on the *Council of Green Wizards*. And I also know from him that you've been assigned to retrieve the statue of the Red Dragon on their behalf. What is it I *don't* know?"

"Darling girl, I do regret not sharing that tiny bit of information sooner, but it was more urgent that I come into your search as an invited guest, rather than an assigned agent.

The *Council's* work is never made public or known, even to Magic Users unless they are on special assignments for the *Council*. Somehow, that information leaked out and cost Dr. Chung Wu his life in this realm.

Directly following that unfortunate occurrence, I was assigned to take his place in the hunt for the Red Dragon. Oh, and also to assist you, dear, in the destruction of the Dark Wizard and the Lady Bao."

I had had my suspicions about mom's involvement in my investigation from the start. She knew the back story on Chung.

Also, she was a time bender and Voyager and knew about dad's pledge to the Lady Bao.

Mom, it was turning out, was a deep cover agent. *Who knew?*

Jason stirred in his chair and turning to me said, "Honey, time to sort out your mom's role later. Right now it's time to get this show on the road."

Turning back to mom, Jason asked, "Can that guy following us do that time-bending thing, Brighid?"

"Most assuredly he has some ability in that area, Jason. Good of you to note it, dear. Let's all do a bit of sightseeing shall we?"

The dome of silence evaporated into thin air with only a slight vibration around our table. After much scrapping of chairs, and smiling like we were off to a big excursion in China Town, we exited the Café.

The driver suddenly became animated, but only momentarily. I looked back quickly to see him leaning back against the brick façade of the coffee house. He blinked out like the guy at the airport.

Anfa must have been watching, because she came close to me and said, "Lady Bao's pet rat has scurried back to her. I think the bait has been set."

She looked very pleased with that assessment of the case and I admit, I felt better that we were one step closer to rescuing Joanie.

I stopped a few feet from the hotel and said 'Here's where I leave you and mom Jason."

He looked shocked and confused. "What do you mean, Cathleen? I thought the plan was to get Joanie."

"I need to start my search for the statue, Jason. It's the reason I'm here, to fulfill that pledge. Right, mom?"

Mom looked very calmly into my eyes and answered, "Of course, lass. You know I will free our dear Joanie and keep her safe. Jason and I will return to that hillock we marked with the sign of the dragon and I will do what needs doing from there!"

Jason took my arm and steered me a few feet away for privacy.

"Cathleen, I'm not happy with this arrangement. It seems like you'll be out there facing this Feng guy on your own!"

"I have Anfa, Jason. She's not just a Faerie. She's a *Colossus*, which means she's the equivalent of a Special Forces trained soldier. Having her with me means she can dispatch Feng Xi's Warriors and anything else he throws at her. While she mops the floor with that bunch, I can find their master and entertain him until she can rejoin me to finish him off."

Jason still looked unhappy, but resigned.

"Jason," I said, taking his hand, "you know how important it is to get to Joanie before anything really bad can happen to her. Please, I need you to trust me here."

I heard mom clear her throat for the third time and realized they needed to get going if they were to find the marked patch of ground before it got too late in the day.

I stood on my toes as Jason leaned over and we kissed goodbye without speaking. I squeezed his hand and turned toward Anfa.

"Let's go, Anfa," I said softly, and looking over at mom I gave a curt nod and a smile.

"Have fun, ladies," mom called at our receding backs as we entered the stream of growing visitors to the world of the Red Dragon.

314

Chapter 57

The crowds were definitely swelling as it got later in the morning.

I felt invigorated by the enthusiasm of visitors from all over the world to this fabled city of oriental wonders and mystique.

Anfa seemed more interested in peering into the dark alleyways and nonchalantly glancing behind her shoulder. I noticed when she stopped in front of a display, she was actually scanning the street behind us for a possible tail.

After twenty minutes of walking we found ourselves being jostled and elbowed by bigger and bigger crowds of tourists and locals. There was some kind of celebration going on directly down the street from us. I strained my neck trying to peer over and around the many people lining the sidewalks in front of the stores.

There was a palatable rise of excitement in the air.

A huge red head, streaming long, catfish-like barbs around a tooth-filled mouth and long snout poked around the corner at the end of the block.

The sun glittered off gold leaf piping around the eyes, making them snap with life as the head moved forward.

An immediate rumble of delight rolled through the throngs of people, with some small kids screaming in fear at this red apparition.

The heavy, papier mache dragon began to emerge from behind the bend in the road. Little by little, it presented its full serpentine body to the ogle-eyed crowds.

Even knowing that this dragon was powered by the strength of many human actors, it seemed formidable as it bobbed its head from side to side, as if sweeping the spectators for tasty morsels.

I was so entranced by the length of the body and the life-like movement of its progress, I nearly missed the feet beneath it, propelling it onward.

There were at least two dozen pairs of the same dark boots with tucked trousers, peeking from under the red and gold flecked scales of the body. The same boots and pants I saw on the crazy Terra Cotta Warrior back in Iron Mountain.

I touched Anfa on the elbow. "Let's get out of here before…"

I never got to finish. Without any warning, the dragon's wings were unfurled and a blue steam began to spray onto the tightly packed onlookers.

I acted as fast as I could, pulling up a ward around me and Anfa, only to realize she had moved a fraction to follow the dragon's progress down the street.

The ward dropped, leaving her stranded like a gulping fish out of water, breathing some blue mist deep into her lungs.

Within seconds, both sides of the street were covered with people lying on the ground. Many had their arms wrapped around loved ones, most just fell over where they stood, in various contorted positions.

The eerie scene took on the look of a body dumping ground, where several truckloads of humans had been unloaded and scattered on both sides of the street.

As the dragon continued slithering down the main street, more people were falling over, succumbing to the blue mist.

I didn't dare leave the safety of the ward, but instead used an air spell to lift Anfa off the sidewalk and carry her down the alley behind us. I lowered her near a pile of crates smelling strongly of garlic and onions. I tested the stale air for traces of the sleeping compound just used to subdue the people. Finding it clear, I left Anfa where she slept and darted back to the gruesome scene of hundreds of fallen bodies.

Feng Xi would likely send out clean-up crew to gather up as many of the victims as he could. He was trying to fill his food stores for his growing army of warriors and these innocent people had been transformed into a smorgasbord for the taking.

As I got closer to the street, I used another spell for concealment, breathing the ancient words of Magic, *fulla fiada.* I stepped out from the side of the building.

The dragon had made a slow progress, but was nearly at the end of the street. I couldn't figure out why no one had sent up an alarm about what was happening just feet away.

And then I realized I was witnessing the work of a very powerful wizard.

My father had told me about a Sorcerer he had been hunting once, with a warrant from the *Council of Green Wizards.*

He had managed to avoid dad over and over, by simply taking control of threads of time. By doing this, he in effect froze the circumstances on that thread, continuing to replay them as if in real time.

The crowds ahead of the dragon would see a repeated reflection of what *had* been reality before the calamity occured. The distortion of time like this took an enormous magical strength, but the *Green Mother* would never allow such corruption of the natural order.

I waited at the end of street, looking back at the fallen bodies, strewn around like dolls by some petulant child.

The dragon was now just opposite of where I stood, invisible to all eyes. The several pairs of boots stopped short of crossing into the next block. I watched for signs of movement, when the paper dragon was lifted high and dropped onto the street like an abandoned kite.

Despite the fact that I had already identified them as the Terra Cotta Warriors, seeing about twenty-four of them arrayed in perfect, military formation, shook me up a tad. Facing one of these guys had been scary enough; now I was looking at a small army of well-trained, well-armed soldiers.

Just as I was trying to think of a way to disable the assembled warriors, the entire group of soldiers turned toward me. I heard the clear hiss of swords being slipped from scabbards and the distinct sound of heavy chains rattling with their studded iron balls, ready to cave in heads.

Uh oh...this isn't good...

I knew my invisibility spell was working, but the line of soldiers seemed poised to come straight at me. Or was it at the sleeping, vulnerable crowds?

I had to act fast.

I began using my wind charm to move the still bodies lying around me. I couldn't take the chance that they might be the targets of the warriors.

When I had pushed the people back toward the buildings on both sides of the street, I was careful to stand them up, propping them with the heavy air currents. I had to get them awake soon, or risk a huge loss of human life.

No *Protector* could allow that to happen, even if it meant my own life.

Most of the people were moved. I could get to the rest as soon as I dealt with the band of Chinese troopers.

They were all advancing forward now, in lock-step, grimaces twisting their reddish tan faces into fearsome grins. They held their assorted weapons ready to strike. They might have been using ancient weaponry, but it scared the crapski out of me!

I tested the air around me. Slowing it down to a pliable sludge, I used it to fashion a shield in front of the rows of unconscious people I had propped up behind me and across the street. Just in time. Several of the front soldiers let loose with a volley of arrows. A streaking javelin came next, sailing past me.

Now I was positive they couldn't see me, but they were clearly trying to make pincushions out of the defenseless humans.

I was feeling pretty cocky behind my shield of invisibility and the ward I had dropped around myself earlier. Both were protecting me nicely. That's naturally when I screwed up.

I heard a soft, muffled sound from the alley where I had parked Anfa's limp body. Even in that state, she had managed to somehow keep the Joanie thing going.

There was no way I could leave this area as the warriors were now moving steadily forward. I had to engage them in battle, because that's why they were here.

I dropped my first ward of protection, but was still an unseen enemy to Feng's bunch of clay-headed soldiers.

I began to back up toward the store window directly behind me. I never saw the little boy laying directly in my path and fell flat on my back, my legs sticking up in the air like a tipped turtle. Somehow, I had missed the little guy as I was picking up the other folks. He was curled into a ball and looked totally exposed to the coming horde.

Scrambling to my feet, I scooped up the unconscious toddler at the same time and put him behind a tiny dome of protection. There was no time to do more than that when two of the soldiers rushed onto the sidewalk and began hammering away at the frozen people with swords, spiked clubs and those lethal looking iron balls dangling like cannon balls, from their chains. Sparks flew in every direction from the power of their blows against the shield.

One of the warriors redirected his attention and was swinging his sword in a wide arc, as if he was trying to slice up something he knew was there, but couldn't locate.

He knows I'm here, I was thinking, as I moved to the side and nearly off the sidewalk.

Feng Xi had to be directing his movements. Was he somewhere close by?

A soldier stopped directly in front of me. His eyes narrowed into two black lines and I knew he was ready to bring the long curve of his sword down on my head.

I conjured a twister of wind and was able to push him back two feet, but he only looked more determined and leaned into the stiff air current like a sailor on heavy seas.

I was calling up fire to my hands when I heard a sharp clap of thunder and the blue sky seemed to tear open in a deluge of lightening directly above us.

A bellowing voice froze every warrior into action figures with raised weapons. The soldiers that were still on the street stopped in their tracks as if waiting for a command to move forward.

The only voice they would hear would be the last voice they would ever hear in this realm, Crom Croich god of Storms.

321

Chapter 58

He appeared like a towering glacier, all diamond blue light, dazzling to the eyes of any human, or non-human, without my Inner Eye. Thank the *Mother* I had slipped into that mode of seeing hours before, so was protected from retina burn, or worse.

Crom stood before the assembled warriors who had definitely reverted back to time worn artifacts, not a spark of life in any of them.

His very presence was enough to scare any being senseless, but he was looking pretty good to me about then. I dropped my spell of invisibility.

"Crom, I didn't call you, but I am very grateful for your intervention!"

As usual, the God of Storms had brought a severe change in the weather along with him. I began shivering in my sweatshirt and jeans when I dropped my invisibility spell.

"Young Wizard, I know you didn't call! It seems the *Teacher* has his own eyes on your undertaking. I believe that being approaching us may be his own?"

Anfa was slowly making her way toward us, avoiding the soldiers that stood in their various wooden positions. She looked disheveled, and dark smudges covered her shirt and jeans. Her thick red hair was decorated like a salad with various pieces of discarded vegetables she picked off as she ambled over.

"Great Crom, Lord of Storms, I greet you!" she said, while touching four fingers to her head and heart.

She straightened her shoulders and now stood before us both as her true Colossus-self, Anfa. She dropped her Joanie persona so quickly I was disoriented for a minute.

"Greetings to you, Faerie of the Second Realm. Your human visage was most convincing." Crom smiled like an old grandfather at the tall Faerie.

Looking back at me, he continued, "I have come to dispatch these hooligans back to the Dark Pit of the Sleepless Dead, only to find they never truly held the spark of life. Ah, well, a few bolts and they will be no more."

The sky overhead began to waffle and rumble. One bolt of yellow lightning after another streaked downward into the close line of standing warriors, reducing their fierceness to small piles of red clay.

Those that had made it to the sidewalk I destroyed with the *Mother's* own *Green Fire*. She would never accept the use of her earth for such evil.

At the end of the small cataclysm, Crom sent the whole mess swirling off into the deep hole I opened.

The twenty-four Terra Cotta Warriors were returned to the earth without a trace of their passing through this realm.

Now I had to deal with the crowds of people who still lined the street in their very unnatural state.

I needed to get rid of Crom graciously before I could bring the human statues back to their fun-filled day.

"Crom, you have again done a great service on behalf of the *Green Mother's Protector*. However, I need to return these humans to their lives immediately and Anfa will need to assume her false persona."

I now appealed to his vanity as God of Mighty Storms.

"Would you do one last favor before you leave us? Bend time just enough so these people will be living in a moment where they watch the last of the dragon as it disappears around the corner? That way, it can vanish and they'll be none the wiser."

"I shall grant you this last boon, young wizard, but before we awaken the mortals, are you interested in the whereabouts of your mother and your life companion."

"Life companion?" Did he mean Jason? Sounded right somehow. "Of course I am!" I answered quickly.

"I will restore these people to their future time now. Then, you and the lovely Faerie, Anfa," he said, leering a bit at her, "shall have the situation described in full."

There was a clear and sharp snapping noise that hung in the still air and the smell of ozone after a rain. Suddenly, all the people on both sides of the street were shouting and pointing and taking pictures with cell phones as the swishing tail of the red paper dragon turned the corner at the end of the street and vanished from sight.

I looked over at Anfa and saw with relief that she had assumed her Joanie look. It would be hard to explain a very tall Faerie, no matter how attractive Crom had found her.

I touched her elbow and we stepped off the sidewalk and into the street where we followed the receding tail of the dragon.

"Let's cut into this alleyway, Anfa. I don't think the Storm god would want an audience for his next appearance."

As we stepped into yet another odor filled passage way between shops, a wind began to stir the paper and discarded boxes, strewn around the area.

With this as our only warning of his presence, Crom had us scooped up like two grains of rice and deposited on the roof of the nearest building. I immediately felt the spell of invisibility he'd cast over our ascent and relaxed knowing we were unseen.

Crom was lounging on a small couch accompanied by four comely looking *Baisleac*, wise women from the Druid cult that often served the Storm god in mortal matters.

Each wore a dark purple toga cinched at a slender waist by a circlet of gold mesh resembling a lightning bolt. Their hair shone like burnished silver, flowing in thick tresses to the hem of their togas and spilling over creamy yellow arms. One was more beautiful than the next.

They were captivating to look at, but Anfa brought my attention back to matters of life and death.

Giving my arm a small tweak she said "Your mother and Jason may be in mortal danger, Wizard."

Crom cleared his throat and a smattering of sleet flew out of his mouth. *I wouldn't want to be around him if he sneezed!* I thought.

He got my full attention when a dark frown clouded his face like a thunder head hanging over us.

"The Wizard Brighid, and your male companion have been able to penetrate the wooded area.

Your shrewd mother turned the mirage that clouded the entryway, inside out, pulling the fabric of the spell until the trees popped into place. Quite a clever trick, that!"

I interjected my question quickly.

"Crom, are my mother and Jason at the cabin now?"

"You needn't concern yourself, Cathleen O'Brien. While they are near that humble abode, they have not entered and are safe enough for now.

"You know I need to locate the statue of the Red Dragon and the Wizard Feng Xi, Crom. I wish to call in my promised favor now."

"Hmm…I thought as much, young wizard."

You wish me to lend assistance to your mother and companion in the rescue attempt of your friend. Am I correct?"

I wanted to say "No, help me with the evil wizard," but I had to rescue Joanie before she became a vampire juice pack, or worse!

"My companion, as you call him, saw me in a dream at that very cabin. If I'm there, how can I search out the Red Dragon and Feng Xi here in China Town?"

"Ah, your friend is a *Vision Seeker* it would seem. Well, my fine young wizard, what he saw is this…"

The couch, the *Baisleac* women and Crom, instantly melted into a bubbling puddle of color. Reddish-brown, peach, blue, and some subtle greens finally congealing into…ME!

Crom was gone and I was facing a mirror image except for the broad smile on the other's face.

My doppelganger stopped grinning at me and said, "Cathleen O'Brien, you have called in my promised aid. And now you understand why the *Vision Seeker,* Jason, saw you in those woods."

I stood in stunned silence and felt Anfa move toward me.

She said in Joanie's voce, but in her stilted way of speaking, "It would appear Crom, God of the Storm, will be of great assistance to your mother and friends. This would be an appropriate time for us to begin our search, Cathleen O'Brien."

"Listen to Anfa, Wizard. She is wise despite her tender years of two."

I turned to Anfa. "You're only *two*?" I asked incredulous.

"Thousand," she said, as she took my arm and we were flying.

Chapter 59

We were still invisible to the eyes of any person that happened to be scanning the afternoon skies for aliens.

We made a soft landing thanks to Anfa's talents, close to a boarded up shack on the outskirts of China Town. Though still in view of the Bay and wharfs, the only commerce taking place here was between the seagulls and the rotting garbage floating in greasy tidal pools.

Anfa stepped in front of my field of vision. She leaned down to study what looked like a worm-eaten wooden door in the front of the shack.

"This is where we shall enter, Wizard."

She began to pull at several wooden boards, nailed together, likely placed there to stop trespassers like us.

Standing outside, smelling the salty sea air and hearing the muffled noise of everyday life off in the distance, I felt a strong urge to postpone this underground hunt. I re-ran in my head what I'd learned about the buried city we were about to enter.

After the 1906 earthquake, when the world in this area shook and rolled and shook again and again, China Town was brought to her knees.

This was not the tourist Mecca it is today. It was a neighborhood of immigrants, where ancient traditions, from an ancient culture, still thrived and were passed on to new generations.

The original China Town was no more than a frontier town that, like others of the time, grew into a city after the discovery of gold.

By the late 1850's it was crowded with hotels, businesses, shops, restaurants and gaming places. There were also many Chinese Pharmacies offering traditional Chinese herbs for healing and health needs. In short, a little China had been founded along the shores of an American city.

All this bustling life stopped dead on April 18, 1906 when the San Francisco area was devastated by a powerful earthquake. Fires consumed much of China Town's wooden structures and the quake and after-shocks, leveled most of its brick ones.

It was reported that this cataclysm took place in less than one minute.

During my research I had uncovered an old newspaper clipping filed on the day the earth rose up and took down the dreams and lives of thousands. The article was dated April 20, 1906. Los Angeles.

The headline read: "Hole Where Chinatown Was". The reporter, a W.W. Overton, filed his article from Los Angeles after viewing the horrific aftermath of the historic quake.

"No heap of smoking ruins marks the site of the wooden warrens where the Orientals dwelt in thousands. Only a cavern remains, pitted with deep holes and lines, with dark passageways from whose depths some smoke wreaths."

Overton went on in his Apocalyptic description to take note of the "...*hundreds of crazed yellow men fleeing*"

This article also mentioned the place Anfa and I were now headed into.

"White men never knew the depth of Chinatown's underground city. Many had gone beneath the street level two or three stories, but now that Chinatown has been unmasked, men may see where it's inner secrets lay."

Reading about passages, one hundred feet deep, gave me more than a moment's pause. I hate being underground, but unfortunately my many experiences as an investigator of the paranormal, seem to put me more than the proverbial "six feet under".

Anfa had completed dismantling the boards blocking the entrance and already entered the tunnel. She was just a smudge of movement in the blackness ahead of me.

The dark seemed to attach itself to my every breath as I inhaled its dampness, and exhaled its gloom.

Anfa reached back to me until she touched my hand as I groped along, hoping not to touch anything, or anyone.

"Wizard, this structure is most unstable, but it is surely the entryway we seek. A tunnel lies ahead. You would do well to give us a small light before we proceed."

I brought a handful of *Green Fire* to my left hand. Anfa's shadow popped onto the dirt wall of a narrow passage where she stood directly ahead of me.

I was sure she could have used her own *Faerie lights*, but I think she wanted me to be busy doing something besides cringing in the darkness.

As we slowly began to descend, I went over in my mind all the notes I had made from old news clippings from the time of the quake. Remembering the particulars and speculations, didn't do much for my nerves.

The one story that kept rattling around in my head as we crept forward, was a more current magazine article from the early 1940's. It mentioned China Town's hidden catacombs, built before the 1906 earthquake. The writer described them as frightening, saying this "subterranean world was nightmarish."

The secret of this dark realm wasn't reveled until the earth tore itself open.

A reporter in the area at the time of the quake, suggested that it was carefully hidden by leaders of Chinese Lords. Allegedly, they used the damp, carved-out areas like dungeons, to carry out their reigns of terror and run private empires built on opium, prostitution and gambling.

These facts and speculations kept pace with me as I followed Anfa's lead.

The floor of the tunnel took a precipitous drop and we both reached out to the close walls to steady ourselves.

The dank air smelled like a mix of dead fish and graveyard dirt; not pleasant, but breathable. Anfa turned her head slightly toward me and asked that I turn up the volume on my fire so she could see further. If I wasn't mistaken, even *she* sounded a little nervous in the claustrophobic atmosphere of the tunnel.

Faeries are known to love the freedom of movement they enjoy in the wild woodlands they inhabit. Being in this place of fetid air and narrow passages, must have made Anfa feel more like a mole than a sprite.

After forty-five minutes of alternating between walking as if through a mine field, and hunching over like old hags, we came to a halt.

Anfa tested ahead for any depressions in the tunnel floor, because we could feel another shift in the pitch of the ground. There was a definite upward trend to our movement. We went forward about twenty feet when we agreed things were leveling out.

I did a slow circle when we stopped. I turned up the flames in my hand. Suddenly, we were both bathed in green tones,

Anfa's *Joanie* face, taking on a rather sickly hue. Not far from the truth of how I was feeling in actuality.

Even Anfa seemed a bit off just then and she seemed impervious to anything less than Bubonic Plague!

"Anfa, I don't feel too well. What's going on? Do you think… there might be some kind of poison gaaaa…?"

I left that question dangling like a vampire bat on a cow's neck.

Not an unapt description either.

When I woke up, I found myself staring into the lifeless eyes of an undead.

He had to be one of Feng Xi's small army of worker bees down here. Anfa and I must have stumbled into him while we were groping around in our limited light.

I was tied up like a calf at branding time and searching the floor of the tunnel for Anfa, expecting her to be lying nearby.

All I saw in my limited field of vision was the gray, hairless creature.

I figured he was guarding me, although he didn't look particularly alert. His huge head seemed to have sprouted from his shoulders. These were sloped, causing a permanent curve to his back. I guessed this demon spawn was likely made that way, to accommodate the low ceilinged tunnel system.

The gray man moved slightly to my left and stood with his stooped back to the wall across from me. His hands hung limply at his sides. Each had only three digits ending in long curved claws like a bird of prey. Guess that was why he didn't have any other weapons on him; that plus he could *ugly you to death*!

The eyes that stared back at me were completely opaque, but had a sort of phosphorescence in the depth of the orbs. *Probably lets them see in the dark,* I thought, as I studied him.

This particular specimen of Feng Xi's handy-work was not discernibly male or female, but I thought of it as male because it was easier and I needed easy just then.

I was beginning to get uncomfortable in the tight bindings around my feet and hands. Whatever had knocked me out, had given me a throbbing headache and I was fairly ticked off to have been taken so easily. And where was Anfa?

I needed to do something about my current status as prisoner to the gray lump thing.

I began to whisper a charm to unbind the ropes and while I was at it, another to loosen the packed dirt floor beneath the stubby feet of the gray guard.

My bindings slipped off me like butter off a hot knife. I stayed perfectly still, until I was sure gray man hadn't noticed I was free.

Suddenly, he let out a chilling howl as his feet began to sink steadily into the earth past his lower legs and up to his waist. Because his hands were down by his sides when he began his decent, they were captured in the gritty loam.

Gray man was looking about himself for some way out of the ready-made grave. He gave out another bellow of anger and frustration as his large, probably empty head, slipped beneath the earth.

Chapter 60

I was standing with *fire* lapping at my fingertips, searching the immediate area for Anfa.

Walking slowly behind a pale funnel of light, I began noticing side tunnels dotting the narrow passageway on both sides. I wondered where they would take me, and where the Colossus Faerie was in this underground maze.

I concluded that Anfa had been taken prisoner by Feng Xi's minions while I lay unconscious.

I peered into a side-tunnel, where the darkness was so complete it felt thick as sludge. I was looking for a starfish in the depths of a black sea.

That thought spurred my hesitant feet. I began a slow jog, my feet stirring an earthy smell. An awful dread twisted my stomach as I reflected on the fate of my only ally down there.

With all the strength she had, Anfa was still vulnerable if taken while unconscious. Even now, she might be lying at the feet of the dark Wizard.

I reached my hand out to the chilled dirt of the tunnel wall. It was time to seek more power. There was a vibration of energy flowing from the *Green Mother* like a mild electric jolt coursing through me.

I had been using my Inner Eye since getting up that morning, but I had no idea how long ago that was. In the eternal night of the tunnels, there was no way to measure time.

I figured I had traveled more than a mile when outer structures of the legendary Underground China Town began to appear like ghosts ships from a grey fog.

At first, I thought I was looking at a livestock barn, but as I got closer, I saw pieces of tables and chairs, tumbled over and broken. A few large oblong tables lay tilted like ships on a sand bar, ornately carved legs rising up like broken masts.

They appeared to be used for gaming, felt cloth coverings, aged into shreds of blackish-green streamers.

Nearby, I spotted a pair of ivory dice, carved with black Chinese characters, staring up like detached eyeballs.

Everything was covered with a thick coating of dirt and grey soot reminding me of the fires that must have raged among these shacks when the conflagration rained down from above.

A spongy mold grew wherever water had seeped through the natural earthen works overhead. The smell was one of decay and the mustiness of unmoving air.

There was one crushed wooden structure after another as I moved further into the passageway. An occasional partial wooden wall sported a billboard sign hanging from rusting nails, announcing what thrill could be had within, in both Chinese and English. There would be no shortage of prostitutes, gambling and the very popular opium dens.

I moved forward and began checking each warren and alcove for signs of life.

I knew I could detect Anfa's life force easily; it would feel pure and untainted. Anything else I would encounter in this hell-hole, would feel like something from the Dark Pit where it came from, and where I intended to return it!

The tunnel split. I wished I could turn my fire up for a better look, but I didn't want to alert any of Feng's roaming gray men to my presence. They didn't appear to be very bright, but they would know an enemy when they saw one. And I still hadn't figured out what they had used earlier to subdue me.

I crouched closer to the packed earth, studying the left-turning trail for any clue of current usage. There was a section of dirt that had definitely been recently disturbed. It was smooth in the center with small mounds on either side. Something had been dragged. *Anfa?*

I leaned closer to the dirt and smelled. I was certain she'd passed through there. It did little to comfort me, since now I was afraid *she* was the one being dragged along behind a gray man.

My nose began twitching like a coon dog on rabbit scent. The odor was distinctly unpleasant. It wasn't Anfa, however, there was a pale undertone to it, an effervescence that clung to the rutted dirt floor.

"There you are, my friend," I said under my breath.

Taking a minute to use my invisibility spell, I could now safely approach any of the gray creatures without being seen.

I was wondering if Anfa was able to maintain her Joanie appearance, or if they already knew who and what she was. Capturing another of the *Teacher's* folk, would be a rich gift for the perverted Feng Xi.

The unlikely metallic sound of machinery suddenly shot through the dead air.

During my research, I found reports of unearthing pieces of equipment after the fires were out in old China Town. Authorities of the day stated they were used by drug lords to torture victims.

There were several piles of rotted wood on both sides of the collapsed warrens. I spotted what was left of several ornately carved couches, crushed almost flat by the fallen dirt and debris. They looked a lot like pictures of the opium dens. Customers, like lizards in the sun, would lounge upon bed-like furnishings for hours, or days, sucking at opium pipes, drifting into oblivion. A twisted nursery for the addicted.

There was a large mirror lying on its back, in the remnants of a house likely used for a different kind of addiction. The rotted, red velvet curtains, were heaped together like vast pools of coagulated blood. They were next to the shattered mirror in its overly ornate gilded frame. Strangely, the mirror had a large rock piercing its middle, making the fractures look like a sun burst under my green flame.

I crept forward, following the drag marks until I saw they abruptly stopped at a slight elbow in the tunnel road.

Wonder what this means, I was thinking when I heard the sound of the engine again, somewhere up ahead.

That mystery would have to wait to be solved. I had to locate Anfa before Feng Xi had her in his torture chamber.

Now that the marks had ended, I had to rely on my senses to pick up the trail again. I sniffed until my nose almost clogged up from the dust motes that clung to the thick air I stirred in my passing.

I turned down my breathing a few notches, so I wouldn't be distracted as I listened to the depths of the tunnels. With all the fallen structure littering the ground, my hearing was pinging off too many objects and was only confusing my search.

Just as I was about to turn around and retrace my steps to see if I'd missed something, I heard a burst of maniacal laughter.

It seemed to be coming from further down the passage way.

The gray men would be unlikely to find anything humorous in life and Anfa didn't seem prone to uncontrollable peals of joy.

Besides, this happy outpouring had my skin crawling like it was trying to detach itself from me and run for cover.

I turned toward the direction of the abrasive cackling, tuning in with senses on maximum alert.

That's when I detected the voice of the Joanie imposter.

"Uh-oh," I breathed out, like someone had wrapped cold hands around my throat.

Chapter 61

They arrived at the marked hillside nearly an hour after they went their separate ways. Jason drove the car he had rented, observing all speed limits, which put his passenger into a bad mood. Good for demon fighting, bad for Jason.

Cathlene's Mom seemed distant, then, as if she had slipped into her Inner Eye, the way Cathlene often did when on a case. He wondered if she was looking for the dragon Cathlene told him they had painted on the stiff, waiving grasses.

They exited the car and her mom took command of the operation.

"Jason, dear, the wooded area our girl is being held is shielded behind a mirage charm. It's right in front of us, but all we can see is the next hill and open fields. I will use my own magic to remove this slight impediment."

He wisely said nothing, allowing her to work her, "This and That" Magic without any annoying questions.

With a flourish of her hands, which he couldn't help wondering if she included to impress him, she began to unravel the spell.

She appeared to grab hold of the fabric of the mirage, sensing its fine edges and called out, *"Bain cnoc!"*

Having witnessed magical interventions over the years, the sudden appearance of the deeply wooded area didn't give Jason a jolt.

"So, there you have it my dear, our entrance," she said, giving him one more chance to redeem himself and be awed.

"Fantastic, Brighid! Better get going before we lose the light. I'll go straight in like we planned while you circle behind the cabin."

He looked over at her quickly and added, "I'm glad to be working this with you, Brighid. I wouldn't want to face these guys on my own."

She looked very pleased with his admission of needing her to make things work.

They split up as soon as the thick trees closed off any sunlight.

It was like a preternatural forest under the gathering gloom of the branches. Jason shrugged his shoulders, unconsciously trying to lift the burden of darkness.

He lost sight of his companion five minutes into the woods. He suddenly felt very alone. Even though he had grown up a true mountain man, roaming the wild terrain and tree-covered mountains, Jason had a healthy respect for all the surprises nature could throw at you. He'd seen many a scary thing pop out of shadows just like these when he hung out with me.

After another ten minutes, he began to feel a slight chill. There was no wind and no bird calls or the expected scurrying feet among the fallen leaves and brush.

As he went deeper into the tangle of trees and scraggly bushes, it got cold enough that he regretted not wearing his heavier jacket. He stopped to take a slow look around at the area to see if he recognized anything from his first vision. As he concentrated on the ground around him, he saw a wide swath of broken and crushed weed stems, tangled in brownish clumps. Something, or someone, had passed through there. He figured it had been several hours ago, which coincided with Joanie's being taken.

Jason squatted down on his haunches, settling comfortably like a large ape in a wild forest. This was *his* environment after all. He cleared his head to force himself to remember that vision of the cabin.

It felt like the lights were diming just before the movie started. His eye glazed over and his breathing became shallow; his heart rate slowed.

The cabin jumped out of his reverie, looking as empty as in the first vision. The front door opened and there was Cathlene...*how can that* be, he thought, frowning at the mystery.

Then, just as he remembered it, the large dragon came around the corner and right at her. Just like in his vision she never looked afraid of the beast, which seemed crazy since it didn't appear too friendly. But this was no vision and there wasn't a minute to lose. He had a hunch about the "Cathleen" he was seeing. Getting to his booted feet, he was now in hunting mode.

Chapter 62

Well, well, Brighid thought to herself as she saw the cabin begin to take form through the thick spread of tree limbs. Mom studied the small structure very carefully, using her discerning Inner Eye.

She was never one to rush into any new situation like a novice wizard. Taking on a vampire's thug would be no real challenge; facing the ancient vampire needed more magical finesse.

"One door in front, three life forms inside, but only one of this realm, Joanie." She was speaking softly into the stillness around her, when she heard the snap of a twig off to her right.

She crouched down and covered herself with the heavy moss and detritus from the forest floor. Suddenly, she was transformed into a medium sized-boulder, lying snug, up against some thick, fallen tree limbs and smaller branches.

She loved doing these tricks, but hoped she wouldn't have long to wait before she could shake off the scratchy grit. There was a louder rustling now, like the shuffling of a card deck, as heavy feet pushed through the undergrowth of the woods.

Her breathing was taken down to the speed of a bubble rising in a mud pool. She wanted nothing to give away her position. She was still several yards away from the back of the cabin, but the hearing of most Magic Users was as keen as a shark's ability to smell blood in the water, several miles off.

She was brought sharply back into focus when two large splayed feet stopped near her bogus rock formation. They were very red and covered in interlocking scales. Three thick toes ended in long curved talons.

The feet moved out of her range of vision, but then a long spiked tail swished into view.

Hmm, she thought, as she stoically continued her boulder state.

The scales, the tail, the size is surely very large. I do believe we are seeing a Dragon here!

She was still as the stone she was impersonating until the creature moved off. Gradually Brighid dropped the spell and all the boulder materials fell off as silently as a whisper among the trees.

The back of the dragon receded down the slight incline behind the cabin. There was no sound in the woods. Only the soft swish of the heavy tail and the muffled thump of broad feet, stirred the heavy silence.

I don't like the woods, so unnatural, she thought, while she moved soundlessly in the wake of the red monster. *And that is no beautiful Dragon of our ancestors. Nay, what we have here is a beastie fashioned by some Dark Magic.*

She brought her attention into a keener focus. Her hyper-sensitive hearing picked up a voice that was as familiar to her as her own daughter's. *There you are, our Joanie.* She wanted to move forward, but the dragon seemed to be guarding the small back door of the cabin.

They must be expecting company. They shall have a wee bit of a surprise instead.

Her only way forward was through the dragon. It didn't seem particularly bright as dragons go and had taken no notice of the shift in the air around its body. Mom called down a powerful Druid spell upon the creature, taking care not to use the wrong inflections on the complex wording.

Farc feath fiadaha.

The dragon was immediately immobile and invisible to the mortal eye. Mom used a wind binding to drag it up the hill, where she said a quick prayer to the *Mother,* sending the inert creature to the Dark Pit.

Oh good, she was thinking with a broad smile. *Now, I get to play a new part in this investigation...and red is a powerful shade for dragons.*

Chapter 63

I was certain I had heard Anfa speaking in Joanie's voice, but couldn't make out all the words.

It didn't make sense unless the Colossus was now the one in charge.

I was hoping that was the case, until a piercing scream of agony filled the tunnel, bouncing back and forth in the stale air until it faded to a murmur.

Peering into the murky passage, a building jumped out of the shadows. I wasn't expecting anything but more ruble. Looking further ahead, I saw other similar structures, more like crude lean-to shacks, but standing, unlike anything else down there.

I stopped moving and heard the same sharp peal of laughter. This time, it sounded like gurgling water through a crusty pipe. It was time to find out.

The heavy clicking of moving chain links hit my ears as soon as I passed through the opening of the crude building.

In one corner I saw a machine turning a spoked wheel very slowly. This wouldn't have been too alarming except my friend Anfa was attached to it!

She had slipped out of her Joanie persona and back into her Colossus Faerie self. Her arms were outstretched in an agonizing pull against the gold chains that held her wrists, ankles and middle. There was no apparent wrenching on her limbs until the wheel began its downward turn.

Anfa's muscled arms and legs were fighting against her restraints, but to no avail. Whoever did this knew that Faeries were unable to bear the touch of a dead man's gold upon their skin.

Down here, there would be lots of that to plunder; stripped from the long decayed bodies of the Chinese gamblers, madams, and patrons of the prolific opium dens.

I could see the chains had torn grooves into the skin where they bound her. A thin stream of yellow blood was dripping down her arms and feet and then, reversing itself as the wheel turned.

The room was empty except for an ancient looking device and the wheel it turned in excruciatingly slow circles.

A single gray man slouched nearby, one hairless arm draped almost casually over the crude, but effective machine. I had no doubt Feng had restored this torture device and I immediately set about disabling it.

I threw a spell like a wrench into the teeth of the works, jamming it up nicely and causing the wheel to stop. Unfortunately, it didn't stop with Anfa standing, but with her head down and gravity pulling mercilessly at her body.

As Faeries go, the Colossus are known for their sturdy, durable bodies. They have a reputation for endurance under most adverse circumstances. But this wasn't going well for Anfa. From the deep oozing abrasions she had already sustained, it looked like she'd been attached to the wheel for some time now. There was one other being in the torture chamber, one who was obviously enjoying Anfa's plight.

When the wheel stopped turning, Feng Xi screamed like a cornered Tasmanian devil.

"You stupid …creature! I have not… told you to stop the wheel!" he gasped between words.

His anger must have gotten the better of him, because he dispatched the stupefied gray man with one jagged bolt of red lightening. A putrid odor of fried blood was added to the smell of decay clinging to the gritty air in the room.

I used the distraction to throw a powerful *Knotted Hand* spell at Feng, knocking him off his silk slippers and onto the dirt floor. His boney legs kicked feebly, trying to free themselves from the heavy silk robe.

He was beginning to shout his own counterspell. I had to act fast. A second round of *Knotted Hands* was now pounding him around the head and mid-section. I threw an extra *Hand* in there to muffle the curse and diffuse its power.

I saw Anfa's eyes turn a bright green. She knew I was there. Why the wizard hadn't sensed me was a mystery, but he was likely too engrossed in watching another living being suffer.

I focused my attention back to Feng Xi, watching for a second to be sure the *Knotted Hands* were doing the job of beating the snot out of him!

When I was certain he was being suitably maltreated, I began to release Anfa from her restraints.

I shouted a spell for unbinding and watched the gold links of the chains melt into yellow puddles on the floor.

Even though they were bound tightly around the Faerie's wrists and ankles, it appeared her mid-section took the worst of the punishment. Being exposed to the constant shifting of the golden chain had all but peeled the skin from Anfa's slim torso.

I almost gagged seeing how raw the silvery skin was on her midriff, but the seeping line of yellow was most distressing. I knew as a Faerie of the first rank of power, Anfa could heal herself given time and rest. Two things in short supply.

Feng was still thrashing about on the floor. He managed to free himself of the *Knotted Hand* covering his mouth.

I was lowering Anfa to the floor when a red bolt of fire shot past my ear and hit the spot she'd been hanging seconds before.

I unceremoniously dropped her and put up a shield around us. Feng still couldn't see me, but he knew another Magic User was present and that was enough.

His next bolt hit our shield squarely, reversing its course and sending it back to the struggling wizard.

The Hands were still getting in a few jabs when Feng dropped his own shell-like shield over his body. He was struggling to get to his feet when I noticed the staff he was clutching in his gnarled and yellow hand.

While he was using it to support himself as he regained his footing, I realized this was no ordinary wizard's staff.

It was an extraordinarily long thigh bone. The length and girth indicated it was plucked from the skeleton of a very tall, very strong being.

The bone was as yellowed with age as the Wizard. Since Feng was slight of stature, he was able to use this to right himself easily. His wide smile revealed a partial row of small teeth, deeply stained, some black and rotting in his mouth. Even with my own shield in place, I detected the odor of corruption radiating from his body like an awful sun.

Feng seemed to have regained not just his feet, but his ability to locate another Magic User. He knew it wasn't Anfa, lying on the raised platform where the wheel now looked like a game found at a carnival. That left a Wizard who was using an invisibility spell.

With unerring accuracy, Feng stared at the space I was presently occupying. He shot another red bolt, smiling when it bounced off my shield.

"So, there you are, Wushen. I believe we have reached a stale-mate."

He had a sickly rattling wheeze in his voice, sounding like he was trying to take deep gulps of air to fill his withered lungs.

"Our meetings have been quite non- productive..."

I believed Anfa and I were safe enough behind my shield spell that I could show myself. I dropped my invisibility charm.

He quickly reached out his arm and hand with the bone staff and before I could say, "Uh- oh," Feng had called up another creature, uglier than the gray men.

I called fire to my hands. I knew this new demon spawn and felt an involuntary shudder, making my shield waver slightly. It came from the blackest corner of the Dark Pit of the Sleepless Dead. This was one of the *Geilt*, beings of fabled Druid lore.

My dad had often referred to these creatures as the "madmen of the wilds". They shunned any contact with other beings. Unfortunately for me, they had Shamanistic powers they could use when provoked.

I could easily see this *Geilt* had taken an instant dislike to me and the fire that burned brightly in my hands. My shield would hold, but my fire would be useless on this side of it!

I picked up movement in my peripheral vision and taking a quick look saw Anfa struggling to her knees.

She looked up at me with a burning hate as she spoke the name, "Feng Xi."

The bleeding from the various parts of her body had stopped. The only sign of her torture was a dimming of her aura from its slivery tones to an ashy black.

In her rush to get to Feng she came into immediate contact with my shield.

"Anfa, we have another to deal with now."

She followed my eye back to the strangely formed *Geilt*.

His eyes shifted between us. They seemed as void of natural life as the untamed woodlands it roamed, before it met its fate in the Dark Pit.

Feng Xi must have caused its transition from its wilds, to the Dark Pit, knowing he could use the *Geilt's* Magical powers in his evil schemes.

I noticed the *Geilt* was beginning to slip into something more comfortable.

Its hunched form, covered with a thick pelt of thick tar-black hair, began to shift and grow like a champion weight lifter.

It already had a head the size and shape of a deformed large pumpkin, left too long on the vine. Now, this knobby, empty gourd, became elongated until the face was altered by a long, toothy snout.

The dark body hair bristled and stirred and the *Geilt* suddenly sprouted what I wished I had at the moment; another set of arms. These were massive in muscle bulk and ended in spiked clubs rather than hands and fingers.

Feng stood back and waited until the transformation was complete. He seemed to enjoy watching ugly become grotesque. There was a serene smile on his thin purplish lips.

"Do you feel safe now, Wushen?" He was still gasping to suck in more of the sour air.

I didn't want to give him an answer. He was scrutinizing my face closely. Looking over at the Colossus as she gracefully rose from her knees to stand beside me, I said, "Anfa, he can't understand your language, so we'll speak only your tongue."

She blinked and answered, "Very good Wizard. But there is something I had meant to tell you, before I was taken."

The *Geilt* looked like he was moving toward my shield to test its strength.

"Better speak quickly, our friend is getting ready to make his move."

"We have been under the *Teacher's* observation since we entered this City of Death."

"What does that mean, Anfa? He's watching us, now?" I took a quick look around me.

With those questions hanging between us, the *Geilt* moved directly in front of our position. Feng Xi glided close to his hairy side.

I didn't much like his look of confidence as he withdrew yet another artifact, possibly from either this buried China Town, or from his own ancient loot.

"This was a little token taken from the battle of Clontarf. From your own...ancestor, Wushen. Brian...Boru."

His robe fell away from his withered, jaundiced-colored arm, to reveal a large gold pendent with the seal of the High King, the Golden Harp.

This meant Feng had taken his trophy upon the King's death. I was fairly certain the Lady Bao had been instrumental in retrieving it for him.

"So now I hold...a special key, Wushen...a key to your...Powers."

Before I could call him a robber of the dead, a crime of the lowest of beings, he reached out his bony, yellow hand and touched my shield.

Dad had taught me that using a wizard's own source of magic against them could reverse, or even corrupt it. He also said not to worry over that possibility, as it was so rarely achieved.

Ha! I thought, as I watched the spell for my shield begin to unravel like a ball of yarn.

Feng's eyes began glowing with the power now surging from the pendent through his wasted veins. I saw his growing excitement as he watched my shield dissolve under his attack.

I chanted a counterspell to grab and hold the shield until I could do something else to protect us. A sound like the ice crackling in a water glass penetrated the silence, as the *Geilt's* club wielding arm smashed a neat hole just above Anfa's head.

Chapter 64

Jason made a short reconnaissance of the area around the cabin. So far, he hadn't seen any sign of Cathlene's mom. He did notice a large swath of trampled ground directly behind and slightly above the cabin.

What the heck did that, he thought, as he slowly looked over the ground for more signs of activity.

His heart was beginning to beat faster as he felt the nearness of something or someone else, circling the cabin. He quickly and quietly made it back around to the hill directly overlooking the cabin; the hill of his vision he realized with a start.

On some level of awareness he understood that paranormal activity was taking place inside the rough-looking shack. That's when he heard the scream and froze.

He knew the next sequence of events by heart; Cathelene would exit the cabin alone, and the dragon would be coming around the corner from the back.

Sure enough, the heavy cabin door was flung open and she stepped out into the twilight of the woods.

Jason shouted as loudly as he could, "Get back inside, Cathleen!"

She looked up as if searching for the caller. He yelled again.

"Cathleen, run! The dragon…"

The cabin door opened again and this time Joanie stood in the pale light. She seemed to stagger forward toward her friend. Jason began looking around himself, frantic to find something he could use to help defend them. He ended by snatching up a heavy branch and taking off at a run.

There was another scream from the cabin just as he planted himself beside them. It raised the hairs on his neck and he knew it wasn't human.

The dragon was standing several feet off to their left and made no effort to attack.

Jason took a breath to ask, "Cathleen, how did you get here? Who just yelled in there?'

He grabbed her arm to focus her attention and felt a nasty shock zap him like the end of a live wire.

"What the…?"

"Calm yourself, mortal. The scream is merely the mewling of Lady Bao's driver. He took offense at being bested by a mere girl--little did he know."

A mirthless laugh, sounding more like a rumble, changed "Cathleen's" face from its natural paleness, to a rosy red.

She looked away from Jason's questioning face in a dismissive way. He was beginning to get a little irritated and even more curious at her nonchalant attitude.

Cathleen now turned her full attention to the dragon that had inched into fire-breathing range.

"Brighid the Beautiful! I greet you!"

Jason looked from Cathleen to the dragon, and back again to his girlfriend. His look of an impending outburst must have stirred something in the dragon.

While a small stream of smoke escaped its gaping jaws, the voice of Cathlene's mom could be heard speaking in the old Druid tongue.

Thinking mom had been swallowed whole, Jason stared open-mouth when she suddenly stood in front of them.

There was little to be said except, "Wow!" Jason looked over at Cathleen with wonder and amazement still playing across his face.

"Did you know all along it was your mom?"

"Ridiculous thought, mortal. My mom indeed!"

As suddenly as Brighid shed her scales, Cathleen alarmingly began to quiver. Her skin coloring changed from rose, to a deep puce, and then to a dead white. It then sloughed away like wet tissue.

Jason stood transfixed as he looked at Crom, the God of Storms, where his love had been standing.

"Joanie, dear lassie," Brighid was saying as she went to the dumbfounded girl, draping a protective arm around her shoulders.

Joanie hadn't spoken or moved since leaving the cabin. Her mouth had dropped open and quivered slightly without making a sound.

"You have been through quite an ordeal I dare say, but all is well, pet."

As she held her tightly, Cathlene's mom began a whispered charm of healing to help erase the last several hours of terror.

Remembering the driver, she looked over at Crom saying, "Would you care to remove the vampire from this realm, Crom, while I explain to these young people a bit of what's happening?"

The God of Storms smiled broadly and vanished from sight. Jason knew exactly where he was when the driver let out another long wail that seemed to be swallowed up by the earth itself.

"Jason, apologies, dear. I didn't realize Crom had assumed Cathleen's persona until I saw her, or rather him, step outside. A mother always knows their own child, you see."

"I understand, Brighid, but perhaps you can explain to us the dragon role you just played. Scared the life out of me!"

"Well, dear, Cathleen had been visited by one of Feng Xi's avatars as you already know; it was this dragon. I found it lurking about the rear of the cabin and after dispatching it, decided to conceal myself using its form."

Joanie finally seemed to wake up to what was happening around her.

"Brighid? Jason? Did I just dream about a dragon and some kind of god person?"

Brighid hugged her and assured her everything was under control and she was safe.

"But where's Cathleen? I think Lady Bao has her."

Mom chuckled saying, "Not to worry yourself, love. Cathleen is probably mopping the floor up with Feng at this moment!"

Chapter 65

I was holding onto my spell for dear life, literally. The hairy beast Feng Xi had conjured raised his club-like arm for another blow against my shield. It was already fractured around a small hole he'd made; causing an arcing of energy around the opening

If I lose the shield, I'll put Anfa in a dome of safety and fight with fire I was thinking.

Feng stopped the creature, raising a boney hand. I saw his fingernails were long, and thick, curving back on themselves like tusks on aging elephants.

I looked over at Anfa and felt something was different about her, but didn't have time to sort it out.

Feng was watching me closely, his thin lips twitching in a sneer. He took the King's medallion, a relic I knew was a *creadair* because it possessed magical power, and placed it against the shield's pulsing outer skin.

There was an enormous sizzling sound reminiscent of fries being dumped into a basket of hot oil.

The fissures radiating from the small hole flew apart, scattering in a rainbow from the golden light of the pendant. These dancing motes of Magic were immediately absorbed into the blackness of the room.

I was ready for this. I already had Green Fire making jittery shadows on the walls around us. I had learned a few tricks from dad that were far outside the usual Druid mix he practiced. Now I drew upon one of the best.

Throwing my arms up as if surrendering, I hurled my fire like a lasso and wrapped it around Feng's creature. Its bristling black hair burst into dark green flame upon contact. After a minute of the beast beating himself senseless trying to put out the fire, the creature was reduced to a smoldering ash pile.

I watched long enough to see it extinguished and sent another spell to open the earth beneath the remains, sending them back to the Pit.

I knew Feng would be expecting his beast to be expendable and would not be made vulnerable by its loss. While I focused Fire on his beast he saw his opening.

Before I could react, his right arm elongated like a piece of soft taffy, shooting across the short distance to my exposed body.

A sharp pain hit my mid-section, radiating outward until I doubled over. I was on my knees with my head down and my hands empty of the sacred Green Fire.

Mother, help me, I prayed as I desperately tried to fight for control of my magic.

Feng stepped closer. With that cruel curving fingernail, stained like an old tombstone, he moved my hair from the side of my face, where it hung in a long auburn curtain.

"I would...see your pain...young Wizard. My...greatest pleasure!" He gurgled out a contemptuous laugh.

I was struggling to get my breath as a searing pain moved throughout my body. It felt as if I was being roasted from the inside, out. There was a long howl of agony and I wondered if he was now torturing Anfa. Then I realized... I was the one screaming!

This isn't going wel,l I thought, as I gritted my teeth against the next flare I expected to tear through me.

The small room was beginning to darken even more when my consciousness started to fade. The only thing I saw clearly was Feng's hideous smile as he watched my agony increase.

Anfa was no longer visible in my peripheral vision as things clouded over.

My father, Liam always told me, "Use the tools you can count on lass, if all else fails!"

The only thing I could remember with my insides turning to molten lava was a spell dad had used to stop a particularly nasty *Athelmort*.

This *Shape Shifter* had been terrorizing a village, when my father was a young wizard apprentice in Ireland.

He was assisting my grandfather when the *Shifter* cleverly changed into a small insect and flew into his father's ear canal. His father was batting his head and yelling for Liam to do something before the insect bored through to his brain.

The only thing he could think of was one of the first spells he'd ever learned.

Standing back from his flailing father, Liam yelled, "Branan Bain!"

Instantly a black raven was sitting on his father's shoulder and with his long beak he extracted the deadly insect from his ear. With a jerking motion of its head, the insect disappeared down its gullet.

 Liam's father suffered only bruising he inflicted upon himself trying to dislodge the deadly bug.

I now called on the raven to do some necessary diversionary antics on Feng Xi.

The raven I called forth was huge. It was so black it blended into the shadows of the room, until it twitched its head around toward the Dark Wizard.

The bird's eyes glowed like twin search lights as they clearly fixed on Feng Xi.

He was slow to react at first, but threw his hands up in a defensive gesture. In doing so he hurled the golden amulet away and onto the floor near my feet.

Luckily for my feathered champion, the bird had ducked its large head to peck repeatedly at Feng's legs and lower body. On a normal mortal being, there would have been blood pouring from the deep wounds. But Feng wasn't normal, or wholly mortal. He quickly began healing the gashes and retaliated with a gush of carbolic acid he belched up from his withered gut.

It hit the tall raven squarely in its massive chest, quickly burning through its black plumage, but before the bird was eaten whole by the acid, it made a leap and grabbed the slight Feng in its talons; lifting him off the ground. The mortally injured bird opened its wings to their full expanse and carried Feng Xi out of the torture chamber.

I could hear Feng screaming curses into the dense night of the underground city. I knew he wouldn't be contained for long and quickly went to Anfa who was crouched down with her back to the whole scene.

"Anfa, are you alright?" I asked, as I placed a hand on the muscled shoulder of the Faerie.

With a jolt that was nearly as frightening as seeing the raven consumed by the foul smelling acid, I jumped back a foot, staring into the handsome face of the *Teacher*.

Chapter 66

Cathelene's mom and I stood outside the cabin in a quickly descending twilight. The woods were already in deeper shadows as the sun moved off toward its resting place, but now it grew chilled too.

I took my jacket off and put it around Joanie's shoulders as she was dressed in the usual tourist T-shirt and jeans.

Crom had returned to the cabin at mom's invitation, dispatching the vampire who'd been guarding Joanie. Because he was a being of Lady Bao's making, there was a pretty good chance the Lady wouldn't be too pleased with his return to the Pit.

It was only a matter of minutes before Crom reappeared and from the broad smile on his blueish lips, he was pleased with his handiwork.

"All is well here, dear lady," he said to Cathlene's mom.

"I have sent the vermin scuttling back to the Pit of the Sleepless Dead and in so doing, have fulfilled my promise to the *Teacher* to perform one good deed on your daughter's behalf."

"We are most grateful for your intervention Crom Croich and will not detain you in this realm further."

It was those words which seemed to release the God of Storms from further delay on this plain. He simply vanished. The three mortals stood blinking in the murky light that was beginning to close like shades around them.

Joanie seemed more herself by then. It appeared she had not been physically hurt, but seemed edgy and ready to bolt at any moment.

I had been studying Cathlene's best friend from the corner of my eye.

"I think we'd better be heading back to China Town, Brighid. Cathleen may need some help."

She was quick to approve leaving. She was concerned that the vampire, Lady Bao, may have rejoined her master, Feng Xi since she didn't return to the cabin.

"You are absolutely right, Jason. We need to get into the underground city as I fear our Cathleen may be meeting head-on with the vampire and her Master.

Taking a long look at Joanie, Jason checked to be sure she was up to a fast run through the woods and back to their car. Brighid simply grabbed both of them by a hand and used a wind charm to speed up the process.

Forty-five minutes later Jason was pulling into the garage across from the Grant Hotel. As they began getting out, Cathlene's mom stopped moving, one foot already on the running board of the rented SUV.

"Wait. After considering this situation, I believe there is a point of entry from the hotel into the underground China Town."

"What makes you think that, Brighid?" Joanie asked, sitting back down in the back seat.

"It was something only mentioned in passing, but our allies, though few in number, have allowed several interventions on our behalf. As you've already seen, the God of Storms himself has been able to lend us help at crucial moments.

When I first arrived at the Grant, the clerk behind the desk…"

"The tiny older Chinese lady?" Joanie interjected.

Jason sat quietly listening.

"The same one, lass. There were other staff milling about the front desk, but she managed to drop a well-placed hint, when I asked about places of *significance* in China Town that I would not want to miss touring.

Her words were most instructive."

Jason blurted out "What did she say?"

Mom looked pleased as she exited the car with them following suit immediately. They looked like a small group of tourists waiting on a street car as they huddle closer together.

"She told me, *"The Grant is happy to show the way."*

After a moment to reflect on this puzzling message, Jason said, "Let's get to the Grant cellars. Now!"

They entered the lobby to the hotel and strolled casually toward the restaurant as if planning to eat a late lunch.

Mom had shared that the old Chinese lady had looked over toward the restaurant when she made that cryptic comment.

Jason spoke in hushed tones. "We'll go straight to the back, and through the kitchen. If there is an entry to the cellars, it would be accessible from there."

They hurried back toward the last table near the swinging kitchen doors. There were no other people in the place, not even a waitress to see them before heading for the kitchen.

They bunched up almost immediately when they encountered a cook wearing a greasy, stained apron over his embroidered oriental jacket and dark, blousy pants.

He was lounging at a tiny round table in a corner of the fragrant kitchen; a cigarette dangling from his lips and holding a steaming cup of tea. No other staff were present.

He jumped up when they entered and said, "Hey, what you doing here? This not allowed. Go away soon!"

Jason tensed, ready to clock the guy if need be, but Brighid was mumbling a few choice words and he instantly sat back down and closed his eyes.

"There we go! He'll sleep for a much needed hour's rest and we'll be totally forgotten when he awakens."

She looked pleased with the spell's effectiveness and continued, "The doorway is likely behind one of these tall cabinets. I'll have to move them."

As she was revving up a good wind charm, so Jason put up his hand and said, "Wait, Brighid. If I wanted to hide a passageway into the hotel, I'd put it in an uncomfortable, limited access, place. The walk-in freezer."

Chapter 67

"I'm sure your instincts are finely trained, Jason. Joanie, are you up to this next bit, lass?"

Joanie inhaled deeply before she answered. It was like she needed to fill her lungs with clean air that wasn't tainted with fear.

"I'm good to go. I just want us to find Cathleen before the wizard teams back up with the vampire! I've seen what that creepy Lady Bao can do and I can't even imagine what Feng Xi can do!"

Jason handed a long carving knife to Joanie saying "I don't want any of us to go in there without some kind of defensive weapon."

He grabbed hold of a heavy wooden rolling pin and in answer to Joanie's questioning look said, "Feels just like my favorite flashlight."

Jason had leaned into the walk-in freezer and found a wall light to switch on. There was an eerie, bluish light radiating off the many shelves and boxes. The frigid air immediately began to suck the warmth out of their bodies as they stepped deeper into the large compartment.

They each began scanning the room for a possible entryway into the hidden China Town.

Jason touched Brighid's shoulder lightly.

"Do you think you could detect our access point using your special gifts?"

She smiled at his sweet reference to her powerful brand of magic.

"Of course, dear, but though I believe you are right in choosing this place as the portal to below, Feng Xi would have placed a strong ward over it to keep it from discovery. I need to search that out first, and then we can proceed. Patience dear."

She turned back to her methodical scan, using her Inner Eye to identify any Dark Magic clinging to the cold walls or floors.

"Ah ha!" she said softly, but clearly as her companions turned as one and looked over at her crouching form.

"What did you find, Brighid?" Joanie asked, the fog of her words hanging briefly in the chilled air.

Jason had squatted down next to her.

"Where is it?" he asked.

"I'll need to move this shelving just a tad…" she said, as her hand swept a ton of boxed goods and the heavy wooden shelves over about three feet.

"There!" she said with a satisfied look on her face. "No one will be the wiser as I'll move it all back when we're through the hatch, so to speak."

Another sweep of her hand and several floor boards pushed back into one another like an accordion.

The top two steps of what must have been a steep staircase, were revealed in the hazy light of the freezer.

"This is it. Let's stay close together. Remember, we're no help to Cathleen if we get caught." Jason's words hung between them like warning flags on a ship.

"Or worse." Joanie finished his thought.

After all three were on the stairs, mom turned and repositioned the heavy food shelving and floor boards. As they descended, Jason took out a small pen light, but it was barely able to show the next step. Mom mumbled a few words and a hallo of green surrounded the small group.

"Good." This was Jason's only response to the light as they continued down. Joanie felt like she was walking under a cloud of lightning bugs.

Mom counted thirteen steps to the bottom. The light from her hallo had shown how rotted through they were in places and rickety at best. They were likely built after the quake as a way to continue illicit business and trade when the dust settled.

The little group was transfixed for a minute. They stood, staring into what appeared to be the outskirts of a devastated town as far as the light extended before it hit a wall of blackness.

Flattened shops and businesses were stacked on one another like lovers in a tumbled bed. Many of the wooden structures leaned against their neighbors in a cataclysmic domino event.

There was complete silence in this dead settlement; only the dust motes stirred by the living intruders moved in the glow of mom's hallo of light.

"We need to move out," Jason whispered to the women. It sounded like a shout in the dense stillness.

Mom whispered back "I'll lead my dear. You cover our backside."

Not waiting for any disagreement, she started to walk down a roughly made dirt lane; no more than a wide path through the mounds of debris.

Jason took up the rear position. He felt a distinct prickling run up and down his arms as they went deeper into the jumble of the China Town of 1906.

There's been Magic Users here he was thinking.

The hairs stirred on his arms and neck and he had the sensation of being watched. He kept looking back over his shoulders, but all he saw were the tracks they were leaving in the well-aged dust.

"Stop," he whispered.

He moved to Brighid's side with Joanie quickly following suit.

"Brighid, I think we are being followed. How about I take up point and check for tracks and you guard our rear which feels pretty vulnerable just now?"

"Indeed, dear. I have been aware of another life form traveling along with us, but I don't think we're under threat from it. It's doing reconnaissance I believe. But, I agree that I should keep our exposed position safe from attack."

She moved immediately to take Jason's place as rear guard.

Joanie felt better knowing she was sandwiched between two determined and strong fighters. She regretted her own position was weaker by far, but it matched theirs in resolve.

They moved deeper into the unrelenting darkness, only faintly illuminated now since mom decided to mute the glow from the hallo.

They could barely make out the shambles of rotted wooden buildings, crushed by the weight of tons of dirt and an eon of time.

Jason suddenly held up his hand to signal a stop.

Once more they huddled in the gloom, trying to make-out one another's faces.

"There are standing buildings straight ahead, and I have a prickly feeling in my gut that they aren't empty."

Brighid didn't speak for a moment, and both her companions waited for her comments.

"We have a more immediate threat, my dears. I have identified the being that has been shadowing us since we came below. It is directly to our left now and trying desperately to stay out of the light from my hallo. I will now deal with this rascal while you two move ahead. I'll catch you up in a wee bit."

Before either of her companions could object, she vanished from sight.

"Vanishing spell," Jason said under his breath.

Joanie nodded her head in agreement. She'd seen this magic performed hundreds of times.

"Let's get going, Joanie. We know Brighid has this!"

As they moved off they heard a guttural sound like the warning growl of a dog ready to attack. They didn't pause to investigate, but were keenly aware of every muffled sound coming from the darkness behind them.

After five minutes of walking, the pair stopped when Jason took Joanie's arm and leaned into her ear.

"Did you hear something?"

"I thought I heard someone laugh, but it didn't sound like a happy laugh; it was just creepy. Know what I mean?"

"Yeah, I do. Let's get off the middle of this trail and stay close to the rubble piles."

They began to find roughly built structures as they walked toward what could have been the center of the ruined city.

Besides the wet smell of rotting wood and the miasma of odors coming off the decaying rubble, there was a smell more familiar to both of them.

As an Emergency Room nurse, Joanie was very familiar with the smell of blood. Its sharp, tangy iron odor clung to the stale air of the lifeless town they moved through.

"Jason, I…"

"I know. I smell it too. Just keep close to me; we'll stay in the shadows as much as possible."

They hadn't gone ten feet when they clearly heard Cathlene's voice calling out in the tongue of the ancients. It was clear she was using some kind of spell.

They froze in mid-step while a series of blood-chilling screams bounced around the thick walls of dirt and debris.

Unconsciously trying to escape the ear-shattering shrieks, they crouched low to the ground. They were huddled there when a gigantic black bird soared low over their heads like a missile. Gawking at this midnight apparition, they spotted the ancient Chinese man, clamped securely in the deadly talons of the creature.

The whoosh of air as it passed over the crouching figures, caused the loose dirt to fly up, enveloping them in a gritty cloud. They covered their eyes and mouths with their shirts, but the grit of dust still filtered through, bringing on fits of coughing and gasping for breath.

Jason reached out an arm to grab Joanie before he could lose her in the aftermath of the dust storm. He found her as she stood up and was shaking off several inches of dark grit out of her hair and off her clothes.

"I think we have Cathleen to thank for that" she gasped out with a small laugh.

"I think that bird was in trouble, Joanie. Did you see its chest feathers? Looked like something had been gnawing on him."

"Actually, I smelled it when it shot out of the dark. Did it really have some old Chinese guy in its talons like a carry-out dinner?"

Jason was bent over trying to use his fingers to brush out the dirt from his thick curly hair. He didn't need it getting into his eyes at a critical moment.

"I'm thinking we'll get that answer up ahead, Joanie. Let's go find Cathleen."

Chapter 68

I was staring at the perfect, muscular form of the *Teacher*. He was as handsome as I remembered. I didn't know how, or when, he replaced Anfa during our journey to this dreadful tomb, but he had.

We stood staring into each other's eyes.

He watched me intensely. I unconsciously moved toward him, drawn by something magnetic in his eyes. When we were merely inches apart, it dawned on me.

"Quit trying to use your *hypnoglamour* on me, *Teacher*. I don't appreciate that kind of manipulation. And how did you find me? Where is Anfa?"

"Quiet yourself, valiant girl. All shall be explained." A small smile lifted the corners of his beautiful, full mouth.

"I have been in communication with Anfa since you began this journey to the dead city. I had already discerned its location and awaited your own entrance so that I might make the body exchange with Anfa.

I merely used the opportunity of her capture by the gray man, as you called it. I caused it to drop into a sleep state and then took over as its prisoner. Anfa is awaiting my further orders and will assist upon being called."

I didn't like his charade one bit. I figured he carried it out to gain entrance to Feng Xi's inner sanctum of torture. The fact that he allowed himself to be strung up as the victim, showed his single-minded purpose.

It dawned on me that I had ruined his plans by calling up the great black raven.

"You must be upset that Feng Xi was carried off by my bird, *Teacher*. If you had shared your presence sooner, it might have been avoided. Now, I don't know if he's been sent back to the Pit, or where the statue of the Red Dragon is either!"

I didn't care if he found my raised voice disrespectful. He deserved a good dressing down for his blowing my investigation.

The Red Dragon was still out there and with Feng possibly on the loose, things could definitely go south.

"Your giant raven will be destroyed by now. Feng will take the only route open to him back to the statue of the Red Dragon. Your biggest threat now is the vampire, Lady Bao who still walks these streets like a hunting cheetah."

I shuddered inwardly at that particular mental picture. I needed to find the vampire before she hooked up again with Feng Xi, if she hadn't already done so,

"*Teacher*, I know you want to rain your vengeance down on Feng Xi's head and I want that too. If you know where he's gone, you also know the location of the Red Dragon. I need to be there when you find Feng!"

He stood impassively watching me as I went on.

"The statue is mine to take, and my mother's, to return to the *Council of Green Wizards*. She is here by their direct command, to bring them the Red Dragon before any of the blood it holds can be used by the Dark Ones."

"I am aware of what you speak, Cathleen, but I fear there may be some on the *Council* who would use the drop of Dragon Blood for their own empowerment."

I didn't want to argue the finer points with him. I was anxious to learn what route he felt was open to Feng Xi since he apparently had escaped.

All I accomplished by conjuring the raven, was to remove Feng before he turned my insides to hot sludge. I hoped that didn't make me a craven coward, but self-preservation seemed more productive than becoming the "Late Witch of Appalachia".

I asked him again to tell me where Feng was headed.

"I will do better, Wizard. I will show you."

With a quick flourish of his hand, the *Teacher* opened a panoramic screen in the mote infested air of the torture chamber.

What jumped into view was a spit of sandy beach bordering what appeared to be a small island. There was dense, wild vegetation just a few yards from the shoreline, leading to some kind of path.

"Where is this place, *Teacher*?"

With another flourish of his hand he produced a rudimentary map that indicated the location of the island off the coastal the town, Half Moon Bay.

I came across that name when I was researching water routes that Feng could use to escape to China, if he got the chance. It was about a two hour drive from where I currently was, but then I did have other modes of transport if necessary.

"I want to go with you," I said firmly, hoping he'd catch on that I was in no mood to argue.

He studied my face closely, maybe looking for a crack in my resolve. He must have been satisfied that there was none.

He folded his well-muscled arms across his chest and said, "Absolutely, young Wizard."

I had begun to protest when I realized that he just agreed.

"Oh, OK then," I said lamely.

Just as we began a joint wind spell to move us out of the China Town catacombs, we both stopped and strained to listen to what was clearly two voices.

"Jason? Joanie?"

It was as if I'd fabricated them out of air.

"Oh, dear Mother, it's really you, Joanie," I said, running to where they stood in the doorway.

When I finally stopped hugging Joanie, Jason swept me into his arms, a public show of affection that would normally make me uncomfortable. Wizards tend to be a little prudish I've been told.

Jason, his arms still around me, said, "We heard you talking, love, that's how we found you back here."

He looked around asking, "Who was it and where'd they go?"

I spun around to look back at the empty space that the *Teacher* should have been occupying.

"He's gone! The *Teacher* was here. Now he's taken off without me!" I said, anger dripping from each word.

Jason and Joanie both knew about the *Teacher's* role in the effort to secure the statue of the Red Dragon and the vendetta he had sworn centuries past.

"Where's he gone, Cathleen?" Joanie asked, a frown creasing her forehead.

I didn't want to alarm them with my suspicions that the *Teacher* would try taking out Feng Xi and lady Bao by himself.

I remembered the *Teacher's* vague comment about the possibility that some on the *Council of Green Wizards* would be tempted to use the blood rather than destroy it.

But what about him? If he had the blood, there would be heavy retribution paid by the Dark Wizard and his Vampire Mistress and any other being, demon or deity.

And no one could ever stop him...ever!

Chapter 69

The three of us had begun making our way back to the entrance I found with Anfa earlier. Thinking about her stirred a curious notion in my head.

What if Anfa was never "Anfa"? What if the Teacher had assumed her persona from the beginning? It would have been easy to have the Colossus Faerie appear to me as the Teacher, while he posed as my special ally. He could learn everything we discovered and then be on hand to take over when Feng Xi was found.

I didn't like thinking he was capable of such devious planning, but the *Teacher* was a skilled and ruthless assassin and Feng was in his cross-hairs.

We were past several of the buildings I'd seen earlier, but something new had been added to the landscape.

There were several new piles of gray ash on either side of the dirt road. They seemed randomly placed and a few still sent thin plumes of an oily smoke into the sour air.

"Mom, where are you?"

I heard Joanie suck in her breath when mom suddenly appeared next to her.

"Sorry, pet. Didn't mean to startle you. We need to hurry, Cathleen. As I was roasting the gray men, Feng Xi released himself from the raven I presumed you conjured. In any case, he is in the wind."

Jason had not spoken since we left Feng's idea of a fun house. Now he took my arm and drew me away from the others.

He had an intense look on his face as he said, "This is it, love. This is where my second vision comes into play; I'm sure of it."

"You mean *us* in that little fishing boat and going to an island?"

"Yes and it still gives me the creeps when I remember it. Do you have any ideas where that island is located?"

"The *Teacher* told me just before he vanished. He said it's off the coast of Half Moon Bay, and I know where that is. I'm not sure about the actual location of that particular island though."

Jason took only a second to consider our quandary.

"Let's get ourselves to the town and ask around at the docks. The fisherman will have worked that stretch of ocean for miles. We can hire a boat to take us out," he said.

His confidence was contagious. When we walked back to where we'd left Joanie and mom, we explained our plan.

Naturally, mom had listened in on the whole conversation with her keen wizard's hearing, but clearly she approved since she raised no objections.

We decided we needed to drive to Half Moon Bay. It would give us all time to exchange stories about our experiences and make plans for our next move.

As usual, mom thought she should drive, but fortunately Jason impressed upon her this would be a bad time for getting a ticket. *She must really like him,* I thought, as he was still breathing through his nose and not a new set of gills.

Our trip took under two hours. While we pulled into the first open parking area near the docks, I noticed several small groups of men huddled together and occasionally pointing out to sea.

They seemed pretty engrossed with some kind of distraction. We walked up behind one group and were barely noticed. There was a heated discussion going on between two of the men, fisherman still holding rods and tackle boxes.

The biggest one had a shock of white hair, his face tanned to a nutty brown and lined from long hours squinting into the sun reflecting off of water.

He was nearly shouting at another burly looking man, though the other man merely stood, shaking his grizzled head in denial.

"I tell you, I know what I saw! It weren't no falling star, neither! It was like a streaking rocket is what it was."

That's when the speaker looked over at Jason for support of his statement.

"Hey, who the hell are you? You aint some kind of reporter are ya?"

Jason looked un-phased by the speaker's aggressive greeting.

"Actually, I'm a Sheriff. Care to tell me in detail what you saw, sir?"

The man immediately responded to Jason's authoritative air and seemed relieved to have a lawman on site.

He went on to describe how he and his buddy had been hauling in a good catch when "this comet thing zoomed close over us. Nearly took the top of my head off!"

Jason continued to question the group, looking for any others who might have witnessed the passing of the streaking object. I motioned mom and Joanie to move back from the group.

"Let's let them all think Jason is investigating the sighting. I don't think they really noticed us, or they just thought we were nosy tourists."

We moved further down the sandy beach, looking off into the distance for any obvious land mass.

"That island has to be near here if those guys got buzzed by Feng, right Cathleen?" Joanie asked.

I looked over at mom who was studying the horizon and mumbling some words I couldn't make out. From her intent look, I knew she was using one of her discernment spells to divine the location of Feng's island hideaway.

"So… there it is," Mom said,"

"You'll need a boat dear to reach it, but the island is only a few miles off this coast. The vampire is traveling as we speak, trying to get to Feng before he can access that statue."

Mom was looking back at the constantly moving ocean and then continued chanting so softly, the waves washed her words away. She turned back to me.

"It dawned on me earlier as we were traversing the tunnels of the old China Town, that the statue must have been hidden on the island by Dr. Chung Wu. He had it in his custody from the very beginning, but as a Shadow Walker he was limited in his time in this realm. He knew he was being hunted by Lady Bao and would forfeit his life if she found him.

Ultimately his plan to retrieve it from the island or use it as bait to catch and destroy the Dark Ones was thwarted. He also knew I was sent by the *Council of Green Wizards* to secure the statue and bring it to them for destruction."

This was a lot to take in at once. The mental image of Chung Wu braced against a tree, his life force gone from this plane, flashed through my mind.

"Mom, the *Teacher* warned me that there might be some on the Council that would take the Dragon's blood for its Magical powers. He wants to destroy it himself or…"

"Or so he says, Cathleen. The *Teacher* is already very powerful. The Dragon Blood would make him a direct threat to the magical balance in this realm and even into the next.

Your father warned me, the *Teacher's* great hate for Feng is matched only by his great ego; a bad combination. He is reckless in his scheming and puts us all in jeopardy with the dark wizard and the vampire."

It all sounded like plots within plots and my head was starting to buzz with doubts when Joanie cleared her throat.

I almost forgot she was standing within easy hearing and probably scared out of her wits by our talk.

"Joanie, are you ok? I know this must all be confusing right now."

"I'm used to you and your mom going on about realms and magic, Cathleen. It's just that, well, I didn't want you to worry, but…"

"What is it, Joanie?" I asked, concerned.

Mom quickly reached for Joanie's hand. "The vampire has infected you, hasn't she?"

"What?" I screamed out.

The men talking with Jason about using their fishing boat turned to look over at us.

"Calm yourself, Cathleen. I can fix our dear Joanie up in no time. All I need is the spell she used to turn her."

"Turn her? Into what?" I was beginning to come unglued.

Joanie looked back into mom's eyes and then looking over at me said, "It's the way she makes the gray men for Feng Xi. I heard her tell the driver, "One more from the slag heap for

Feng." She dipped her finger nails into some kind of liquid and then, did this."

She took her hand from mom and pushed back the rolled up sleeves on Jason's jacket. There were two long welts on her forearm, but rather than the deep red you'd expect, they were an ash gray. They went unnoticed by everyone in our hurry to get to the docks.

Mom said, "Cathleen, this needs my immediate intervention as you can see. I will now take our Joanie to the *Healing Garden.*"

She began to chant softly, using arcane words, long stored in her subconscious and known only to the initiates of the *Garden,* chosen for their own purity of spirit.

I knew this meant time travel for Joanie, travel to the land of Faeries and the Emerald Isle of Antiquity. That's where the *Healing Garden* grew an abundance of remedies against the Dark Magic inflicted upon the innocent.

This was a place only the highest among the *Council of Green Wizards* are permitted. For my mother to have such access indicated her standing was far greater within the magic community than I ever suspected.

"Are we going now?" Joanie asked timidly.

I knew this was a critical situation, but she had grabbed my arm as if she wanted me to say she didn't need to go.

"Joanie, dear girl, we will be back here before you even remember what you ate for breakfast."

She had taken both of Joanie's hands and with those last words, they vanished.

Chapter 70

Suddenly, I stood alone, seeing only the never-ending waves wash up on the sandy shore. I noticed the wind had picked up quite a bit now and wondered if that was part of mom's mode of travel.

I felt terribly alone, knowing it was going to be Jason and me facing the dangers on that island.

That brought me out of my reverie and I walked over to the small knot of men huddled around Jason. They all looked over as I approached. I was smiling, but it took all my effort not to run up to Jason and tell him about our friend.

"Hey guys," I said, by way of greeting. In return I got nodding heads and a few, "Hey there's."

Jason quickly made me feel at ease as he slipped his arm possessively around my shoulders.

"Hi, Cathleen. We can use Mike's small skiff over there for a few hours to tour that island they found. They've drawn a map, but it's pretty much a straight shot from here."

I heard a few chuckles at Jason's comment.

The man Jason referred to as Mike said "Aint no straight lines on the water mister."

They all laughed out loud now and Jason must have realized he looked pretty much like a *land lubber* to these seasoned veterans of the sea.

Jason smiled at the remark and agreed that he felt more at home in the forests, but that he used to do lots of white water canoeing and thought he could handle himself.

"Besides," he went on, "As a Navy Seal, I guess I logged some nautical miles on my rep sheet."

They all stopped laughing and there was lots of head bobbing and agreement. Gods above, men love to wave their plumage at other males.

We shoved off with the help of Mike and another fisherman from the group. The others had wandered back to their net trimming and boat swabbing and whatever else goes on in a fishing boat.

Jason proved every bit the sailor as he was a woodsman. He immediately steered us clear of any obstacles like dinghies, buoys and underwater boat moorings and set us on a course toward the island.

"Jason, mom and Joanie are gone."

Before I could say anything else he said, "I knew there was something wrong with Joanie, love, from when we got her out of that cabin. I saw your mom watching her like a hawk and figured she was looking for signs...kind of like I do in the woods."

"You were right, sweetie. Joanie showed us where Lady Bao had infected her by scratching something into her skin. Mom has to get her to a special place to find the cure to the spell, otherwise..."

I didn't need to finish. Jason took one hand off the wheel for a minute to give my hand a squeeze. "Your mom will do what needs doing, love."

I had to put everything, but our current challenge out of mind. We'd be getting to that wretched island within the half hour and I needed to focus.

"Cathleen, this is going to be my second vision we'll be stepping into. I haven't had a minute to really try to recapture it, but it has every element so far."

"The island of your vision. I remember. At least we know we're on the right trail."

We stood together at the wheel, my arm was now around his slim waist and I felt his energy flow through me. My long auburn hair was whipping across my face, blurring my vision. I slipped into my Inner Eye. I wasn't sure if the Gray Men could swim, but I wasn't betting against it.

The wind was sharper out here, without the benefit of buildings and other boats to block it. I huddled as close to Jason's warmth as I could, without distracting him from his work of locating the island.

After another ten minutes of listening to the sea gulls squawking in our wake, hoping for a toss of fish entrails, we spotted the curve of an island just ahead.

As we got closer, we could make out a patch of narrow beach-head and a dense, wild thicket of trees and foliage behind.

Jason cut the motor and we drifted closer. When he knew he could drag us onto the pebbly beach, he slipped down into the chilly waters with a small splash. Towing us onto land, he tied-off securely onto an outlying tree trunk, using the heavy rope that Mike left on board for that use.

"This looks like it, let's do some scouting before we go charging in." Jason was almost whispering, but I wasn't certain we could make an unannounced entrance in any case.

Feng Xi would have made sure this scrap of land was guarded with what was left of the Terra Cotta Warriors he animated. And soldiers like to patrol.

"Jason, I think we should separate."

"What? No, Cathleen! We need to find Feng together so we can have each other's back."

"I know you want to work this together, but you need to let me call the shots here," I said as forcefully as I could, considering I was as anxious as he was obstinate.

"Your vision clearly put me *inside* a cave, and you, clearly *outside*! Jason, Lady Bao is likely to be here too. She'll sense your presence if you get anywhere near the cave's entrance. And we don't know if she's here as Feng's Mistress Killer, or just as *his* killer!

Let's not take the chance that she's working with him again. If we separate we can come at them with some element of surprise."

He was studying my face intently, as if looking for flaws in my reasoning.

"OK," he said. "But what am I supposed to do to give you support?"

"This island isn't that large according to those fisherman. I'm heading straight in to locate the cave entrance; you take a more circular route to find it. I should be inside by the time you get there. That should keep the vampire from sensing your presence and give you a chance to secure the island for our eventual departure."

Jason grabbed my arms in a strong grip saying "Cathleen, remember my second vision.   The cave and the screams I heard; someone is getting hurt. Please, make sure it's not you!"

I gave his hand a strong squeeze and kissed him. Then we each began walking. Jason went left, while I stayed the course and began to quietly move forward.

Chapter 71

The fishermen were right about this being a small pile of sandy dirt with lots of wild plants and trees. These acted like an effective screen, blocking the view of anything ahead.

I wished I had a machete, but didn't want to use magic to conjure one. Feng would be alert to magic being employed anywhere on the island.

I'd been pushing through fibrous, unyielding plants for ten minutes when I made out a slouching hump, rising from the ground a few feet ahead.

Peering through the clammy green gloom, I knelt on the spongy ground to make sure I was looking at the outline of a hill.

It was not very high, heavily covered by vegetation, making it nearly indistinguishable from the natural contours of the area.

A narrow slit in the mound appeared at the left of the path I was making, so I veered over in that direction.

I hadn't yet stepped out of the thick foliage dangling around me, when I saw a movement out of the corner of my eye.

I quickly whispered a cloaking spell and stilled my breathing. I sensed whatever it was, it was close by.

I moved my back against a nearby spindly sapling. It was being chocked of life by the thick vines that I noticed earlier. They were attached to everything that could support their weight, or crawled along the sandy floor of the island.

There was a rustling among the dead leaves and fallen tree limbs. Glad I had slipped into my Inner Eye earlier, I saw what should have been one of the nonthreatening vines, begin to rise up like a dark green sea serpent.

Sprouting wicked black thorns up and down a thick, ropey body, it stood suspended for several seconds, seeming to sense the air around the area, before it stretched itself out along the sandy earth and became inert once more.

Guess it didn't detect me, I thought, wondering what other little traps Feng Xi had placed in his little Garden of Evil. I didn't have long to speculate.

I was about to move toward the narrow cave entrance, when a fully armed Terra Cotta warrior stepped out of the shadows, its heavy spear glinting in the shallow light.

Now, I had the threat of the soldier and the creepy creeper to deal with. I needed to hurry as I knew Jason would be showing up soon. I had to defuse these dangers so he didn't step into some serious dodo.

I decided the vine had to go first, but rather than waste a nasty piece of work, I decided to use it on the bigger threat, the warrior. The vine was probably designed to stop intruders whose feet unhappily stepped on it, or made vibrations it could feel. Simple and effective guard dog.

The warrior stayed close to the slip of entryway. He was peering intently from side to side into the impenetrable foliage, screening it from intruders like me.

He appeared to be unaware of the vine creeping along the ground nearby.

Picking up a handful of sand and small pebbles, I used a strong wind spell to blow them directly at the soldier. He jerked violently at the assault and went immediately into a defensive posture, kneeling on the ground with his spear at the ready exactly as I hoped he would.

That sudden movement alerted the guarding vine, making it react with a sudden rush as it propelled itself at the kneeling figure. Within a few seconds, the entire mass of the thorny creeper had wound itself around the Warrior. Its long barbs had dug deeply into the reddish flesh, gauging eyes and piercing face. The soldier never screamed out in pain as the vine pushed into his open mouth and back out through the padding of chest armor.

Still concealed, I moved toward the cave opening. I was sure the creeper couldn't follow into the cave itself and took advantage of the shelter to throw out one last spell.

"Bilebiss Nocturna!"

The words turned the vine into a pulpy mass of rotted material, dropping to the ground where it could never revive. The Terra Cotta Warrior dissolved under the weight of the inert goop, its body turned to lumps of reddish clay.

Done and done I thought as I looked on, satisfied that Jason wouldn't have to face the creep and the creeper.

Moving further into the cave, I was losing the pale light filtering through the mask of vegetation.

I had slipped out of my cloak of concealment, needing my senses totally aware in this new environment. I sniffed the air as I moved forward, because I remembered that the Gray Man had a pungent odor coming off his body, like a dead carcass in the heat of summer. Only musty air. I started forward, using my hand to make sure I stayed close to the cave wall. Suddenly, I picked up the distinct vibration of another magic user.

The power of magic is as subtle as the energy radiating from a cell tower, but it lights things up in a receptive magic user like a light bulb.

I couldn't determine if this was the Dark Wizard, or Lady Bao. There was one other possibility, too, the *Teacher.*

Chapter 72

When he disappeared from the labyrinth of tunnels, I knew the *Teacher* was pursuing an agenda forged like steel in the fires of hate. Driven to avenge his brother's murder, the *Teacher* was blinded by this blood vendetta. I was afraid this could make him more of a liability than an ally.

I quieted my breathing because the nearness of another Magic User had accelerated it as it always did. My Inner Eye was searching the darkness surrounding me. I thought of Jason on his own in this evil morass of an island.

Earlier, while the fisherman was readying his boat for our short trip, I had slipped Jason the Golden Harp amulet I picked up after Feng lost it. I explained that if he needed to disarm a Magic User, the touch of the amulet would help protect him from the magical powers of the enemy. It was clutched in his hand when we parted earlier.

The earthy smell seemed to work its way into my pores; I could almost taste the dirt and sand as I moved deeper. There was no ambient light so I brought a small Green Fire to my free hand, helping to illuminate, without shining like a halogen lamp.

There was a new odor moving on the air. I got a whiff of something definitely not expected inside the cave; something I'd smelled before …Jasmine. It had a spicy scent, distinct from the thick, loamy smell.

This small clue confirmed my expectations. The vampire, Lady Bao, had rejoined her master, Feng Xi.

I considered this a likelihood from the beginning of our trip out here, but there was always the possibility that she wasn't here as an ally.

Her loathing for Feng seemed genuine. She wanted his destruction to assure herself complete freedom.

The statue of the Red Dragon would agive her total dominance over any magic user, even those on the Council of Green Wizards. She was already an Immortal. The blood of the Dragon would make her a god.

Thinking about gods triggered a thought about the *Teacher*. He was bound to be here and that gave me some measure of confidence until Jason could rejoin me.

Even without magic, Jason had always proved himself resourceful and surprisingly intuitive when we were dealing with the paranormal.

I was heading deeper into the low-ceilinged cave. My body, moving through the stagnant air stirred a stronger scent of Jasmine.

I stopped and pressed myself into the dirt wall.

Lady Bao was close by and I was getting closer to her.

I had shut off the fire in my hand earlier to arrive unnoticed at the cave's center. I stood in utter darkness, smelling the perfume of the ancient blood sucker.

The last thing I wanted to do was to bump into the vampire until I could determine if she was back to serving Feng's wishes. The two of them against me were not the best odds for a happy outcome.

As I moved in a steady shuffle, trying to stay close to my guide wall, my foot hit something on the ground.

I quickly took a step back. Whatever I hit didn't move. I stuck out my foot again and probed the object for a reaction. There was little resistance and I pushed harder.

The mystery blob grabbed my ankle and I fell squarely on my butt and started to scoot backward using my free foot to kick out at the thing. I hoped to do some damage even though I didn't have a clue what I was fighting.

I decided to relight my fire for a better look. There, lying at my feet was Anfa, the Colossus Faerie.

She was trussed up like a boar at a hog roast; her one hand was still tucked behind her back and secured to her feet. She had managed to wriggle out of the golden threaded rope and free one hand and arm. Her mouth was sealed with some kind of waxy substance, she later told me was secreted by a thorny vine.

I coaxed her steely fingers from around my ankle.

"Anfa!" I whispered, as I stooped down close to her head. Her hair was matted with a sticky substance as I discovered trying to pull it away from her face.

I took out my pocket knife and cut the remaining ropes with a few fast strokes, the golden threads disappearing when they hit the dirt floor and cleared her mouth with an unbinding spell.

Anfa whispered in her own tongue, how the *Teacher* had called her back to duty after Feng Xi was carried off by a huge black bird.

"Though I do not know where that interfering creature sprang from." I didn't bother to enlighten her.

She continued, "The *Teacher* used his skill as a *Voyager* and we followed the Dark Wizard here. He then ordered me to perform reconnaissance of this mound of earth. I was shamefully caught unaware by the vines that move like thorny snakes.

But now that you are here, Wizard. I will share my intelligence with you before you do battle."

The intelligence part sounded great, the battle part, not so much.

"Anfa, we can't stay here, so give me the short version of what you know."

She was standing at her full height by now, though that meant she had to stoop because of the low ceiling.

She told me about being dragged by the vine after being subdued, into this part of the cave and simply dropped where I found her.

"I am certain I would have been dealt with within a short time since I heard voices in the near distance."

So now I knew I didn't have much further to go in the endless night. Soon, I would find the pair of power-hungry creatures who sought the Blood of the Red Dragon.

I suspected that Lady Bao kept close tabs on Feng by placing her own spies among his Terra Cotta Warriors. The one that was destroyed by the vine outside the cave entrance seemed less of a guard and more of a look-out. Perhaps he was waiting for her to show up to the party.

I suspected Jason would have finished his circuit around the island. So, where was he?

Chapter 73

"Anfa, Jason was to enter this cave shortly after I did. He's very late in showing up. I think he's encountered some of Feng's nasty creatures and may be in a world of trouble."

Without a moment more lost to discussion, Anfa lifted her arms and looking like a lightning bolt, went streaking toward the cave entrance.

The well-honed warrior skills of a Colossus Faerie are legendary among Magic Users. Many a Demon has fallen to their take-no-prisoners code in battle. Anfa would be a formidable ally for Jason and I could put that concern aside as I faced the ancient powers of the wizard and the vampire.

Now that I was alone, I returned a small flame to my hand. This time, I made it arc like a rainbow, so I could see both sides as I moved forward.

A sudden chill ran across my back. I shrugged my shoulders in reaction, but the chill moved like sliding ice down my arms.

I snapped my head back, looking up at the cave ceiling.

My skin censors had picked up the disturbance to the air made by the movement of a Gray Man hanging from a thorny creeper vine like a grey bat.

The hairless thug seemed blinded by the Green Fire as I held up my hand to see it more clearly. Jumping out of the way, shot a stream of hot green lava at his hefty body.

A few seconds later, it came to earth with the sound of a loud plop. A blackish-gray sludge spread into a lumpy circle near my foot.

The next sound I heard was a scream that sounded as if someone was having their beating heart ripped from their chest.

I wondered if I had one less adversary to face now.

Wrapping myself in a blanket of darkness and shadows, I extinguished my fire. I didn't hear any other sounds.

Moving like a phantom, I speculated about what evil being I'd be facing in a matter of minutes, the master or the mistress.

Whatever the answer, one of the deadliest foes I'd ever encountered was now the victor. And to the victor goes the Blood of the Dragon.

Chapter 74

Jason had been following the perimeter of the small island, moving silently, like the well-trained woodsman he was.

Finding the entrance to the cave was important, but it had to be done without being discovered by Feng's thugs in the process.

There was an unnatural feel to the surrounding woods and the thick clumps of sharp-edged marsh grasses, growing around the swampy areas and mud flats he crossed.

That's it, he thought, stepping over a nasty looking vine.

This place has nothing making any sounds. No birds, no insects buzzing, even the air is completely still. He tilted his head slightly, to sniff the dank air.

A shiver ran down his spine. He thought for a second he saw that vine move.

Wow. I'm losing it here.

He reached into his jacket pocket and took out the Golden Harp amulet. It felt warm and somehow reassuring in his hand. He closed his fingers over it and started moving.

He'd been warned that his presence would be detected by the Lady Bao if he entered the cave too soon. He understood that the vampire had a nose for human blood, like a dung beetle has for a cow pie.

The thought of a vampire sucking his life out of him put all his senses into high gear.

He'd only gone a few yards when he picked up a sound. It was very soft, but his trained ears identified it as the smooth slithering of a snake. It definitely came from behind him.

He spun on his boot heels in time to see the thorny head of the massive knotted vine rising up from among the fallen leaves and dead grasses.

The island must have been infested with them. He'd spotted them everywhere on the island he'd covered already, never suspecting they were a threat.

Jason wrapped the heavy gold chain of the amulet around his wrist, leaving enough dangling for a longer reach. He began to notice an odd heating up of the already warm piece of jewelry. It seemed the amulet got hotter as the vine moved closer. Stranger yet, the talisman wasn't burning his hand or wrist. It was hotter, but not painful.

Jason stood still and waited for the vine to make its move. He knew it was being directed by Dark Magic and wondered for a second what other natural life had been perverted like this.

The vine was standing a good three feet off the ground, its ropey, yellowish-brown body, studded with sharp thorns. It began to sway like a curtain in a light breeze. Then, it lunged directly for Jason's face.

The momentum of the vine took it squarely into the large Golden Harp medallion of Brian Boru. There was a sharp sound like a lightning blown tree getting hit in the forest. The smell was a mixture of sulfuric acid and rotten fish.

Jason gagged and was unconsciously stepping away from the blackened scar marking the length of the vine.

He now had proof of the sinister creatures he was warned he might encounter. He decided to keep the amulet wrapped around his wrist, to have it handy if something else sprang up.

He could tell he was nearing the cave entrance because he'd spotted the slight swell of the land as he rounded a mud flat. He had backed into the tree line for some cover as he got closer to the mouth of the cave.

The stillness of the air was suddenly shattered by a scream that might have risen from the Dark Pit itself. It clung to the damp air like moss on a rock and hung there in an echo state for another beat.

Jason had crouched down at the first sound of this tortured cry. Now he slowly got to his feet whispering, "Cathleen…no…"

He knew his second vision took place on this island, in this cave. The scream he heard could have easily been mine. He wasn't waiting to see my head roll down a sand dune.

He checked the amulet to be sure it was secure and then reached into his pocket for the small Mag-lite he'd brought on the trip.

By now, long shadows were lying on the ground near the entrance to the cave.

He checked his watch. Time here seemed different to him; it felt later than his lighted dial read.

He took one last look around before he approached the narrow opening.

The perfect stillness of the air, the silence where there should have been some kinds of bird and insect life, formed a picture in his mind.

This place is dead he thought grimly.

He left the cover of the trees and slowly made his way toward the squat looking mound and its dark opening.

He used the flashlight and the beam fell across a pile of reddish dirt and a similar scorch mark made by the thorny vine he destroyed.

"And that's just out here"…he murmured…"What's in there?"

He took his last breath of damp air and went to find out.

Chapter 75

The tortured scream was reverberating off the dank walls of the cave as I carefully moved closer to the source.

I needed to determine if the Dark Wizard lived, or if indeed, the Vampire had destroyed him.

There was a sharp turn in the tunnel's slightly defined path as I moved in that direction. I still kept one hand against the dirt wall.

I felt the hairs on my neck and arms begin to stir. I was nearing a powerful source of Magic. My breathing and heart rate would sound like bellows and hammer strikes to a highly alert Vampire, or a powerful Dark Wizard.

Using dad's method of stopping a body's life support, without turning into a dead Wizard, I went into a kind of shock state. Feeling a deep, bone-numbing chill set in, I shook off the effects of being mostly dead. I pulled in more darkness to fully restore my shadow spell and moved on.

Without the sound of my breathing, my hearing became like sonar. I picked up the vibrations of something being dragged along a dirt floor. Then a gasp and a high pitched laugh.

Someone was clearly delighted with life at that moment. That could only mean one thing. They were now in possession of the statue of the Red Dragon.

I felt light-headed from lack of oxygen and my movements became painfully slow; as if I was wearing lead shoes. Being covered in the shadows, I began to feel claustrophobic in the tight space between dirt walls.

Unconsciously, I had begun looking up to see if the ceiling was pressing down on me, and it was!

There was a garish red light penetrating the glooming of the cave. I must have triggered one of Feng Xi's little traps with my movements; now the dirt ceiling was inching its way downward. The long tendrils of roots moved like an inverted pit of vipers.

Raising both arms and drawing on the *Mother's* great powers, I pushed back against the force of the descending tons of dirt. I knew I would tire if I couldn't end this contest of strength quickly.

Just as my arms began to tremble, a flash of light exploded so near to my head that my eyes watered.

When I blinked, Anfa was standing beside me.

With a small grunt of effort, she pushed back against the would-be crush of earth. I stabilized it with a quick binding spell so we could move ahead.

I was happy to see her, but concerned about why she wasn't with Jason.

"Your man is here Wizard and will join us shortly. I can bring him to you now if you wish."

I was tempted to say yes, but I needed to judge the situation first. I didn't want to expose Jason to any more danger if I could help it.

"I would appreciate if you would stay close to him Anfa. I need to assess this threat before I expose him to it."

She merely nodded once and was off again riding her bolt of golden light.

I looked ahead where the reddish light still invited me forward.

At least I can see better I was thinking.

I heard another high cackle like a chicken pleased with her clutch of eggs.

I kept the shadow wrap in place and moved forward; a spell on my lips ready to shout out.

The lighting got stronger as I approached what appeared to be a deep depression in the right side of the tunnel.

There were two Terra Cotta Warriors standing rigidly, in front of it, fully armed and looking like the stone-cold killers they were, in every sense of that description. When Feng Xi animated them he had likely used the spirits of the worse scum bags found in the fourth realm.

The guards seemed to sense my presence. I could see them shifting their coal black eyes back to my direction and slowly pivoting their bodies slightly away from the opening.

They were armed with swords and wore the heavy padded armor. Their flat faces were like death masks; expressionless under the tight top knots of hair on their heads.

I had to get past them and I had to do it quietly.

None of the warriors I'd encountered so far, seemed to have the ability to speak. Feng Xi must not have deemed that a necessary skill for killing. This was a stroke of luck for me, since I didn't need a charging warrior shouting ancient Chinese obscenities at me just then.

The thought of them screaming reminded me I'd better step-up my game.

I had to speak my spell out loud to direct its full power at the soldiers. They were now moving toward me as I stood a few yards away. I stayed cloaked in the darkness I'd drawn to myself and in one long breath, hit them squarely.

"Faaabaaht!" This had the effect of a wrecking ball; undoing the strength they possessed at their very core.

The weapons fell from their hands. I dropped the cloaking shadows and threw Green Fire until they were both reduced to reddish-powder mounds.

I moved on when I was sure there had been no alarms set-off by my Magic. Which seemed strange to me, since I knew both the Dark Wizard and the Vampire, should have detected both me *and* my Magic by then.

Perhaps they thought the warriors had dispatched me already. Whatever the cause of their lack of response, I was grateful. I moved silently toward the red glow, stopping a few feet away from the now, unguarded opening.

There was still one thing I could use to change the odds in my favor. I might still be facing two powerful Magic Users and maybe a few Terra Cotta thugs.

I'd been in dread of this moment because it meant I was alone on a really slippery slope.

I reached into a deep inner pocket of my jacket and pulled out my last defensive position; the Shadow Box Library.

I knew I could use this charm to call upon the *Librarian,* Bandi for his help, but I would have to step into the Library to do that.

Dad's words kept my feet rooted to the ground. "Thinking over yer plans more than one good time, let's you see the light shining through the holes!"

Without another thought, I opened the door to the Shadow Box Library and knew I'd made the right move.

Chapter 76

There was no bursting light or quiver to the air as it opened, the Library was just suddenly around me.

It was now shaped to conform to the height and width of cave's tunnel dimension, but I knew this too was an illusion. I felt safer now, because I couldn't be detected while in the Library and no one could detect the Library from the outside. In essence, it wasn't there so neither was I.

I also knew that by bringing the Library into this realm, the Librarian, Bandi, would soon join me. I did a slow scan of the room. Ban Briathar didn't keep me waiting. Standing near the book-covered walls was the handsome Second Librarian of the *Shadow Box Library of Celtic Magic and Myths*.

"Greetings, Cathleen O'Brien! I have been waiting upon your call."

"Bandi, thank you for coming. I'm about to face Wizard Feng Xi, or the Lady Bao, or maybe both, in just a few minutes. I don't think my father would have given me access to this Library unless he kept a powerful spell secreted away here for my future use. If I'm correct, I need you to find that for me now."

The Librarian smiled warmly during my brief speech and said, "Very good, Cathleen O'Brien! Your father Liam was wise to have seen your potential to ferret out his clues.

This is what you'll need to defeat both the Dark Wizard and his Vampire Mistress."

He held out his hand to me.

"The talon of the Dragon King, *Hong Wang*! While the Lady Bao had harvested those few drops of his powerful blood, the Shadow Walker, Chung Wu, took this formidable weapon.

The last Dragon King knew of his coming demise soon after being lured into eating the petulance-ridden humans by Feng Xi.

He had begun to store his prodigious destructive powers in a most natural place; the hardened bone of his spur talon. This, along with the inscription your father thoughtfully wrote upon the bone, is all you'll need. Well, and the courage to face both the wizard, Feng, and the vampire."

I extended my hand. Bandi gently placed the large, claw-like spur onto my palm.

I felt an immediate shock go through me. There was a tingling down to my toenails as I studied the artifact. It was as if the last Dragon King was breathing down my neck. I fought the urge to check over my shoulder for a fire-breathing snout.

"Bandi, these words are in the old Druid tongue. I've never encountered them before," I said, my concern tinging my voice.

"Toghairm tribhas," is a *Summoning Invocation*, to bring down a triple death upon your enemies, Cathleen."

I didn't dare speak the spell out loud for fear of causing some kind of calamitous result to Bandi.

He was watching me closely and must have sensed my discomfort at using this new spell without knowing its outcome. Dad always warned, you can't just toss spells off like a high school cheerleader; they had to be precise and carefully delivered.

"Bandi, what are the three deaths and will they destroy Feng and Lady Bao completely?"

He must have taken my questions as doubt of the power in the talon.

"You need only say the words and let the Dragon King have his revenge on these two wretches."

I asked, "How does this fulfill my father's pledge to Lady Bao if I'm actually planning on destroying her?"

Bandi held up his hand as if to stop any further discussion.

"You have already found the Red Dragon, Cathleen. Your father's promise is now done with and you must now return these two abominations to the Dark Pit of the Sleepless Dead."

There was a shuddering under my feet and when I looked down, I was once more standing in the cave. The Library was gone, along with Bandi.

The long, sharp claw of the last Dragon King suddenly felt heavy in my hand. It began glowing a deep crimson, as if infused with the blood of *Hong Wang*. I closed my fingers around it as tightly as I could considering its large size, afraid I'd fumble and lose it at a critical moment. It gave me a feeling of confidence to feel its weight and heat.

I said the words over and over in my head and knew I had the spell ready on my tongue. All I needed to do was hold out the talon and repeat my father's words of magic.

That, and stand exposed to the evil powers of two soul and blood eating monsters from the fourth realm. I moved forward and stopped just inside the recently guarded opening. The red glow was much brighter here. My Inner Eye gave me a clear view of what looked like a hall of the damned from a horror movie!

Two wooden casks were placed in the center of what had the appearance of a killing ground. They were both filled with a blackish sludge and giving off a strong metallic smell that I prayed to the *Mother,* wasn't my blood type.

It appeared there had been a recent harvest of living creatures from all the realms. Body parts, tails, tufted ears, scale-covered torsos, lay in piles like a junk yard for the slaughtered.

The chamber was fairly large for a cavern. Unfortunately, some of the space was taken up with two short lines of Terra Cotta Warriors, with a smattering of knuckle-dragging Gray Men. I did a quick count; they were fourteen strong.

I spotted the beautiful vampire, Lady Bao, standing near the vat furthest from the entry way where I stood.

There was a heavy loamy scent coming off the tunnel walls, but this was nearly smothered by the stench of ancient bones and the breath of the dead. All mixed in with the coppery smell of fresh blood.

The Lady Bao must have disguised her own strong odor of an ancient undead, with a frequent dose of Jasmine perfume. But here, in the bowels of the unnatural cave, she probably didn't feel the need.

I bet her victims didn't complain about her body odor... at least not for long, I thought with a shudder.

Sensing another being just out of sight in the garish red glow, I wondered if it was the Dark Wizard, or another of his abominations.

As if in answer to my question, Feng Xi stepped from behind a large Warrior. He was gripping a broad sword in gnarled but seemingly strong hands.

His skin was nearly translucent with his great age, revealing an intricate network of blue veins, coursing with his unnatural life. His skin was taut against sharp cheek bones and the color of a weak cup of tea.

Like the vampire, he exuded an odor of a disinterred body, one that had been buried for many months.

He wore a red silk robe, embroidered in gold thread. It was covered with black cymbals of Magic that I'd never seen before.

He held the sword at waist level, letting his arms poke out from the silk sleeves like shriveled stems on a petrified plant.

Because I was again concealed with the shadows of the cave, I couldn't be seen, but that didn't mean my presence went undetected.

There was a ripple of alarm going through the rows of soldiers. The Gray Men started to make a humming sound which had the effect of a bee swarm on my ears.

They must have been warning Feng of an intruder nearby. He snapped a look at the front of the cavern and seeing only shadows, narrowed his tar black eyes.

I stopped breathing for a minute so my hear beat wouldn't be detected by his sensitive hearing.

Lady Bao had been watching Feng closely and made a high pitched sound to get his attention. He twirled around as this call vibrated through the dank air.

She then lazily dipped a three inch, well-sharpened index finger into the vat of gurgling blood. Slowly, swaying like some kind of exotic dancer, she moved her tongue in circles around the long, pointed finger nail and digit, until all the gooey mess was gone.

I wanted to gag at the scene, but Feng Xi was entranced by her seductive show and moved like one in a trance, toward her.

"My gifts are waiting upon your pleasure to indulge yourself my Lord." Lady Bao continued her swaying display.

She still has some power over the old coot I thought in amazement. *How did he miss the memo on her wanting to destroy him?*

As I was thinking about her powers of allure, the two moved slowly to within touching distance of one another. They were centered in my vision now, and I felt the hard talon of the Dragon King get hotter in my hand.

I wanted to hurl my spell at them when they were closer together; hoping to destroy the two of them. I wasn't certain, but I thought the Gray Men and the warriors would drop out of existence with the demise of their maker, Feng Xi.

Lady Bao had a sly, teasing grin on her perfect porcelain-like face. The black sheen of her long hair swung gently at her back; a metronome marking her fluid movements.

I was almost as mesmerized as Feng Xi and hesitated momentarily to pronounce my spell.

The Dark Wizard had dropped the broad sword to his side and let it slip from his hands. It clattered onto the hard-packed dirt floor.

As one, the warriors and Gray Men dropped their own weapons in unison. The noise was startling, but Feng seemed unaware of the mirror actions his minions had taken.

He stood transfixed by his once enslaved Mistress, submitting totally to the power of vampire glamor. Lady Bao reached out the finger she had scrubbed clean of blood with her delicate pink tongue.

Teasingly, she traced the wizened face of the Dark Wizard with delicate touches. His mouth hung open in anticipation of her next touch.

Suddenly, striking like the blade of a guillotine, she drew the nail so quickly across Feng's exposed throat that he barely emitted a gurgle as his ancient blood spurted onto the pale face of the vampire.

Without hesitating for a second, she threw Feng down to the floor. In a blur of motion, she grabbed the sword he had dropped, to sever his head in one startling quick and powerful move.

Blood ran in rivulets from her forehead and off the perfect bridge of her nose. It was spattered all over the front of her cream colored silk gown. She looked more like the victim of a massacre, than the crazed killer.

I looked over at the warriors and gray men and they suddenly disintegrated into piles of ochre dust and ash. I was right about their demise being linked to Feng's.

I thought it was odd that the Lady Bao still had such a hold on Feng Xi's passions. Then, I reflected on the fact that he was keeping himself viable by sucking the life essence from other living creatures. This must have renewed any dried up urgency he felt toward her. He wanted to be immortal and have it all.

It was just the vampire now and I was ready for her.

"You can drop your shadow spell, honorable Wushen," she said sweetly while looking directly at me.

I was thinking about the great spell I thought I had used and now I was beginning to wonder about the claw I held tightly at my side and out of sight. Had she sensed that too?

Chapter 77

The Vampire inched toward me. As she did so, her small boot hit the severed head of her old Master. It was enough of a shove to roll it a few inches.

With a twisted smile on her face, she gave the head a stronger kick and sent it spinning into the pile of dismembered bodies. This seemed to please her and she smiled sweetly in my direction.

I struggled with the decision of exposing myself to her or not. I didn't fancy getting to the top of the heap. In the end, I heeded the voice of my father as I imagined he'd tell me.

"She is clever and very sure of herself. Beware the former and take advantage of the latter."

I knew she had somehow sensed my position so I couldn't exactly sneak up behind her with the talon. She thought of herself as invincible, now that Feng Xi had literally gone head over heels for her. I would use that smugness to my advantage.

Reversing the shadow spell was easy enough. They fell away like a light gauze and were absorbed back into the surrounding cave.

"Ah, I am delighted you have joined me young Wushen. As you have seen, the worm, Feng Xi has been returned to the dirt where he belongs. It is now time for you to fulfill your father's pledge to me and bring me the statue!"

I looked at her without responding to this obvious order. Giving her a thin smile and staring at her blood-spattered face, I pressed the talon closer to my side.

"Lady Bao, I think you already know the location of the statue of the Red Dragon, or you wouldn't have returned to Feng Xi. In fact, I believe it's near this very chamber. The question is, why can't you take it into your possession?"

"So, you have more of your father's discerning talent than I credited you with. For a young Wizard you seem to deserve some of your reputation as a competent Magic User. I discovered that your mother, a rather meddlesome woman, had the statue in her possession after your father, the Wizard, Liam O'Brien left this realm.

It disappeared into a place shielded by heavy wards and spells. I had to wait patiently, until she moved it from behind that wall of magic, to try to seize it for myself. Your mother took the statue to the China Town gallery where it was displayed for a short time. This was reported to me by my spy network. Rather ingenious of her I must admit."

She had smoothly taken a few more steps, bringing her within a few feet of where I stood.

The heavy scent of Jasmine moved with her; a pall of cloying sweetness. It clung to the air around me. I breathed it in like a putrid fog.

I was riveted to her eyes now, trying to judge her next move. They had changed from a dead black color to the vivid red of newly spilt blood. She had likely eaten her fill before dispatching her old Master. He likely enjoyed watching the victims as they died.

I didn't want her getting any closer and started to raise my hands. My father's words were buzzing around in my head. Something about not going into caves without my Green Fire at the ready.

But something was terribly wrong.

I couldn't lift my arms and the only thing burning were Lady Bao's dead eyes, as she glided closer on her silent feet. Oddly, I had noticed one tiny boot was spattered with clots of blood from Feng's shriveled head.

She moved as if she was testing the water before committing herself to the plunge.

I tried to lift my foot and got no response. I couldn't let her see my panic as it began to rise. I remembered an old adage dad would repeat to me whenever I became afraid and couldn't seem to act.

"Panic and anger make perfect mates!"

As the vampire slithered closer to where I was rooted, the fear began to subside and I was getting my Irish up!

"Stop moving, or face the consequences!" I ordered her.

She came to a halt and narrowed her eyes as if trying to see why her powerful glamour wasn't working on me. I checked to see if I was able to raise my arms, and when I couldn't panic began to creep back into my head.

"I know you are now immobile young wizard. I've always enjoyed the fragrance of Jazmine. The effect it can have on mortals can be quite rewarding. For instance, you are able to speak, but not to move until I allow it, making you a perfect tool to me."

Her confidence seemed to grow while mine diminished with each footstep she took closer to my rooted body.

"You need not fear me wizard, as I intend no harm, I assure you. The statue of the Red Dragon is nearby as you have so cleverly surmised, but it needs the will of a Pledged One to retrieve it. As soon as I have made you my servant, you will act as I command. Though your father would have been preferable for this task, you will have to suffice."

I felt my arms and legs beginning to go numb. I looked down briefly at my hands and they had a wrinkled, frost-bitten look that was slowly creeping up my arms. I was sure my feet were in the same condition. I still had the Dragon's claw in my hand, but my fingers were now frozen around it like a blue vise.

She had now glided within touching distance. When her smile drew back over her teeth, I saw the perfect white incisors lengthen and curve at the end.

The smell of Jazmine faded under the new smell coming from her now gapping mouth; the odor of decomposing corpses. She was death on the move and she was moving in for the kill!

She bent her head slightly to the side as she pushed my jacket aside using that killer fingernail, exposing the pulse hammering in my throat.

I screamed out to the only ally capable of helping me now. This ally would come because I knew his story was incomplete without his revenge upon his destroyer.

"Toghaaa...irmcoming ... Hong Wang! Come forth!"

There was a deep rumbling sound from directly behind Lady Bao. The walls and floor of the cave began to shake and then sway.

The vampire had reached out to the cave wall to steady herself. There was a look of confusion on her face; her eyes wide with surprise. The beauty of her face was erased by the twisted look it had, now that her fangs protruded from her once delicate mouth.

The shaking continued as a hole was punched through the thickly packed earth. A long toothy snout was thrust forward, quickly followed by a heavily muscled foreleg covered in scales so red, they almost looked black in color.

Lady Bao gave a sudden intake of breath. I blinked several times like a swimmer trying to clear her eyes and was immediately set free of her glamourizing spell.

I felt a terrible heat begin to fill the cavern. The Vampire had moved well to my left and was edging her way toward the opening, with one eye on the emerging Dragon King.

The massive chest of the creature broke through the wall bringing down large clods of dirt that looked like mere pebbles as they rolled off its back.

His whole head appeared. He stopped shoving and turned his golden gaze on the Vampire. A look of fierce hatred came into his eyes. A deep roar rumbled through the cave, sounding like the powerful waves that crashed upon the shores of the tiny island.

Lady Bao held out her hand and screamed some kind of warning, but the dragon was through the gaping hole, bringing down another ton of dirt as he charged at her.

I moved when the dragon did and pressed myself into a newly made fissure in the cave wall.

I knew I was not a target of Hong Wang's rage, but that was no defense against his massive tail if it swung in my direction. I used my spell to unbind, to loosen more of the packed earth and pressed myself deeper into the wall.

The vampire looked like a white ibis as she leapt into the air to avoid the first blast of fire from the Dragon King's gaping jaws.

I needed to get to the statue of the Red Dragon before Hong Wang brought the whole cave down around my ears.

Before I had left the hotel in what seemed a lifetime ago, I had stuffed the letter from Dr. Chung Wu into my jeans. I studied the map he had scrawled on the back of it during my flight, and couldn't make sense of the symbols or markings. Now I understood; it was a detailed mapping of this very cave.

While an "X" didn't exactly mark the spot of the treasure, it came close.

I heard the high-pitched curses of Lady Bao and felt another tremor in the cave walls.

The Dragon King had come from outside of the cave when I called to him. I could see a streak of light on the cave floor. While he punched a hole big enough for a city bus, he also brought down lots of dirt and debris, effectively closing it off for my exit.

I knelt down and placing my hands on the damp earth, I called to the *Green Mother* to reabsorb this tainted ground around me.

There was a shallow movement under my knees followed by a sucking sound. Like water running out of a tub, the black dirt was draining away until I had a clear way out.

I ran for the exit, clutching the map and heading for the place where I knew the statue of death was hidden away.

Chapter 78

Since I had no way to find Jason and Anfa, I had to rely on the Colossus Faerie to protect him if they ran into the cave only to find a Dragon and a Vampire.

Anfa was clever and brave, but mostly practical and she'd get them away from any contact with the Immortal Lady Bao. I wasn't so sure of her reaction to seeing the Dragon King in the flesh; flesh revived by Dr. Chung and me for just this time of extreme need.

As I made my way to the *Dragon's Pool*, Chung had marked on my map, I was thinking about the secret I had to hold deep from all the others.

Not even my mother knew about Chung's clandestine visit to my home.

He came shortly after she revealed that Chung Wu was an elite *Shadow Walker*, working on behalf of the Masters on the *Council of Green Wizards*.

He came while I was studying the books from the Shadow Box Library. Jason had left earlier and I couldn't sleep.

I sat at my kitchen table sipping a cup of tea, the four books scattered about me. I was reading about the Dark Wizard, Feng Xi when the tea cup began to shake in the saucer. I felt a chill run up my spine and the hairs under my pony tail stirred.

"OK," I called out. I know you are here, so show yourself!"

This was no Demon from the Dark Pit, or I would have had a different reaction to their presence. The Dark Ones always bring along the cold shiver of death.

With a loud pop that I now associated with a Voyager who bends time, Dr. Chung Wu stood before me.

"Welcome, Dr. Chung Wu," I said, with a slight bow returning his deeper one.

"Greetings to you, Cathleen O'Brien. I fear I am disturbing your studies, as you prepare for your trip, but my visit here is of utmost importance to that outcome."

I had gotten up from my chair when I first felt his presence and now he indicated I sit again. He remained standing.

"Young Wizard, while my hologram has been made known to others whom you trust, tonight's visit must become your deepest secret. Not even your mother, Brighid, can be told of our meeting. Will you give me your solemn oath to this?"

I never hesitated, understanding his role in this search was at the behest of the Master Wizards.

"You have in your possession, the map that will lead you to the hiding place of the statue you seek."

He flicked his index finger and the letter he had sent me slipped from beneath the mess of books and notes I was making.

"Know this young wizard, the *Grand Masters* have arranged for this entire search as a means of luring two of its most dangerous renegades from the Dark Pit, out into the open, where they can be destroyed for all eternity."

I was stunned by this news. "Do you mean that I have involved people I love, who trust me, in a complete charade…a charade that could get them killed?"

He spoke so softly I had to strain to listen.

"Remember, young Cathleen O'Brien, you are not the only wizard of your clan to have worked on behalf of the Council. Your father and mentor, while he lived on this plane, answered to the Grand Masters as both *Protector* and *Voyager*. His pledge made to the vampire, Lady Bao, was made freely, to insure the very existence of your clan throughout the ages.

Can you now turn your back on your own role as a *Protector*? You can use your unique place as seeker of the statue, to send these evil creatures to dwell where they belong…the Dark Pit of the Sleepless Dead and end forever, their incursions in this first realm of life. Can you as a *Sworn Protector*, do less?"

It had taken Chung Wu only this one question to confirm my loyalty to the scheme.

Now, I was heading toward that pool of water Chung had drawn on his map. I was following the crude drawing, figuring it was only a short distance ahead. The sound of voices coming from that direction, brought me to a quick stop.

Slowing my pace, I kept low, finding as much cover as I could. I picked up more conversation and knew for sure who had beat me to the hiding place of the statue.

I crouched behind a thick clump of sand grasses, drawing in some of the shadows from the woods to help conceal me. I was not surprised by what I saw, but sorry I had to deal with him now.

The *Teacher* hovered over the dark, scum covered waters of the pool, his arms outstretched. The green cloak he wore had an iridescence about it that made him look like a large dragon fly.

His movements stirred the surface, creating small ripples in the brackish water. He peered down intensely as he hovered, studying the scene below.

Movement under the water made it slosh in small wavelets onto the sandy dirt. I watched for his accomplice to resurface.

My attention was drawn away from the scene for a second, when I heard a muffled sound.

I peered into a tangle of scrub undergrowth and debris, deposited there by past storms blowing in from the surrounding ocean.

There was another, louder noise; definitely human and if I was right, someone I loved was protesting their confinement.

Finally, I spotted him.

Lying against a long piece of driftwood was the six-foot-four body of my boyfriend! He was not visibly tied up, but I saw the quiver in the air around his body and knew he'd been put under a binding spell.

No time to undo that, I thought, as I waited for the next shoe to fall.

Now that I saw him lying on the gritty dirt, I guessed who was below the surface of that murky pool.

The *Teacher's* next words confirmed it. "Anfa! Bring it to me!"

I watched as large bubbles and eddies began to break the surface of the stagnant waters. A hand's width of sunlight had managed to penetrate the tree canopy for a brief moment. It acted like a spotlight on the center of the pool, where the movement was greatest.

Suddenly, two long arms shot up with water coursing down them in greenish rivulets.   Griped between her muscular arms, the Colossus Faerie, Anfa, held the life-like statue of the Red Dragon.

I heard the *Teacher* gasp out his surprise at its extraordinary beauty. The water only enhanced the sharp color of its gleaming red body and smooth curve of its tail as it curled around the lower body. Its jaws were gapping and the rows of slightly curved teeth, looked like daggers standing on end with points exposed for deadly combat.

Even in the thin sunrays, the golden eyes of the statue pulsated with power.

I recognized at once, that Feng Xi had infused the gold pigment he had used, with a strong spell. I suspected it would literally draw life from whatever touched his creation; be it man or beast… or Faerie!

A last snare I never saw coming!

Anfa cradled this ceramic leach to her chest, stepping out of the murky waters. The *Teacher* had drifted back onto the ground nearby, ready to take the statue from her arms.

She slowly approached him, her long hair and body shedding water until she was completely dry. I was so mesmerized by her that I almost missed the *Teacher's* changed expression from an admiring gaze, to one of sheer, ugly greed.

I couldn't let him take the statue from Anfa, or the spell placed on the statue would affect him as well.

I could see the tall Faerie was already showing signs of losing some of her natural strength. She began to falter and lowered the heavy form as she approached the *Teacher's* outstretched arms.

I broke from my cover, and sprinted between the two, before the transfer could be completed.

Anfa was staggering by then and offered no resistance. The *Teacher* was transfixed and barely noticed me.

I was shouting my spell *"Corrbolg creadair!"*

Immediately, the statue of the Red Dragon was taken from Anfa's slipping grip and put into the Magical Treasure Bag I had conjured.

The bag's drawstrings pulled together, wrapping the statue into a snug darkness where its eyes could no longer pull life to itself.

FRANCESCA QUARTO

430

Chapter 79

I knew snatching the statue and bagging it like a common garden gnome wouldn't make me popular with the *Teacher*, but I wasn't prepared for the extent of his anger.

Without a word, he glared over at me from a few feet away. He lifted his hands and the Corrbolg stirred on the ground at my feet. He was trying to draw the bag and its contents to himself prompting me to place a binding over it for good measure.

"*Teacher*," I said sternly. "The statue is *not* yours to take. I have the authority to secure it for the *Grand Masters of the Council of the Green Wizards.* You will not interfere with that directive!"

He didn't bother to respond to me, but refocused his attention on Anfa.

When I had plucked the statue from her arms earlier, she collapsed onto her knees and stayed there until now. She slowly got back on her feet and answering some unspoken order from the *Teacher*, began to walk toward me.

I liked the Colossus Faerie very much, but now I wasn't sure if she was prepared to help, or attack me.

Anfa was still weakened from her contact with the statue, but seemed determined from the set of her jaw, to answer the *Teacher's* unspoken command.

"You are the *Teacher* and must comply with the orders from the *Council* and the *Grand Masters.* You are pledged to this role." I called over to him before Anfa could move any closer.

He blinked at my words and responded to them as if I'd challenged him to a duel.

"When my brother and I were held captive, and he was tortured to death by the Dark Wizard, the *Grand Masters* lifted not one jeweled finger among them, to rescue us. This, even

though we were doing their bidding. Your own father, Liam O'Brien, tried over the long span of time, to find and save my brother after I escaped. The *Council* has much to answer for in the sight of my clan and as leader of that clan, I will extract the toll."

I screamed back at him.

"If you try to take the statue, Feng Xi will have won! He will defeat you as surely as if he murdered you, like he did your brother. You can see how, just touching this monstrosity for a short period of time, causes Anfa to weaken. Imagine how it will change you! It will corrupt all that is good in you and taint your clan forever."

I wasn't sure what part of my speech was having an effect on him, but the *Teacher* turned his eyes to Anfa. His face looked stricken as if he was seeing her distress for the first time. She was struggling to stand and finally collapsed onto the sandy ground.

Her skin had taken on a sickly green color; she didn't try to move when her hand trailed back into the brackish water.

"Anfa, my love!" he said as he rushed over to her side.

His love? I tried to comprehend what the *Teacher* had just blurted out in his obvious distress.

I knew I had discovered the key to lock away his passionate desire for the statue and the drop of Dragon blood it held.

His love for the Colossus Faerie had surfaced like the statue. It brought with it, a hope to save the *Teacher* from an unforgivable treachery.

"*Teacher*, unless I send this statue and its burden of evil, back to the *Grand Masters* Anfa's life is forfeit and so likely is any of your Clan that comes into contact with it."

He looked back at me. I noticed his eyes were changing color from deep green to blue and then back. It was a sign of the conflict that must have raged inside his head.

By now, her color was nearly as green as the scum on the face of the still pool. I reached out with my senses and could feel her heart slow and begin to skip beats. She shuddered as a yellowish bile was released from the side of her slack mouth.

The *Teacher* had been kneeling close to Anfa's still form, holding one limp hand in his own. After a minute, he gently lowered it to the ground.

He stood back up and began to chant, holding his arms out over Anfa's body; his palms held flat over her.

By then, I could hardly recognize the lovely Faerie. Her skin had taken on a deep, sallow green hue and had begun to pucker like something was sucking every bit of her life's juices from her.

Her once vibrant body seemed to be shriveling up into a dry husk. Her hair, once filled with lovely honey hues, fell away from her scalp in large matted clumps, leaving oozing patches of bare skull.

"She's dying!" I screamed at the *Teacher*. He went on chanting even louder as if to drown out the plea in my voice.

Anfa had been twitching in agony, then suddenly became still as the corpse I feared she was.

I was unable to react for a second when a smoky mist began to rise from her desiccated body.

I knew the *Teacher* had not been trying to save Anfa, he was killing her. He called her his *love*, but destroyed her like an enemy.

I brought Green Fire to my hands, expecting the worse. I knew I was badly out-matched if the *Teacher* had become my adversary.

"Cathleen O'Brien, do not think me your enemy, when one will soon stand before you."

I didn't want to look away from him, but the *Teacher* had turned his own eyes to look back at the soupy mess that had been the Colossus.

I followed his gaze, watching the strange mist linger over what had been Anfa's body.

If this was Anfa's spirit, it was materializing and taking some form.

I noticed the *Teacher* had moved further away from it and closer to where I stood. I felt no imminent threat from that quarter, so refocused on the shape that had begun to thicken, taking on the definite proportions of a woman.

The long black hair, had been transformed into a squirming mass of eel-like creatures spitting thick red streams that ate the very ground they touched.

The once beautiful body was as corrupted as one whose burial was a simple pit of lime. There were gaping holes in her face, fractured, yellowed teeth and pitted tongue showed through. A greenish puss escaped the open tears of her flesh.

The only thing about her that brought her name to my lips, were her coal black eyes. They stared at the *Teacher* and then me and flared a blood red.

"Lady Bao!" I breathed her name and the vampire moved like a lightning flash!

BLOOD OF THE DRAGON

435

Chapter 80

I was quick to ignite a stronger flame in my hands and the vampire stopped short of my reach.

"What have you done with the Colossus Faerie called Anfa?" I screamed at her.

She attempted to make her rotted lips smile, but they peeled away like old brown tape and fell to the ground with a hiss.

"Your friend was quite delicious, young Wushen. Alas, she didn't keep well after she was drained, but I did manage to capture her spirit life and make her mine. As you can see, her last act was to retrieve the statue of the Red Dragon for me. Soon, I shall be restored in body and nothing will prevail against me!"

"You told me only one who had pledged service to you could retrieve the statue."

"Ah, I should have added a small detail to include any ally serving the pledged one in the quest."

She looked over in the direction of the large log where Jason lay like part of the flotsam carried in by the storms.

*Jason...*I had been so drawn into the scene of the *Teacher* and the vampire I nearly forgot he was a prisoner...but whose prisoner?

I threw a quick unbinding spell in his direction and the spell dropped, freeing him. He stiffly rose to his feet, but looked unhappy when I contained his newly gained freedom with a Dome of Protection.

He was standing with his hands pressing on the invisible shield..

"Cathleen, she has the medallion!" his voice was muffled inside the Dome, but I heard his warning loud and clear.

I knew Lady Bao had defeated Anfa, as strong as she was, but I was surprised she could touch the Golden Harp pendant of High King Brian Boru. It should have destroyed any demon spawn that entered this realm on contact.

Then it dawned on me.

The Vampire had possessed the Colossus Faerie after sucking her dry of her life essence, consuming her Magic and invading her body. The Magically imbued pendant, would not have recognized her as a Dark One, but it could be used against my own Magic.

I looked back at Jason. He looked ready to explode, but I had to keep him out of the way until this standoff was resolved, one way or another.

I did the math. If I won, the vampire was sent back to the Dark regions, Jason would be safe. If I lost; he'd still be protected for a while, until the vampire smashed the Dome which I knew she could. But there was one ace I hadn't turned over yet; the *Teacher*.

He was looking at the muddled goo that was once his lovely Anfa. He must have felt my eyes boring holes in him because he slowly turned to face me. I blinked and he was at my side.

The vampire must have decided we offered no real threat, even if we were united against her. She gave us a lipless grin, her blood-stained incisors glinting in the pale light. She began to move toward the liquefied remains of the Faerie.

I hadn't spotted the Golden Harp until Lady Bao reached out a skeletal arm. Pox- like sores, covered the patches of flesh left on her.

There was a metallic ring when her curved fingernails scrapped a blackish lump from the center of the mess.

She passed fleshless fingers over the object. The sludge fell away, exposing the golden gleam of the Harp pendant of the High King.

While the vampire continued to study her newly acquired treasure, I softly asked the *Teacher* how he knew Lady Bao had possessed the Colossus Faerie.

"My clan is connected by *ChiFlow*. When the body of my Anfa approached, I found only darkness when I moved into her spirit essence."

This also explained the *Teacher's* deep suffering during his brother's torture and murder.

Our immediate challenge was the Lady using the pendant to help break Feng Xi's powerful Magic and possess the statues powers.

I had to stop her from taking the *Corrbolg Bag* that was now slightly behind me and the *Teacher*.

I looked over at Jason and gave him a hand signal. Jason and I often had to communicate without words in some dicey situations.

He gave me a sour look; letting me know he didn't like my plan.

"Lady Bao, you may want to reconsider your next move," I called to her.

She was still several feet away trying to size up her adversaries no doubt. Having the *Teacher* on my side, was not something she'd foreseen. He had a reputation among Magic Users in all realms for his prowess in battle.

The *Teacher* also had a secret weapon that added metal to his Magical armor; he had a burning hatred of the approaching vampire.

She stopped moving at my warning, but seemed to waive my threat aside as her skeletal hand fanned the air in a jerky movement.

Suddenly, the *Corrbolg Bag* shot up into the air and descended at Lady Bao's tiny booted feet.

My reaction time was a breath too late. She had both the harp medallion and the statue.

I heard Jason yell a warning, but missed the exact words. Could have been, "Look out!"

Chapter 81

The *Teacher* was the first to respond to Jason's warning. A blast of wind blew my hair into my face and eyes as the *Teacher* streaked over to attack Lady Bao.

At least, that's what I thought he was doing until he changed trajectory and headed over to where Jason stood inside the Dome of Protection.

He smashed into the invisible shield like a wrecking ball, bringing it down with the force of his Magic. Jason seemed transfixed as the shield dropped. He reached out a tentative hand and the *Teacher* grabbed onto it.

This all happened so quickly that the vampire barely had time to turn her head to register what had occurred.

As soon as her eyes began to follow the *Teacher's* action, I saw why Jason had yelled out his warning; the *Corrbolg* bag was open and the statue's blood-red head was leering out at me.

I could feel a kind of magnetic pull on my body and I realized I was inching forward, toward the vampire. The statue of the Red Dragon was using its Dark powers to drag me closer to my own destruction.

The Lady Bao must have sensed my movement as she snapped her head back, the bones of her neck making a loud clicking sound.

She hissed, "Yes, Wushen. Come to me and the dragon. When I taste your blood, your powers will be mine."

I knew it was the dragon's power, not hers, that was bringing me closer to the vampire.

I wasn't sure where the *Teacher* had taken Jason because my eyes were riveted on the dragon. I needed to break its hold on me and couldn't be distracted until then.

My father was always big on spells within spells. He had actually woven some of mom's *This and That Magic* seamlessly into some of his strongest Magical charms. I used one now that would get to the heart of the problem; the Blood of the Dragon.

I let myself be pulled, concentrating my energies on the words of the hybrid spell. If done correctly, the statue would be bound to the earth, while a fog shrouded its mesmerizing golden eyes to break its hold on me.

The new spell was awakened once I summoned the elements, *"Cuir Ceobhran!"*

Instantly, the bag holding the statue stopped moving. A thick gray mist fell over the dragon head, shielding me from the pull of its piercing golden eyes. The Vampire's face registered what must have been a perplexed look. It was hard to tell, since most of it had rotted away.

Taking advantage of her surprise, I hurled a *Knotted Fist at* Lady Bao's midsection and she doubled over.

This was no time for niceties. I followed the thumping she was taking, by casting a spell of restraint, binding her to the earth like the statue.

With both the vampire and the statue secured, I turned my attention to the *Teacher* and Jason standing near me now.

Rather than relief, I saw fear on Jason's face. He and the *Teacher* were both riveted on something approaching from behind us.

I spun around in time to see the body of Feng Xi, his decapitated head tucked like a football under a boney sallow arm.

He glided like a shadow, his silk slippers whispering across the sandy soil.

I immediately brought *Green Fire* to my hands, hurling it at the headless wizard.

I heard the *Teacher's* voice as he and Jason moved to either side of me.

"Saighean!" he shouted bringing up a sudden flash of white light as he faced the oncoming headless corpse.

Feng Xi's severed head let out a howl when the unworldly light seared his black eyes. He began to grope around with his free hand only to encounter the Green Fire I had suspended over his ragged neck.

A second scream from the disembodied head ripped through the dank air as Feng's hand caught fire like the wick of a candle.

Before I could throw a second green ball at him, the *Teacher* had moved within striking distance of the Dark Wizard. He hurled his own dire magic at the struggling Feng.

I saw a claw, the size of a heavy garden rake, materialize directly in front of Feng Xi. With a downward sweep of his hand, the *Teacher* tore into the emaciated body, shredding it like a head of cabbage. Feng's torso hung in ribbons, taking on the appearance of a multicolored skirt around his legs.

The Dark Wizard's head slipped from his arm. I saw the grimace of shock and pain twist his mouth into a silent scream.

I looked over at the *Teacher,* his handsome face twisted in hatred as he used the claw to tear out the Dark Wizard's eyes and totally destroy any vestige of the once human face.

Feng Xi was no more. Raising my hands, I sent Green Fire to reduce the shattered remains of the Wizard to gray ash. The act of sending him back to the Dark Pit of the Sleepless Dead was interrupted when the *Teacher* turned to me.

"Send this wretch back where he deserves to spend eternity, Cathleen O'Brien, and free me of this vendetta."

I opened the ground directly under Feng's ashes and as the earth absorbed his remains chanted a quiet prayer to the *Mother*. He would be sent to the Dark Pit and never regain his powers in this, or any other realm.

I felt Jason move closer to my side.

He took me into his arms and held me for a minute whispering my name over and over as he held me tightly.

The *Teacher* had moved toward the Lady Bao.

He was within arm's reach, but strangely didn't make any effort to destroy her as he did her Master, Feng Xi.

I gently disengaged from Jason's strong arms and called over to him.

"*Teacher*, I must send the Lady Bao to the Pit. But first..."

While his attention was on the vampire, I undid the binding on the bag holding the Statue of the Red Dragon. It streaked past the *Teacher's* head and was firmly deposited at my feet.

"You do well to secure the treasure held within the Red Dragon, young wizard. I must confess to succumbing to its allure and power. Now I see how it cost me dearly and I will pay its price for the span of my days."

He was looking over at the sludge-like remains of his love, Anfa.

I threw another ward around the statue to be certain of containing its evil glamour.

I wasn't sure what to do about the vampire. She stood transfixed by my rooting spell, only her eyes shifting between me and the *Teacher* as he stood over her.

"You have taken the last innocent spirit from the many realms of the living, Lady Bao" he said.

He spoke softly, but his words penetrated the heavy air like shards of glass.

"Your undead legions will no more walk upon the *Green Mother's* earth, or stalk the unwary of the Fey peoples. I return your mortal remains to the Dark Pit where your old master awaits you for his eternal retribution!"

He raised his hand and covered her in a tarry black shadow. When he dropped his hand, Lady Bao, the beautiful Chinese vampire was gone.

Chapter 82

Jason and I watched as the *Teacher* knelt over the tarry slick, that was once his lovely Anfa. I heard him mumble a few words in the Old tongue and the puddled sludge was absorbed into the sandy earth.

After a minute he stood up and walked back toward us.

"I have achieved my goal in this realm, young wizard, and it cost me dearly. I assume the Red Dragon and the powerful blood hidden within its stone heart, will be destroyed by you."

"The statue will be given over to the Elders of the Council. My mother, Brighid, will…"

My statement was cut short when a blast of Artic air blew into our small circle. A loud pop and sizzle crackled around our heads.

The *Teacher* backed away from a whirling pillar of gritty earth that had formed in the center of our small group. I had already raised my arms and was beginning a defensive spell, when a bejeweled hand jutted out of the spinning threat.

"Mom!" I yelled, as I recognized the many rings that she favored wearing like part of a uniform.

Jason must have identified her at the same time. He was leaping forward, eyes squinting against the spinning sand as he pulled her by the arm and hand.

When she was yanked out of the churning vortex, she landed against the *Teacher*. He'd moved toward Jason to aid him and took the full impact of mom's arrival as they fell together in a heap on the ground.

"Oh dear, that was a rather undignified entrance I fear." She chuckled as Jason and I helped her and the *Teacher* to their feet.

I rushed over and hugged her, then pulling away asked, "Where's Joanie, mom?"

"Don't be concerned lass. She's back at the Grant. After we got to the *Healing Garden* I left her in the care of the *Little Mothers*. It took many months to stop the Vampire's poison from totally polluting her body."

She looked over at Jason when she heard him mumble "Months?"

"That would be months in the Second Realm, dear. Joanie and I were only gone a few hours from this time thread." She answered his bewildered look.

She took notice of the *Teacher* and smiled over at him while he continued to brush off his long green cape.

"*Teacher*, it is known to the Council that you lost your love, Anfa and they wanted me to express their deepest sympathies."

"I appreciate your bringing me their message, Brighid, but I am certain more is known to the Elders of the Council than my love's passing from this realm."

"If you refer to your help in securing the statue of the Red Dragon for them, you are correct. None are above the allure of power, but you have given beyond measure, in your weakness and then in your strength."

So, they know he almost caved, I thought, while I watched the emotions of loss and then relief, pass across the *Teacher's* face.

I would never have believed that he could be humbled, but mom has a way with words!

Jason had moved closer to me during this conversation and practical man that he is whispered "Do you think we can all fit in that boat?"

I squeezed his hand and answered, "It might just be you and me, Jason. Mom has to go back to the *Council of the Elders* and deliver this and the *Teacher* into their care."

I looked down at the bag holding the Dark Wizard's ultimate work of evil. Mom had picked up our conversation and gave me a warm smile.

"I do believe the *Teacher* and I will be travel companions, dear. We will make this, delivery, together."

She was smiling at the *Teacher* when she announced they'd be seeing the *Council of Elders* together and it seemed to lift his spirits.

He reached down and took her hand and gently pressed a kiss into her palm.

Before they left together, mom gave Jason an affectionate hug and pat on his cheek, then turned to me.

"Daughter, I will not be rejoining you in San Francisco as you've already guessed. I shall be careful to relate your latest exploits to the full *Council of Green Wizards* and am certain, they will be very pleased indeed! It might make up for the wee incident when you nearly burned down Wizarding Hall while practicing to bring Green Fire!"

"I was only five, mother! Hardly knew what I was doing in any case."

"Of course, pet. She's easily ruffled, Jason. You should be aware of that." She laughed and kissed my cheeks.

She put her left hand over the bag holding the Red Dragon and encased it in a sticky Spider's Net spell, snaring it securely. She used air to raise it off the ground. Attaching the webbing to her side, she curled her arm firmly around it as it floated beside her.

The *Teacher* gave Jason a brief nod and turned to me saying "Perhaps someday in the future, yours or mine, you and I will again share an adventure, Cathleen O'Brien."

He reached down and took my hand, but rather than kissing it as he did mom's, he just looked deeply into my eyes.

I saw his own eyes change color from blue to dark green and back again. I knew this time it wasn't the Faerie Glamour he was using to impress me; this time he was trying to make a deeper impression.

Wow! I could get used to this, I was thinking when mom grabbed for the *Teacher's* hand and they both vanished with a whirl of sand.

"He certainly is charming isn't he?" Jason said with a smirk as I turned my full attention back to him.

"I hadn't noticed, but I did notice he was glad mom would be there when he met with the *Elders*."

"Will they know how his acts led to Anfa's death?"

I didn't want to attribute that terrible destruction of the Colossus Faerie to the *Teacher*, but Jason was right in this cold truth. There would be retribution for the loss of any living being under his care, if the *Teacher* was held as responsible. He allowed his thirst for vengeance to morph into an all-consuming desire for power that nearly destroyed him, but surely did his love.

To quote Liam O'Brien, my own teacher, "The finest revenge in this realm is the happiness of those who have survived tyranny and suffering."

I wondered as I leaned my tired head into Jason's chest, if the Teacher would eventually know happiness.

Chapter 83

We returned to where the fishing boat sat perched like an over-sized clam shell on the spit of gravely beach.

Jason untied it from its make-shift moorings, giving the boat a strong shove while I clambered aboard.

The outboard motor sprang to life and we turned our backs on the wretched island and all its horrors. An eager group of gulls hovered overhead as we put more distance between us and the island. The birds used the salty air currents as they tracked in our foamy path.

I was watching the island's green and tan colors merge into one smudge on the horizon and then sink from view.

Jason understood that I was trying to process everything that had happened during this case. He smiled at me when I looked over at him, but knew he didn't have to speak.

Feng Xi and Lady Bao had brought a terrible evil into this mortal plane. They had left a bloody trail of misery and death, carved out over many millennia in this realm and others.

The sound of the motor purred in my ears with a calming, monotonous hum.

I must have drifted off, my head resting on the back boards of the boat, where I flopped down with my legs tucked under me.

I looked around as I sat back up and saw the small boat harbor in the distance.

"Jason, I'm so sorry, sweetie! I think I fell asleep."

"You needed the rest, love. We'll be landing in another fifteen minutes, I'd guess."

I smiled back at him, letting the love I saw in his beautiful green eye wash over me like the green waters lapping at our small craft. Sometimes it's better not to try to talk about your feelings out loud.

True to his estimate, Jason hit the beach mooring site fifteen minutes later. I had spent the intervening time, trying to wrap my head around the convoluted investigation that was drawing to a close.

I was jarred out of my unfocused mental state by the scarping of the boat bottom on the coarse, sandy beach. The boat's owner must have been watching for our return. He looked relieved as he grabbed for the rope Jason tossed over to him for securing to the stout wooden pilings.

"Thanks for the use of your boat," Jason said to him as we passed by without another word.

Jason had paid the owner more than he would have made fishing that day and he likely enjoyed a day at the local pub rather than hauling in half empty nets.

I took Jason's hand as we made our way back up the sandy boardwalk. He smiled down at me saying, "The Grant Hotel, right?"

"Yeah. I need to be sure that Joanie is doing ok."

He leaned down and kissed my mouth gently and we got into his rental car. I knew we both needed some "alone time," but Joanie was probably feeling pretty alone herself.

As we drove in silence for a while, I felt the constant tug of something that wasn't quite right. I was running through the scene on the island, between the Dark ones, the Teacher and me.

That's when I knew what was nagging at me.

I had given that talisman of the Golden Harp to Jason for protection, but it ended up with Anfa and then, with the Lady Bao.

But where was it now?

Like the flash of setting sunlight on the calm water below our speeding car, the answer came to me.

Oh Teacher, you are a sly one indeed, I thought.

Chapter 84

I shared my alarming thought about the medallion with Jason.

Jason watched the highway signs and said, "Let's hope your mom is aware that the *Teacher* took the pendant, love. This could mean more trouble with him."

As we neared our exit, we could see the city's skyline come into view. It was awash in a golden glow, looking like a scattering of ancient temples spreading out before us.

We parked across from the hotel and I was practically sprinting into the lobby when I heard my name.

"Cathleen! Over here!"

Joanie was getting out of an over-stuffed chair in the lobby and moving toward me. After hugging me, she came over to Jason and planted a kiss on his cheek while he smiled shyly back at her.

"Joanie, let's get up to our room so you can tell us about the Healing Garden and everything that's happened since we left you with mom."

I didn't want to let Joanie out of my sight, after her harrowing experience, so we headed toward the bank of rickety elevators.

Now, I was sitting next to her on her bed, with Jason sitting directly across from us on mine. Joanie took a deep breath and began by telling us about her time with the Vampire. We found out the Vampire had left her alone with the driver on several occasions.

"He was really scary! He never spoke unless she asked him a direct question and he never talked to me at all. Once, when she returned, she looked…radiant! Like she'd been to a beauty spa or something. I swear, her skin was glowing and she was even more beautiful. I had noticed before she left us that her complexion was beginning to look kind of sickly. You know, Cathleen, like a really elderly person."

I heard Jason snort out a little laugh before he said, "She was probably a thousand years old, Joanie."

"She had undoubtedly just fed on some poor creature, Joanie. Thank the Mother it wasn't you!" I said, squeezing her hand.

Joanie gave a visible shudder and went on to tell us how she was infected by the vampire.

Just before we rescued her, the vampire had ordered the driver to investigate a power source she felt somewhere near the cabin.

"That would have been Crom and mom, Joanie. Lady Bao was using you as blackmail, but I don't think she counted on mom and the Storm God.

Joanie continued her story of how the driver had returned to report that he saw a dragon approaching the cabin from the back. Lady Bao looked very alarmed. Joanie overheard her tell her driver to remain behind, to guard her. "That's when she came over to me and before I could even react, she grabbed my arm and tore into it with her long fingernails. It felt like acid shooting through me and then, I couldn't feel my body anymore. I couldn't move, Cathleen. It was like a drug was in my system that prevented any muscle response."

Evidently, Joanie had overheard a comment about the dragon being a different entity than the one Lady Bao had conjured to stop any attempts to rescue her prisoner.

"She said something like, "It may be Feng Xi's work," but I 'm not sure.

I noticed she was beginning to tire and Jason and I left her to catch up on some rest. The story about her experience in the Healing Garden would have to wait till later. After she rested we would have plenty to talk about. Besides, I had other concerns nagging in the back of my head.

What was the *Teacher* going to do with the golden medallion of Brian Boru? And did my mom even know he'd taken it along for their trip to meet with the *Council Elders*?

We went to Jason's room and after placing the excess pillows at our backs, laid on the bed and shared our own versions of events. We were caught up in the story-telling and the kissing and holding and more kissing when Jason looked at the clock.

"It's time to get Joanie, love. In fact, it's past time."

We scurried around throwing ourselves back together because Mother knows, cuddling can get pretty messy!

Chapter 85

Joanie was already waiting for us when I tapped on the door to our room.

"Hey guys! How about feeding me?"

As we were passing through the quiet lobby on the way to the mostly empty restaurant, one of the older managers called over to us.

"Pardon me, Miss O'Brien, but something came for you while I was out. Regrets for not delivering it sooner," he said, apologetically.

I told the others to get a table and I'd join them in a minute.

The elderly manager pressed a heavy manila envelope into my hand. I immediately felt a jolt.

I must have registered my reaction, because his wrinkled face broke into a smile and he said, "It won't bite you, young wizard."

I quickly stepped back from the counter. He had used the Old Tongue and there was a slight quivering in the space around him.

"You need not be alarmed, Cathleen O'Brien. You hold a gift from the *Council of Green Wizards*, a reward for retrieving the Blood of the Dragon."

In the dim lighting of the antique lobby, I saw the shimmer surrounding the old man become more pronounced.

Before I could blink twice, standing before me was the Librarian, Ban Briathon.

"Bandi!"

His name came out in one long breath.

"What is this...why are you here... where is my mother and the *Teacher*...where *is* the *Teacher*...?"

Enough questions, Cathleen. Quiet yourself and take the gift sent in gratitude from the *Council*. You served so well. All will be made clear."

I never thought to see Bandi after he left me with the Shadow Box Library a lifetime ago. He leaned over the dark wood of the counter.

"I wish you well young Cathleen and will assuredly see you again."

With that the shimmer faded into the soft lighting of the lobby. The small Chinese desk manager seemed to shake himself when he saw me standing there.

"Do you need assistance, Miss?" he asked with a perplexed look wrinkling his already creased face.

I shook my head, tucking the heavy envelope under my arm as I went to join Jason and Joanie. It was radiating a warm, tingling feeling, letting me know it was alive with Magic.

A gift from the *Council* could be anything from a pile of petrified bat guano, to a new book of regulations they wanted me to learn and observe.

I was definitely not one of their favorite *Wizard Protectors*-- too much of a maverick like my dad! Dad was always in trouble with the *Elders*, because of his unorthodox methods of employing magic. But he was effective and that couldn't be denied even by his harshest critics on the *Council*.

I got to the table they'd picked and noted it was nearest to the kitchen and a quick exit. They were both on their guard as if expecting more trouble, or at least ready for it.

When I sat down they both looked at me and the package I'd placed in front of me.

"So, what is that Cathleen?" Joanie asked with a trace of nervousness shading her voice.

"I have no idea."

Jason had been sitting with his arms folded in front of him, but immediately pushed back from the table when I placed the manila envelope between us.

"Magic," he said in a hushed voice.

Joanie took in a deep breath and said, "I hope you have your mojo on, Cathleen. I don't think I can take another kidnapping today!"

"Let's order some food before we do anything about this package." I said as casually as I could.

The waiter, a very round Chinese man, approached our table from the kitchen area. I heard someone yell something in Chinese and he answered in a high pitched voice and a deep scowl on his face.

He stood before our table and with a curt bow asked what we wanted to order. I studied him while Joanie rattled off her favorite breakfast and watched as he rolled his eyes every time she paused to reconsider her choices.

His graying hair was swept around his head several times ending in what could have been a bird's nest belonging to a deranged magpie. The waiter had carefully tucked pins into strategic areas to secure what must have been a foot of hair into his personal aviary.

He left with our orders and we sat back, each of us silently eying the mysterious package lying between us like a ticking bomb.

"OK, love. Let's talk about the mysterious package now," Jason said, taking my hand to reassure me it wasn't going to scare anyone.

Joanie didn't seem to trust her voice and just nodded her head in agreement.

"All I know is that it's from the *Elders*. Some sort of "thank you" gift for securing the statue of the Red Dragon for them."

Neither of them looked satisfied with that explanation. Joanie spoke up first.

"Do you think they want you to do something else for them with whatever they put into that envelope?"

"I sincerely hope not! Jason needs to get back to his job as Sheriff and I have to run a radio station. Besides, Ollie misses me!"

After a few more imaginative guesses, I poked at the large envelope to determine the shape of the contents.

"Whatever's in here, it's wrapped in a heavy padding. No telling what it is till we get back upstairs."

We were all famished and dove into our meals with little conversation.

After settling our bill, we returned to Jason's room. I had laid wards around both rooms, but I placed a second around his and felt secure enough there to open the mystery package.

Jason and I sat next to each other on the bed, Joanie was perched on the desk chair. The manila envelope was tapped shut and I took out my pocket knife to cut it open.

Before slipping the contents out, I whispered a spell of protection around us and the room. I reached inside the gapping envelope and pulled out a gauzy material that seemed to shed light as I moved it. The seemingly delicate wrapping was definitely the work of the Fey and likely as strong as a cast iron casing.

I noticed from the corner of my eye that Jason had shifted slightly away from me. In answer to my inquiring look he simply said, "Magic jolt."

Joanie was as tense as a race horse pawing at the gate.

I turned my attention back to the object in my hands and began the chant I'd need to unwrap it from its iridescent bindings.

"Teagar bain!" I said over the object.

The gossamer material slipped off as I said the last word. It draped over my hands and wrists and I felt like a High Priestess as I looked down at the glittering gold medallion of Brian Boru.

Chapter 86

"The medallion!" Jason said, his voice reflecting the surprise we both were feeling.

Joanie stared down at the gold piece, remarking "It's really beautiful, Cathleen. But since when does the *Council* send you jewelry?"

I smiled at her comment and answered "This isn't simply jewelry; it's the Golden Harp medallion of the high King, Brian Boru. It's also a powerful source of magic. I was certain this was lost. I know Anfa took it from you Jason, but the last I saw it, it was in Lady Bao's boney hand. It could never have been sent to the Dark Pit, and I suspected the *Teacher* had taken it for himself."

As if on cue, we heard a rattling of the door handle.

Jason was on his feet instantly and unconsciously reaching for the holster that wasn't there.

I felt confident when I called out a welcome in the Old Tongue because I suspected our visitor would understand my words.

Without opening the door, Dr. Chung Wu stepped into the room.

"Greeting, Cathleen O'Brien, and also to your friends," he said, while bowing to each of us in turn.

"I see you hold the gift sent you by the *Elders*, rewarding your recent success."

"But you're dead!" Jason barked out in alarm. "He disappeared, Cathleen. We both saw that."

"Chung Wu only left this realm until I could retrieve the statue. Am I correct?" I said, looking closely at the recently deceased Wizard.

"May I explain to my friends what has transpired so they can understand your part?"

He bowed his head and answered "Naturally"

"I already know you are an Agent of the *Council of Green Wizards* and were acting on their behalf. You allowed the vampire to believe she killed you, so you could travel freely between this realm and the second and report to the *Council* on my progress."

He nodded his head like like an indulgent grandfather.

"You are correct in your astute assessments and, as a *Sworn Protector* *t*o the *Council*, you will understand how I must always place their directives above any personal inclination. I would have wished to assist you more in this task, but the fact that your honorable mother, Brighid, joined forces with you, strengthened your hand sufficiently."

I wasn't sure if he just insulted my own magical powers, but I let it pass hoping for more details on the status of the statue now.

"Dr. Chung Wu, we are at the end of my investigation; an investigation that you hired me to pursue. Now, I need some answers to a few important questions."

He signaled with a slight nod that he was prepared to answer.

"How did you come to have the Golden Harp medallion and what has the Council done with the statue of the Red Dragon and the Teacher?"

"The Golden Harp pendant came into my care, after it was given to the Elders by the *Teacher* upon his return to their presence, in the company of your honorable mother.

He secreted it away before removing the Lady Bao to the Dark Pit. It was always his intention to surrender it to the Elders, or so he said, but I suspect your mother may have influenced his wise decision during their trip to the *Council* Chambers."

He gave a small chuckle and went on.

"I was instructed to turn the medallion over to you, to reward your important work in securing the statue. I employed the Librarian for the purpose of seeing to that task.

As to the evil statue, the *Council* has destroyed the Blood of the Red Dragon and the powers it contained. The *Teacher* has been reinstated as head of his clan and to his position, with all his powers intact. There was one caveat to his exoneration, however."

We all watched Chung closely, especially me.

"He must spend one lunar cycle in this realm, helping to guard against further incursions from the denizens of the Dark Pit. His directive from the Council included giving requested assistance to the *Witch of Appalachia*. This to be determined at your discretion, young Wizard."

The silence in the room was broken when Joanie, a touch of awe in her voice said, "Wow! Your own assistant, Cathleen!"

I wasn't as enthusiastic with this arrangement as she was, but the *Council* must have had their reasons.

Jason looked even less favorably on this plan for me to work closely with the *Teacher*. A quick look in his direction and I saw his mouth set like he'd just chewed something distasteful.

I got the distinct feeling Chung sensed my attraction to the Fey leader. I had attributed that, to his Magical powers. Looking over at Jason when Chung announced this new alliance, I was pretty sure my boyfriend was not unaware of the *Teacher's* powers to charm any female as easily as he could cast a spell.

This could get complicated, I thought, looking back at Chung.

I was about to tell Chung Wu that I wouldn't need the *Teacher's* help in future investigations when Jason spoke up at last.

"Dr. Chung, as Cathleen's partner in most of her investigations these past four years, I've seen her get out of some pretty scary situations. But if the *Teacher* can help her in any way, I for one would welcome him as an ally."

A slow smile creased the ancient face as Chung Wu gazed at Jason as if seeing him more clearly.

"You have spoken wisely, Jason Tate," he said, bowing slightly to Jason. "I am impressed with your devotion to Cathleen O'Brien, but then, the bond between you is quite apparent even to these old eyes."

Chung's thin gray eyebrows shot up his deeply furrowed brow. "There is something of interest in your own aura, Jason Tate, something of the magical nature. You have the gift of Vison Seer."

Jason shot me a look.

"I don't necessarily think of my walking dreams as a gift, unless they are helpful to my work, or to Cathleen's investigations. And I sure don't see them as magical!"

Chung Wu nodded at him and said, "You are wise beyond your years Jason Tate. It is never good to seek out Magic for its own sake. But be assured of this, as life partner to the *Witch of Appalachia*, you will be called upon to employ all of your own considerable resources, whether magical in nature or informed human instinct."

I'd been standing by listening and waiting to interject a question burning in my mind.

"Dr. Chung, are you saying my services as a *Sworn Protector* will be called upon soon?"

"I am merely preparing you, young wizard, for the inevitable. The forces from the Dark Pit of the Sleepless Dead are ever restless and their thirst for power is unquenchable. They will rise again to interfere with the natural life in this realm. You must be vigilant and prepared. And now, I leave you, young wizard, with your life-mate and stalwart friend."

He was smiling at Joanie at the end of his comment. She beamed back at him for being recognized by such a powerful wizard.

I wanted to ask a million other questions about these future incursions of the Dark Ones, but Chung Wu vanished with that small popping sound and I knew he was voyaging to another time or realm.

Had he journeyed back to the land of his ancestors; back to the earliest days of the Chinese Empire? As I stood in the first realm of natural life, was he in the second realm, giving his report to the powerful *Council of Green Wizards*?

Only the *Green Mother* knew the answers.

Now, my curiosity was ignited by the possibilities of the gift I clutched tightly in my hands, the Golden Medallion of Brian Boru. It was a source of power that would greatly enhance my own.

By possessing the medallion, I now stood, symbolically, shoulder to shoulder, with my wizard parents; a place I never dreamed to occupy so early in my life cycle.

My best friend and my "mate for life," as Chung called him, stood silently while I tried to process the turn of events in my life as a Wizard.

There was no doubt that I'd be given more challenging cases of Demon incursion to deal with; not to mention more training by the *Teacher*.

It was thrilling to hold the powerful Golden Harp Medallion in my hands and to know, only I would wield it.

While my mind raced around the corridors of possibilities, Jason took my elbow.

"Cathleen, sorry to interrupt your thinking, love, but we need to make some changes to our plane reservations. I want to fly back with you two to Pittsburgh, so why don't I go with Joanie and contact the airline to make that happen?"

"Jason, you are a gem! You always know when I need my alone time. I will take advantage of your absence and finish packing."

I leaned in and gave him a long kiss and only broke off when Joanie cleared her throat to remind us she was still there.

After they left for the guest computer room off the lobby, I returned to my room and started throwing things back into my carry-on and suitcase.

The monotony of sorting dirty clothes from clean was broken by thoughts of new adventures to come. Now that I'd been elevated within the ranks of Magic Users serving the *Council of Green Wizards*, I wished my dad could have shared in my proud moment. He would surely have some sage advice to share, along with his usual casual disrespect for the stiff hierarchy among the *Elders*.

I remembered once, when we were out of earshot of mom, dad had described the powerful *Elders* on the *Council* as "…a bunch of nattering old monkeys who delight in throwing their magical weight around like poop!"

"Oh, dad…you sure knew how to put things in perspective!" I laughed out loud.

I knew dad believed in the lofty work of the *Council* and died while still serving their needs. The fact that he was a powerful Wizard never changed his fun-loving zest for a life lived simply, with grace and humor and love.

I stopped my packing for a minute to hold the heavy Golden Medallion I'd laid on the pillow. I slipped its heavy chain around my neck and felt the buzz of magic flow through my veins.

The room began to darken and as I watched, frozen with surprise, a familiar figure shimmered before me.

"Dad," I whispered.

About the Author

Francesca is part of a large Italian family where she discovered early on, that a love of reading was as much a part of her DNA as her mother's skill at baking. Growing up in a house filled with laughter, screaming, banging pots, fighting and loving family bonds, shaped her life and heart.

Having moved from the east coast where she was raised between New York and New Jersey, Francesca left for the midwest where she spent several years outside the Chicago area raising a family of three children, completing her college degrees and writing introspective poetry like other young mothers.

Francesca has worked in local television, a small city zoo, founded a non-profit tutoring agency for an inner-city neighborhood which eventually served local school districts, worked for an International Evangelical Television and Radio Station and for a non-profit organization serving challenged adults.

Francesca Quarto resides in a small town outside of Indianapolis, Indiana with her husband Patrick. She still has a great love of the written word and while she enjoys her E-Reader immensely, she still treasures the excitement of turning the next page.

Young Cathleen O'Brien comes from a poor Irish immigrant family, but she was enriched from her earliest childhood by a father who gave her the perfect treasure, magic.

Cathleen is part of a clan of Celtic Mages with Magical roots going back to the Dark Times. Her father taught her the mystic arts of the Magic User and after she purchases a radio station in a remote mountain town, she'll need this magic to survive.

Iron Mountain was a booming coal mining town in the late 1800s, but there is a sinister cloud hanging over this beautiful mountain setting. Old news clippings from those times, tell of town folk being hunted down and murdered and visitors disappearing off the trails, never to be seen again. Legend held that there was an ancient Indian Shaman who was responsible for all the mayhem and his flight into the high mountains was proof enough to all. After his escape from the town's suspicions and justice, there were reports of giant wolf-like men and other creatures roaming the mountains as part of the Shaman's twisted pack.

While researching the town's history for herself Cathleen uncovers these old news stories and concludes there was more myth, than magic, at play in the old town. Never one to scoff at any sort of reports of magical powers, she tucks the tidbits of information away.

Her detective work takes her high into the densely forested mountain where she finds the howling snow storm is not the only threat to her safety. Her encounter with one of the Shaman's pack puts her into a life and death race for safety and an unexpected champion who is as terrifying as protective.

Cathleen discovers she is up against the evil magic of a Skin Walker whose tentacles reach into the quiet town of Iron Mountain, and can touch all that appears innocent and destroy all that is good. Her life is pitted against the changing face of this evil and she cannot predict who or what the enemy is. Cathleen is only sure of one thing; her Magic has grown as powerful as the Green Mother and she can make the world tremble.

Hidden away on a secluded ranch, the Wiccan sisters hold their Coven retreat, searching for peace and communion with nature among the towering Buttes of Utah.

The tranquility of their days is shattered when the girls begin to disappear like water under the sizzling desert sun. They are under attack by unknown forces and even their dreams will make them vulnerable.

The Witch of Appalachia, Cathleen O'Brien, has been called upon to rescue the missing girls; if they still live. Searching among the ancient pillars that soar like giants rising from the sandy floor, brings the young Wizard face to face with Morgayne. This half lizard Demon is known in Celtic folklore as "The Queen of Rot"

Cathleen soon uncovers a devious scheme by one of the Coven's own sisters. Her allegiance is now bound by blood to the Queen, whose evil has subverted her very soul.

Helping Cathleen to locate the missing girls, her mother, Brighid, uses her "This and That" Magic to protect her untested daughter from the powerful Morgayne.

Time is running out for the abducted girls. Soon, they will have only dark dreams in a never-ending night.

Tell-Tale Publishing would like to thank you for your purchase. If you would like to read more by this or other fine TT authors, please visit our website:

www.tell-talepublishing.com